# Chasing Shadows:
## *Back To Barterra*

J.M.N. Reynolds

*Cindy —*
*You are such an*
*— image of God to*
*all of us.*
*Thank you*
*so much*

Chasing Shadows: Back to Barterra
Copyright © 2012 John Mark N. Reynolds

For information, contact Unlocking Press
www.UnlockingPress.com

Unlocking Press titles may be purchased for business or
promotional use or special sales.

Cover Design by Joyce Odell and Renee Jorgensen

10 – 9 – 8 – 7 – 6 – 5 – 4 – 3 – 2 – 1
0–9829633–6–4
978–0–9829633–6–4

To Father Michael, Rest in Peace

To Michael Fatigati, Carry On

# Preface

This account is based on events that took place in the late seventies into the early twenty-first century. The dates are not exact to protect privacy, but correspond roughly to the time of the events as they happened.

How did this manuscript come into my hands? A person claiming to be a visionary or prophet sent me a collection of notes about what he had seen. With these dreams was a story that was even harder to believe from a man who claimed to be an old friend, though I have no recollection of him. This book is my attempt to put the two pieces together as a novel.

Writing this book is what was requested of me by the visionary who sent the manuscript, in fact, it was what I was paid to do. I will have more to say about this later.

The notes came with money and a contract from this publisher and the story you are now reading fulfills the terms of that contract. I did not write this book, however, mostly for the money. The story became part of me and even seemed familiar. You will learn the reason why I think this might be true if you read the story.

Recently a very sensible colleague at Torrey Honors, the sort of person who closes any book quickly in which the word "elf" appears, asked me if this story is, in fact, true. Obviously some elements are not true, but disguise the truth to avoid certain problems with the authorities. About the rest of it, I am only willing to say that the fact that such a question occurred to my friend, who is very skeptical, says much about the times in which we live.

# Preface

My son, Ian, criticized the book for leaving out important, but controversial issues that I thought would make a story already hard to believe even more difficult for the reader.

A person who works for the Church read the book and his reaction was much less sane, but then she is much more involved in the sort of events that inspired this book. She suggested we pray for Holy Mother Russia.

This is excellent advice.

John Mark N. Reynolds
Saint Anne's
The Feast of the Martyred Tsar 2009

# Chapter One:

## Going Down to the City

17 January 2009, Saturday: Rochester, New York

Peter Rupert Alexis opened the flip tab of his morning diet cola. He was stocky, in his mid-forties, with a sedentary job and could not afford the calories from a glass of orange juice. It would take ten minutes of riding on his stationary bike to work off even one glass. He glanced through the day's appointments. A few papers to grade. A seminar on Plato's view of the human soul. Accountability meeting in the evening. An easy day in the secure life of a tenured philosopher at a small Christian college.

He carried his cereal bowl over to the counter and began to swish it clean with the sponge. His mind was elsewhere. Blue eyes, a bit near sighted, gazed blankly out of the little half-window over the stainless steel sink. The window of his apartment looked out on the window of someone else's apartment. It was a gray day, but was snowing lightly, beating the usual Rochester drizzle. An old mug with the University of Rochester logo stamped in gold on it had his carnation from last night's banquet stuck in it, the white carnation turning a bit brown at the edges.

He grabbed a stiff dishtowel looped over the stove door handle. Swiping the water off the bowl, he put it back in the white metal cupboard that was the norm in his one bedroom flat. The towel curved back over the stove handle neatly. He did not even have to think to do these things, and so he moved about the apartment efficiently. There was little in it to get in his way. A very good audio and visual system was in one corner near the best computer he could afford. One fraying couch took up the longest wall. His indoor bicycle for exercise dominated the middle of the room. A few folding chairs for the meeting of the group tonight completed the furniture. There were books piled everywhere, but few shelves to store them. The major part of his collection was in his office at the college where he did most of his writing and research. The books at the house were just there temporarily, though the dust on some of them showed that temporary could be a long time since, like most academics,' he was working on three or four projects simultaneously. Unlike most academics, there was little focus to his interests since Peter had always had trouble focusing on any one subject area.

Peter was tired and running as slowly as last years computer, purchased with too little memory. His weariness was understandable, given another night disturbed by the Dream. As regularly as a Windows crash, Peter had a dream that ruined any slumber. For years Peter ignored it or passed it off as an eccentricity, but now he was getting worried about the Dream, because it was getting more frequent and the feelings it stirred up in him were not going away after he woke up. Last night was the second night his sleep had been destroyed since Christmas. It was getting on his nerves more than usual and he could not stop thinking about it. What did it mean? Why did he keep having it?

Some of the imagery in the dream was clear enough and did not require much reflection for Peter to recognize the sources. A youth spent reading Plato, Russian history, and fantasy novels accounted for almost all of it. Most of the details could be explained after twenty years of academic reading ... though Peter had to admit that much of his eclectic taste in literature had been shaped since he was sixteen by an attempt to understand the Dream. The Dream came before the reading.

It was becoming a dominating factor in his life, and by now he was more familiar with the details of the Dream than an old school Trekker with the original series episode City on the Edge of Forever.

It was the intensity that frightened him, though, of course, there were also historical details that had turned out to be accurate. He had diary entries from his childhood in the seventies describing the Dream, and newspaper clippings from the last decade announcing discoveries from the nineties that confirmed some of the details in it. At sixteen, he had known things about the death of the Royal Family of Russia nobody could have known had not been there.

To Peter the information he seemingly possessed was less important than the feelings. He knew how it felt to be in the room where they had died and those feelings had shaped his life ... starting in his personal Purgatory of the second year of high school. He had found a Virgil during that awful year of high school, but had lost his Beatrice.

His sophomore year had been bad, very bad, but it had not started that way. Peter had been happy enough in school. He drifted through freshman year and much of the fall of his second year content to play soccer and try to master Gauntlet. He kept his grade point average barely at honor roll level since that sent him on a field day with the rest of the school. His father sent him to the tiny Christian school for God knew what reason, but the religion had stuck anyway, enough to make him want to be a missionary for a short time.

He even had a girl friend at the start of the year, and Classmates.com somehow knew this and periodically reminded him that he could pay to get information available for free on Facebook about a still single Mary Yurislav.

When he was a freshman, Mary Yurislav had transferred in with her Holiness mother, no makeup, and enough ambition for two. She came, he saw, and she conquered. Mary had been allowed very little freedom by her mother, but they got to do the little there was to do together anyway, since Peter fit Mrs. Yurislav's idea of a virtuous young man. This was not quite accurate, which proved something, though Peter was not sure what, but Peter's intentions had been honorable.

They fell quickly into a daily after-school pattern. Mary studied while he listened to Trek carefully recorded on cassette tapes from television. His grades actually improved a bit, since she was the main reason to work for the outing on honor roll day. They were headed for a senior yearbook title of Best Couple until his accident and the year out of school that followed it.

The accident was the only memory he had worse than the Dream. It was simple enough; his school bus crashed on a bad turn and then he did not remember anything for a long time. TV shows about "to jump the shark" and Peter both had gaps in their back-story. His father had taken him to expensive clinics and had spent thousands of dollars trying to help him, so he was told, but Peter knew nothing of it. Eventually he was pronounced ... not quite cured ... but well enough to return to life outside the hospital.

When he came back to school, he was different. Some of it was good, he studied harder for one thing, but there was something missing and that something was not the Dream. The Dream started the night after he returned to school and never really went away.

His teachers were happy with his attitude, but a few missed his sense of humor which had, almost entirely, vanished. His first day back in school, he volunteered an answer in class without joking about it.

Not everything was different. He kept playing soccer and eventually watched every Trek movie except V on opening day, but Peter had moved on from high school. He had grown up or grown old while he was unconscious in hospice care.

Mary had waited for him, of course. She had decided to marry him after their first month together and Mary had all the will required for waiting, but the relationship had not survived anyway. Peter did not want it. He wanted someone, but Mary Yurislav was distinctly, suddenly not her. She was too tall, too grating, too angular and her mother was too Russian for Peter's comfort. He wished he could blame the Dream for the rotten breakup, but it had mostly been him.

She had looked at him impatiently when he tried to explain, "But you said you loved me ..."

"I did love you."

"Then you should love me still. Love does not change."

"Mary, you can't win this argument. I am not the same person ..."

"After the accident? You cannot blame this on the accident. Lots of people are faithful after something bad happens to them."

"Good grief, Mary, we are only sixteen. It's not like we were engaged or something."

"You said you wanted to marry me."

"That was stupid ..."

"You think it was stupid? Our love? Or wanting me?"

"No. You don't understand."

"I only understand I love you, want to marry you, and thought you wanted to marry me."

She was taller than he was by a good bit and this was emphasized by her straight back and his growing slouch. She spoke again, but softer this time. Each word came out as if it was going to be the only one.

"Who is she?"

"Who?"

"The other girl."

"There is no other girl. Not really."

"Not really?"

"I just want something, someone ... I don't know."

"Someone not me?"

"I am sorry."

"No. You are glad. I know you well enough to know you're glad. God help you, Peter, but don't ever come near me again unless it is to ..."

Peter was shocked. Mary was rubbing her eyes as if her contacts were irritated. Could it be that she was crying? Mary did not cry. Well, why not cry now? It was a normal thing for most people to do, but Mary was not most people. She was strong. Peter blinked; Mary definitely was crying. He wished he could cry too, but all he felt was burn out.

He also knew that he was being a jerk, but he could not stop.

"Mary, I have to go."

And he had the last word.

Not that Mary had given up on life or had suffered much by

the loss. She moved onward and upward and out of any contact with Peter Rupert Alexis. He was no Facebook stalker but her success had been hard to miss. Mary had earned a great degree and had flourished in every job she held. She became a first rate college administrator, though that was damning her intelligence with faint praise.

Peter had been sad to notice her religious status was now "other." At one point, Peter had a big enough ego to think that lost first love had turned her from God, but he was older and wiser now. He didn't have the gravity to disturb her trajectory. He had seen her once or twice at academic functions and she glittered, which, Peter reminded himself, was more than could be said about him. Maybe they had never belonged together anyway. Some people are Tolkien people and some people are Salinger people. Mary was a Salinger person, but with the strength to move on from high school, still hot, still smart, and wildly successful. He was a Tolkien person: haunted, single, and pretty mediocre. Peter felt reasonably depressed.

He decided he would bring the whole thing up when the fellows gathered that night.

Saturday night was his book discussion group and he needed to prepare the reading. Peter dropped into the sagging couch with his much abused copy of the Republic. The two volumes in the Loeb were filled with notes from every year of his life since he had purchased them in grad school. He had better copies, shrines to his love for Plato, but this was his working copy. The Dream faded away as his mechanical pencil traced the familiar words. He feasted on Plato followed by some Boethius for devotions. Some poetry by Charles Williams was his dessert and a break from study. He looked up at the clock and it was one, looked up again and it was four, glanced at it after a trip to the bathroom and it was six. The day was done and it was time to greet his guests.

The first to arrive was Max, the Virgil who had guided every stop of his career. Peter always felt his career should carry an acknowledgement to Max giving him credit for the successes, but excusing his mentor from blame. If Peter was a mediocrity, it was not because Max had failed. The pupil simply was not up to the teacher.

Max certainly would be the last to leave and would be illuminating any topic right to the end. It was as predictable as the tick of the cuckoo clock on the wall, but the best things in life are exactly this predictable and interesting. Anybody can be dull and predictable or wild and untrustworthy, but only a few can, like God, generate excitement without changing. Professor Arthur Maximos was predictably brilliant.

Max's wild gray hair, combed back, but still sprouting in all directions was the first thing one noticed about him. The second thing to capture the attention were his eyes, the bane of deceitful students, and capable of destroying the most talented academic bluffer. Once you had seen the Eyes of Maximos, the saying at college went, no sane man lied.

He was a professor of literature at one of Rochester's many schools, this one a too expensive Catholic men's college, and he was easily the best-known scholar in Peter's small circle of friends. His college had gradually become more secular than Christian ... Catholic-In-Name-Only, critics inside the Church said. It was fat with the money of faithful souls from an earlier generation whose actual beliefs were mocked daily inside the buildings bearing their names. The college president pointed to Maximos as an example of the diversity of the college and Maximos would not-so-quietly note that the college had hired nobody else like him since the day his Berkeley degree had fooled them into a bad guess about his views.

Max had more than one irritating trait, but only one that particularly irritated Peter. Married to the same woman for almost forty years, Maximos had a fanatic's distaste for the single life. He approved of singleness in principle, but not in practice. He knew somebody must be called to the life of Saint Paul, but other than Saint Paul he could never name a particular example.

Just seeing the dust on the furniture in Peter's otherwise neat house would be enough to send him into his standard lecture on the civilizing influences of the feminine in history. Maximos held views so dated that they were daring, but even his most outlandish opinions came studded with verbal footnotes. He would have been a perfect commentator for Fox News if the cable channel had decided to start a network devoted to the politics of the Byzantine Empire.

Maximos had first formed the little group. They were scholars from different area colleges, interested in their faith, big ideas, and each other. Together, and under the spiritual guidance of their leader, they held each other to the high spiritual standards of the Church. Despite the Spartan conditions, they always met at Peter's house. "What else," Maximos would growl, "of interest happens there?" The house was, Maximos would conclude, "As close to a monastic cell as this group is likely to find."

Max never knocked and Peter never locked his door. There was no danger Max would surprise anyone, since he could always be heard talking to himself coming down the hall. Tonight was no different. By the time Max slung open the door and said, "Good evening, Peter." Peter already knew that his former teacher was in good humor, was stuck on a passage at the end of Book IV, and had enjoyed his dinner.

By instinct, Peter looked around his living space to see if he would pass inspection and felt good about the image he was presenting of single life. The lonelier Peter got, the more determined he became to appear happy. There was nothing pathetic in the house that night. He had even run a dust rag over a few of the surfaces in the main room. He felt the righteousness that only comes to those that do housework they despise. He would not be teased tonight.

He glanced into the kitchen and saw that his hopes of appearing domestically competent were going to be dashed. He had left his cola can prominently displayed in the middle of his little table as if a shrine to the cooking gods. The kitchen and the living room were all one room and nobody could miss the message of zero calorie consumption today. Eating more than his day's calories of snack food during discussion would not compensate in the Eyes of Maximos. Peter knew what was coming next and it came quickly. The all seeing eyes of Maximos missed nothing and Max came to judgment: Peter was weighed in the domestic balance and found wanting.

"I see that you are keeping your usual dietary and household standards. Meaning, of course, no standards at all... As I reminded Maggie last night, you are in dire need..."

But Peter was delivered from the shame of his cola can by the arrival of Bartholomew White. The youngest member of the group, in his early thirties, he also was notably thin in a group always tempted by binges of donuts. His undergraduate days had mixed physics and track. "A natural combination," he had once explained to everyone's astonishment, and his explanation had become sufficiently mathematical to stun the rest of them into silence. He worked in Maximos' not-so-Catholic university, in the huge, lavishly funded government projects that no one ever talked about, but that formed the basis of the school's expansion. He had purchased the exercise bike for Peter, and made sure he used it or at least periodically started to use it. The bike was the one piece of furniture in the apartment that was never dusty.

"Max, leave Peter alone. His moods are bad enough, and single life is miserable enough, without your running on and on about it."

Peter looked at Barth gratefully. Maximos snorted, "Then why," the old professor had just begun to fight, "Why ... doesn't he do anything about it? It is not as if Maggie and I have not tried... It is not as if..."

"As if what?" came the clipped and precise words of the last member of their fraternity as he too entered without knocking.

"Don't interrupt me, Jack."

"I would never think of it. I am changing the subject altogether." John Warren Smith was tall, much taller than even the Chestertonian size Maximos. Smith flopped down on the couch, dripping coat and all. He was the only member of the group to work most of the time in the "real world." A psychologist with unconventional habits, he taught part time at the local community college, toyed with obscure ideas, and published in all the best journals. His income was fantastic, almost a legend in the group, from a thriving practice that he supervised from a distance. He tossed a fedora to the opposite corner of the room, snagging it expertly on the handle of the cycle. Jack turned to Peter and said, "It is your night to pick the topic. What shall we discuss?"

"I have begun work on Boethius," Peter replied, "and his notion of Divine time."

Barth looked thoughtfully at Peter. "Time. Interesting topic. Some of the lab types at the University are messing about with that on a theoretical level."

The conversation was beginning well and the group began to enjoy themselves, which was more than could be said about a discussion in the boardroom of Douglass University a few blocks away. There, an administrator had called in a researcher to, as her email put it, "hear his reasons for certain situations that have been brought to my attention."

The professor was not there yet, but the administrator was. She sat at the head of the table drumming her nails on the hard, dark oak ... the sound was very loud in the silence of the room. She was wearing a comfortable tweed jacket and her nails and lips were a bubblegum pink. If she had closed her eyes, one might not feel threatened, but her eyes were staring. If you looked into the blue of them long enough they began to pulse with the rhythmic tapping of her cotton candy nails.

At last the door at the other end of the room opened and a very small man stood framed in the light from the hallway. Portraits of past university presidents contained eyes more alive than her own. The administrator spoke very quietly and confidently to the little man and her fingers never stopped drumming.

"Yes." she said. "What is the status of the request?"

"We will not get the funding."

"What?" The tiny man looked even smaller as the College vice-president stood up. She was a very tall woman.

"The political situation simply does not favor such esoteric projects..."

"Do not tell me about the political situation. Get me the money."

"It can't be done."

"Then quit..." And she looked at him now, sitting back down. This made the small man twist his hands. She somehow looked larger in the high back chair.

"I will see what I can do."

"Yes." The door shut again. One of her shiny nails moved to a small pin on her collar, a double headed eagle. She began to tap on it. A smile, tiny at first, jerked her face into motion. Her breathing became more rhythmic. She began to hear the sound of the Wind again. It was coming: the Message. She did not know she shared her very private dreams with anybody else. Her goal was privacy and she was well on her way to total isolation.

Across town at Peter's house the conversation was simmering. The wine had lubricated the flow of ideas nicely and the preliminary banter was out of the way.

"But what can it mean, for God to be outside of time..." Jack looked disgusted. His analytic training was offended by anything that could not be quantified.

Maximos turned, "Of course, it may be a Mystery. Like the Holy Trinity. Perfectly possible, but super-rational."

"Bother that!" Barth said. "What does it mean?"

Peter grunted, "But isn't that the point, Barth? It has meaning only from within..."

"You mean we would have to experience timelessness to understand it fully?" Jack seemed unconvinced.

"But the idea is coherent... There is a related discussion in Saint John of Damascus... blast it, Peter, you have spilled the wine! And it was good stuff too... Maggie bought... Peter?"

Peter gazed forward. His near sighted eyes were too focused, but not on anyone in the room. His mouth was open. The wine from his glass dribbled over his trouser knee to the flour. He was hearing the wind again and he could not hear anything else. He had never had the dream when he was awake, but he was having it now.

Wind. All he could hear was wind. The voice of Max and the others vanished in the gale of his waking nightmare.

It was dark, the kind of perfect darkness modern people rarely know and so find disorienting. And then he saw a circle, spinning like the outside rim of a wagon wheel and the dreadful sounds began, as he knew they would, and he watched the wheel spin, faster and faster. It was the howling of a gale passing through a space too narrow for the force. It was the sound of despair.

His vision of the scene become more expansive and the first spinning wheel became part of a larger system. It was joined by a second inner wheel turning in the opposite direction. This second wheel had parts, smaller spheres perhaps, attached to it. He couldn't capture it fully and this infuriated him, because he was dimly aware that Max would have understood, but Max was outside the Dream. It was maddening. He wanted to shout out a question to his mentor, but he could not speak.

He knew what was coming and he did not want the dream to continue. "God let it stop," Peter prayed, but he knew it would not stop. It never did after this point. He was passing right through the center of the spinning circles. His body was burning and then as he reached the center his chest began to feel heavy. It was like being buried alive, but with no coffin, only mud and matter pressing down on his face and soul. Alive. Buried. Buried alive. Until he was in that room, the room he hated once again, and the real dread began.

His body pressed against the rough stone of the basement wall. Or was he the wall? Objects were easy to identify in the Dream, but he was not. He could not see himself and everything was washed out ...soft focus.

He was watching what amounted to fragments of a movie or pieces of history. The fragments were not more comforting as they became familiar: the angry men, loud orders, a father, a feeble mamma, four daughters, an invalid boy, friends of the family. All of them leaning on the wall ... leaning on him.

The voices of the angry men filled the room, but he, as always, could not quite understand what they said. Orders. Shouts. His vision blurred and his hearing became even more confused. He was not so much seeing and hearing as feeling his dream now. He could sense bits of emotions from the people in the dream room: mostly fear.

Finally, as he knew he must, Peter saw Her and once again realized that he must save her and that once again he would fail. She would die. This woman, his She, was being murdered with all her family. He knew her name, but could not say it. He could not pray, could not move, but merely be the wall against which this young woman leaned as she died and into which spent bullets flew through her to him.

He felt pain, but not from the lead burying into him. Instead he felt her nails, as she was dying scratching symbols into the wall ... into him. He could feel that scratching, desperate writing cutting into his plaster skin. What was her final message? He could not tell.

Her face filled his mind, becoming so sad and beautiful that it felt like a blasphemy not to venerate her. This last part of the Dream was always, almost, bearable. The hatred that filled the room did not touch her. The greater the pain inflicted on her, and it was horrific, the less she seemed aware of it. She did not die in fear or the desire for revenge.

He was, for just a second, overwhelmed by perfect love.

And then his mind began to awake, driven away from the best part of his Dream by the hatred of the men with guns. She was lost to him. Gone. In the whole scene he could soon make out only a few things: the yellow stripes on the basement wallpaper, the odd cap on the chief of the angry men, and the sickening smell. The great wind that brought him to the room began to suck him out. As he was yanked from the room, moving back again through the images and sounds and the last word of her father, the bearded man, dominated his mind. The word drowned out all thought.

The father said it softly and patiently. It began to echo with authority and righteous anger. The start of a question spat out right before a bullet made speaking impossible. "What?" "What?" "What?"

His friends saw Peter slump in his chair.

The noise in Peter's Dream was like the noise in the basement of one of the lab buildings at Douglass, very much like it. The little professor from the boardroom was a big man in his lab down stairs and he hated being yelled at. He resented everything his bosses, especially her, told him, but he was usually more obedient than he was vengeful. He need money and in a University money came by loving your boss like yourself. When he left the boardroom, the little man was determined to do something, to act, which for him meant flicking a great many "off switches" to "on" in his huge laboratory.

The large motor growled. Men and women in white jackets scurried about like so many acolytes of a greater god. The experiment, the last if they got no more money, was beginning. Switches were pulled and noise increased as the turbine began to whirl more and more loudly. The little men at Douglass were making a mighty wind.

# Chapter Two:

# In the House of a Friend

18 January 2009, Second Sunday After Epiphany, 2:00 PM: Rochester, New York

Peter woke up refreshed after a sound sleep. Lately, all by itself, this was a fact worthy of mention. Sleep was more exhausting than being awake, but waking up after the Dream often was worse. The minutes after a nightmare ends are some of the worst in a man's life.

He stretched and then stopped in mid-thought. When had he gone to bed? He seemed to have a faint memory of Max, and a discussion of time, and then the Dream had come to him awake.

This was new and not with the Obama "hope and change" kind of new. It was rotten and depressing and was probably insane.

Some people go crazy and then cheer up. Other people go crazy and become evil, but laugh a great deal like the Joker on Batman, but Peter felt crazy and miserable. It was hell to be bad at going mad.

He once heard that the crazy never think they are crazy. For a minute this comforted him, but not for very long. He feared he was crazy, but this meant he was not crazy. If, however, he came to believe that he was not crazy, then he might be crazy. He shook his head and realized he was missing a step. He started to pull out a piece of paper to diagram the argument, but stopped himself just in time. He realized that formalizing nonsense would have been conclusive proof he was a lunatic.

His head started aching, the way it always did when he was lethargic for too long a period of time. Every muscle in his body decided to sympathize by aching too. His eyes did not ache, because they just hurt. The text for today's sermon should be: "Thou shalt never sleep with thy contact lenses in place." This reminded him that he did not know the time and that today was Sunday: church.

Peter rolled over to look for his lens case and realized that he was not at home in his own bed. He glanced around. The room was bright and sunny with a late afternoon sort of cheerfulness. Where was he? Not at the hospital? The closest place, Saint Thomas General, was much too antiseptic for the chintz drapes by his bed. Where was he?

Susan Smith came through the door. "You are awake at last?"

"Yes. I take it Jack brought me home with him last night?"

"He thought he should."

Peter groaned, "I am sorry to be such a nuisance."

"It's not like you're company Peter. You are family."

"Except I am not really. Is Jack around?"

"No. He had an early afternoon appointment, but he should be back soon."

"What is wrong with me?"

"I don't know and you don't either. Jack will know, but he needs to figure it out first. Now lie down. Jack gave strict orders that you were to rest."

Peter gladly flopped back on the pillow. He was still wearing his clothes from the day before; at least he thought it was the day before. He began to panic:

"What day is it?"

Susan laughed. "Don't be so melodramatic. You just slept through the night, something Jack doesn't believe you have done for a great while by the way, and a good part of the day. Now be quiet."

"What about Church?"

"Missed it by hours. Go to sleep."

Peter gave up and decided to obey. He knew legitimate power when he saw it and Susan had it. There were times when Peter understood his friend's impulse to get married. Looking at Susan Smith, her dark hair, just a tiny bit gray, reminded him of loss. Susan was good at almost everything, especially at creating a home; a job she called "the most important work."

Jack, she felt, was defending civilization or helping sick people discover it. She **was** civilization. A big part of that job was home schooling their three children, and Peter noticed with a start that he had not heard a sound from them.

"Where are the kids?" he croaked, realizing that his throat was still unnaturally dry.

"They went to Jack's mom's after Church. You needed quiet. And the boys are not good at providing it..."

"Thanks, Susan."

She smiled at him, held her finger to her lips, and closed the door.

What had happened to him? This "dreaming" wakefulness had been much more intense than his nighttime dreams. He could still visualize some of the images from the room. And her. He could still see her clearly. Peter knew, of course, the person behind that image. He knew she had been dead decades before he was born. He knew you could see pictures of her bones on the Internet with a quick search. Still he had seen her so many times in his dreams that it felt like her knew her. She was part of his reality. He fell back asleep with her face still in his mind.

"Peter," someone was shaking him, "Peter. Wake up."

His eyes met other eyes. Brown eyes. Brown face. Jack. His friend, his psychologist, had pulled a chair next to his bed. The room was dark, but it was still afternoon. The weak sun had given up and was back behind the real sky of Rochester: grey clouds.

Peter felt better after a Dream-less sleep and Jack's welcome presence made him feel almost euphoric. Jack was strong and bright, and his friend. Everything would be fine.

"Peter. Are you ready to talk?"

"Yes. Thanks for putting up with me."

"Susan did all the work. And wait until you see my bill. Insurance companies give me a great deal of money for the kind of service you have been getting."

Peter smiled.

"You went a bit gaga last night, Peter."

"What did I do?"

"Not much other than sitting muttering to yourself."

"I was seeing things, Jack."

"Tell me what you saw, Peter."

And so Peter told his friend the Dream and felt better once it was out. Someone else knew. Can a forty something feel like a little boy? Like a boy confessing secret sin to his father, Peter told Jack all that was in his mind and everything that he found in his heart. Jack knew, understood such things, and was wise. Dr. Jack Smith, his friend Jack, would take care of everything and be the grownup in charge. So Peter talked, felt release, and then looked up at Jack knowing his friend had understood. In a moment his childish confidence was gone; Jack looked frightened.

Hope became terror and Peter nearly shouted: "What is it? Am I mad? Have I done something horrible in my sleep?"

"Nobody, Peter, is quite sane, but your dream is not part of your particular madness." This man who **was** his friend, Jack, was acting like somebody else just now. Peter had gone from friend to patient. He would put up with anything from Jack, but hated dealing with Dr. Jack Smith. Peter had avoided psychologists other than Jack ever since getting an overdose of them at sixteen after the Accident, and even as his therapist,, Jack had avoided sounding clinical. Now he did, and Peter hated it.

Peter wanted to ask, "What is wrong with me?"

He wanted to ask, but found it hard to get the words out.

Finally drowning in the Dream he repeated the single word he never forgot.

"What?"

There was only one clear word in the dream, the last word spoken by a father about to die with his family in a Siberian basement.

"What?"

The evil man in the cap read his paper, the doomed father asked his one word question, and then the smoke, blood, and death began.

"What?"

The question. Then the explosions as an answer. What? Bullets. What? Smoke. What? Butchery. What? Death.

She was the last one alive ... running back and forth against the wall until they caught her with bayonets.

Peter was shouting. He was shaking. No, he was being shaken. It was Jack. Jack. She is dying! She must be saved! She is gone! Peter was weeping.

"How long," the doctor friend gazed at him, "have you been seeing the death of the last Tsar of Russia?"

19 January 2009, Monday, 3:00 PM: Rochester, New York, Douglass University

Mary Yurislav was in a desperate hurry. The building was empty except for those working on her project, and now her project was at the make-or-break point. What would they find today? What would they see? What would the payoff be for a decade's work and billions of government dollars? If her machine was going to work, it was going to work today.

The process could not be stopped, only completed, and now it was nearly finished. If it had been Christmas Day, they would have come to work, because nothing could stop what was going to happen today, if anything was going to happen today. She was paying triple time to get her workers to forgo a long weekend and find out the results, though most of them were so curious they would have come for free.

Her bosses needed results, and she would deliver today or they were never going to get any return from this particular investment. Mary was either going to be very powerful by the end of the night or perpetually unemployed. The people paying the bills were generous to success, but never dealt twice with a failure and they were well connected.

The next day marked the inauguration of a new American president, but Mary laughed at how little that mattered. The bosses first funded her during the Bush years and would continue to do so under Obama. The man at the top of the government changed, but the real players never did. It was not small changes like a new president that brought the need for speed, but the demands of the bosses for tools in the deeper global game. Deep change was coming, but only the Israelis even pretended to be ready. Mary's job in the lab had been to prepare a tool for this change and her tool would be ready today.

It had to be finished or she would be. It had to work or she wouldn't.

Her heels clicked down the tile floors of the hall of the science building and she could smell the new wax the cleaning staff had put on the floors. She had to know the results of the weekend's experiment and so she opened the door to room nineteen. Frosted glass. No names on it. Mary swept past the grad student qua secretary. The secretary started to protest, saw who Mary was, and retreated to her studies. Mary strode into the office of the Project Director without knocking.

His back to her, he was typing away. The keyboard, carried from one computer to another, clanked and rattled under the force of his blows. His monitor was glare proof, but he had installed rear view mirrors on the side. He never needed to stop his work to deal with the distraction of people.

"Mary, how kind of you to knock." The typing continued.

She glanced quickly around the office. Concrete blocks. No pictures were on the wall. It a was cell whose only windows to the outside were multiple computer screens. The scientist could see the street outside with Google Earth if he needed to see it. Stacks of papers were everywhere. There were few books, but many journal articles. Bobby Kennedy's projects were too cutting edge to be in books.

There were two interesting things about the scientist: his work and his name. Even at his very liberal technical school neither had been enough to get him a date. Bobby did not care, as any social interaction, "a controlled interface" to use his language, was a waste of time. He could get all the socialization and comfort he wanted online.

Still, Robert Kennedy was a preposterous name for the dank little fellow in front of Mary. Bobby Kennedy went out of his way to lose contact with the outside world. Other men, for the pleasure and glory of man, had created this virtual world and RFK was thankful and grateful enough to do his duty to it. Kennedy's job was to explore and populate virtual reality. He was a creator of shadows in the shadowlands.

Bobby Kennedy liked to rant on numerous discussion groups, but his favorite message was how lamentably overrated reality is. Virtual reality promises an improved "real life" and delivers on that promise, much more than reality has ever done for anybody. "Reality," he would fiercely type, "promises pleasure and produces pain."

You could be whatever you desired on line; limitations were slowly falling away as the interface became more complete. Kennedy had on-line avatars to match his mood. Some days he was a big man, a truck driving man, cruising parts of the Net where he received respect for his blunt chatter. Other days he was a better-looking version of his nerdy self teaching any newbie the ways of the dark Net. He had scores of identities on-line and when he messed up with one, he just trashed it and began again.

Fortunately, thanks to Red Bull, the hours away from virtual reality were shrinking. He hardly slept and never dreamed dreams. Shadow life was life for Bobby Kennedy and he was increasingly irritated when people insisted on speaking to him instead of sending a sensible email. Why had Google invented chat if people kept talking to each other face to face?

Mary Yurislav tolerated him, because he was good, no, great, at what he did. He brought home the research bacon, but he was difficult and she never looked forward to meeting with him. His smell alone was noxious enough to ruin her day, but today it was necessary to get him moving, and nothing disturbed him more than facing a real human being. She stared at his back as he multi-tasked, and cleared her throat impatiently.

"Yes?" Bobby muttered at her and did not even break the rhythm of his work.

"I got word on your funding last night." The typing stopped. Bobby looked up. His pudgy eyes focused on her reflection in his mirrors. Money was computer time, and so money mattered.

"Deak says you might not get it. I told him to get it."

"God damn Republicans." Bobby began to jerk his mouse around the desk. Windows opened and shut on his monitor at a furious pace. "God damn Republicans. Can't anyone stop their interference with science?"

"Spending is tight. Both parties claim your research is pork. It doesn't help that we cannot really describe it, but we have not given up yet."

"You promised me the money."

"The economy is making things hard. Esoteric research is never a priority in a recession."

Bobby had started the day irritated with Mary and his mood was not improving, "I want this money. I am not the only spendthrift in this office you know. Your little experiment last night was not cheap. The power alone cost thousands."

Mary was blunt: "I ordered Deak to run the machine."

"So he told me. I don't appreciate your going around me like that with Deak."

"He was on duty. Do you want me to bring you in every time I run an experiment?"

For the first time, Kennedy turned his head, "Yes. Anything that uses my machine? Yes. You bet I want to be called." Kennedy paused and his tone changed to a something more pleasant, "Still, Mary, we did it last night. Or almost did it." Bobby was typing again on a screen full of numbers and names. A printer in the corner began to hum.

"You broke through? You saw them?"

"Who knows? None of your new-age crap here, thank you. We did something. I don't know what we did."

Mary ignored his knee-jerk naturalism with practiced ease. "What did you see?"

"We saw exactly nothing. The machine recorded an event, perhaps the Event."

"And?" Mary reached for the throat pin, the double headed eagle.

"And I don't know. The machine is having its problems. I tell you I need Barth White."

"You know the problems with getting Dr. White and getting him on the project."

"I have told you I don't give a rat's ass for your scruples. He is the best man for this kind of work so I want him. This is science, not some sort of Inquisition. He is an idiot creationist, but he does the math I need."

"Will send me a copy of the tape, if the Vision is fully actualized?"

"If you don't let me have White, it will never be actualized fully. Getting the models right doesn't require computational power, it requires genius." The typing actually slowed down. "He is the only one who knows this area as well as I ... and..."

The time had come, as it always did, to be brutal. "You can't have him. You know why. Get me results or kiss your funding and your computer time good-bye."

She turned and walked out of the room. She knew the images would be watchable and in her inbox by late evening, because threatening his computer time was Kennedy's weak point. It was expensive and he used a great deal of it. Not all of it was university business, and she monitored everywhere he went on line. Whenever better offers came, a choice word about his habits was enough to keep him at Douglass University. She could put a healthy dent in even his stellar career, and so she controlled the door of the wardrobe to his private Atlantis.

Mary knew once the machine worked she would let the repulsive sexist lizard go to another school to live on his reputation while she finished the project using his assistant.

19 January 2009, Monday, 4:30 PM: Rochester, New York, the 19$^{th}$ Ward

Arthur Maximos loved Rochester. He could go to a world-class concert at the Eastman School in the evening, enjoy some city nightlife, and sleep in a country bed and breakfast at Letchworth State Park ... . the sort of Grand Canyon of the East. It was fifteen minutes from downtown to cows. As for housing, it was perfectly possible to buy an aging Edwardian mansion in the 19<sup>th</sup> Ward and renovate it to splendor. The worst neighborhoods in the City were an urban paradise compared to places like New York City. The hardwood trim alone in some of the houses in his neighborhood would have fetched thousands in a place like Los Angeles. He simply could never see why anybody would ever live any place but the Flower City.

Martin Luther King Day was a big day in his neighborhood. He had walked to a street fair, eaten some popcorn, heard some jazz, and held his wife's hand. Maximos stretched with content as he put his book down and listened to the tick of his mechanical clock in his office. He hated sounds in his home that were synthetic, and so even his phone had a real bell. His real bell suddenly jangled. He sighed, fearing telemarketers, and cursed the insufficiency of the do-not-call lists.

"Hello, Maximos."

It was no telemarketer.

"Yes, Jack. What is it?"

For the next few minutes, he listened and watched his small fire burn. As he listened to Jack, he felt a strong urge to look at it, the box with the mirror that sat by the fireplace. His office was full of interesting objects collected over years of travel, but nothing so interesting just now as that box. Jack kept talking and Maximos kept listening.

Maggie was reading in her chair by the fire, Max saw her, and was for a moment distracted. He smiled at her and forgot what Jack was saying.

"Say again Jack?"

He sat listening for a long time and Maggie went back to her book. Their large Irish setter, another bow in the direction of comfortable stereotypes, stretched, yawned, and went back to sleep. Finally, Max hung up the phone and sat looking at the box.

Maggie, knowing his moods, waited for a bit before speaking. "Well?"

Her voice was perhaps the only thing that could have called him back from the far place where his thoughts had led him.

"I think, my dear, that the time has come."

It was, perhaps, the only thing he could have said that would have startled her. She knew him so well. She had seen him declaim over the putative discovery of a new meaning in some obscure Byzantine text. He would announce it "earth shattering" and be off to phone Peter. This quiet statement was not like that, and she knew what it meant. Maggie placed her book on the end table. It would go unread for many days after that and when she picked it up again a few weeks later the "thriller" seemed too tame after the events she had experienced.

"I am going to look in the mirror."

"Why?"

"The shadows are stirring, Maggie, even more than they did forty years ago."

Max got up slowly, crossed himself, and knelt before a dark oak box. It was about six feet long and might have been a hope chest. It had no lock and there was a mirror on the surface of the lid.

"Is this safe, Max?"

"I had communion today."

"Did you receive it worthily?"

"God helping me, yes."

"Max."

The old scholar looked into the mirror on the top of the box. "Lord Jesus Christ, son of God, have mercy on me a sinner."

Maggie was quiet, waiting for Max to tell her what he was seeing. She knew he had not looked into that mirror for over twenty years. It was too exhausting after a certain age.

Max finally looked up, crossed himself again, and slowly stood up. Finally he spoke to her:

"We shall have to go to Jack's."

"Tonight?" she asked.

"Yes."

"I have a few calls to make. We must get Father to come."

Maggie looked thoughtful. "Of course." She got up and pulled the weights up on the clock to give it another seven days of life. Neither of them would be there when it ran down a week later.

19 January 2009, Monday, 5:30 PM: Rochester, New York, Saint Michael Orthodox Church

Father John closed the door to the Saint Michael Orthodox Church. There had been a time in this little parish in the 19th ward of the city when the doors had never been locked. The times and the neighborhood had changed, and locks were multiplying as property values sank. Some of the icons in the building were quite old, and art collectors were known not to ask too many questions about their latest prize. Of course, the church could never be made really secure, so locking up was probably a waste of time, but it comforted the parish council. A big part of the practical life of an Orthodox priest was comforting the parish council.

He paused to light a candle before the Blessed Theotokos. Her face, pure and serene, looked alive in the candlelight. It is not as common as one might wish for an over worked parish priest to devote hours of his "free" time to prayer, but Father John was exactly that uncommon sort of priest. If locking the door comforted the parish council, his prayers in the quiet church comforted Father John.

He began his prayers, "Holy Mary, mother of God, pray..."

In the far corner of the nave a glow began. It passed without notice at first. The priest moved his fingers with practice over the smoothed knots on his black prayer rope. "Jesus Christ, Son of God, have mercy on me a sinner."

John shifted his weight off a knee gone dodgy through college soccer long ago and too many food festival fundraisers recently. This shifted his gaze for a moment from the Theotokos and a growing light caught his eye. He was immediately on his feet. Remembering, through practice making perfect, to bow briefly before the Host, he rushed to the far back of the Church.

His heart sped up: fire? Disaster. He knew what fire could do to an old building like Saint Michael. All wood, it had been a Catholic Church before being purchased by his Western Rite parish a few years earlier. Suburban bound Italians were fleeing the neighborhood, just as college professors and students were moving into it. His young group of converts loved all

26

the wood. It was so "authentic," they would mutter in awe, but authentic or not the building would, in the words of the Fire Marshall who inspected it, simply "go up like a match" in a fire. As a result of insurance priorities, the building had bad plumbing, but a state of the art fire system. It was overly sensitive, and once the candles on the altar from an Advent vesper's service had set it off. Father had been firm that electric candles, like a praise band, were not happening at Saint Michael.

No alarm? It was quiet. Preternaturally quiet. His heart was beating in rhythm to his last prayer, "Jesus. Christ. Son. Of God. Have. Mercy." He stopped. The prayer rope slipped from his left hand and touched, for the first time, the ground. The glow came from an icon and it was on fire.

In the rear of Saint Michael was a shrine to the New Martyrs of Russia. Simple, yet impressive, a prominent member of his Church had put it there as a warning and a call to faithfulness and it reminded his comfortable parish of the thousands, millions, who died for the faith during the reign of Soviet unreason: the New Martyrs.

The shrine was full of icons done in the Western style. Angles circled the outside around the main arch of the shrine and Saint Michael crowned the top, his sword eternally drawn and ready. Images of children and martyred believers crowded the center of the shrine lit by flickering candles representing the prayers of the faithful. More windows to heaven surrounded the main icon: Saint Elizabeth, sister to the Tsar and New Martyr, Saint Tikhon, patriarch, murdered by Communists, icons of Nicholas, Alexandria, and the Imperial family.

The holy fire wreathed a small icon of the Imperial family in the very center of the shrine, one of the first ever made: Nicholas, Alexandra, Olga, Tatiana, Maria, and Anastasia wreathed in flames. The light did not hurt his eyes or even dazzle them. He could see each detail of the icon more clearly than he had ever seen any physical object. The cracks in the varnish of the image were beautiful, the gold background staggering, and the figures luminous. He could see through the paint to the texture of the wood and through that to the wall and still his eyes were drawn further inside the image. He could see everything.

The eyes of the figures in the icon began to stream with holy oil, but the sweet aroma of myrrh did not destroy his sense of smell. He could smell the leather of the book on the altar. He could smell everything.

Father John fell to his knees. The priest had never stopped praying the Jesus prayer: "Jesus Christ, Son Of God, have mercy on me a sinner." Each time he spoke the Name every bell in the church from the largest bell in the steeple to the smallest bell on the thuribel would chime.

The phone began to ring in his study.

19 January 2009, Monday, 7:00 PM: Pittsford, New York

The friends gathered on the evening of Martin Luther King Day in the dining room of Jack and Susan's sprawling Pittsford home. The huge, round oak table in the center of the dining room had hosted the group's Christmas feast a month ago, but this meeting was much less formal. An eclectic group of mugs sat before each place, personally chosen for each guest.

Jack was at the head of the table, but he had nothing to say. Susan was next to him and she was talking quietly to Barth. The physicist was nervous and kept looking down at his RIT mug and wishing he would stop seeing patterns in the swirl of the English-Breakfast tea.

Father John was sipping cafe latte from his dishwasher-faded Oxford mug, still shaken by his experience in the Church. Maximos had called him to this meeting and had shared a disturbing story about Peter and his dreams. Both events were similar, though his vision in the Church had brought him great peace while Peter's dream was disturbing his friend's sanity.

The priest rubbed his beard out of habit while he checked the spiritual temperature of his congregation. He looked at Arthur and Maggie Maximos. It had been their money that had helped furnish the shrine. Maggie had found the icon of the Royal Martyrs in a pile of junk at a Moscow outdoor market, bought it, and brought it to the church. Both Maggie and Arthur Maximos knew enough about the world to expect that icons would weep. Jack and Susan were recent converts and were having a harder time understanding the story. They believed in such things in theory, but it was harder to understand in practice. Barth did both his metaphysics and his physics with faith so he was quite calm. His physics contained weirder things than Holy Fire. All his parishioners were handling things well except for Peter and the distracted look on his face worried the priest.

The bay window of the dining room looked out on the greens of the Pittsford Country Club. The grass was winter brown waiting for nearly constant rains of Rochester to bring them back to life. There was nothing to see, but Peter sat looking out across the fairways anyway. Meaningless, really, all that grass and order for a game. It was not quite a park and certainly not a forest. What was it for? Peter had never been much for games. Barth, on the other hand, loved golf almost as much as Jack and Susan who played several times a week. To Peter, golf was pointless and golf courses looked sterile. They were not just nature tamed and domesticated for service, but nature forced into a mold. Were you really outside when on a golf course? It was the outside most like being inside all leading to a drink at a 19$^{th}$ hole. With weariness he realized that Max was at last talking and he would have to listen.

"Many things are beginning to happen together, friends." Max was working up to his full lecture style. "Pieces of the puzzle only visible to one or two of us are now evident to all."

Peter could not keep his mind on the words. Something was happening and some of it was happening to him, but he was too tired to care. His eyes drifted back down the fairway. In the distance, the steeple of a white church showed against the black Rochester sky. The clouds were low, so low that the steeple seemed cramped for space and soon would pierce the low hanging clouds and bring the snow.

19 January 2009, Monday, 7:00 PM: Pittsford, New York, Faith Baptist Church

Peter did not know it, but the inside of the church was hopping. The Faith Baptist Church of Pittsford was holding a revival service. The members of Faith were fundamentalists untainted by Evangelicalism, and the congregation was content to be their grandparents' church. There were church ladies in abundance. They had dish-to-pass suppers in the basement. There was an altar rail where sinners came to kneel and cry away their sins. Faith Baptist may have been the only place in Rochester more intentionally anachronistic than Max's study.

The only thing new in the church was the carpet: royal blue, and synthetic. You could shock a friend if you scooted across it with the proper shoes and did not lift your feet. The church had an organ and a piano, but no guitar every played in the building. In fact, any music with a "back beat" worried some of the mothers of the congregation almost as much as Cabbage Patch dolls and super-hero movies had worried their mothers.

The waves of theological liberalism had utterly missed Faith. As the senior pastor noted, "If it is in the canon, we shoot it." There were no hesitant and sly disclaimers regarding the Faith once delivered to the saints; the Old Story was bellowed and believed.

The revival was in full swing. The workers of Pittsford, the people who cleaned, built, and repaired, were touching the Eternal. The visiting pastor was striding up and down the platform and he was enjoying his work. His bald-head was wet with sweat mopped with a hankie he carried in one hand as he waved a worn black Bible in the other. His tie was wide across an even wider belly and his strained tie tack was an American flag. The air was cold coming in from the half opened windows of the Church, but the sanctuary was hot. Hot as if the fires of Pentecost were burning in their souls, though in this church the Spirit would not have dared to move a soul to tongues. They did not believe in such things in this age and dispensation.

"Jesus is alive, I tell you. Whatever men may say, whatever the professors and pundits may proclaim, Jesus is alive. He wants your heart, he wants your soul, and he wants to bring you salvation. He will give you new life. It is the message of Easter, of hope. You must come to Jesus. He won't force you. He is a gentleman. He is waiting. He has a good gift, a better gift, a gift as sure as the promises of this Bible. Tonight can be your night." Pastor Henry moved to the center of the stage.

"Amen." The congregation leaned forward in the hard wood pews. The tears were beginning to flow. There was no doubt that the Spirit was beginning to fall at Faith Baptist. "His sacrifice, His death, what He did for us on Calvary! Who can put a price tag on it? Who can fail to rejoice with that old song in knowing that "We Are Bound for the Promised Land?" But it might be..."

And Tom Scott sat in the back hearing it all. Of course he knew the story. He knew also what his mother wanted him to do, but what Tom wanted to do was to escape this Church, escape from Pastor Henry, to breathe free air. He wanted to get out of Faith, but somehow he knew he was not going to go. The lights were too bright, the words too loud, and God was closing in on him. It was loud, and he wanted quiet, but he was afraid to move, for all the motion in the room seemed toward that man and his Bible. He knew that there was no escape from the love of God that made the Church so powerful. He could escape the silly cultural additions, he could deny his family, but he could not deny that Story. It kept pounding into his skull. He was a sinner. God knew his sin.

"And what will you do with Jesus?"

Tom squirmed on the unyielding boards of the seat. He stared at the names scratched on the back of the pew in front of him by little children with access to Daddy's car keys. What year were they put there? How could he be a Christian, at least this sort of Christian? What about the lies, the lust, the rebellion? How often had he told his Mom, in need of a lot of support after Dad left, to leave him alone! Damn. Would this service never end? How absurd it all was! That preacher. What should he do? He knew what to do, but he did not want to do it.

"All to Jesus I surrender ... all to Him I freely give."

The song was starting. How many times had he made it to the last verse without moving that fatal first muscle? His mother would be praying ... again. She said, she always was saying

31

something, that he had a calling and she always said this in hushed and reverent tones, though Tom thought that everybody in his Church ended up with a calling. When he was a little boy, Tom knew, he had told his mother whatever popped into his head and said it was from God. Mom had been amazed and would have sworn, if she believed in swearing, that he was a prophet or called to be a prophet. Ideas were always popping into Tom's head, and sometimes they even served him well in creative projects, but an irritating idea was popping into Tom's head just now. Was his mother right?

He looked up at the face of the pastor who was no longer sweating. With the music playing, the man of God stood quietly in the pulpit praying. For one moment, the face was unguarded as it looked down at the worn, black, red letter King James on the pulpit. It was the look of devotion like in a David C. Cook picture of an apostle and it was the look that seized Tom's soul. The man was, perhaps, absurd: Tom's friends would call him a clown. But he was in touch with something else, something that could transfigure a sagging middle-aged face into beauty. What was it? What was it that pulled at Tom's heart? What was making him get out of his seat?

The words to the old hymn, "The cross before me, the world behind me..." filled the little Church. People began to murmur as the hardest young man in the Church youth group moved up the aisle.

Tom was kneeling before he knew it. And then he lost sight of Pastor Henry, and forgot his Mother, his gift, and his fear of Hell. He saw. He saw what cannot be described, but only known in the seeing. If Peter could have seen inside the Pittsford church, he would have been happy. He would have been less happy if he had known what was happening at the same time in his own college.

19 January 2009, Monday, 8:30 PM: Rochester, New York, Lyons Christian College

Arthur Maximos once told Peter that the cosmos was all God's, but that Hell loved to pretend that it was hanging in the balance. The masters in the infernal regions had convinced themselves that evil existed as a real power opposite from goodness. The policy of Hell tended to be reactive as a result. Every fundamental defeat, and they had no fundamental victories, would lead to some petty reaction from evil that would soothe the nerves of the devils. In this way they could pretend that they were creating something new and not merely breaking something good.

What was happening in Rochester was part of that pattern. Killing was easy, but they could not yet create life, nor had they any power over the dead. Even murder could turn out badly, as they had discovered in the case of Jesus. The harrowing of Hell still stung, God claimed even Hell as his, but they were about to strike back again to reclaim some lost dignity.

The conversion of Tom Scott was very irritating. The devils have some idea of the value of a human soul and the loss of even one disturbs them considerably, but they do not value all souls equally. Some humans could, after all, do things, and it was Tom's extraordinary abilities they craved. Demons cannot tell the future, but they are very clever and could make a good guess of the damage a sanctified Scott could do. An irritated devil, Maximos would say, is apt to strike back quickly even if it distracted them from their main plans. Tonight's defeat in the Tom Scott affair led directly to an overreaction at Lyons Christian College.

Dr. Robert DeLong had not felt such a spiritual passion in a lecture in some time. If he spoke that way, he would have said he felt an "anointing," but DeLong did not use religious jargon. He had been asked to give the Spring Scholar's Lecture at this small Rochester Christian college on the evening of Martin Luther King Day, was being paid well, and was earning every penny of his money. He was really, from any point of view, at the top of his game. Dr. DeLong was a fixture on the small Christian college lecture circuit and rare was the Christian college student who had not read one of his books.

His most recent, Fear of the Intellect: How False Piety Makes for an Impotent Church, had become a rallying cry for the Christian college professor that felt stifled by the culture. A stellar review in Christianity Today led to a commencement lecture at Wheaton College and a regular column in Books and Culture. The average Christian layman had never heard of him, but he owned Christian colleges.

DeLong worked hard at God's work and was not afraid to speak the truth in love. He attacked fundamentalism, those who would marry religion to the Republican Party, and the anti-intellectualism of the average Evangelical church. His book jacket called him a "voice crying in the wilderness." Christian Scholar's Review marveled at his courage, irenic spirit, and erudition. His seminary gave him an endowed chair and he was up for a book of the year award. In short, he was brave, handsome, daring, and very bright. Tonight the campus chapel was full to overflowing and he was giving them everything he had.

The applause was just dying from the last point. He had compared Billy Sunday to Bertrand Russell and found Sunday lacking. He had moved from the Enlightenment to deconstruction and now he was winding up to the climax of his talk. His suit, perfect pearl gray, soft without edges, matched his pale blue eyes and neatly trimmed gray hair, all merging into a whole without any parts. The audience, which after all was mostly undergraduate, may not have understood all the references, but they knew it was very authentic and not the kind of thing they would have heard at Pittsford's Faith Baptist: full of stories and relevance.

"And so the fundamentalist has defended the Bible. And we must give him credit for it. The theologian turns to him, and she applauds this willingness to believe, to have courage, in an age he thinks is evil and secular. Sure, the fundamentalist has embraced a dualism, a false dilemma. This age is not so unlike any other. There is no golden age, no Eden to return to with guilty faces. But he believes there is, and so the fundamentalist is brave. On so much we can agree." DeLong leaned forward. He spoke without a glance at his notes. The teleprompter in his mind give him every cue and tonight it was running fast and hot.

"But the fundamentalist, by his hasty condemnation of the Enlightenment and of the post-modern age, actually imbibes in the worst forms of their spirit. He has made objective truth an idol. He has raised his ideas about God to the level of the Very Words of God. And it is this we cannot applaud. The fundament-alist looks at modern science and is afraid. He cannot see God in the workings of chance and natural causes and so declares God is not present. Does he think he can capture God in a sentence, or the Truth of His creation in the dry and dusty logic he be-lieves he finds in Genesis? I suggest to you that the failure of your home Church to understand your questioning spirit, your desire to grow, is based on fear. Their burning desire to control and wipe out your youthful quest for something more than a mere formula or creed is the last move of the Old against the New Wine of the Spirit!"

The room broke into applause. The bulk of the student body was rolling with DeLong, the hard right of the student body sat impotent, unsure if they agreed or disagreed. A few of the faculty looked bemused. One could not be quite sure where this talk was going. There were the trustees to consider, and the alumni were quite conservative at times. Still, they controlled official college news. If word of this lecture got out on some passionate right-wing student blog, a few missionary alum stories in the college paper would balance everything out. Besides, donors old enough to have money did not believe blogs; they trusted the newsletters from Mar-Com.

DeLong continued, "On this Martin Luther King Day we must face our own bigotry and intolerance. We must speak the truth to power in the name of the oppressed."

He paused to take a deep breath. He sipped some water. "I know of a girl, the leader of her youth group. She wanted to be a pastor. She wanted to serve. The Holy Spirit, best reason, and the true traditions of the Church were with her. I know of a young man. He struggled with his sexuality. Was he gay? Was he straight? He knew one thing; he wanted the sort of relationship he had seen between his Mom and Dad. Whatever else, his partner would be his partner for life. Two stories, but the same reaction from our community."

The chapel was very quiet. "The response of the Church was not love for this young woman and man. Instead it was anger born of fear. They were afraid of something that might not fit into their neat little worlds, but the Bible tells us perfect love casts out all fear."

DeLong's voice trembled with emotion, "That young man is outside the Church and shunned by his family. They had no room for him as the rigid never have room for the Lord. And the young girl ministers to the poor, but is no longer in Church, because we had no room for her call and passion. We must be better than that. We must reach out. We must think. We must reason. We must embrace the best of science, literature, and the arts. We must see that all truth is God's truth. We must no longer have false piety in an impotent Church and it will begin by our repenting for the sins of our fathers and mothers." DeLong felt humbled by the reaction, enthusiastic even by his standards. "Not by my power," he muttered to himself.

The applause died down. The janitor began to quietly clean up in the back. The last students were shaking Dr. DeLong's hand. A few angry students were quoting Bible verses. DeLong had a sad smile on his face. He had been just like them once, so sure of himself and his rightness. He must remember to pray for them.

Mostly, however, the crowd around him was excited. The chair of the sociology department who had organized the event felt utterly vindicated as he stood at DeLong's side. He drew a strained breath and noted grimly, "I can only feel sorry for the faculty who chose not to attend such an anointed lecture."

"Every Christian college has people who struggle with new ideas ... and," DeLong smiled, "older donors."

"It is time that something was done. It is the twenty-first century and we are dealing with issues of justice, not of taste." DeLong and the sociologist walked out of the chapel.

Shadows poured from the box in Max's study.

19 January 2009, Monday, 8:30 PM: Pittsford, New York

Peter turned his eye from the Church spire across the golf course and blessed the Christians there under his breath. He wished he were with them, he wished he were anywhere rather than here.

Peter smiled a bit as he realized that this was not quite true: he would rather be at Jack's, even talking about the Dream, than at the DeLong lecture schedule tonight at Lyons.

Father John got his attention. "You have heard the story of the icon of the New Martyrs. What does this miracle mean?"

Jack stopped Peter from replying. "You know that my colleagues would say that you were both hallucinating. Religious devotion can manifest itself in many strange ways."

"But then there is the question of my dream combined with Father John's miracle. It seems to fit together." Peter commented.

"Fit what?" Barth growled. "We have pieces, but no idea if we even have a puzzle."

Maximos lowered his hand, palm open, slowly on the table. "The last Tsar, that is the key. What of him Father John?"

The priest paused and then spoke. "Many in the Church view the death of the last Tsar as very significant. Of course, Orthodoxy has no single eschatology, but many argue that the death of the last Russian, the last Roman, Emperor in 1918 was a turning point in history."

Barth groaned. "No eschatology please! I have spent a good lifetime in the Church studiously avoiding all discussions of the end times."

"Agreed. Totally agree." Jack muttered. "What in God's name does the Tsar have to do with the end of the world?"

"It has been suggested, and mind you this is only speculation, not Church teaching, that Orthodox emperors existed to restrain great sin and wickedness. It is certain that after the death of Nicholas all hell broke loose for the Faithful."

Jack spoke. "Of course many of them were not good men themselves. Look at the Russian pogroms. The Byzantine Empire itself was no paradise."

Maximos agreed. "You have misunderstood me. We did not fall from a golden age, but lost a barrier to human wickedness. The rights of the individual and the rights of the state are hard to balance and a Christian emperor may have been part of that balance. Even when it did not work in practice, the office was there and some evil may have been restrained.

The emperors, West and East, were often quite wicked, but their position prevented a greater wickedness. They restrained a certain sort of moral chaos and reminded men of the best parts of the past. The worst of the Christian emperors never dreamed of the gulag. Something changed in the scope of evil and its attack on man's basic humanity when they were gone."

Susan said, "Liberty was lost in the name of perfect equality."

Jack still looked troubled, but wanted to hear more. He was blunt: "You don't have to agree with the politics or the eschatology Maximos is suggesting (and I don't think I do) to know something must be up. I will admit that natural explanations for what is happening here don't satisfy me right now."

Maximos looked at them all. "I would caution all of you to keep an open mind. We mustn't turn into a group that is going to look at the world just like our secular colleagues. There is a deep mystery here. We must follow the trail wherever it leads us."

Maggie looked at her husband fondly, but laughed, "That includes you, Arthur. Your highly speculative theories are not holy tradition. Don't invest too much in them, or any one of them, and keep an open mind."

Barth turned to Maximos. "This is all too strange. There are things I know from my work, but I cannot talk about them due to the nature of my University grant. I can say government funders in two nations have an interest in certain, related, historical events."

"Perhaps," Maximos turned in the direction of the physicist, "you could hint at the connection you see to the Miracle of the Icon and Peter's dream."

"This much is no secret: our government and another major power are working hard to understand the nature of time." Barth looked at the ceiling, unsure how much he should say. "The team leader is eager to recruit me, but I am even more eager to have nothing to do with some of the scientists in the project. Still they keep in touch and I am informed overall." Barth paused and chose his words with care, "At least one of the project leaders is using July 17, 1918 as a reference point."

Father John crossed himself.

"I take it from the general reaction this date matters?" Jack asked.

"That is the day the Tsar was murdered by his slaves." Peter replied.

19 January 2009, Monday, 8:30 PM: Douglass University

Mary and Bobby were sitting in his office, having heard, at last, from the funders. There had been good news and bad news. The good news was that, despite the recent drop in the price of oil, the main international grant was still coming. The bad news was that the donor wanted faster results and more access to project data. Only the whine of the computer connecting for periodic downloads broke the silence.

"They want it done now," Mary said gently.

"I cannot do it safely right now. The machine is not ready."

"They don't care. We have to bring back the body," Mary said at last.

Bobby Kennedy was at a loss for words.

Finally he spoke: "My god."

"Exactly," Mary responded.

# Chapter Three:
# A City in Words

20 January 2009, Tuesday, Inauguration Day, 1:00 PM: Douglass University

Mary Yurislav turned off the Inauguration with satisfaction. Thank the gods the Chimp-in-Chief was gone and thoughtful adults were back in charge of the nation. Today was already a good day, maybe even a great day, and Mary was determined to add to the history making. This day would change her life, and Mary was in a reflective mood.

Who was she? Where was she going?

Mary's mother would not have known what to make of her daughter. Or perhaps, Mary thought, she would have known just what to make of her. From her mother's point of view she had gone the wrong way, so far the wrong way, perhaps, that her old-fashioned Russian mother would have viewed her as evil. It was sad, really, the bondage that bound that old woman, the most strict sort of holy-roller Russian Pentecostal. Of course, though no one at the University would have guessed it, Mary Yurislav herself, had once been "washed in the blood of the lamb." She could never bring herself to join the sneers of her clever friends about religion because of that. There had been something warm and real about those days and nights in the church.

If Mary was anything, she was honest and she wanted to be fair. She had gotten a good academic start from the tiny Christian school her mother had picked out. The teachers there were very wrong, but they had not known any better. They had done the best they could, despite the beliefs that had warped their thinking, and the attention they gave each student had worked.

Church revivals gave a socially acceptable emotional release to blue-collar men and women. There was good to those warm nights, full of passion and shouts and imaginary victories over Sin and Satan. The battles they won were no less real to the folk in the room, though no less imaginary than the triumphs of Bush in Iraq, only Bush should have known better.

Like most people with wit and promise, college had helped her by giving her better ideas than her mother could. Her brains and Regent's scholarship had won her a ticket into the intellectual class. There she met her peers, and the questions raised by her studies moved her out of her mother's church. Why no women pastors in her home church? Why trust a Bible that was out of date? Why didn't the Bible condemn sins like slavery more forcefully? There had been many questions, and only dog-eared paper backs from the Church library with titles like, "The Bible has the Answer!" to guide her. Self-educated "doctors" who had never seen the inside of an actual college classroom wrote these books and they were full of condemnations of "evolution" and the "higher criticism." They were pretty bad and she had none of the sympathy for their pretensions that she had for folk religion.

In short, the more she learned in school the less she believed. It had not made her happier, sadly. Truth might set you free, but, in her experience, rarely made a woman happy. Her mother proved that innocent ignorance was be bliss, and Mary was honest enough with herself to admit that occasionally, **very** occasionally, she wanted to believe all of it again. She wished she could find a head covering, and go back and speak once more in tongues under the power of God's Holy Spirit. She supposed that at thirty-eight everyone misses childhood sometimes.

Whenever she went home, especially at Christmas, she could pretend that she did not know better. She could believe for a minute, and it was not all bad. Leaving behind family ways left her feeling, always, a bit rootless.

Her life was a very full and satisfying one in other ways, however. She had a job that meant she would be the president of a very good university before long. Mary was waiting for the right offer, but meanwhile had easy access to men, money, and power. Mary did not care much about any of that, except to keep off their horrid alternatives: loneliness, poverty and weakness. She knew what all three were like, and did what was necessary to avoid them.

One good gift of her childhood was, thank the gods, an aversion to the cold irreligion of lizards like Bobby Kennedy. She knew that his facile materialism was as dated as her mother's religion. Her mother had been a saintly Victorian Christian, while Kennedy was a loud-mouthed Victorian atheist. Mary wanted nothing to do with Victorians of any kind, but supposed if she had to choose, she would pick the saints.

Mary wasn't a Christian, but wasn't interested in being a Not-Christian. What was she? She had done Eastern religion as a grad student, but then hadn't everyone? Some truth was there, like all religions she supposed, but no power. She either got mystery with no thought or thought with no mystery. She might as well be a Christian!

All the trendy religions lacked the historical depth that was one of the few charms of her childhood Pentecostal experiences. She had friends who stuck with the eclectic "choose-your-own-religion" path, but did not like what she saw. Choosing her own religion meant ending up with a religion that looked a good bit like her ... and Mary had no desire to worship a god in her own image.

Mary did not know anyone she thought could be trusted to be the founder of a religion! Since most people knew they needed something else, her friends ended up looking for one more thing to do: vegetarianism leading to a simpler life style leading to further rules that made her fundamentalist childhood look positively libertine. You could sleep with nearly anyone guilt-free, but had to boycott most stores, use plastic grocery bags, and only eat most meat with guilt.

Mary had grown skeptical about all of it. A woman must

do what grownups do and face the terrible ambiguity of the universe. One could not take comfort, like silly old Bobby, in the emptiness of the Universe since it did not appear to be empty, but one could also not find any other easy answers either. There is Something More and no one knows what it is. Mary was determined to keep poking in the odd corners until she found a piece of that Something More, and lately it had seemed that she was closing in on it.

The physics people had been working on problems dealing with time and some of the worries without solutions that seemed to be the heart of contemporary physics. One interesting colleague said everything we thought we knew about the cosmos was based on ideas that could not all be true. This situation was, as Professor White once put it in a paper she heard him read, "not good."

Her faculty kept ripping pieces of the cosmos up until at last, using the University's pride and joy—the billions-of-dollars machine, laughingly called Magog—they had stumbled onto a discovery. She was quite proud of her part in it. She knew she was not the class of scientist to have made the break through, but she was a fantastic administrator who brought together the team and made sure the staggering bills got paid. Magog, the mere machine, was worth more than the rest of Douglass University. Mary was a good enough scientist, a first rate practical engineer actually, to know that Magog was a splendid bit of work.

As usual when she felt burnt out, Mary returned to the moment of her greatest triumph. She could remember the moment of the discovery better than she could remember any event of her life. It was the start of the adventure that had not ended yet. Last year, July 17 to be precise, Bobby Kennedy had come to see her. It was so unusual to see Bobby away from a keyboard that she had been at attention instantly.

He was sweating and stammering, "We, we…"

"One more and you can go all the way home," Mary said with a slight smile.

"This is serious, Yurislav. It is Magog! Magog!"

"Have you broken our multi-billion dollar baby?" and real

fear gripped Mary's heart. Some of the military types had nasty ways of getting even with people that wasted their precious grant money. A university could disappear off the grant list forever for the wrong kind of snafu.

"No. Not that ... never that!"

Speaking slowly, to help her project chief get control, Mary placed herself in the iron cocoon that was becoming a second skin, "What did you do to Magog?"

"We have gone back in time."

"What? Is that possible?"

"Well, we don't have a theory to explain it, if that is what you are asking. Though Bartholomew White has a thought about it."

"I don't care about the theoretical end of it at the moment. You're telling me that Magog took you back in time?"

"Well, in a manner of speaking. We were watching the computer reconstruction of the events occurring in the main chamber. And were, as you know, manipulating the Lego-matter around in as many geometric patterns as possible and Magog started showing us pictures."

"What?"

"I know. The machine started showing us coherent three dimensional images."

"Get to the point." She was impatient and in full control now. "What did you see?"

"It was like looking through a cloudy window into a room." Bobby was calming down now. "And it was full of people. Of course, there was no noise. We aren't wired for sound, though how the hell we would do that anyway is beyond me. Of course, I don't know what is going on down there now."

"It is still going on?"

"Same scene over and over again. Pretty violent. Looks to me like turn of century. But I don't know. We don't dare turn it off, for fear of losing it."

"You have everything recorded."

"Of course."

"I want the upload and a hard copy in my office now. If you can really go back in time, get it to me yesterday. You're not to turn Magog off for any reason. Call R.G. and E. and lie about our power needs. Burn the power grid for the rest of the city, but keep this going."

She had known the minute she downloaded and played the file on her office computer what they were seeing: the murder of the Imperial family. Why that? Her mother would have called it indecent to watch the death of the last Tsar. Her family had been utterly non-political except for a hatred of communism.

Her grandparents had fled the Revolution simply because things were bad, but her poppy had always believed that the Old Country suffered a sort of blood guilt for the many deaths of the Revolution. She remembered him saying, "They killed the Tsar. And then? It all came crashing down." Her family had the old Biblical superstitions about regicide: "Touch not the Lord's anointed." Her poppy said, "Lenin did what David would not."

Eventually they had to shut Magog down or risk burning it up, but every time they turned on the great machine, the images reappeared. It was a great strain on the machine and each attempt cost the school hundreds of thousands of dollars out of dwindling, off the record, military grants. They had to push further and see what it was they had.

Last night, less than six months after their first success, they had sent a probe, a tiny microscopic needle into the inner chamber of Magog. It had come back dirty. Analysis had reported it was just dirt, plain ordinary garden-variety dirt. They shut Magog down and cleaned it. The whole project was dust free in any case, but Bobby had gone almost mad to see dust and debris on his precious probe. Magog had been clean. Nothing, almost literally nothing, on the clean metal and stainless steel walls of the chamber. Clean.

Another probe was sent into the chamber: more dirt. And then they came to the answer that would have been obvious to anyone who did not know how impossible it was. Magog was allowing the needle probe to touch the walls or floor of the room. They had sent a piece of metal back in time and brought some earth forward.

Mary was delighted, of course. Just remembering the moment

when they knew, when the University had become the most important scientific institution on the planet, brought the ecstatic feeling back to her. She tapped on the desk, excited. They were going to grab a larger bit of matter tonight. She had questions, but tonight might be the start of getting answers.

Mary suffered from restless leg syndrome and as always when she was nervous or excited it began to annoy her. She began to do her breathing exercises to re-center her thoughts. The coolness returned. She smiled. She was going to put her school on the map.

Her life was about to get much simpler and much more pleasant. The worst part of any University administrator's job is asking for money, and Magog's cost had forced every waking hour to asking, groveling, for money. Some of the funding she had been forced to accept had come from outside the United States from people she hated dealing with. They had demanded to know everything she was doing that skirted post-9/11 law. Those days were over. She would never have to ask for money again—the entire world would throw it at her.

She might, given time, be able to direct Bobby and his team to explore all of history. She would know the true story of humankind. She could show the world, dimly, for there were still problems in resolution, the reality of its heritage. Myths vanquished, truth triumphant, she could bring to the world the Word that would set it free. Her mind, as had done so often of late, began to soar. She could vision heaven or hell. She could see what she wished with her inner eye. It came to her that she was, at last, on the edge of a new and better spirituality. It was the end of the childhood of humanity, perhaps, and January 21, 2009 was the beginning of a better age. They were going to found a new religion by giving humanity the truth.

The best way she knew to start was with a resurrection. Her team was going to do something so remarkable nobody could doubt or argue with it. They were going to bring back a body. Dead or alive, they were going to rescue Anastasia Romanov, one of the last Tsar's daughters. Her body, her corpse in reality, would shout the truth to the world.

Why Anastasia? Why not someone religiously important like

Jesus or the Buddha? Mary knew the answer to that ... she had always wanted to save Anastasia, even as a little girl. She was in charge and she got to pick. Of course, she had fed her committee some bull about needing a person recognizable, but not offensive to a big part of the world's population. Snatching Mohammad's body would not just put their funding at risk. It had helped that the machine seemed to want to view 1918. Any other date gave them greater headaches and more breakdowns. She had pushed for her project and Magog had cooperated.

But in private reflections, she was not fooled by her own public reasons. Mary wanted to save Anastasia, because that is what her grandfather would have done if he could have. She wanted to do something to make her family proud of her, given that over the next few years she would look back to the past, record what had really happened, and almost surely destroy the foundations of their faith.

She smiled to herself at the "almost" she had inserted into her thoughts. What if she found an empty tomb? Mary knew she could not stop hoping that Jesus was alive, even though the implications would undermine most of what she had done. She had loved Jesus and been furious with him for not being the God-man He said He was.

Mary felt contented. She was open minded enough to know her deepest desires, even uncomfortable childish desires, and was acting on the best information she had. Her conscience was clear. She was one with the order of things, because she knew her place in it and accepted it. She was not passive, but joyful in acknowledging her role. In her mind's eye she saw the planets wheeling about the earth. She saw the stars as gods and as persons. She saw the thousand-year journey of her soul to truth and knew she was finally beginning to come out of the darkness. Mary was unaware now of the room. Her hand stopped its motion. They were going to bring the dead back to the living. Anastasia would be here and would know a better place and a happier ending. Time would be broken, its hold on humankind no more and the problem of evil would be solved. Is could be molded to ought by the faculty of a Rochester university: the brightest and best.

She was happy, grimly happy. She began to hum a simple song, full of new meaning with none of the old baggage, "Praise God, from whom all blessings flow. Praise Him all Creatures here below."

20 January 2009, Tuesday, Inauguration Day, 1:30 PM: Lyons College, Hart Hall

Tom Scott woke up without a hangover. That was good. He was "saved." And on thinking about it for a moment that was good too. He had made his mother happy; she had hugged him at least half a dozen times before letting him go to bed at about two in the morning.

He slept an unconscionably long time, but he felt marvelous. Light, like a middle aged man who had just lost ten pounds from around his middle in a moment, and he was almost afraid of doing something wrong and losing the feeling. He glanced at the clock radio. WHAM had failed to wake him up with its usual mix of talk and commercials. It was then that he noticed that the green numbers were telling him that it was thirty minutes until his sociology class.

He almost swore. Almost. Do Christians swear? He laughed out loud. It was amazing how good he felt. How did one shower as a Christian? He was going to be late for class. He hustled through his getting ready routine. Mother would have been long gone to work. She would be cleaning houses to help keep things going. It was that sort of sacrifice that had made him willing to go to the Christian college after two years at Monroe Community College. It made his mom happy, and it was a decent school. In a grade-inflated world, Tom was a perfect "B" student, but a good man at a party.

He grabbed a bagel and headed for the door. If he drove about ninety miles an hour on 490, he might make it to class before attendance. As he slid into his 1979, very peppy, Buick Skylark he noticed it was not snowing. He felt grateful to God for that small mercy since it radically increased his chances of getting to Lyons on time. He caught himself; he simply refused to become the sort of person who found a spiritual meaning in everything. Next he would be seeing visions of Jesus in the primer and rust spots on his car. And he laughed out loud about that as well.

He hustled into class and saw with relief that Dr. Mott was slowly getting on to the stool in the front of the room. He was in time, because his professor was never on time. Mott ran on a schedule that his body could tolerate and that meant moving slower than Uncle Joe at the Junction. Dr. Mott was boldly and gloriously fat. If Santa were a sociologist, he would have been the skinny member of the department. In fact, his fat was the best thing about Mott, an act of defiance against the politically correct skinniness of most professors out of keeping with Mott's usually predictable opinions. His fat was his one rebellion against the spirit of the age, but it did slow him down.

Mott tended to teach perched on a stool at the front of the room and he never moved if he could help it. Sociology was taught from the overhead projector that was nailed to the floor next to his over-burdened stool. Many students had never seen an overhead and the University had removed them from every classroom saving his, but Mott was unapologetic. No computerized whiz-bang graphics for Mott, he distrusted any change in lectures he had polished over twenty years of teaching. He had been through this material many times before and he lectured with a self-assured wheeze. Half the time he showed videos, actual VHS tapes, to the class and he was always on the lookout for a good guest lecturer. Simultaneously he had ferocious attendance requirements. There was not much to his class, but you had to attend it.

Today, however, Dr. Mott was in a rarely energetic mood. He had watched Obama sworn in, that was good, and someone else was going to teach his class, and that was better. He had a real treat for his student; his satisfaction with the world filled the room. Tom prepared, as he always did, to count the wheezes in everything the sociologist said as a kind of mental exercise, but could not quite settle into classroom catatonia. He kept feeling that something bad was about to happen, but Tom knew that nothing good or bad ever happened in a Mott class. He twisted in the seat and tried to ignore the feelings.

"Today, we have the honor, wheeze, of having, in our class, Dr. DeLong. I have known, wheeze, Bob DeLong since we were in seminary together." A moment of heavy breathing followed this exciting announcement. "Dr. DeLong is, and has been, wheeze, a leader in the movement to bring real, evangelical Christianity into the academic world. Without further ado, wheeze, Dr. DeLong."

There was a smattering of polite applause and then DeLong came to the podium. Tom did not bother to listen to a word of it, of course. It would not be on the final since it had not appeared on the overhead.

He had Dr. Alexis next for Intro to Philosophy. Alexis was pretty religious, not as common as you might think in a Christian college, and maybe he could talk to him. Alexis was not the best teacher ever, all over the place and pretty distracted, but he was a Christian. Maybe he could explain why Tom felt doomed and happy at the same time.

A fly was attacking the fluorescent light just above DeLong's head. The light buzzed. The fly kept hitting the light with a popping noise.

20 January 2009, Tuesday, Inauguration Day, 2:00 PM: Somewhere on the 441

Dr. Alexis should have been getting ready for his four o'clock class, but instead was speeding to Penfield to meet with Barth White and a few of his physicist friends from Douglass. He couldn't concentrate and his stomach hurt. While he drove he tried to prepare for class, but it was insanely difficult. At least he had the comfort of knowing that once back on campus and class had started, he would have some peace. Teaching always stopped the world for Peter and right now he needed the world to stop.

The meeting at Jack's house last night had gone well enough, but there was so little to go on, and so much that could not be said. Until you experienced the Dream, you could not know the horror of what was happening at their neighboring university. They were still guessing at what was going on with the machine

Barth called, very off the record, Magog. It all reminded Peter Alexis of something. What? There was the word again: "what." It hurt to think it.

His schedule? He knew it was shot. He had to drive back to Lyons after this emergency meeting with Barth. He would drive back to Lyons College, park, and walk directly into class. Thank God it was not snowing and that Lyons had good faculty parking. He could never have made it from Douglass, but of course if he had been a more productive scholar, like Barth, he would not have had late afternoon classes anyway. As a stud researcher, Barth taught no classes and made his own schedule. "Think about your day. Relax." Peter tried to govern his emotions, but that only made his stomach ache.

He had to concentrate. Think. What had he done today? What did he have to do? He had to teach in two hours, but first this meeting with Barth. He had gotten home from the meeting at Jack's house, slept very late, and woke up to find a message from his friend on his iPhone. Odd really, that Barth should call so soon after the meeting, but there had been an emergency meeting of the physics department at Douglass this morning and Barth must have learned something new. Barth wanted to see Peter after that meeting and whatever he had to say was too important to put on a mobile phone. Barth hated cars and refused to buy one so Peter, despite being the one with a schedule, got to drive. Where Barth could not bike or run, he would not go.

What were Barth and his colleagues at Douglass up to? Normally the physics crowd was too sane for Peter. They were the most romance free bunch one could hope to meet. Most were married to their work and viewed any non-scientific enthusiasm with scorn. So, what were they doing having secret meetings at five in the morning?

He drove to the address Barth had given: a very old house in Penfield. The brick house stood near the corner of Five Mile Line Road and the 441. Its brick was so old that any repairs would have been too expensive and so the present owners had slathered it with red paint. The red paint now needed paint. He parked his car. Old houses in such a state of disrepair always made him sad.

He walked up the porch and the stairs creaked. They were un-painted and a splintered gray. The many cards by the front door bore witness to a proud old mansion torn into apartments. He was to meet Barth in Apartment 2. He rang the bell.

"Come on up." Barth's voice. The buzzer sounded and Peter opened the outer door. He was relieved. It was as if he had half expected something or someone else. Something familiar was lurking at the back of his mind. There were things, not quite for-gotten, that kept creeping back to disturb him.

The stairs on the inside were in worse repair than those facing the weather, though they did not creak or groan. Each step simply sagged under his tread, lacking the life to protest each passing per-son. Now his stomach and his head hurt. For some reason, he felt like the idiot people in horror movies who keep going into the dangerous room, despite the background music telling them not to go. He knew now why the people kept going. They kept going because the script in their head refused them choices. Surely noth-ing could be bad up ahead? Step. What had happened when he was sixteen? Step. Where had that thought about his sixteenth year come from? Step. He had gone to summer camp. Step. He could not seem to remember much that happened at the little church camp. Step. He was remembering green, and clouds, and a girl's face. Blond hair. Blue eyes. Step.

Peter stopped in the middle of the long flight of stairs. Why couldn't he remember sixteen? What had happened? It was the year after his parents died. He had gone to live, where? Had he known Max then? Terror. He was remembering. Or he was go-ing mad. At this point he actually decided to turn around. He discovered that turning around was impossible. The glass on the door behind him was very dirty, and frosted. The early morning sun, rising just outside, could not light the hallway.

He suddenly knew what he had forgotten, not a lecture and not his laundry, but the most important events of his life. It was so simple, yet so impossible. He recalled that in his sixteenth year he had been on Barterra: another world with another sun.

"God, my God."

Madness and truth were both very close to him now. He

slumped against the dirty wall. He had failed that year to do something very important. What was it? Someone had died in the year of our Lord 1985. His parents? No, his parents had died in 1984. He was confusing his dates; the horrible murder in 1985 was not his parents'. Blonde hair. Blue eyes. Blood. He was recollecting. Trembling against the wall, he wanted to forget, to be born into a new world where memory could be lost. What had he failed to do? How could he have forgotten?

Suddenly, without any transition, in his mind, half mad, Peter was no longer in Penfield. He stood on the top of a very high tower. He was holding in his hands two birds made of crystal. They shimmered, full of fire. Cool to the touch, they burned his soul without touching his body. They filled the sky, lighting the darkness of the world. His thin young body was shaking. He knew what to do. He turned to the girl. He must place both the birds on her brow. Lisay. Her name was Lisay Macbor. He knew. And then blackness, and ruin, and smoke. Someone had betrayed him. He was slipping back through time and coming back to his Uncle Max. But first he saw the face of his foe, his mortal foe.

At the top of the stairs, the door swung open. Peter, the forty year old philosopher, looked up with sixteen year old eyes. At the top of the stair stood a fair haired young man of no more than thirty who was physically perfect like a god. He could have been Apollo come back to Earth, except for the dark patch covering one eye, but there was something child-like in the message of that ornament, like a pirate in a Victorian children's book. It said, "Despite my fair form, I am a bad person. Beware." The man had never been politically correct in his own world.

"Come now, Peter." god said, "We are old friends you and I."

"Bandor, Dragon Lord." Peter choked out

"That is a title better left to fairy tales. It would make your friends roll their eyes if they heard it and it is too simple for my complexity." the fair man was laughing. "This isn't a good world for dragons! You saw me and knew me then with a childish mind and used childish language to describe me. You can know me better now."

"I remember... I think I am beginning to remember."

Bandor spoke with Barth's voice, "Yes. You've forgotten. But I have not. You left me a world ago, but the time has come for me to pick up your quest that failed. It is time to bring the long struggle Home."

"Why did you bring me here? Simply to tell me this?"

"No. Nothing quite so melodramatic. I am not foolish enough to believe you would follow me and we both know I cannot kill you."

"Then what?" Peter was frustrated with his memory, with the situation, with the man at the top of the stair.

He began to speak. It was in her voice. The girl, he had failed so long ago. "Peter, my goal, my sole desire in this meeting, and the need of my heart, is to drive you mad. I need you insane, dear Peter"

The sound of her voice brought it all back and threatened to Blue Screen his mind. Nimlandor. Earl Macbor. The Narva Birds. An utter failure and a ruin ... and all of it was mixed up in his mind with the death of the Russian Tsar, the Dream, and a machine named Magog. He had held it all back for too long. Peter simply slumped on the step and began to cry.

"I cannot harm you, dearest Peter." The young man came down the stairs without making a sound, scarcely touching a stair. "But I can lock you in this room. I need your body out of the way for a few hours, and your knowledge." He touched the unconscious philosopher on the brow. He smiled gently to himself. "Yes. Now I know." He picked up Peter Rupert Alexis and carried him gently, like a mother with a sick infant, to the room at the top of the stairs.

A bare bed was in the center of the room. The blue stripes of the thin mattress were the only color in a room painted gray. Softly he placed Peter on the bed. No need for rope, Peter was scarcely breathing. Bandor reached down and touched Peter once again and smiled as he changed.

The image of Peter Alexis walked briskly to his car. He would be late for class, his class, if he did not hurry. "I believe," he said with an infectious grin, "that I shall lecture on time and virtual reality in class today."

20 January 2009, Tuesday, Inauguration Day, 2:00 PM: Rochester, New York, 19th Ward

"I don't know." Max was back in his study. The Democrat and Chronicle was untouched. What did the papers know about what was really happening in Rochester?

Maggie sat in her chair on the other side of the blazing fireplace. He had just watched the new President take office with her. Max had not voted for Obama, but was glad for much of what his victory represented. Today's paper would have none of those half-measures, the election of the new president would be the only story ... even the weather in the D&C would be useless.

A lifetime of living in Rochester told him exactly what he could anticipate this evening. It was cold but there was a fair night ahead, Max believed. Why read a paper to have his opinions confirmed or obvious reality denied?

Maggie spoke at last, "I don't like it, Max. Peter is becoming very unstable. How much does he remember?"

"Very little I think. It was almost thirty years ago. He has never said a word about it and he shows no sign of understanding me when I ask even the most leading questions." He looked at his wife, "But you know that since you have tried to speak to him about all of it yourself. He does not remember most of what we did for him in those years."

"But these new dreams? Why Peter? What do you really think it means?"

"What do I think? Or what do I believe?" Max stopped and looked at the ceiling. Maggie waited on him to speak knowing that if she interrupted him now she might not get him to speak of his worries this bluntly for a long time.

"I imagine, perhaps this is the best word "imagine", that the idiots in the lab at the University are using what they think of as science to play with time."

"Could that ...?" Maggie sat her Bible down very carefully.

"Open the Path again? It might. It would explain Peter being the one to dream. He is the only one of us who has been down that road so far. He has followed the windings of time to their very core. I have been to the Spindle at the center of the World, but he has been within the Earth. His soul remembers the way."

"So this machine that tears at time, what it does, impacts him?"

"I think it does. It tears at the forgetting that blocked out whatever happened to him. Those who visit that world drink of forgetfulness, but that mercy is fading. The machine is bringing back what had been forgotten. Peter may see what it sees."

"Why the Tsar? Odd. It seems so horrid and so repulsive. Unconnected."

"That is where I must confess to ignorance and to dark imagining."

"Go ahead. I know you are not sure." The house was silent.

"If something is Inside Earth and wants Out, then it might direct the images of the machine."

"I don't understand."

"Turn to Second Thessalonians, the second chapter."

Maggie picked up her Bible and turned to the passage. Max looked at her and said what he knew by heart, "Let no one deceive you by any means; for that Day will not come unless the falling away comes first, and the man of sin is revealed, the son of perdition, who opposes and exalts himself above all that is called God or that is worshiped ... and now you know what is restraining, that he may be revealed in his own time. For the mystery of lawlessness is already at work; only he who now restrains will do so until he is taken away. And then the lawless one shall be revealed."

"Yes? What does this have to do with Peter?"

"We must recollect. We must recall 1986, for there may be something that happened twenty-five years ago that might help us. When he returned up the path that July day in 1986, he could only talk about an evil man. He had failed at something, failed to do something. He had lost, or so he said, 'Barterra,' the other world. There was a girl, and a betrayal, and a crushing blow and then he was simply ill for a long time. You remember all of that."

"I remember. I paid no attention to his words. He was very sick."

"He was in hospital a long while. The doctors said, when he came out of it, he remembered nothing of his 'trauma'."

"And we helped his healing by staying away from him for a very long time, only making contact again when he went to college, but what does that have to with this verse, and with his dream?"

"If they are playing with time, and there was an evil at the heart of Time, what would keep them from unchaining that devil?"

"My God. The beast. But the Tsar?"

"He was, my dearest, the last man to rightfully wear the crown of Rome. Tsar is simply Caesar, you know. A few theologians have believed the Christian emperors of Rome, from Constantine to that last Tsar, Nicholas II, to be the rulers, with all their many faults, who restrained lawlessness."

"And after their fall?"

"Communism, fascism. Millions of dead. Empty churches. The beginning of the End. A confused and meandering middle time, full of peril, before the real doom falls."

"So," she looked at her man and said, "we are nearing the End. Those idiots at the University have at last gone too far."

"I think so. They shall, if they have not done so already, release whatever evil has been buried in Time, chained within Earth during the Age of the Church. We don't know what that Place was like. Only Peter has been there. Now the End is picking up from his failure. And the University types of course are too clever to see it. Our Peter, who failed once fighting it, is now back in the fray."

Both Max and Maggie looked at the box. Despite its size, it was rare for anyone to look at the box. Neither noticed that the shadows in room were coming closer. The logs in the fire popped and the light dimmed. Max rubbed his eyes and Maggie reached for the light.

Between the two of them a darkness grew and eventually Max spoke, "Maggie, someone is in the room."

"I know, Max."

"Saint Michael defend us."

The shadow lifted and Max and Maggie sat in silence for a

great while. Finally, Arthur Maximos turned to his wife and said, "Perhaps I should go see Peter after his class."

20 January 2009, Tuesday, Inauguration Day, 3:20 PM: Lyons College

Tom Scott started to leave his sociology class knowing that if he rushed, he just had time for a bathroom break and a Diet Coke before sprinting across campus to Cather Hall and his philosophy class. DeLong, not surprisingly, had talked far past the dismissal time. You could have walked out on anyone else. No one dared try with Mott physically blocking the door. The thought of trying to shift all that weight was positively frightening.

Tom tried to slip past Dr. Mott and Dr. DeLong. Both men were engaged in jovial after-lecture conversation. Unfortunately, Mott was still blocking his pathway to the door, Tom could not even see the hallway around the large sociologist.

"Excuse me, Dr. Mott. I need to get to Intro to Philosophy."

"Fine, fine." Mott began to creep to the side. Tom could see a flicker of light to his right hand side. The mountain was moving.

"Excuse me," DeLong spoke while passing his hand through his perfectly brushed silver mane, "Is that Dr. Alexis' class by any chance?"

Tom groaned inwardly. His day was already over crowded with things to do, and now he could sense an un-refuse-able Request coming. On top of that, he really had to go, but then he really had no choice but to say, "Yes, sir. It is Dr. Alexis."

"Could you by any chance walk me over there? Alexis and I went to college together, longer ago than I would like to say … and we are supposed to have dinner after his class with you. Thought I would sit in on the poor old fellow's class and provide a bit of balance." Dr. DeLong gave an experienced little chuckle. Everything he did was an unintentional stereotype, and Mott rolled his eyes sympathetically. He finally shifted enough to let Tom out the door.

Dr. Mott wheezed and snorted his way down the hallway with them. He then left them to cross the campus alone. Tom forgot his Diet Coke, but still hoped for a bathroom break ahead. Still DeLong was quite friendly, "I am imposing on you I am sure," the academic said softly in his rich, deep voice. "But I would get lost in my own home, let alone another campus. So I am most thankful to you."

Tom was irritated, guilty, and afraid to offend: "No problem."

"What did you think of my little talk last night?"

"Well, my home church was having a revival and my Mom wanted me to go."

"Yes." DeLong smiled in a kindly manner. "I remember them well. The preacher, always a bit on the heavy side, and the pressure to be 'saved.' I must have walked to the altar a dozen times! Did me no good, but no harm that I can tell either. Still it was good of you to support your mother. Such acts, a crisis of faith, are real moments of God's grace in our lives."

Tom felt deflated. Listening was worse than blocking a penalty kick with your stomach like he had done once in highschool. Catch it in the right place, and you can't move coherently for five minutes.

"Yes, sir."

"Please don't call me "sir." It makes me feel older than I am. Call me Robert."

"Yes, Robert."

DeLong was good at chatter, actually interesting, and they soon got across campus. Tom pushed through the double glass doors and dropped DeLong off in the classroom where he could wait for Professor Alexis to come in a half hour or so. Tom made it to the bathroom and hung around waiting for class.

He made it back to the classroom just as Alexis began to take attendance, fashionably barely on time as usual. Tom slipped into a middle row and tried to drop back into his invisible mode. He felt flat and discouraged. He noticed that Dr. Alexis was looking very pleased with himself, never a good sign in a professor. Tom settled in for the class.

20 January 2009, Tuesday, Inauguration Day, 5:05 PM: Cather Hall, Lyons College

Upstairs in Cather, about an hour later, Professor Maximos walked to Peter's office where he would wait for his young protégé to finish his lecture. Max was growing increasingly fearful about Peter. Up the stairs. Turn a corner. What was unfolding before them all? He stopped in front of the office door and felt his stomach flip-flop.

The wood of the office door was nondescript. The bleached blonde veneer to the woodwork had been favored in the late fifties when the building was constructed. The nameplate read: Peter R. Alexis Ph.D. Next line: Associate Professor of Philosophy and Classics. Nothing else. Max slumped against the door. He felt ill, overwhelmed with an old man's vertigo. The door was solid and blank, yet all at once he could see through it ... all the way through it. The office was full of darkness. No light.

Max looked down at the hallway carpet. He expected to see evil oozing across the floor under the crack at the bottom of the door. There was nothing. Of course, there was nothing. He looked up and the blackness returned. More of it swept over him, churning, boiling, like the artificial clouds in a cloud chamber. He actually began to pound on the door.

"Peter!" Max stopped. He pulled his jacket down where it had bunched around his waist as he hit the door. He looked from side to side, but the hall was empty. Peter was not in his office. He was still in class and that could be confirmed by the schedule taped next to the door.

Peter never closed his door anyway when he was there. He kept it always open in case of students in need of help parsing a tough verb in "Republic" or was just in pursuit of a chat. Max wandered how Peter Rupert ever got any work done, and smiled for just a moment. His colleagues had been wondering that regarding his own career for years. Peter's office was empty, at least of Peter, and yet something was seriously wrong in there. Max began to puzzle out how to find out.

Max had, of course, seen some strange things in his time. The oddest events of all had centered on the professor of philosophy who worked in the office before him. Had it been thirty years ago? The events leading to the death of Peter's parents still had the power to churn his stomach. Max faltered. The battle had been difficult as a young man. How would it be now? He leaned against the door again.

Peter's shape turned the corner feeling content with his success as a college lecturer. Nobody had gone to sleep today! Associate professor! Give him a few months and he would be a full professor. Peter saw an older man waiting, eyes closed, with his back to the door. Who? Arthur Maximos. The soul that looked like Peter knew a great deal without being told.

"Max!" Peter grinned and stuck out his hand.

Max opened his eyes. There was no doubt from the first moment. This was not the son of his truest friend. It was something else instead. His palms grew moist. His mouth hardly worked, "Who are you?"

"Max?" Peter looked about, but the hall was still empty. "Perhaps you should come into my office, Max. You don't look well."

"Where is he?" The intense eyes of Arthur Maximos tried to tear away flesh and see who it was that had taken on his friend's form. Or was it the body and had Peter's soul been destroyed? There was no way to know.

"Curiosity," Peter began to unlock the door, "is a commendable thing in a professor. Come in and let's talk."

Max looked into the office. It looked normal, and he glanced briefly at the piles of books and the many artifacts of the life of a middle-class professor at a low-rent college. Max noted the two computer monitors with Peter's screen saver picture of the School of Athens. Peter had too many gadgets for Max's taste. Max only reluctantly had let Maggie talk him into email. The pressure on his arm reminded the professor that on this particular late afternoon, his mind would not be allowed to wander, but Max resisted doing anything the person next to him wished him to do.

"I don't think so."

"Have it your own way," Peter smiled politely, "Besides, I have a dinner meeting and have to rush downstairs to meet a friend."

Overcoming his reluctance, Max reached out and grabbed the sleeve of the Person's jacket. "Who are you? What have you done to Peter?"

Max was desperate now. He was almost shouting again. The Peter before him just kept smiling. Max hated that grin, stupid and without meaning. He wanted to push in that face with his fists, but his time for fighting physically was long past. Of course, Max thought, he had never been much for fighting, though he could recall that singular incident with Mr. Forbes fondly. Max caught himself again and realized that Maggie was right. He had waited too long to break the multitasking habit. He had to concentrate on the issue at hand and find out what had happened to Peter.

At that very moment, the body that looked like Peter's body turned and pushed Max inside the office. The door closed automatically. The body grinned at him, "Well, well, well." Max looked around in near panic. His arrhythmia was acting up.

"You helped Peter come to Barterra. I know that much from joining his memories to what I already know. You are a very experienced man, Max, which is unusual in this age for a professor of literature, eh?"

Max crossed himself. Immediately the smile vanished from Peter's face. "None of that, unless you wish to make me angry."

Max began to pray, "Our Father ..."

The reaction was immediate. The room became dark. It was as if the ceiling had vanished and Max was looking up into a night sky without moon or stars. The form of Peter blurred. A young, fair skinned man, almost a boy, stood before him.

The darkness seemed to confuse Max's thinking. His prayer slowed, "in Heaven." and then stopped. All he could remember were sins, big and little, every sin he had committed. Every lust, passion, and desire he had ever indulged sprang up with fury inside his body. Max accepted his sin, but he did not enjoy feeling the force of all of them at once. He could not move, he could not think, he could hardly listen. He was simply and totally unmanned.

"It is my time, Maximos." Bandor, lord of Samov, master of the Halls in Metcalf, and Enslaver of Dragons, raised his right hand. In it was a crystal bird which began to glow and burn with a strange light. He moved to the side of the literature professor's head and began to stroke the iron gray hair as gently as a lover. Max began to tremble.

"I am inevitable, coming forward like a great ship into port. Equality and liberty are in my wake, Professor Maximos. Action that does not humbly wait to be called, but fraternity that acts boldly. Join me and become part of me. Love my cause. Follow me." All Max could hear was the sound of the voice of the Beast, and the cicada-drone was driving him mad. Max was imploding, drawing into himself and his sins, seeing them over and over again. There was a knock at the door.

Instantly there was an almost tangible lifting of the blackness. Max still could not move. He was trapped in his own sin, but he was sinking no deeper for the moment. The shimmering form of the Dragon Lord returned to the form of Peter. "Who is it?"

"Tom, sir." The voice was unsteady. "Dr. DeLong says he needs to get right to lunch. He sent me to bring you over to the Caf."

"I will be right with you," said the kindly voice. Peter turned to Max. "Sleep for a while and dream. Dream of what might have been had you chosen different paths." Scarcely opening the door, Peter left to join Tom.

20 January 2009, Tuesday, Inauguration Day, 5:11 PM: Douglass College, Old Quad Dining Commons

Jack and Barth usually had lunch with each other on Tuesdays, but this week they had decided to make it dinner. Jack had wanted to give himself to the joyful enjoyment of the Inauguration and did not want a single Republican nearby to spoil his pleasure ... not even as good a friend as Barth. Tonight he would collect on a dinner bet from his friend over the election. It was sweet to win after two lost election dinner bets in a row. It was a good day to be Orthodox, Democratic, and African-American.

Both Jack and Barth enjoyed their lunches, their differences, and their friendship a great deal. Most days they discussed a book they were editing on the place of the human soul in science. This was a book in search of a publisher, and had been in the works for roughly ten years, but they still had firm faith in its eventual success. They were meeting, as usual, in Jack's favorite place near his downtown office that was reserved, he often said, for his paying customers and not for his friends who needed much more help. There is scarcely a decent restaurant in all of the area, but Jack had finally found Huburt's on State Street. It had cheap food and warm yeasty house beer.

Jack was not really a drinker, but he enjoyed watching his friends drink. He smiled as Barth took a large gulp of his favorite microbrewery house label stout. "You know that you order exactly the same beer every week."

Barth took another swig, "I run it off."

"I am not talking about the calories, but the predictability."

"I prefer to think of myself as reliable."

"I know that if I need you, and if Regional Transit has a bus there, then you will be there for me."

"You have something on your mind other than beer and our book."

"Yes. I can't tell you a great deal, but I think we are doing something big in one of our projects in the next twenty-four hours. They are throwing incredible power demands on the entire system at midnight tonight."

Jack picked at the brim of his black fedora sitting on the bar. Was this good news, bad news, or just plain old news? "Can you tell me any more about what is going on down there?"

"I don't know much myself, at least for sure. The Executive Veep herself has frozen me out of the project in the last twenty-four hours, maybe. It is hard to tell. The team leader is not the communicative sort. But listen, this is not what I want to talk about, I have a problem and I need to speak to someone about it. You listen to a lot of people and I figure you could listen to me."

Jack knew enough not to say anything. He picked at his plate of vegetables.

"This is a beyond top-secret government project. I think I know what they are going to do, are doing, with a very important device and it is bad. But if I tell anyone, there is jail time in it.

Some of it, some of what I might know..." Barth stopped in frustration. "How much of what I know should I, can I, tell to Max or Peter?"

"What do you think?"

"I think that tonight, tonight for God's sake, that my University is going to do a very dangerous and wicked thing."

"And you want to stop it."

Barth sighed, "If we can. But I can't stop it by myself."

"You could tell the D&C. They are good at destroying things." Jack smiled faintly. His low view of the local press, after its coverage of a malpractice suit he had eventually won in a walk, was a group legend.

"It means jail either way. The Feds ignore the First Amendment in a case like this one and I am pretty convinced that this one-paper-town has a pretty snug relationship going between the top editors and the University. We give them academics for Op-Ed pieces, they protect our state budgets. If I blow the whistle to them, they still may print nothing and also turn me in."

Jack stared for a moment at the ceiling. "Do you have a dollar?"

"Ah. Yes." Barth passed a crumpled bill across the table. "I take it this means you are now my psychologist."

"Let me give you a receipt." Jack jotted down the receipt. Barth continued speaking "Now at least for most things you say to me, I cannot turn you in to the authorities. Speak in a normal tone of voice; don't raise or lower it. Look me in the eye and move in a casual manner. Tell me what is bothering you."

Barth paused, sipped his drink, and only after a full minute spoke. "We have built a very powerful machine to study time."

"Yes. I gathered that the other night."

"We have distorted time. I know that much for a fact."

"So you have said. What about it?" The psychologist stared at the pressed and highly decorated tin ceiling and seemed barely to be listening to each word Barth said. In reality, every syllable was going into storage in Jack's nearly flawless memory. Both Barth and Jack were quiet as a server came to the table with their plates. Barth had sausages with his baked beans, but Jack was staring at a giant plate of beans without any additions.

Jack took one look at the plates and groaned. "This food, using the term loosely, is going to wipe me out. Now, keep going. Speak as if to yourself. Outline the problem."

"I believe ... I think ... but then perhaps, you should know that Bobby Kennedy, the project leader for Magog, brings me in at times on the side to solve mathematical and physical problems."

"And?"

"For some reason one of our primary international donors wants all our results, but also wants Magog turned off. He wants results without running the machine, but this is impossible!"

Jack sat listening as Barth continued. It was rare to see the physicist so worried.

"Nobody is sure why the interest from abroad. They want something from us, but nobody is sure what ... at least Bobby Kennedy does not know and it is driving him crazy. He doesn't think Mary Yurislav knows what they want either."

Jack asked, "Why aren't you involved in the project?"

Barth answered quickly, "They refused to put normal ethical protocols in place for dealing with any subjects. These are the same kind of rules you use in psychology. They keep us from abusing people or the environment in the name of science. When I pointed out the problem, Mary Yurislav got mad."

"She can do that," Jack noted. "Does Peter know Mary is in charge of the project?"

"I don't know. Does he keep track of her?"

Barth cleared his throat, "They both have Facebook and we went to a small high school."

"High school was a long time ago, Barth, people change."

"Mary Yurislav certainly has."

Jack changed the subject, "So how do you get involved even a little?"

Barth sighed, "There are problems that Bobby can't solve. So without telling Yurislav, he brings me into the mix to solve the problems. I am not sure I should help, but it is so tempting. The math is really very elegant. Of course, there is also the advantage of getting information, since letting me work on the math involves telling me certain things, quite a few things."

Jack nodded, "I get it."

"The bottom line is this. And it is hard for me to believe. They are going to use Magog to bring someone back from the past."

Jack did not blink or move. His heart was beating very quickly now, but he merely said wryly, "Yes? Who are they going to bring back? Tell me it is John Coltrane."

"You are never really serious are you?"

"I am very serious about my music. Why are bad guys always bringing back people that everyone was glad to see go the first time? We could use more Coltrane, but you could bet nobody is thinking of bringing him back."

"I don't think they are."

"Who is it then?"

"My bet, just from hints that Kennedy kept throwing at me, is that they are gong to bring back one of the Imperial family. One of their major donors, the difficult one, is demanding it. Yurislav herself was more than willing. She is Russian you know."

"Funny, I would have guessed Irish with a name like Yurislav. Nothing more about Mary, please." Barth rolled his eyes.

The psychologist poked at his food. "Can they do it?"

"I don't know. No one really knows how Magog works. It isn't supposed to be doing what it is doing now, but weirdness is not all that uncommon in science, you know. Half the things we find are by accident."

"I know. Some people, after all, view psychology as a science." Jack smiled for the first time in a while. This was an old discussion.

"Oh, no you don't, I am not going down that road!" Barth visibly relaxed. He began to munch his "white hot," as any Rochester native called his hot dog. It was a strange regional quirk to eat the mildest possible sausages and then chase them down with the hottest possible chicken wings.

"If they do it, and if some of the things Max believes are true..."

"Then we should know what is going on..."

"Don't speak with your mouth full, young man. Didn't your mother teach you anything?"

"I missed breakfast."

"What are the odds of your being at their little midnight party?"

"Nil. I am strictly off limits." Barth had calmed down now that someone else knew all that he knew.

"What kind of security do they have around a project like this?"

"Well, we are in Rochester after all so security will not be great. This is not Berkeley. Besides, nobody really knows the thing is there, so it is not considered necessary to draw attention to Magog with extra security. It is supposed to be an alternate fuels project. I even think that is where the Department of Defense gets the money. So what is there to guard?"

"So a few checkpoints and what else?"

"Necessary identification. I can get you to Magog, if that is all you want. Like I said, they are keeping a low profile. They are not really supposed to be doing anything all that interesting. I doubt more than five or six people know what is happening tonight, and half the people in the know are on a different continent."

"Sometimes," Jack said over this port, "sometimes, I wish we could return to the old days. You know, last year when Peter was morose, Max was verbose, you were bellicose, and I was happy."

"Yes, I miss your grandiloquent persecution of Max. You know, I need to go for a run. We are getting too retrospective and serious."

Jack grinned, "As you evidenced in the last five minutes of conversation." Jack looked at his expensive drink, "We cannot just talk, Barth. We are going to have to do something and that something is going to have to be done tonight."

"What are you thinking?"

"What about messing with the machine? It must plug in somewhere. Let's pull the plug."

"I know you know it's not that simple. They are not heavily guarded, but they aren't stupid either. What good would it do to get to Magog just to get kicked out and then find our own funding curtailed for the next seven hundred years or so?"

"I am not sure funding matters since if Max is right, then..."

"Then if they bring back the Tsar or part of the family, it could trigger the End."

"Or an end. The West, after all, could crumble without the Return."

"Yes..." Barth was serious again now.

"And if we are not there..."

"Then we will not know what is going on, short of Peter having another dream."

"How is our Peter anyway? The wife and I have been worried about him. He did not seem his normal morose self at our house this week, he was much more so."

Barth looked up, "I haven't seen him since the Monday night meeting at your house."

"Why did you cancel your meeting with him this afternoon? I hope he did not cancel it. I have been worried that under the pressure he would start withdrawing from his friends."

"What meeting? I had to run some errands since on top of everything else my roof is leaking. I haven't seen Peter today."

Jack stood up quickly, though his outer calm remained. "Check please." He brushed off his jacket. "Curse the people who started taking decent coat racks out of restaurants. Didn't you tell Peter you wanted to meet this afternoon? He called me to say you wanted to chat with him in Penfield."

"I never called."

Neither man said another word to the other. They paid the bill and began the long drive to Lyons College.

# Chapter Four:

## Seeing the Forms of Evil

20 January 2009, Tuesday, Inauguration Day, 7:30 PM: Lyons
College, Café Banquet Room

The dinner was going very well. The special banquet annex
to the main cafeteria at Lyons was pleasant, and the chicken
was more interesting than was usual in such institutions. Dr.
DeLong was in a very good mood; the entire day was turning
out splendidly. DeLong was radical in his theology, but quite
conventional in his pleasures. It would have shocked him how
much the quality of his dinner impacted his mood, but it was
true. Tonight the dinner was passable, and since he had expected
less, his mood was excellent.

Professor Peter Alexis contributed to his good feelings by being much more sensible than the last time they had met. Discussion then had degenerated over the ordination of women; today
there were no such fireworks. Things were really progressing.

At the moment, DeLong was making one of his better points
to a surprisingly appreciative audience: "He couldn't be made to
see the point, but then people like he is never can see anything,
let alone points. He kept insisting it was a question of authority.
I kept arguing it was a matter of charity, but we were going in
circles. Finally, I said to him, 'You seem obsessed with questions
of sexuality, my dear Bishop. Perhaps you should seek professional or clerical guidance!'"

Peter chuckled appreciatively. "Go on. You haven't told me what your plans are for the up coming year."

"More of the same, Peter, more of the same. You can't believe the sort of battles I fight. Some of these colleges are still struggling over evolution! I sometimes feel, really feel, like my life is a bloodless martyrdom to the cause of intelligent Christianity. Some of these schools seem determined to throw the whole relationship between the Church and the modern world back a thousand years, with only me and a few professors to stand in the way."

"Yes." Peter had not touched his food. "How many contacts have you made with colleagues at secular schools?"

"It is delightful to speak with a man who gets the point so quickly. To God be the glory and all that, but my career has been severely hampered by the teaching demands the seminary must make on my time. There are many of God's children who see the problems of our sick civilization and know something must be done. But I am so busy putting out these useless fires that there has been no time to engage the real issues.

Of course, the modernists are just as bad as these fundamentalists, but we must put our own house in order first. Such a waste of time, however! Wouldn't I love to be able to get a Richard Dawkins on a platform and dialog with him about the real issues? We must get him to see that there is more to religion than the method of creation! He does not realize that we have more in common than separates us, you know, tolerance and all of that."

"Exactly." Peter looked at DeLong quite closely. Their eyes met and both men smiled.

"Frankly, and you must hear this charitably, but I did not know you felt this way. Since college you have seemed, a bit, enthusiastic compared to me ... more of a Campus Crusade man."

"And both roads have led us to the same place, as religious roads so often do. Enjoyed your meal?"

"Tremendously, Peter. What is on your agenda for the up coming march of Old Sol?"

"I have been looking pretty closely at my life, Bob, and I haven't liked what I was seeing."

# Chapter Four: Seeing the Forms of Evil

The gray-haired professor leaned forward, "Clearly you have been really seeking God of late, Peter, and that can be hard and life changing. Don't I know all about it! Shifts in thinking are never easy, as you know mine have cost me a great deal."

Peter picked at his food. "The Church is getting all wrapped up in this eschatology nonsense again. First it was Y2K, then we were all going to be left behind, but the crack-pottery keeps coming. Every lunatic with a Bible and his cousin with a blog are predicting the end of the world."

"Did you see my CT piece in 1999? I warned that this was exactly what would happen over a decade ago, but naturally nobody remembers." DeLong was growing excited and his handsome face grew flushed.

Peter sighed. "It comes of taking a piece of literature and making it into something it was not intended to be. These folks find their science in Genesis and their global outlook in Revelation. They are simply doing injustice to both, but then you said it all in Deliver Us From Textual Evil."

"Right. And I followed up with Without A Progressive Vision the People Perish. You should get it."

Peter's nod warmed the author's heart. Peter said, "Once I started opening my mind to your work, I saw what an idiot I was."

DeLong leaned forward and looked at Peter with real compassion. "That is a beautiful story, and it does my old heart good that I had some hand in your intellectual awakening.

"Have you thought of writing your pilgrim's progress? It would make a terrific journal article. You have been wasting some real talents, Peter. I don't mind telling you that some of my friends have been fairly critical of things you have written, but I knew your heart from when we were together in seminary.

"After all, who can forget those late night card games in Waring Hall? But still, it was hard to defend some of your more extreme positions and I was losing hope. I will never lose hope again. The Holy Spirit gets to us all, doesn't He?"

Peter nodded and DeLong continued triumphantly, "I have had my bouts of self-centeredness too. Don't doubt that for even a minute."

"It is hard to believe." Peter looked sadly at the teacher across the table.

"How can I help, Peter? Beth, you remember Beth from seminary, and I will do anything we can to nourish your new life in Christ. I know Mott and some other members of the school have some negative opinions about you, but that can change over time. We all have to start somewhere. You know I did ... since I am sure you read my booklet Beyond Good and Evil: A Young Student Finds Faith Without Fundamentalism.

You should download the teachings I did over the summer that deal with the oppression that can plague a man on his way to the truth. The teaching series was very well received in some of the Orthodox churches in Colorado before their reactionary Bishop blocked their sale, and I could let you have them for half the normal price."

The false Peter looked interested.

"Just type 'skopeia' in the discount box for half off," DeLong continued.

"I can't wait," Peter gushed, "Don't you have any with you now?"

"I have a few. Would you spend a bit more time in correspondence twith me? I would make it worth your time."

The false Peter eagerly reached into his jacket for a checkbook in the Café Banquet Room, while in Penfield the real Peter Alexis was rolled up in a fetal position on the bed in an empty room. His eyelids twitched. It was the Dream. Over and over again. Alone.

20 January 2009, Tuesday, Inauguration Day, 8:30 PM: Lyons College

Jack and Barth ran up the stairs quickly.

Barth heard Jack wheezing. "You should stop smoking cigars."

"I don't intend," Jack sucked some air into his lungs, "to live a long time miserable." He inhaled again. "I will have had more fun," quick breath, "in any one year than you have in ten you crunchy-con."

"I am not the one gasping over one flight of stairs." Barth observed as the burst into the second floor of Cather Hall.

"May I help you, gentlemen?" Paula, the philosophy department secretary believed that the entire edifice of philosophy depended on her keeping her hapless philosophic children, the faculty of the school, in line. She recognized the need for the imposition of discipline in the two in front of her. "Aren't both of you a bit old to be running in the halls?"

Barth spoke quickly, "We are looking for Dr. Alexis' office. We know the way."

Jack got his breath back and added, "We are good friends of his."

"Well, yes." Paula looked at the two middle-aged men, recalled seeing them with Peter in the past, and decided she liked them. "But I think Peter left for dinner with an old college roommate. I am only here because I am getting ready for the students' return next week. Somebody has to do it."

"Rats." Barth interjected. "We were supposed to meet them. Do you know where they went?"

"Could be the Café, but I am not sure. They might have gone off campus. You know, Peter might be back, the man has no life and sometimes I see his light on as he writes deep into the evening. Somebody should help that fellow get some interests outside of his work. I mean commitment to the Department is one thing ..."

"I am sure that is true. We do what we can with him." Jack interrupted gently. He knew how long Paula could go.

Paula thought, "I am so glad. Professor Alexis is a nice fellow ... but so absent minded, not that most people in this Department wouldn't forget their own schedules if I were not here to remind them, but still God gives everyone individual gifts."

Jack spoke up quickly, "Yes. The Department is lucky to have you. You have no idea how hard it is to get such commitment from the help at Douglass."

Paula positively glowed, "Well, of course. I have always said that Douglass University might be bigger than Lyons, no offense, but they cannot match the service that comes from true Christian commitment."

Paul glowed.

"Could we wait in Peter's office?" Jack gave the secretary his most trustworthy smile. Like it had since he was ten, his most trustworthy smile worked without a hitch.

"I suppose. If you two will walk down the hall with me to my office, I will give you the key. Just bring it back when you are done with it. You two don't look like the types to steal anything."

"No, ma'am." Barth looked at her with innocent eyes.

Moments later, they were in front of the door of Peter's office, key in hand. Paula had clucked at their hurry. "Hurry up to wait, gentlemen," she said maternally.

Jack reached forward to unlock the door, but something made him stop. "There is something wrong, Barth. Sense it?"

"Yes. I sense it and it's not good. Open the door."

Jack stuck the key in the silvery door knob. It went in smoothly. "I can't do it, Barth. I can't turn the key." Jack was so used to total mastery over self that this inability shocked him more than seeing Paula suddenly nodding off at her desk. He turned to Barth, but Barth was sitting on the floor. He was muttering to himself.

"Barth?" Jack suddenly felt alone.

Barth suddenly looked up, "Jack, help me. Memories. Bad ones. All the evil I have done. God forgive me. Lord have mercy, Christ have mercy." Barth began to cry.

Nobody had seen Jack confused since fifth grade when he figured himself out. If the examined life was worth living, Jack was living well. But suddenly Jack was confused, a fact which would have frightened his friends more than if they had seen him cry. He turned from Barth and absently put the key in the door and then took it out again. He looked down at it, not sure what he expected to see. There was nothing there of course. What did he expect? Blood? Blood.

Jack remembered. He had seen blood, a great deal of it, at college, on the pavement, under his window, at night. He had seen the normal amounts of cuts and scrapes in childhood, but nothing like this. There had been nothing wrong with the party, but there had been something wrong with Tim. He had come drunk and gotten drunker.

Jack had seen it all, but been unable to stop it. The hell of it was he understood the problem, but he could not get anyone else to help. Tim decided to hang out the window and shout at some girls passing the dorm. Some of the guys were laughing at him and Jack had told Tim to stop it. He should call Campus Safety; he turned towards the phone, heard someone scream, and then saw Tim falling out of the window.

He had known what to say to Tim then, but had not had a chance. He had no idea what to say to Barth now even with a chance. Jack grew impatient with himself: he was a man with a degree in psychology. He knew what to say and what to do and he had to get control of himself.

Barth was weeping to himself. "I am so sorry. I did not know. I did not know the bus was going to crash or I would have said good-bye."

"Lord Jesus Christ, son of God, have mercy on me a sinner." Jack stopped trying to master himself and gave his will to Christ as Max had taught him. He was no hero and he did not have all the answers. Jack put the key back in the knob and turned. The door opened smoothly with a slight push.

The office looked normal, but in the chair there was someone. Peter? Jack tried to turn on the light, but nothing happened. He moved forward and saw the figure better in the light from the parking lot coming through the window, "Max!"

Concern for their friend seemed to break the impotence of evil memories. Jack rushed into the room and Barth began to struggle to his feet. Their friend and mentor sat slumped in the office chair. His mouth was hanging open and he looked years older. Jack reached for his collar.

Barth stood in the doorway, "Is he alive?" Jack was examining the older man unsure what was wrong.

"Yes, very much so, thank God, but Max is in some kind of trance-like state. He is breathing very deeply, and his heart rate is very, very slow. Close the door."

Barth went to the door and pushed it shut. Barth reached for the light switch, but nothing happened.

"I already tried that. There is some sort of power failure." Jack said as he finished his examination of Max.

The light from the window created shadows and neither of their nerves could handle shadows. "Jack, we need to get Max out of here." Barth said.

Jack stood up. "Good idea. Any suggestions of how to do this without alerting the whole world?"

Barth spoke slowly, "Let's alert the whole world. A frontal assault, old friend, is the one thing whoever did this will not be able to counter. This great evil must lurk in shadows or it is dispelled before its plans can develop. Call 911."

"That makes sense. We can get Max to a hospital and he needs to be in a hospital." Jack reached across the desk for the phone.

"Don't touch that phone." Peter was there, though neither man had heard the door open. To men who knew him well it was obvious that the shape that looked like Peter was not their friend. He looked younger, in many ways better than they had seen him look in years, but the person who looked like Peter was not their friend, and neither man could ever be sure later how they knew.

"Dr. John "Jack" Smith and Dr. Bartholomew White. You are an interesting pair."

"What have you done to Max? Where is Peter?"

"Isn't it more interesting to wonder what I am going to do to you?"

Jack crossed himself and the phantasm of Peter backed up. "What are you going to try to do to us?" Jack said.

The being that was not Peter spoke, "I am going to do nothing to you. There are too many loose ends already."

Barth broke in. "What are your plans for us?"

The phantasm laughed. "Don't expect a monologue outlining my plans. This is not a movie and I am not really the villain."

"You are evil if anything ever was." Jack was angry.

"Well of course I am evil, but that has nothing to do with whether my desires are best for me. As for you two, in many ways we have compatible short-term aims. As you shall see."

Jack and Barth stared at the phantasm. They could think of nothing to say to him.

"I have done what I needed to do here today. It is amazing the clarity of vision one can gain in your Air. Marvelous. Tell Max, when he wakes up, if he wakes up, that I made the contact I need. Good day, gentlemen."

The phantasm grinned and waved at them. He turned, walked out the door, and closed it behind him. They heard him say goodnight to Paula as he passed her desk. The light came on suddenly in the office and the darkness in their hearts dissipated. Max groaned in his sleep.

20 January 2009, Tuesday, Inauguration Day, 9:00 PM: Lyons College

Tom Scott was feeling pretty bad. He had been "saved" and now was wondering if he should be sorry about it. The day had started out so well, but now he felt like a dupe. Somehow the one off hand comment by Professor DeLong had gotten into his system. There had been something toxic about this entire day. Even his philosophy class, usually a time to catch up on needed rest and relaxation, had an edge to it. Dr. Alexis had not been his usual distracted self.

Was he going to end up just like the combed-over men in the Church basement? He could sit on folding chairs at dish-to-pass suppers until Jesus "came for his own." Where was his "new found faith" going to lead him? Tom could only imagine handing out three color tracks with titles like "God's Last Name is Not Damn" and "Heaven or Hell: The Choice is Yours." The flames would be lurid red to match his neck. Next he would be sending money to television preachers. Soon he would be reduced to watching them twenty hours at a time, mailing them his social security checks. He would get prayer clothes from them and use them to heal his gout or cast out "demons of doubt."

Tom had not moved from the bench outside the building where his philosophy class had been held. He just sat in the dark in the parking lot light that made his skin look undead and tried not to think. The two professors had left long ago for dinner, but Tom wanted no food.

Dr. Alexis came back from dinner by himself. Tom watched as he went upstairs towards his office and then returned in just a few moments. He seemed in a bit of a hurry. Waving with an unchar-acteristic grin, he left Tom alone again on the bench. Time to get going, Tom decided. He had been "saved" and lived to regret it.

Tom slowly got up and began to saunter up the hill at the side of the humanities building. As he walked by the side door, he nearly ran into two men. One very tall and solid, the other was smaller and very lean. They were carrying a third, rather large, older gentleman between them. They nearly dropped him to avoid Tom. Reaching out automatically, Tom grabbed the shoulder of the man they were carrying.

"Sorry." he said looking at Jack.

"It's all right. Our friend is troubled and we are trying to help get him home."

"You wouldn't want to help us get him to the car, would you?" Barth looked hopeful.

A drunk. And an old man too. What was the College coming to? Tom shrugged. "Sure. Where is your car?"

Jack pointed to a Mercedes in a corner of the lot next to the building. It was dignified, classic, old, and every expensive look-ing. "We can take my car, and Susan or I can come back for Max's later." Barth looked at Max's battered off-white, rust primed, 1970's Buick Skylark parked near the Mercedes.

"You should do him a favor and drive his car into Letchworth Gorge." They reached Jack's car. Barth turned to the student who had so graciously helped them. "Thanks a lot. Max is not getting lighter with the years. What is your name?"

"Tom."

Jack shifted his position. "Thanks Tom. If you can take his legs, we can get him into the back of this car and home to his wife. There is nothing wrong with him that a good night's sleep will not fix."

Tom felt offended that they would think he did not know a drunk when he saw one. He was not a baby or a naïf. All he said was, "I get it, sir."

The two older men waited as Tom reached down and grabbed Max's legs. "O.K. Got him. You lead and I'll follow."

As they headed for the car, Tom's depression deepened. The

sight of this drunken old man on a campus founded by the Women's Christian Temperance Union was more than he could stand. He stumbled on a stone in the lot.

"God damn it," Tom said in a fit of temper.

Instantly a wave of darkness clouded his eyes. He dropped the legs of that foolish old man. He could not see. He opened his mouth to talk, but he could not speak. Motion suddenly seemed impossible. Tom was smothered in velvet, throat raw as if he had had too much whiskey, unable to move or speak. Could he breathe? Trying, concentrating, he felt air coming into his lungs. Force it out. That was all he was able to do with maximum concentration.

Jack watched a black cloud strike out from Max to the young man. All expression was wiped from the student's face in an instant.

Barth turned his head to see why Max had suddenly grown heavier.

"Dear God, what happened to the kid?"

"He is being oppressed by It, whatever it is."

"How? Why?"

"I don't know. He seemed unhappy, maybe he was spiritually vulnerable. I don't know what is happening. How can I say?" Jack looked very unhappy at not understanding what to do.

"Well," Barth looked at the sky and as was usual in Rochester, clouds obscured the stars. "We can't leave him here."

"No." Jack looked even unhappier. "It is for sure that no one in the school infirmary knows how to deal with this. I don't know how to deal with this."

"Father John..." Barth looked hopeful for the first time in an hour.

"Yes..." Jack responded quickly, "It is worth a try. Max is in his parish. Science isn't going to help either one of them."

"Do you think the young man is a Christian?"

"My guess is that if he was not, then he would either have not been bothered at all or would be in much worse shape. Instead he seems to have responded like Max ... Let's get out of this parking lot before Campus Security notices."

Barth laughed. "If we are parked in the wrong space, they would be here to give us a ticket already, but stand around with two bodies and you can be sure that they will be someplace else."

Lowering Max to the ground, Jack went to his car. Fortunately, at that time of night the back lot was nearly empty. They had managed to avoid Paula's desk by going down a back staircase, but they did not want to press their luck.

Jack moved the car over to where Tom stood stiffly with Barth, who was trying to look like nothing was out of the ordinary. Barth and Jack slid Max into the passenger side of the car and then maneuvered Tom into the back seat. The young man was totally out of it. Barth squeezed in with him to keep him from falling over while Jack walked calmly around to the driver's side, picking up the backpack that had fallen off the young man when he came to help. Jack picked it up and tossed it into the car with them and got into the car.

Jack turned the ignition key and said, "We are going to my house, geting these two inside, and having a good drink. While we are on the way, you might figure out what is going on, where Peter is, and what we are going to do next." Jack pulled out of the lot with a grim smile on his face. In the back seat, Barth buried his face in his hands.

20 January 2009, Tuesday, Inauguration Day, 10:30 PM: Pittsford

Jack and Susan's three boys were sitting at the dining room table finishing their day's schoolwork. They had watched the Inauguration, and that had thrown them behind schedule. Their home school support group met the next day, and several of their co-operative classes met at the church. Mom and Dad might let them skip an assignment, but the co-op teachers would not.

The colorful work texts in front of them were fairly self-instructional, which helped provide a little time for Susan to run the house and provide for educational extras. Despite the late hour and the need to finish, they were having a hard time concentrating. Something strange was going on in the house. Dad called Mom from the mobile and then Mom had called Father John.

They heard a great deal of interesting conversation, but could not follow most of it. Father John had come directly from his evening prayers carrying a large satchel and had not even spoken to them. Mother had taken him directly to Dad's study. The boys could hear him talking on the phone almost in the next instant. Mom never returned.

Charles, the image of his Dad at ten, looking at John, the oldest, asked, "What is going on, John?"

"I don't know."

Doug, the model student, went back to the math problem in front of him. "I have three more pages on my goal chart for math and I am getting sleepy. Be quiet, you guys."

Charles was thoughtful; "Father John isn't talking on the phone now."

John nodded, "It is very quiet in there."

"I bet I could see what was going on if I looked under the door."

Charles never had the chance to get out of his seat. The garage door banged open. Dad was home with Barth, which was not unusual, but he was very quiet, which was very unusual. He was out of breath and out of sorts ... and that was just weird. He began giving orders from the moment he swept into the house through the side door.

"Charles, get your Mother."

"John, I am going to need your help carrying some people who are very sick."

"Dad, Mom is in the study with Father John."

"Good. Get both of them. We will need their help. Doug, follow us to the garage and get two of the fold up cots and carry them to my study."

The boys went into action. John and Doug followed their father out the side door. Charles scrambled off to the study. Doors banged everywhere. The wind caught a Science workbook and turned the pages. School was over for the evening.

Jack's office was always a bit crowded, packed with books and mementos from family trips. Max and Tom were each gently placed on a cot, filling the little remaining space. The boys wanted to ask questions, but kept their mouths shut and stared. The priest had placed an icon of the Christ at the head of each bed.

"A new image to capture their imagination?" Susan pointed at the icons at the head of the cots.

The priest responded carefully. "Their souls have been exposed to evil stronger than most of us have to endure. This is a window to the greatest reality of all."

"It is hard not to hate those people who help cause such things."

"It is the evil in our hearts that give room for these attacks. Still, it is difficult to understand what is happening here. A great many of the things happening lately have not fit my preconceptions, though they are not foreign to Orthodox possibilities, so I am just praying and waiting."

"A sword pierced the heart of the Mother of God, Father John. It is not always our evil that hurts a man; sometimes, compassion causes pain as well. I know Max well and he is as likely to be suffering from seeing a soul that has rejected God as from his own sin."

Father John accepted the implicit rebuke. "You are right. We cannot know what caused these two to suffer. Our job is to love them and do what we can. You are certainly doing that Susan. This chaos must be hard on your family." The priest noticed the children. "Are you boys all right?"

Susan spoke quickly. "Too excited to work or sleep, I am sure, so you can use the Wii ... even though it is way past your bedtime on a school night. Just keep the noise down."

The boys vanished.

It was midnight before the good priest let them back into the study. Father John looked very tired, and much to their shock, Max was sitting up in his cot. "Could I have a glass of water ..." he asked with a slight smile.

Jack and Susan both began to talk at once. They rushed toward their old friend, only to have Father John step in between them.

"He is tired now and soon must sleep, but he insists on speaking to you. Given what is at stake, I agreed to let you in to see him."

Jack nodded, "And the boy?"

"He is asleep now. Normal sleep. He should be fine. He is a young Christian and God protects His lambs from certain kinds of harm to the soul. Young Tom will remember what happened, but I think he will recall none of the horror."

"You act as if you do this sort of thing every day."

Max spoke from his cot. "In a sense, he does." Father John shrugged.

Susan went over to Max. "Jack, get this poor man a glass of water. We are glad you are back with us, Max."

"Yes. I am glad to be back with you as well! Now we must decide what is to be done."

"Done?" Susan asked.

Jack returned with the water. He brought Barth with him. Father John leaned against the window at the back of the study. Barth stood by the door. Jack handed Max his drink, waited while he drank, and then spoke: "Max, we know now a few things we did not know before."

Barth spoke quickly. "They are going to use their machine tonight!"

"What are they going to do with this great stinking machine of theirs?" Max growled.

Jack said, "We think they are going to try to bring someone or something back from the past."

Father John crossed himself.

Max groaned. "Disturb the Holy Martyrs? They do not know what they are doing, and God alone knows what the results will be. They can bring back the body, but the soul will be a trickier proposition."

Jack said, "If we are committed to a substance dualist view ..."

Barth interrupted, "Which of course has been the traditional Christian position, but..."

Susan spoke firmly, "We don't have time for this right now, gentlemen."

Jack grinned at his wife. "Sorry."

Susan spoke softly. "It is just that our dear friend is still missing. Where is Peter? Does anyone know? And who is the spirit that Jack told me has taken his body?"

Max turned to the woman, "We have no idea where Peter is, we cannot even be sure he is alive, but I think I know who has his body ... or a body that looks like his."

Father John spoke, "Don't say that name, Maximos. It is not time yet for you to say that name. You are still weak. Try praying another Name." The old scholar pulled out a worn prayer rope and his fingers began to move over it.

The priest turned to the rest of them. "We are at the beginning of an end even if it is not the End. You, gentleman, have just faced a power long kept back from us. He is free and may Christ have mercy on us all. Human power will be useless against a being that could fight Saint Michael and the angels and live."

The bad news made them as quiet as Milton's heaven, but oddly enough not afraid. Susan later commented that this was the most frightening moment of her life, but the least fearful. The news was so overwhelming that there was no need to plan. The plan was God and that was strangely comforting.

A light wind stirred the curtains where Susan had opened windows to try to freshen the air in the room. It was a January evening in Rochester and the breeze was chilly and perfectly appropriate. It woke them up to important things.

The warmth of friendship made them happy as they looked around the room. When Jack tried later to explain what he felt, he described it as not at all giddy about the men and women around them, since they knew their faults and failures, but contentment with their place. Their fate was in the hands of God. Barth would later write that at that moment he understood friendship. Friendship was risky; it could fail and cause great pain, but there was no avoiding it. Men and women would be friends no matter what the circumstances.

Then the absurdity of the situation struck them: here was an odd collection of souls to battle the forces of evil! Barth even managed a faint smile. "He will have mercy, Father John, and after all you are here. He will. Now, what are we going to do? If we cannot do anything else, then what should we pray?"

20 January 2009, Tuesday, Inauguration Day, 10:30 PM: 441 outside of Rochester

The phantasm of Peter Alexis had agreed at dinner to drive Reverend DeLong to the airport to catch his Red-Eye West Coast flight. The traveling minister was always getting ready to fly somewhere and he thought of himself as an "aero-apostle." His conversations with Peter were the high point of his entire trip. Giving the same general message can grow tiring, but this conversion, that word was not too strong he thought, was utterly invigorating to DeLong.

They had spent several years together in college and seminary and DeLong had always respected Peter's intellect, even when he berated him publicly for wasting it on defending reactionary views. Peter was one of those people he longed to see join the good guys ... and now he had! Delong wanted to tell Peter ideas that he was usually hesitant to express to others.

The chief topic on the ride was a new less hierarchical understanding of the Trinity and the incarnation. DeLong believed that there could not be social equality in the Church until "our image of God reflects what we know about humankind. Any difference in function is inherently unjust and the Trinity must not make such an injustice part of doctrine."

Finally there was a break in his passionate disquisition and Peter said, "You really are coming up in the world, Robert. They tell me that you might be the next Billy Graham ... if Billy Graham were crossed with Martin Marty!" He looked at his liberal friend teasingly. "You could even be the next president of the N.A.E, if thing progress in the proper ways. You have friends."

DeLong was jubilant, "All in God's time, Peter. All in God's time. But I think there are some exciting days ahead for men who become the Spirit's agents. Just pray we can get it all done! There is so much to do and so little time to do it in this Age of the Holy Spirit!"

Peter laughed. "Time! Given the low standards of my school and my non-existent social life, I have plenty of time and am ready to change directions. You are going to have to tell me how I can hitch my little academic wagon to your rising star."

When DeLong got excited he knew he tended to wave his arms

around. He knew it was a bad habit; it had embarrassed him more than once, but he could not stop it any more than he could stop talking. The car was small, his mood eager, and he bumped the rearview mirror with his arm during a particularly telling point. As he tried to straighten it, he saw nothing where he should have seen Peter. The only thing Reverend DeLong could see in the rear view mirror was his own image. There did not appear to be anybody at all with him. The car engine raced as they rushed around a tight curve near Penfield.

20 January 2009, Tuesday, Inauguration Day, 10:30 PM: Penfield

Peter Alexis woke up. The mattress was soaked with his sweat and he was groggy. The room was very dark and he had no sense of any passage of time. What time was it? He looked at his watch: 10:30.

The date?

He hit a side button on the black digital. Same day. What day? My God.

Peter remembered: Bandor, terror, blind panic. He got up and staggered to the door of the room. He made it down the stairs, but fell the last few to the landing. Why was he alive? He clutched the confirmation cross around his neck. That was it, perhaps. His faith had saved his

body. His sanity? At the moment, he could not be sure. He fell in a heap at the very bottom and emptied his stomach. Jack. Max. He had to call them, but somehow he had lost his phone. He began to crawl towards the front door.

20 January 2009, Tuesday, Inauguration Day, 11:45 PM: Douglass University

Magog was being turned on bit by bit. The great machine began sucking all the energy the Ginna Nuclear Power Plant could send them. The foreman, yellow hardhat firmly in place, stood and chewed on his pencil. "I don't like this, you know Jim."

"Sir?"

"What the hell are we doing anyway?"

"What do you mean?"

"I mean this is looking less and less like science and more and more like some sort of screw ball New Age religious obsession on the part of upstairs."

"You better be careful, boss. She has ways of finding out things."

"All I know is that we are about to blow a good bit of the budget on this night's work. And there are no controls, no proper double checks."

"I know. And she is bringing in a bunch of M.D.'s and psychologists to watch the show tomorrow evening. What is up with that?"

The foreman, an engineer who had learned his math on a slide rule and took his naturalism straight, grunted, "If she pushes much further in this direction, I am going to blow a whistle or two. If we wanted religious crap in the lab, we could invite some creationists to come read Bible verses over the machine."

"I don't think it is religious. She is determined to do something big on the first day of Obama ..."

"Yes, I know. I voted for the guy, but he is becoming a guru to some people around here."

"Meaning her, again."

"Yes, meaning her, again."

A computer screen flickered. The two men turned to the job of getting Magog ready for the night's work.

Mary looked down on the men in the pit working on the machine. She knew many of them disliked her. Some of the men were still uncomfortable with a woman running a major scientific project and others hated her metaphysics. Both sorts of stupid bigotry were all right with her as long as they delivered. In fact, it worked to her advantage as she had enough stupid comments on file from most of them to fire them whenever she wanted. Mary was not vindictive or politically correct, but she believed in self-preservation.

Tonight would put her ideas to the test and sometime tomorrow she would know if her dreams were possible. She was going to prove that Plato, the Indian sages, and her own intuition were right after all. She was going to bring a soul back from the dead.

20 January 2009, Tuesday, Inauguration Day, 11:45 PM: Rochester International Airport

Reverend DeLong smiled at the sign announcing Rochester "International" Airport. Canada was another country he supposed, but this was not one of the world's great transportation hubs. Still, he rather liked the scale of things in this airport; it tried hard to be big, and it was easy to find a plug for his laptop. He would make it to his Atlanta connection on time, and then on to California. It would be good to be home.

The woman behind the counter handed him the ticket. He smiled at her and moved his luggage to the scale. He would have to pay extra for the carrier, but he was content. His dog whimpered a bit and DeLong reached a few fingers inside the bars of the carrier and patted the muzzle of the large black hound that was stretched out inside. It licked his hand and quieted.

"I hope you had a pleasant stay here in Rochester, Dr. DeLong. I see you bought a pet here?" the agent asked. She was ambitious and did not want to stay in Rochester. She chewed her gum slowly and waited for the answer. That East Rochester was no place for a woman with her talent was the essential element to her creed, and so she had chosen work in the airline industry. Avoiding Kodak meant a better chance to get the prized transfer to Any Place Bigger USA. With luck and outstanding customer service, she could spend her evenings in Manhattan and not at the Lilac Festival.

"No, no, I bought him years ago and he goes with me everywhere." Delong responded. He was irritated by her question. "Is there a problem ..." his reading glasses were in his pocket and he was too vain for bifocals, and so he strained to read her tag. "Is there a problem, Ms. Durante?"

"No. Just wondering."

DeLong paid the extra freight and headed for the gate. His allergies to pet hair were bothering him, which was the chief reason he had never ... but DeLong felt irritated again and decided to call the airline to complain about the service tonight at the counter. Durante never made it to New York City, which was a fact that her future husband, who in a few months would come to Rochester on a mission to Palmyra from Salt Lake, would find providential.

20 January 2009, Tuesday, Inauguration Day, 11:50 PM: Pittsford, New York

They brought Peter Alexis to Jack's house. The group that gathered there would not split up until they had come to the bottom of the adventure whose pace seemed to be quickening. Peter's hair seemed visibly grayer to them and he was in pretty bad mental shape. It was fortunate he had been able to dial the phone at all. In a few hours, if he had not met some friendly faces, Peter would have been completely unable to do so. They would have ended up going to pick him up at R-wing in Strong Memorial.

The mobile phone has nearly killed the pay phone, but small town stores change slowly. The Pen-Deli on Five Mile Line, just doors from his place of captivity, had a pay phone and Peter called Jack collect ... the first collect call Jack had received in ten years. Jack and Barth had gone to get him. Max had called Maggie and she rushed over to Jack's house.

Meanwhile, the young man, Tom, had woken up and Father John already had spoken to him and was probing for plans. Tom was a young Christian, of course, but Father John saw something very unusual in him, a unique spiritual sensitivity. The old priest knew Tom was confused and had no desire to rush him into a commitment to the group, but it would be difficult to let him simply go after what had happened. What did he want to do? Tom was not sure, but he knew one thing: he was staying. He wanted to stay; was demanding to live at the house.

"Would you want to be out there knowing what I know by yourself?" he said to the priest. Tom actually looked excited. Father John shrugged his shoulders. It was easier if the boy stayed. They could keep an eye on him.

Father John called Tom's mother, told Mrs. Scott her son was staying with some college friends, and that was that. It was nearly midnight by the time they brought Peter home. If Barth's information was correct, the Magog experiment had already begun, but would not reach a critical point until the next evening.

When Peter came, he sat for a long time talking to Father John, Max, Barth, and Jack. It was not really wisdom he needed, but security and friendship. Peter could not forget what had happened to him—forgetting was not something he wished to do anyway—but he needed space from it. They did not talk about the events of Inauguration Day ... not yet, but just being together helped Peter.

21 January 2009, Wednesday, 9:30 AM: Pittsford

They slept, or at least tried to do so. The house was big enough that they could each have their own room, but Peter would not sleep. He sat in the living room waiting patiently for them to finish their rest and tried to stay awake by drinking gallons of Diet Coke. Sleeping meant dreaming and he was determined not to dream until he confronted whatever was going to happen that Wednesday. He tried watching television, but the slightest wickedness hurt his overly sensitized soul. He finally quit trying to do anything and just sat in the room waiting for morning. In the early hours of the morning, he actually fell into a dreamless sleep for a short while. Peter woke up as soon as anyone stirred. He heard Susan preparing her children's breakfast and then driving them to their grandparent's house. He heard everyone else slowly wake up and begin this day that would determine so much. Today they would discover the meaning of his dream.

The members of the house gathered after breakfast in the living room and waited for Peter to speak. Jack sat in a chair brought from the dining room next to the couch where Peter stretched out. Susan sat next to Jack. Max stretched out in the large recliner on the right side of the room near the large screen. Father John stood, claiming he was too impatient to sit. When Susan urged the priest to take a chair, Barth noted that Father John's time training in Russian churches had made him capable of standing for hours at a time. The physicist was leaning in the doorway to the dining room, having just finished his morning run. Tom sat on the floor with his back to the wall. Maggie stood over him protectively as if he were her own child.

"I could not remember a great many things. I still don't recall most of it." Peter began as if in the middle of a thought or a story. His voice was strained and he looked like either a prophet or a mad man. There is usually little distinction between the two. "When I was sixteen, Max can tell you, my father was involved..."

Max broke in, "Some of this is not necessary for now, Peter. We should share as little of other men's evil as possible. Spare your father's memory as much as you can."

Peter persisted, "My father was doing certain experiments. He was involved ... the group he associated with wanted to explore the soul. They believed that there were other worlds, other possible places, and that these could be reached by looking within a man ... their techniques became frightful." He stopped and just sat for a minute. Nobody spoke until he resumed. "It is enough, at least for now, to say that they ended up sending me away. I passed up and beyond this world to what Plato called the spindle of the cosmos. I came down in another world."

Jack whistled. "You know what people would say about such a story in my profession, Peter."

Max turned to the psychologist. "He knows. And there is little or no evidence of what happened except his word, but I was there with him part of the way. It was God's mercy that I found out what was happening and joined him. They would not stop, and I could not follow all the way, but I know this for certain: Peter left this world. What happened next, of course, is beyond me."

"I ended up in a world that is a shadow of our own. All the imaginations and creations of human beings, the little creations of God's image, end up there to resolve their subsidiary existence. I called it Barterra. Human imagination changes Barterra, but in very subtle ways. Since 1901 by our own calendar, Barterra had been in decline. A century for us was a thousand years for them.

"A force foreign to Barterra was oppressing her. A being from our own world, or time, from what they would have called the Center, tormented their peace. He was fair to look at, but twisted. He was bound to Barterra, and had been there for many centuries. I do not know totally his connection to our own time."

Tom spoke from the floor, "Now that is weird, really weird. When I was dungeon master of a group in high school, we played out a scenario just like this ..."

Max looked interested, "Did you create the scenario, Tom?"

"Yes," Tom pushed his hand through his hair, "I thought Barterra, son of Earth, a great name for a campaign."

Father John said, "Tom, I suspect that you have peculiar and important gifts."

Tom said, "But I was just making up a land with stuff I liked: singing dragons, battles, fair maidens. Pretty standard stuff."

Peter smiled faintly for the first time, "Singing dragons? They are not so common in the role playing games of my youth, but they do exist on Barterra."

Tom looked excited, "You mean my imaginations were real?"

Peter laughed, "It is a good bit more complicated than that. You may be one of those rare folk whose imagination creates reality in Barterra, and that can also sense events there. It is too complex for any one man ... at least any one man not a Shakespeare."

Max looked serious, "Even Shakespeare could have only comprehended some of it."

Tom replied, "So I wasn't just making stuff up?"

"Nobody just makes things up, Tom," Max responded, "You were interacting with a subset of reality in a bi-conditional relationship."

"I sort of get it. What were you doing there, Peter? Were you the hero of a quest, three dimensional gaming?"

"That's just what I thought at the time, but there was no quest and I was nothing special except for one fact: it turned out that, for whatever reason, Bandor could not kill me. In all that world of war and battle and smoke, I could not be killed by the ultimate evil or by anything else for that matter. I was invincible, or so it seemed. And so I decided to try to deliver Barterra from him."

Peter stopped and drank from the water glass next to him. He seemed to be slipping back and forth between his dreams and the room.

Max said, "It did not work out, of course. Peter came back having forgotten most of it. Travel along the Spindle does that to a man."

"Why did I fail? My own pride, mostly, I suppose. The pride of my friends was part of it, and there were good friends there who were proud of my triumphs. We failed, but we gave that Man of Sin reason to hate us in the end, and left him weaker than we found him. And now, somehow, he has come here. Whatever power he represented is back on the earth."

Father John said, "Maximos and I think it is some of the power behind Nimrod, Nero, and the infidels who sacked Hagia Sophia. It is lawlessness, the spirit of anti-Christ."

Susan groaned, "And we have let it loose here with our probing and poking into time?"

"It isn't our science," Barth said softly, "it is our unbelief chained to our science. We have said that all truth is God's truth, but we have acted as if it did not matter if impious hands touched the building blocks of creation. We don't seem to realize that being able to do a thing does not mean we should do it." Barth was building up to his usual attack on the overuse of technology.

"Enough of this," Jack muttered, "We can talk all we want, but this Man is loose on the world. Can we stop him? What does he have to do with the experiment at the University? Barth tells me that they are going to make some profane attempt tonight to disturb the past of our own planet."

Father John was firm. "We must do all we can to stop them. What might they profane with their unclean hands?"

Susan spoke. "Why not just go to the press or the University? Tell them what is going on in their own back yard. We don't have to tell the whole truth, just tie them up in an environmental impact study or something."

Max looked up at the ceiling. The room was quiet for a moment. Maggie slipped her hand into that of her husband. He was considering his words, and finally he spoke. "It is my belief, and

Father John agrees with me, that a real battle, perhaps the End of All has begun here in Rochester. The town, the community, all the pieces in the game are going to be used, if not openly, more directly than we have ever seen them. I do not think there is much hope in the secular world. Their new prince is not part of it, but he cannot stop it. He lacks the maturity and the faith."

Jack growled, "Let's not get political."

Max responded, "You are right. Bush could not have done anything either."

"And he would have done nothing incompetently." Jack said.

"Now who is political?" Max laughed, but quickly became serious. "Even if we were to unmask him the process has started and he will see that this thing will be done."

"Why?" Barth spoke forcefully. "Why all this?"

Peter began to mutter. His eyes were wide. He finally spoke loudly enough to be heard. "There will be a wicked father, and he has come from this other world. He will have a priest, a messenger and advocate of his word. And they must have a Child who will come to rule."

"They want an heir to the last Christian emperor." Max said softly.

Barth looked at his old friend. "You know, Peter, that was pretty strange. Are you going to keep doing that?"

Peter looked up. "I am afraid so. These ideas came into my head since I met Bandor. I thought I might as well express them."

Barth was nonplussed. "I am not going to start taking you seriously now."

Peter actually laughed. It relieved some of the tension in the room.

Father John shook his head. "Too many forces are coming into conflict. It is hard to tell what Peter is hearing."

Max spoke. "The important thing is that what Peter said is essentially correct. If there is a new heir to the Empire it will have great eschatological significance. Such a person, once dead and now alive, will be their answer to the incarnation and the passion of our Lord. An unholy trinity which will set itself up against the Lord and His Anointed." Father John spat the words out.

"Of course, the pieces, even the Dragon Lord himself, are manipulated by the fallen archangel. They do not know, at least most of the time, what they are doing." Peter dropped back on the couch. "The Dragon Lord is beyond us. We don't even know where he is. So far as we know, he has no priest yet to help him in his cause. Our only possible task is, therefore, to stop the horror that takes place in that lab tonight."

"My God," Maggie said, "They are trying to birth an anti-Christ."

"No," Father Max replied, "They are trying to birth the anti-Christ."

21 January 2009, Wednesday 6:30 PM: Douglass University

Mary stood in front of her masterpiece, the fully prepared Magog chamber. It was all stainless steel and very sanitary. She would not be allowed even to breath inside of it. Since the experiment had started last night, the machine had been bending back time. These experiments always began and ended at night to protect the Rochester power grid from the heavy load that those phases of the experiment demanded.

The chamber stood immobile, but full of change. Bright in the reflected lights of the lab, it gleamed. The probe would slowly enter the reality inside the chamber and would capture a body and bring it, through physics nobody really understood, into the room where she was standing. The body was not being moved; only displaced in time slipping from 1918 to now. Space had been made incidental to the entire process. The phone next to the chamber rang.

"Yurislav."

"Mary," it was the distant voice of Bobby Kennedy. "Good. Are you ready to do this at last?"

"We are ready." She could not keep the excitement out of her voice. "Will it work?"

"We will get something. But I don't know how the thing works in the first place, so don't ask me to make any promises. We may get pieces or the entire population of Yekaterinburg, but we will get something. It is logical, after all. Do the same thing, get the same result. This is a tidy universe, whatever your guru of the moment might think."

"Be professional, Bobby. You don't have to like me, just keep the project going."

She began to pace anxiously about the experiment and then held still, impatient with her impatience. She did not want to merely go through the motions; she wanted to savor every moment of her triumph. Too often she won her battles without enjoying the end, but she was not going to make that mistake this time.

It was cold in the lab. The noise of the men became easy to ignore as she rehearsed every carefully worked out step of the Magog process. Her fingers began to work and knead the rail as they locked down the heavy stainless steel doors. She drew her jacket closer around her neck, as the room grew very, very cold. Mary was pleased to notice that she obviously was calmer than the other supervisors, which was as it should be.

Outside the building things were not as Mary would have wished. Max pulled up in Susan's minivan with its **Marriage: the Pathway to Holiness** and **Antiochian Christian** bumper stickers. "Why be subtle?" Max had pointed out. "Barth claims he can get us in the building. Let's go, get as close as we can, and play it by ear from there." Barth pointed out his favorite parking area and they disembarked.

Peter, Max, Maggie, Barth, Jack, Susan, Tom, and Father John had spent the day talking, reading, watching old movies, and ended it with Evensong at Saint Michael. Tom and Maggie had been delegated to stay by the phone at Jack's house to form a fall back position. There was no real plan for what the rest would do when they got to Douglass University.

As they got ready to leave for church, Tom suggested that the group needed a good name. Like any collection of academics, naming a thing was immediately distracting from doing anything.

"What will we call ourselves?" he asked. Peter suggested the Eight Van Riders and then claimed he was kidding. Barth wanted to be the "Scoobies," but Jack thought there would be copyright problems when they went to make the movie. Max was in favor of calling themselves the "Tagmata" after elite units of the Byzantine Empire, but Father Jack pointed out they were not elite.

"We are more like the 'Themata,'" the priest said, "the sort-of-professional part-timers that often saved the Empire." Max agreed, and the two began a discussion about the causes for the decline of the thema that threatened to make them late for service.

Jack would have none of it. "I feel silly enough without using strange group names unless we are going to call ourselves 'Aging-Academics-Who-Should-Know-Better.'" The group decided to remain simply "the group."

They walked up the front steps of the Eastman Science Building. The large brown brick Edwardian structure had received numerous additions, most of them utilitarian and hideous. The experiment was taking place in the basement of a back wing, added with government defense money in the research gold rush of the eighties.

They paused in the front entryway. Science luminaries carved in stone, large and imposing, looked down from their permanent niches in the front. Gods of this age, they watched as Jack dialed home on his cell phone. "Maggie? We are here."

"God go with you, Jack."

"If you don't hear from us in three hours, call the police. It may not do any good, but one never knows. If he is there, I doubt Bandor can or would kill us. How much open power can he use? Take the chance that he will back down if police show up. If you don't hear from us, it will be worth the risk."

"Tell Max I love him."

"Tell him yourself." He gave the phone to Max who listened without much change in his facial expression.

Max finally spoke. "I love you too. Goodbye." He closed the phone and handed it back to Jack. He turned to Peter: "You know Mary Yurislav is going to be involved in this project."

"I am not blushing, Max," Peter replied, "so stop looking. Professor Yurislav is doing a bad thing. We are going to stop her if we can. This is not some Rowling story where high school romance still matters decades later."

"Of course, Peter," Max fixed his Eye on his protégé, "but methinks you doth protest too much!"

"And if I did not protest, you would claim ..." Peter noticed he was sputtering and decided on more walking and less talking.

Jack adjusted his fedora and then felt badly about doing something so Hollywood. Looking around, he saw Peter biting his lower lip. Max was with Susan at the back. Father John was at his right and Barth was to his left. He turned to Barth. "Get us in, friend."

Barth used his card and then led them down two flights of stairs. They passed through hallways full of dark classrooms. Offices were on another floor. A few doors were open with grad students pecking away at last minute papers. Barth waved at one researcher eating a slice of cake in a half empty lab. Everything looked, and felt, utterly normal. At last they came to a blank metal door. On the wall beside it was a black plastic sign with white letters reading, "Physical and Cognitive Science Research."

The door was locked, but Barth pulled out yet another ID card and the door opened. The group went down one more set of stairs and came to a final door. This one had no sign. Barth took his university ID card from his wallet and slid it through the card reader by the door. There was a hum, and then the party was through.

"That's it. This is as far as I can get you."

"How much further do we need to go?" Max moved to the front with Jack and Barth.

Barth spoke quietly and quickly. "There will be security cameras in the halls ahead. Any odd behavior and campus security will be here very quickly. They are pretty much donut eating slugs, but they would be able to keep us from getting to the lab since, except for Barth and Susan, we are also pretty much donut eating slugs." Jack grow0led. "There is one check point with a guard before the machine itself. No gun, but a nasty nightstick. Then it is down a gangway into the pit that holds the machine."

"Not very secure is it?" Susan said.

"Well, no. But then, after the Cold War, they are mostly

concerned about industrial espionage. There is more than enough security for that."

Jack nodded, "And for us. How do we get in the last bit?"

"Could we go in as cleaning crew or something?" Peter said.

"My dear Peter, it is good to hear you getting back to your normal naive self." Max grinned at him, "People don't let the mop and bucket crew into labs in the middle of billion dollar experiments."

"Multi-billion dollar experiments," Barth said, "and that is our hope. If we can foul it up tonight, they are not going to have the funding to mess around with this sort of thing for another good long while. This little bit of action has to be exhausting the research grant. Mary Yurislav is going to be feeling pressure from upstairs already about the money."

Susan smiled. "I get it. Dr. Yurislav would not want to ask for money to be bringing folk back from 1918, yes?"

Barth nodded. "Right. Enough people that count have watched enough science fiction to worry about unauthorized time travel in any direction unless there is a TARDIS involved!"

"Which is why," Max said, "my advice is to walk up, knock down the guard, break into the lab, wreck some equipment, and go to jail."

Peter actually laughed out loud, "You have to be kidding!"

Jack thought and shrugged his shoulders. "Anyone have any better ideas?"

Barth shook his head. "Why not? Let them explain to the press what they were doing in there."

Susan looked at her watch. "We don't have much time for big plans."

Father John said, "Our job is to do what we can. Let's stop this evil thing now, and leave the rest in God's hands."

Max spoke. "I was a bit of a conformist in the sixties," he said. "It will be a pleasure to be on the other side for a change. Mad Max the Campus Radical is a new role that I think I shall enjoy."

Rita had been guarding University facilities for about ten years. It was not a job that required a great deal of actual work. Once a group of animal rights protesters had freed all the white rats on campus, but she had stayed out of the way during that one.

Another time she and the action end of her flashlight had cracked the skull of a frat brother who had imbibed too much liquor. That was just about it. So when she saw a group of people, mostly professorial types, strolling down the hall she did not get too distressed. Her experience was that career minded folks were not particularly dangerous. Still, it was a secure area. She glanced up at the gray haired fellow with the wild eyes at the front of the group. She spoke in her best-bored monotone, "Do you have a pass to be here? This is a restricted area."

"Ah, here is my identification." A younger man handed her a University science building pass. She checked the list but to her surprise he was not on it. "I am sorry, but you're not here Dr. White."

"Yes. I suppose that is right." He was staring at her. Worried, she reached for the two-way on her belt.

"I am sorry, but we are going to have to take that." A tall black man stepped up to the right and grabbed her arm.

"What's going on here? What do you want? This is all on camera you know."

Jack looked at her apologetically. "Yes, so it is. We shall have to hurry. Susan, come tie this lady up, will you?"

Susan hurried to the front of the group. "Jack?"

"Hurry, dear." Jack was looking down the hall.

"Jack, we don't have any rope."

Peter looked to the ceiling, "We have got to hurry. They should be starting the machine any time now." He looked around for something, anything to use.

"Belts!" Susan snapped. "Jack, Max, give me your belts."

"You have to be kidding." Jack looked at his wife.

Max ripped his two-sided belt through the loops and groaned, "We are not very good at this, are we?"

"Just give me the belts, gentleman!" Susan was growing impatient.

Rita laughed. "You don't do this often do you? I'm not going to cause any trouble, but this is a government project right? There are going to be some pretty unhappy people at the end of this crap and I'm not going to be one of them."

Susan began to try to work the belts into knots around Rita's wrists. They could hear the main door being thrown open down the corridor. The belt leather was too stiff to easily tie to the chair or anything else. "This isn't going to work. What if I just stay here with the guard?" Susan said at last.

"Fine with me. I am not going to make any trouble for you until the trial," Rita said. The belt came untied again.

Max was getting winded. "Blast. This always looks so easy in the movies." Max's belt slipped to the ground with a clunk from its big metal buckle.

Max looked at Susan. "You stay here and keep her quiet."

Susan rolled her eyes. "Right."

Jack, Peter, Father John, and Max headed up the hallway. The last security door was ahead, but it had been propped open with a wedge to let the air conditioning from the Pit reach the guard post. They pushed through the last door and looked eagerly at the great machine. Below them was a vast hole filled with the great machine Magog. As they closed the steel security door behind them, a metal bolt slid into place. The humming stopped, and all was still. "They are reaching back into time, Max." Barth said. Peter began to get the dazed look that had become too familiar to all of them lately. Jack looked up over the door. He saw that a silent flashing security alarm had gone off. The door, however, was secure. It appeared that they were sealed inside with Magog and his servants. Pounding on the outside from the campus security told them that they were safe for the moment. The room had been sealed off from the outside world.

"Snap out of it Peter." Barth began to run down the catwalk. "We have to shut that thing down."

"Too late." Max lurched against the handrail.

The room was so quiet that each man could hear his heart beating, thumping against his chest. Then in horror, they all began to see It. The dream that had tormented Peter for years came to life in front of them.

Magog was pulling even the most spiritually insensitive into its sphere of influence. Each man, each scientist, every person in the area began to have the Dream. It began with the sickening spinning. Fire and wheels and wind were sucking them down toward the center of the machine. Every post was abandoned as the human chaff was blown toward the steel chamber at the center and at the bottom of the pit.

Jack, Peter, Max, Barth, and Father John stumbled, fell, and almost rolled down the steel steps. Bruise after bruise as they hit each steel platform, it all made them desperate to scream, to cry out. They could not make a noise. It was heavy earth crushing down on them now. There was water in the earth and then more wind.

Other men and women came crashing into them. Every one of them was forced against the steel wall of the room. The doctors and psychologists brought from the University hospital were mixed up with the pure science types who always worked on the machine. Each of them had gaping mouths and were pressing against the wall as if they wanted to get into the room. Every man was looking into the past and seeing the death of the last Romanov tsar.

The room was full of smoke. They could see the yellow wallpaper of the basement room. They could taste the bitter flavor of gunpowder. What were the shrieks they heard? They could not move their arms even to stop their ears. It was a woman screaming.

Mary Yurislav had created Magog and had birthed the terror. Now she was the only one that could protest against what was being done to time and to the image of God in her creation beneath her vantage point. Her experiment had gone mad and she wished she could go mad with it. It would keep away the knowledge that was slamming into her.

Now that they had a greater work to do, the finite spirits that had filled her and had given her strength left her at the moment when she needed strength so badly. Mary wanted to repent, to be sorry, but she could not speak because she was choking on the reality that she had been used. Her masters, having left her, abused her further by showing her that they existed. Devils delighted to show her just who and what they were and how much she owed to them. Solitary, she stood at the top of the long metal stairs, the others pressed against the wall beneath her form. A dark shadow stretched down from her and came to an end at the steel door at the foot of the steps.

Magog churned with Ginna power and belched out what Magog had been programmed to produce. Electrical fire began to dance along the lines leading from the machine to the central chamber. In the rest of the building, fire alarms shattered the quiet of the University night and the security forces that had been banging uselessly at the door turned and ran for more help. The great machine was being consumed as an offering to the vanity of its creators.

Mary wept.

In a room far across the campus, Bobby Kennedy slammed his keyboard down. Data had stopped coming from Magog. Something had gone wrong. His phone rang and he answered it simply: "Kennedy."

"Something has gone wrong with the project. Security reports a group of people broke in on the experiment and then all hell broke loose."

"Terrorists? Some eco-freaks?"

"We don't know. You better get over here fast."

Mary raised her head and looked down at the room in the center of the machine. The lab workers and the strangers were still pinned by a fierce gale against the inner walls of that main Magog chamber. The blue flames were everywhere, but the room was still strangely cool. In fact, the temperature was dropping quickly, and soon it would be very cold.

Mary could see it all. Nothing she had believed or heard since childhood was apocalyptic or dreadful enough to account for this except rants from pastors on the Book of Revelation. The demons left her body, but were loud in her mind: "You helped us bring about the End." She could not stop looking at the ruin of her great project and, though she knew that it was childish she could not stop thinking that when it was all over her mother would be proved right.

The black cloud swept to the bottom of the stair, and there was silence even from the machine. The wind stopped and every person in the room crumpled in a heap with the release of the pressure. Nobody was dead, but everybody felt as if their souls had withered by facing the Elements directly. Some felt crushing weight, others burning, a few other souls drowning, others that they were nearly blown to pieces by the Wind. It would have been easier to die, but there was no time and so no release into the severe mercy of death for anyone in that room.

Peter raised his head from the ground. Jack was moving slowly next to him. He was reaching out for Susan's hand, already trying to help and to regain his usual poise. Susan looked calm and was already repeating the Jesus Prayer to herself. Max was up on one knee, but any heroic effect was spoiled as he was forced to hold up his beltless pants. Barth could have been dead as he was stretched out on the floor with his eyes fixed on the center of Magog. Father John sat with his fingers moving over the knots on his prayer rope. Peter was sick, and sure he would soon be sicker.

The pit in which the main chamber of Magog sat was full of smoke, but it was clearing quickly. The smoke was being sucked to the front of the door to the chamber. They could see the Cloud in the machine thicken and take the form of a devil standing before the door. The glass windows and the fitfully working video screens on the walls above the chamber showed a woman sleeping on the floor of the chamber at the bottom of the pit. She was on the inside, and the devil was on the outside of the inner chamber doors.

Peter shook his head. Of course, nothing from the spirit realm had a true physical appearance, but simply chose how it would appear to men. He could hear Max lecture, "Devils do not have actual cloven hoofs or horns!" This was true, but the man-figure Peter saw had both hoofs and horns.

What Peter saw was exactly what the simplest believer would have expected to see when a devil became visible to men, but it shocked Peter with his incapacitating modern education. He thought he knew better than Dante, that Dante's images of the residents of Hell were crude, and drawn to the stereotypes of the Middle Ages. He was learning that Dante had described devils as he did, because mostly the very nature of devils forced them to appear this way to men. For angels the wages of sin is a disgusting form.

Peter was surprised by the childish simplicity of what was forming in the center of Magog, an image to frighten little children or wise men. There was a biped in the fire, but from his brow came two sharp horns, a video game image of a devil. Like some painting of judgment from the Middle Ages come to life this devil moved toward the door of Magog that would open the inner chamber and put him in the main area. Peter could not keep his eyes on the girl. The devil was too grandiose to admit any such distraction.

Peter tried to stop shaking, but failed. Flames and horns. Smoke and ruin. The old images of death and evil were coming. He crossed himself and tried to struggle to his feet.

A devil stood before the outer door of the chamber of Magog. In front of him was the parish priest, John, who spoke first as usual: "How do you dare disturb the rest of the saints of the Lord?"

The figure laughed. A red flame curled from his lips as they opened and shot sulfurous fire at the tottering priest. It burned around the man of God. His garments were consumed as if they had never existed. Only his chrismation cross remained, burning on his bare chest like a star. Father John raised his head and said, "Lord Jesus Christ, Son of God, have mercy on me a sinner. Saint Michael defend me on the day of battle."

A white flame shot with each Word at the devil. With a shout, there appeared at the top of the steel shell a being of such intense brightness that to see him was to see for the first time. His was a light that did not dazzle, but only clarified. All the rest of the World was made brighter when Saint Michael came.

The devil's form wavered and the darkness grew less intense. "It is not my time!" The fiery being spoke quickly, "We want nothing much, just her body. It is a small thing, merely her body, which is still part of the airy realm."

"Her soul is with Christ." Max had come to the side of the priest. He took off his jacket and covered the man's nakedness. "You may not have or even touch her relics with unholy hands."

And then from the archangel came a beautiful voice. Calm. Ancient "The Lord rebuke you."

The parts of Magog began to melt away. There was no explosion, and the destruction of that entire work of man was done quietly. The cold vanished as the metal melted with a fervent heat. There came over the place the smell of paradise, myrrh. The Angel that had guarded the door to Eden before the Flood brought with him the odors of the Garden.

Fire trucks were wailing towards them in the distance, but the building itself would not burn. The machine, the computers, the data, all of it was vanishing, but the structure was untouched. The room was being cleansed. The terror was gone and anything that was destroyed had been transformed into an acceptable offering.

Max looked up toward the face of the Holy Angel. He loved this great being and knew he would see something like it again at the hour of his death. The angel was a moon with no craters, perfectly reflecting the light of the Sun. He wanted to write a book, or better, compose a song. And then Michael was gone.

Max wondered about passages in Isaiah and in the **Four Centuries** and what they had to say regarding such visions. What could he say about what had happened? Peter Alexis came up beside his old teacher and friend, and interrupted his thoughts: "We must not forget her." Max nodded and both of them went through the outer doors to the entry of the inner chamber of Magog. The walls were melting away, but for now it was still necessary to open the door. .

Peter turned, unbolted the door of the inner chamber and stepped back as it hissed open. His friends crowded around him. The lights in the chamber had gone out and Peter peered into a dark room. The guards and firefighters would break down the doors soon so there was no time for caution. Peter took a step forward to enter the inner chamber. A motion from within made him stop. Some small sound made his heart almost burst from his chest.

With slow steps, a woman walked from the heart of the dark place. "I am Anastasia Nicolaevna, a friend of God."

# Chapter Five:

# The Great Waves

24 January 2009, Saturday, 9:00 AM: Rochester, New York

The wind blew open a copy of the Rochester Democrat and Chronicle. The paper was trapped in a bush by the side of the road. If one looked down, one could have read an editorial headline with huge type in the center of the front section.

The Community of Monroe:
Our False Sense of Security

We watched the film of the Oklahoma City bombing and said, "How horrible." When the World Trade Center exploded, Rochester groaned ... but after all, "That is New York City." Rochester has always prided itself on its blend of urban comforts and suburban values. Tolerant, diverse, and at peace with our differences, we are "family values." Extremists live in the rural South and Montana. Not here. Not us.

We know better now. The terrorism at Douglass University woke us up from our pleasant dreams. Hatred and toxic ideas lurk everywhere. A small group has destroyed a research project costing billions of dollars motivated by their twisted view of Christianity. We are fortunate that only the equipment was destroyed, and loss of life was so minimal. University Vice-Provost and Project Director

Mary Yurislav is missing and feared dead. The terrorists themselves may have died in their own mysterious attack.

Who did it? The project workers that remain suffer from severe memory loss. The terrorists may have died when they interfered with the experiment, or some may have survived. All of us must do what we can to help law enforcement find the truth.

Police are starting to release names and fill in details. Two University professors had fallen for "conspiracy" theories about a mundane research project at Douglass. The Unabomber should have taught us that the bright are not immune to this sort of nonsense, but it still comes as a shock. How could such men work in a modern University? Did our own tolerance betray us? It is a time for hard questions.

These evil men are probably dead. There is justice in that fact, and it is safe to say that few will mourn for them. Two are in police hands and they must receive a fair trial. Rochester owes that much, not to them, but to the Community of Monroe. These men of science gave their lives for law and reason. The judicial process is our best revenge against the religious zealots who killed them. Are there more? How widespread were the beliefs of this "study group" led by the wild-eyed Arthur Maximos? The City must spare no expense in finding answers.

Of course, we must not blame religion or even the Christian faith. It is too easy to look for scapegoats. Still, as Professor Samuel Mott of Lyons Christian College points out, "As an evangelical, I have to admit that too often members of my own faith community have tolerated, or even promoted, the sort of apocalyptic teachings that lead to this sort of crime." Leading evangelical Robert DeLong adds, "We have too often sown the wind with irresponsible rhetoric, and are now reaping the whirlwind of violence. Leading voices in the evangelical world must condemn the hate and intolerance that too often masquerades from our pulpits as the gospel of Jesus Christ." The Reverend Sarah More of the Downtown Presbyterian Church put it best: "It is time for mainstream Christians to take their religion back from the odd balls and hate mongers who would turn the religion of love into the ideology of the Christian Right."

The most disheartening fact about this crime is the age of one of the suspects. We like to think that our young people will bring a better world. We see promise for a brighter future in their untapped potential. His high school teachers describe Tom Scott as a bright young man, trapped in the tensions of his fundamentalist home. Growing up is a painful time, full of transitions and tough decisions. What services were available to help Tom Scott? The far right was ready to give him pat "answers" and "friendship." Where was the Rochester community? Education and intervention against hate must begin in our schools and continue into the community. The price of doing nothing, even in a time of budget shortfalls, is all too evident in the events that took place in the Eastman Building.

It is a new day. We know too late we are not safe from hatred and unreason, but our new President is a demonstration that progress can be made against hate. While we celebrated our progress in Washington, we were reminded of how far we have to go as a nation here in Rochester. The terrorists of two days ago were black and white, well educated and simple, from the suburbs and from the City. They were part of us. It is time to look in the mirror and admit that they were part of the face of Rochester.

22 January 2009, Thursday, The Day After the Destruction of Magog, 9:00 AM : Rochester, New York

Mary Yurislav woke up and discovered she was lying on a small cot. It had white sheets. She stared at the sheets for a moment. Where was she? The walls of the room were white and it looked like an empty dorm room. Her bed had a white iron headboard. A college room from the forties? Slowly, vague images of what had happened came back to her.

She felt strangely empty. Something important had left and all her strength was gone. She just wanted to be in bed. She closed her eyes again and contented herself with breathing deeply. Her old ability to focus was gone, however. Breathing was just pulling in air and letting it out. The power was gone from it. She heard a noise in the hall. The door opened a bit and a distinguished man came through it.

"Hello." He sat in a plain wooden chair with a straight back.

"Hello. Who are you?"

"My name is Dr. John Smith. You can call me Dr. Smith or Jack. I am a professional psychologist. You are not in a hospital, but you are safe. Do you remember how you got here?"

"I don't want to talk about it."

"Why?"

"I don't want to talk about it." Memories were coming back more quickly now. The realization was returning that she was guilty of something. Where was Momma? She began to pull back into herself.

"Where is my mother?"

Jack leaned over and looked at her. "You are a well trained engineer. You work at Douglass University as an administrator and your project "Magog" has been destroyed."

"No." Mary closed her eyes. "No." She seemed to remember hearing singing during her long sleep. The songs like those she had heard as a child. She began to hum, "Lord as of old at Pentecost. Thou did thy power ... I can't remember the rest. How does it go?"

21 January 2009, Wednesday, The Evening Magog Was Destroyed, 10:30 PM: Rochester, New York, Pentecostal Holiness Bible College and Training Center

"Lord as of old at Pentecost, Thou did Thy Power display. Send the Old Time Power, that Pentecostal power ... that sinners be converted and Thy Name glorified." An auditorium full of students was singing the song Pentecostal Power loudly as the piano pounded out the four parts of the music. Hands were raised and eyes were squeezed together in holy concentration. It was the final evening service of Missions Emphasis Chapels. The students were dressed in what the predominantly white, lower middle class group took to be "clothing of the people groups of the world." It was a motley mix of clothing brought back from the mission field in various decades and what students pieced together from Good Will racks and their own imaginations. It might have been offensive if it had not been so sincere.

The Pentecostal Holiness Bible College and Training Center had been at the center of the city of Rochester since the nineteen-twenties. An old hotel had been converted into a religious training center by a group of former Methodists expelled from mainline Wesleyanism for their enthusiastic style of worship. The miracle that had brought this "valuable property in the center of the city into the hands of believers in the Full Gospel" still had a prominent place in the school history. "World Wide Revival Our Only Creed" was painted over the front of the building and many coats of paint later, it still remained. The second president had added, "For Such a Time as This," and both had by now become familiar Rochester landmarks.

In its great days during the healing revivals of the nineteen fifties, the school registered as many as two hundred students. The charismatic movement and other changing currents in Pentecostalism had failed to revitalize the old place. It had about one hundred full time students now setting out to earn, in the words of their founder, not their PHD, but their PHB.

What they lacked in numbers, however, they more than made up for in enthusiasm. The chosen few viewed themselves as a "Gideon's Band" out to change the world. Their area of the City may have received more evangelistic messages than any other single bit of America. If you weren't saved in downtown Rochester it was not because nobody had asked.

Mary Yurislav was sleeping in a bed in the top floor of the building. Nobody but the Dean of the College could have made that decision and no Dean in the history of the school would have made it except for the incumbent.

Simon Berkeley was the current Dean of Students. In his

mid-seventies, he could still have taken quite a few of his students in a one round fight. A former lightweight boxer, he had left the ring to pursue a call to the mission field. So dramatic had been his conversion that he had been featured in a Moody radio program called, "From Boxer to Believer." He spent time as a missionary in mainland China and Formosa until illness forced him to return to home.

Students told stories about his spiritual insight that had passed into PHBC lore. Many a young couple, engaged in "public displays of affection," had been brought back to the straight and narrow by a mere word from Brother Simon. Self-taught, his library rivaled those of any professor at the University. "Read, gentlemen." he would tell his class in Practical Manhood. "It is the key to the minds of men, but most of all read the Book. It is the best pointer to the person of Jesus Christ who is the best pathway to the mind of God." Brother Simon had an informed opinion on most things of importance ... even when he was wrong. The old man reminded his students that when he was a boy simonizing a shirt would keep it from shrinking ... and by the time he was done Simonizing them, they would not shrink from any task either.

The students, naturally, venerated him.

Brother Simon was standing in the pulpit at the end of a good conference. He need only deliver the last appeal to the "fields white unto harvest" and the week would have come to a predictably rich end. The prayers, the weeping, and the ministry would go on all night for some of the students. The impact of the three days of ministry would be, literally, global.

In the distance, Simon heard the sound of City fire alarms. This was not unusual, since the main branch of the fire department was only a block away. This alarm, however, went on and on and on and it was distracting. The song pounded to an enthusiastic close, but Brother Simon paused. Something was not right and he said a silent prayer.

He opened his worn, burgundy NIV and began to speak, "First, Jerusalem. Then Samaria. And then to the Outer Most Parts of the Earth! We are called. No, beloved, we are commanded. To preach. To preach. The gospel. Of our Lord and Savior. Jesus. Christ." Brother Simon had a staccato delivery that an entire generation of young preachers had learned to imitate. It scanned badly, but with practice was punchy in the pulpit. His familiar delivery matched a familiar theme, and the zealous faces before him would have followed him anywhere.

He simply could not continue. Something was seriously wrong. The nagging in his soul would not stop, and Brother Simon was too experienced a Christian just to keep going.

"I do not know. Just now," he paused, every single eye in the room now riveted on Simon. This was very unusual, though the unusual was anticipated at PHBC.

Brother Simon looked to heaven: "I don't know. Why. But we should pray. Let us bow. Before the throne. Of ... Grace." The students went to their knees bending down before the padded folding chairs. The murmur of many voices crying out to God filled the old hall. The anointing began to fall on Brother Simon. He began to weep.

Why?

He opened his mouth: "Jerusalem. Jerusalem." The tears were flowing now. Water dripped down his cheeks, still as smooth as a boy's. The cry of the fire whistle seemed to blend with the only word of English he could say, "Jerusalem. Jerusalem." He closed his eyes and tried to clear his mind. He had two simple choices: he could say nothing or he could simply repeat that single word: Jerusalem. Pentecostal Holiness College and Bible Training Center began to weep for the city of Rochester.

He looked up at last. The students were praying with great fervor. The teachers had gathered them into small groups and, holding hands, they reached out to God for some unknown need. The clock in the back, white face with black hands, showed him that forty-five minutes had passed since he had interrupted his sermon. He was waiting for something, but was not sure what.

The side door near the platform opened. Much to his shock, he saw John Warren Smith. Jack had been a student at the University and had fallen for Susan Thomas. She had been one of the best Christian Ed students in the history of PHB. He had opposed

115

the match at the time, but Susan had left to marry her Jack, and in later years he had softened and was willing to consider that he might have been wrong. In one tough financial time, an unexpected and very hefty check from the noted psychologist had kept the doors of the Bible College open. They would occasionally come to Revival Services and, Orthodox or not, John Smith had even filled the pulpit. Brother Simon could love anybody who could love his Jesus.

The usually perfectly groomed Jack was shockingly disheveled. He had no hat and his clothes were actually mussed, something that Simon could not recall from his entire Bible college experience. Jack's face was marked and he looked twenty years older. Behind him were an older man and another fellow, hardly dressed, beside him.

Brother Simon recognized Professor Peter Alexis, a friend and colleague of Jack's near the back of the group, since Peter had done some seminars on apologetics for the College. Now, Peter was struggling to carry a woman who was taller than Peter. As he let her down to the carpet of the hall she curled up in a fetal position, but in the next moment Brother Simon forgot the rest of them, even the woman passed out on his carpet.

He was looking at an angel. A girl, a woman, a light, stood at the back of the party... or was she at the front? It was hard to tell. For the old man of God, this woman seized his attention. She was dressed in clothing from the turn of the century, but it was torn and burned. The woman, however, was happy. No, not happy, that was not right. What was the precise word for it?

Brother Simon believed he could classify any student on earth in a moment, but he had nothing to say about this Woman. He was even thinking about her in capital letters.

Given the layout of the old room, nobody but Brother Simon could see the group standing at the side of the platform. The rest of the room was deeply in prayer and Simon Berkeley had forgotten them. He slipped down from the platform and went to the door.

He put his finger to his lips and backed them out of the auditorium. He closed the door behind him and Jack spoke. "We need help, Brother Simon. We are in trouble. Can you give us a room? Frankly, we need a place to hide. I swear to you we have done nothing wrong. Please, sir." Jack was a college student again, pleading his case to the Dean of Students.

If Simon Berkeley had been a man given to obeying only his head, he would have hesitated or called in some help. There was no policy or precedent for this, but then whatever Simon did was policy at PHB. Simon Berkeley was a man of the Book and the Spirit and he would immediately do what the Book said and the Spirit prompted. He could not take his eyes off the Woman and he had never felt the Spirit more powerfully on an individual. If Jack brought her, then Jack must be doing the right thing ... which he was inclined to believe in any case. A lifetime of listening had made him ready to do what he heard God saying. He looked at the Woman and decided, "Follow me." He closed the door to the pulpit.

The hallway was quiet. No noise escaped from the auditorium through the thick layers of insulation recently installed in the walls to keep out the Rochester winds. Brother Simon reflected that Jack had helped pay for it. He began to move them through the empty corridors of the Bible school. He finally reached the central stairway that wound its way up six stories. "Highway to Heaven," the students called it, some suggesting it was from the heart attacks produced by a climb to the top. Brother Simon paused at the bottom of the stairs and turned to Jack: "The top floor is not used now."

Jack grabbed his hand. "Thank you, Brother Simon."

"I am going to want. No. I am going to demand. A very long explanation."

Max spoke. "You shall have it, but before Almighty God, with the Holy Spirit as my witness, I beg you not to tell anyone that we are here before we have a chance to explain what is happening."

"I will ... not."

Having said that, Simon turned and led them up the stairs. In the old auditorium, the students had begun to shout as the spirit fell on them. The piano began to play. A student grabbed a tambourine and shouts began to be raised to the Most High. The worship leader began the favorite PHB chorus, "We have come to the Kingdom, come to the Kingdom, we are in this place, for such a time as this."

Upstairs, Jack stood looking out the window at the west side of the City of Rochester. He could see the banks of the Genesee, though he could not quite see the steeple of the Douglass University chapel. Jack wondered if he would be able to visit Douglass again. He missed Susan, and wondered when he would see her again. Jack refused to allow his thoughts to keep going in that direction. He loved his wife and so he must see her again. Jack could not help wondering where Susan was at that moment. Jack had not seen her since last night, the terrible 23$^{rd}$, when she volunteered to stand watch over the guard in the science building. He hoped and prayed she was safe and that she had escaped the consequences of their actions.

23 January 2009, Wednesday, The Destruction of Magog, 7:30 PM: Douglass University

## Susan

By the time the rest of the team fled the destruction of Magog, Susan had pretty much failed in her efforts to keep the guard Rita under control. The minute the others had left, Rita had pushed Susan out of the way and run toward the door leading to Magog. Susan discovered that she really didn't know how to hit anyone and that she had no desire to hit Rita. The fire alarms began right after Rita started tugging at the door. She gave up trying to follow Jack and his friends and turned to Susan:

"Locked. The emergency locks have gone into place. What the hell is going on in there?"

Two security guards came from up the corridor just as blue fire began to snake down the walls following the path of Magog's wiring. It seemed obvious that the building was burning down, but it was hard to tell why.

"Crap. Look at that fire." Rita gave quick commands to the two guards.

"Take this woman, cuff her, and then let's get out of here. You can forget guarding anything down toward the Machine. The door is hot and this weird blue flame is coming from that direction."

She triggered an external call button as the three of them hustled Susan back up the hallway to the entrance of the science building. Her signal would bring even more help to the University, including the City fire department. Help had better come quickly, because the building was beginning to shudder under their feet.

"Earthquake?" one of the guards panted.

"Nope." Rita struggled for air. "You ever see the machine they have in there?" She sucked in more air. "My bet is that the monster is blowing up and we don't want to be in this building when that happens." She looked at Susan. "You are in serious trouble."

Susan looked at her and nodded, "I know." She knew where she was going: jail. She was glad the children were at their grandparents'. She wondered how they would react to a parent in prison and then she felt empty, drained..

"Where," Susan thought, "where is Jack? Is he dying in the carnage behind that door?" Susan knew that if he could, Jack would come back for her. He had not returned and she hoped that the locked door had kept him away and not something worse. "Where are you, Jack?" Susan said aloud to nobody in particular, and nobody answered her.

## Jack

Where was Jack? When the Martyr appeared from the fire, Jack and the rest simply followed Anastasia. They had to go someplace, and if anyone had turned around they would have seen their escape in that direction cut off by the burning and melting of the great machine Magog. They did not look back, because that would have entailed taking their eyes off the Saint and it was too soon after her appearance for that.

Anastasia walked up the catwalk and the fire died down everywhere she passed. At the top of the stair, they saw her kneel and easily pick up a woman. Peter came beside Anastasia to see that she was holding Mary Yurislav in her arms. Anastasia was crying and Peter looked from Anastasia to Mary and back again.

"We must bring her with us." Anastasia got up and Peter found that he was half-dragging, half-carrying Mary through the room. Sadly, he was weaker and Mary was heavier than when they were both sixteen.

"What about the others ..." Peter realized he did not know how to address the Grand Duchess. "Shouldn't we at least try to rescue the other workers? We can't leave them here to die."

"Nobody will die." She said with poise. "The machine and all its wiring will soon be gone, but then the fire will end. There will be no gratuitous destruction of anything. The room will be scoured of all traces of the machine's foul structure, and then the judgment will end. The others in the room will drink of the river of forgetfulness, but they will not die."

Anastasia did not slow down her progress out of the pit and toward the back of the area that had housed Magog. She reached a back door at last. The group following her held their breath as she turned the handle, but it opened. Thank God it opened! The science building was no longer a safe place for anybody, and so the party followed Anastasia outside.

As Anastasia led them further into a University parking lot, they could breathe again, and the air was cool. Max turned as they left the science building, surprised he had not yet heard massive explosions and expecting to see a raging fire. Instead, aside from a blue flame flickering in a few windows, the science building looked safe.

"Safer than what we are doing," Barth muttered.

They came at last to a rear parking area where old college cars went to die. Peter looked behind them and said, "What is happening with Magog, Barth?"

"Magog is disappearing. Evidently bringing Anastasia back from the past was too much for the Heavenly Powers and they are taking strong actions." Barth said.

"Exactly." Anastasia turned to them. "Take me to a safe place where I can talk to this woman." She pointed to Mary.

"Susan." Jack looked at the building with anguish.

"Don't be afraid," Anastasia said in a kind voice. "She is in danger, but not from this fire. It will only destroy the machine. Even the building will be untouched."

Max spoke: "Gentleman. We dare not go to the van. They are going to think we did this, you know." Max could not take his eyes off the building.

"Yes. With any luck, they will think we are dead, at least for awhile." Father John was grim.

Peter nodded. "Which, by all rights, we should be, but we have to get Mary some place safe. Where can we go on foot? Who would take us?"

"I know a place here in the City." Jack looked into the night.

"Where?" Max was in a hurry to get Anastasia someplace out of view.

"Pentecostal Holiness Bible College. Susan and I," Jack paused, "went there as kids and I think they would help us ... at least for a little while."

Anastasia said, "Yes. That is exactly the right place. Take us there."

"Let's get out of here then." Barth said as he followed Jack into the darkness.

## Magog

Meanwhile in the Science building Magog was failing as system after system melted away. The heart of the great machine was still creating a hole in the cosmos spinning and opening the wall between space and time, but it could not last. The central chamber at the bottom of the pit was now utterly consumed in a cold,, blue fire that destroyed without leaving a trace of what it touched. The fire was directed by intelligence and annihilated only what it wished, leaving the rest.

The scientists who had been left in the room were washed again and again in this flame. They would remember nothing

121

about the project from beginning to end, but many reported being healed of numerous diseases. In the many medical examinations that would follow, some doctors would claim that the smokers amongst the scientists who had been in the fire had clean lungs, and that one scientist who had a serious heart condition now had none.

All over the building and through the campus, the fire followed the cabling from Magog to offices and to classrooms, consuming any trace of the project. The fire followed cable and phone lines to homes and offices all over the country and then the world that were connected with the Magog project in any way. Every bit of data was wiped clean whether on paper, on discs, or on drives. The papers were consumed, the computer drivers were formatted, ready to use, but totally empty. Few people had known of the real purpose of Magog, but of those few, none were left with memories intact. Men and women connected to the project collapsed and when they awoke could remember nothing. No data was ever recovered about the project from Douglass University or anyone related to it.

The fire at the center of Magog kept forming geometrical patterns that were constantly changing. The dominant figure in the fire was a pyramid, but the shapes changed so quickly no human eye could have discerned the pattern. One could barely make out the open door of the central chamber, but passing out of the entrance was a faint flicker of light hardly visible in the brilliant light of the pit. Dampness, a mist, came from within the inner parts of Magog. The form of a man stood looking down at dying Magog and then slowly turned. The shade hesitated as if unused to his lack of a body and then passed through the walls and raced west.

22 January 2009, Thursday, The Day After the Destruction of Magog, 9:00 AM: Douglass University

On the same morning that a confused Mary Yurislav woke up at the Pentecostal Holiness Bible College, Bobby Kennedy read the latest news on the destruction of his project at the Democrat and Chronicle web site. There was a blistering editorial in giant type across the center of this screen and he read it with approval. To look at Robert Kennedy was to see a man born-again. He was wearing a jacket and a tie and his hair had been washed and combed.

Mary was probably dead, if she wasn't a terrorist, and the University President had turned to Kennedy to clean up the mess. The destruction of the complex by religious fanatics had done wonders for the Program. Before, it had been starved for funds, with little hope of renewal at the end of the year. Few had known what the Program was about or cared about its existence. Now it was safe to say nobody knew what the Program had been doing, including Bobby Kennedy, but everybody was sure it should exist.

Of course he had not told the President about his memory loss when he called; Bobby Kennedy knew paid computer-time when he saw it. He lied and told the President of Douglass University that of course he knew exactly the goals of the program and what had and should be done to restart it. Naturally the fire had destroyed many records, but Kennedy promised to bring in a brief outline of the project as soon as he could get the data together. When Kennedy discovered that nobody had anything but vague memories about the experiments within the science building, he knew his future was secure. Any expensive and expansive research program dealing with the general topics of time and psychology would fit what his colleagues recalled about the fire. A computer virus had, he had been delighted to discover, annihilated all the records to which he had access, and Kennedy was pretty sure there was no Project computer file to which he did not have access, legally or illegally. The project could be anything he could recreate on his own system from his own imagination.

He should worry about the memory loss, but memory leaks happened. This institutional memory loss was going to make him rich and powerful. Every single member of Congress was going to vote to fund it, just to show the crazies that Uncle Sam would never run scared. Who was going to be handing out all that research money, designing programs, constructing buildings, and developing new computers to handle the work? Robert Kennedy, of course. He was the big man on the research part of his campus and he was feeling fine.

The more he looked into things, the more he realized that his luck had been amazingly good. Everything, simply everything, had been wiped out in the weird fire and the virus that Barth had unleashed on the system. There was a risk, of course, that someone had a complete file on the Project somewhere, but some risks were worth taking.

His happy thoughts were diverted by a worm-like thought. It was possible that Barth and his merry band of religious terrorists had destroyed the project and infected his computers, but that did not explain the memory loss in so many people. Nothing could explain the memory loss in so many people. He was scared, but then he calmed himself.

This was a frontier of science, and maybe they had done something very bad. Maybe they had given themselves a disease for which science had yet to find a cure. He felt sick, but then calmed himself. Science would find the answer someday, perhaps too late to help him, but science was still the best answer to his problem. His forgetfulness did frighten him more than a bit, but the fear could be controlled by study and research.

Fate had left him the only man with the sense to act in his own interest. He too had been infected by the virus, but was that so surprising? He grinned and realized that he had fallen into religious thinking! He was just a machine with wetware instead of software. The virus unleashed on the computers had also worked on the human brain! Barth, or the people funding him, had managed to infect the human mind with his horrible, no interesting, weapon. Any virus that could be created could also be checked.

What had they been doing exactly? He knew it had to do with time, and under Mary had turned into something quasi-religious, but he could not think what. He could remember most things perfectly, down to the web sites he had visited during the day, but some very important things were just black holes in his memory. If he got too near those forgotten details, they sucked up what, he did recall and caused him to forget what little he had left in terms of specific memories about the project. The harder he thought, the less he recalled. Why?

He knew he had been in the lab earlier, of course, to set up the experiments. It was fortunate he hated Mary as much as he did. As a result he had watched most of it from the safety of his office monitor and avoided, he thought, some of the impact of the event.

He could remember seeing Barth and his gang enter the chamber. He could recall the frantic calls for his help that would make fabulous You-Tube riff-tracks if he had the nerve to upload them. He remembered his certainty that Mary's New Age nonsense had destroyed everything. Magog (he was delighted to remember his pet name for this supercomputer system) had never been designed to take the sort of sustained power that had been pumped into it for days, but of course, religious impulses know no check of reason. But what exactly had they been doing?

Bobby Kennedy pushed himself to think very carefully. He had a sense that Mary had destroyed any real science in Magog in a quest for visions. Kennedy took satisfaction in the memory of heated arguments about whether religion itself was a mass delusion. Surprise, surprise, he had been right about that. Maybe somehow he had been caught in the kind of mass hysteria during a crisis that was the real basis for religious experience. Of course, he was level headed enough not to take this experience of evidence of something "supernatural" or spooky.

Bobby gained some clarity in his thinking. Mary had failed to respect the proper boundaries between sense and nonsense. She had opened the experiment to abuse and manipulation by the religious fanatics on campus. Somehow they, especially that bastard Barth, had harnessed Magog and used it as a weapon against science, but their plans had backfired. He had been too smart to admit his ignorance to the President of Douglass, and now the University would ask a real scientist to do the work. This was his chance to be the strong man and play the part of the hero.

He knew what he wanted from heroism: heroes get grants and prizes. Grants and prizes meant prestige, women, and the end of kissing up to judgmental bosses. He had seen how Nobel winners got away with every form of social folly and envied them their true liberty.

Robert Kennedy would claim that the Magog Project—he would name this second project Gog—had been research on the wetware of the mind, and methods of infecting it with a virus or correcting its failures. Kennedy grew excited and wondered if this was not what the original project had been! Was he remembering? Perhaps, and he thought this might be right, they had been playing with the brain's perception of time and history as part of the experiment?

The defense department would see obvious implications of it in research and the medical community would laud the so-called positive applications. The earlier experiments had gone awry and harmed some scientists involved, but this was merely the **Challenger** disaster of experimental cognitive science. He would build in safety features that Mary had overlooked; he would recreate the memos showing that her zeal had blinded her to danger. Bobby Kennedy really felt **better** than fine.

26 January 2009, Monday, 10:35 AM: Pentecostal Holiness Bible College

Peter Alexis did not have to worry about the Dream anymore. Anastasia had told him that it was gone for good, which was small comfort since now his actual life seemed to be a nightmare. He was remembering more and more of what had happened to him around the time of his sixteenth birthday. His attempts to save the little alternate world, Barterra, and the loss of the girl he had loved there, were now pathetically available for review. They were embarrassing, because he had seen that world and the people in it as a sixteen year old, and his memory had not matured with his mind. His memories and feelings had all the depth of a sixteen year old in his forty-something self and the result was not good. The oddest thing of all was that as memories of his sixteenth year grew sharper, he found he was struggling to recall some of the details of the events of the last week. Barterra often seemed more real than Magog.

One advantage of being in his forties was that he understood this sub-creation, this little world, better than he had when he was in it. Maybe.

Barterra was a world where certain human creations, our imaginative children, lived out their lives when humans were done with them. Our fears of a monster under our bed or dreams of a fairy in the woods lived on in Barterra and gained a secondary freedom. Peter had experienced Barterra through his mind, his dreams, and his nightmares. The form of the characters in Barterra was fluid and dependent on the observer in ways not true in a God-created-world. Like a god, humans had some creative power there for our expectations to shape the very fabric of the world.

Peter had helped create what he had seen.

Even the names used to label the people and characters he met were those fit for a sixteen year old. Bandor, Dragon Lord, was exactly the name he expected in a fantasy world and could comprehend at that time. He had fixed a name on Bandor and made it so. He could not totally control or change Bandor, as the Dragon Lord was the product of many human hopes and fears, but he did name him and give a more concrete form by being in Barterra. It was as true a name as he could give, and just as Adam had in the garden, he christened creation, but unlike Adam's naming, Peter's names had been given no chance to grow or change with time. Now, apparently, everybody would know his juvenile imaginative limitations.

Like many people Peter had recalled his sixteen-year-old self as his forty-year-old self in a young body. One problem with keeping old papers or old diaries from high school is the reminder that this was not quite true! Peter was getting a much more brutal reminder than most people ever experience when finding old yearbooks. He was trapped on the top floor of a Pentecostal Bible college in a room like one from his eighteenth year, and he smiled to himself, eating pathetic cafeteria food just as he had then, but being forced to recall exactly the way the world looked to him at sixteen. He was sure he had lost five pounds and more self-respect.

Peter stared out of the half-closed blinds of the room in which he was more or less a prisoner. His eyes fell to the overloaded electric outline filled with two-prong adapters and tac-strips. The electrical system was not built for modern demands, and it made using any appliance awkward. They kept losing power and he could have sworn he saw a blue spark arc from the wall to a borrowed blow dryer in the bathroom this morning. He had jumped back, but there was no shock ... just a cold chill of fear about fire in such an antiquated building. Of course, according to the radio, since Magog went down, the entire power grid of Rochester was spotty. As might be expected in a city that needed heat in the winter, there was more discussion of that on local talk radio than the "terrorist incident."

He should have been grateful for a few things: they had stopped Magog, and Anastasia was in safe hands and with him, with Bandor.

Anastasia. It was four days since her "rescue" and Peter still could not believe it. She sat by herself mostly in a room that had been turned into a chapel. Quiet. When she spoke, what she said was true. Remarkable. The door opened and he looked up.

Max came across the room. "You look better, Peter. Sleep does you good. On the other hand, you are losing weight, which is a bad sign. Recollect the truth that at a certain age, a happy man is no longer a thin man."

"You have been a happy man for some time now, Maximos."

His friend smiled, "Moderately so, Peter. But I have interrupted your thoughts. What were you considering so carefully just now?"

"I have just been thinking of Her."

"Which her?" Max looked hard at Peter. "We have the Blessed Mother of God, Lisay Macbor of Barterra, Mary Yurislav ..." Max paused.

"Not that Mary, Her: Anastasia. Who or what else is there to think about?"

"Actually, I have been reading the Philokalia with Father John in my room. Remarkable work that contains such insight ... though the Greek is rough, the spirit is profound. Those Fathers knew the spiritual life. Have you read it?"

"Max, the entire nation believes we are dead. They also believe that we probably destroyed the most expensive project at the University in which you were a former employee ... and you are reading the Philokalia?"

"Is there something better to do with my time? That is the best thing about this whole little adventure. There is so much time to read! Our last little fracas when you were a boy had me dashing around all the time. Lord knows what it had you doing, but my guess is that you had little enough time to reflect. We are really most fortunate this time out."

Peter laughed aloud. It had been quite some time since he had laughed and it felt good. "You really are hopeless, you old fraud. You have come to cheer me up!"

"Well, yes. However, I was reading in the room in between my shift watching that lovely woman, Mary. I am mostly here to tell you that it is your turn to go into her room. I came to get you."

"Ah, how is she?"

"Still quiet. She asks questions. She knows our side of the story now from several angles."

"Yes. She pumped me for information, but she says nothing definite about herself or her wishes. Does she want to leave?"

"I am not sure what she wants. She seems content to stay in bed, think, and listen."

Peter quietly responded, "Yes. She is oddly peaceful and at least she looks nicer ... more relaxed, more like herself."

A glint appeared in the Eye of Maximos. "Peter! You are human after all and recollection is a powerful aphrodisiac. Now Maggie would say that the two of you ..."

"Stop that now! I will take it from Maggie, but not from you. Now get out of my way and let me get to my post, you perpetual matchmaker." Peter began to hustle out of the room. He thought of something and turned to Max.

"You must miss her." He saw tears fill the old eyes of the scholar. "I am sorry, of course, you miss your wife. It was silly to ask."

"No, it was thoughtful of you to remember her. My pain comes from knowing that she must think me dead. We cannot make even a mobile call, and she will be hurting. She is hurting for no reason and I would spare her."

"You wonder why I don't get married, Max? I think that is why. The pain versus pleasure ratio is always bad. Love let me down once. I know it hasn't let you down in that way, and that there are plenty of people that would not do what Lisay did, but does that really matter? Won't love let us all down in the end?"

"Death comes. How could I bear that final parting? How will you? The more you love Maggie, the greater the pain of death. If I were to die first, I would hurt the women I loved. How could I wish this? It is hard enough to stand the parting when marriage is hard. Love is too difficult, and avoiding it too easy to justify the risk." Peter shook his head. "Your pain is a good enough reason to close off that part of my heart."

Max nodded,. "But that is too simple, Peter. The pain is good for us, you know. Most pain is. It makes our souls strong enough to bear the joys of paradise. Sounds trite, but I have found it to be true. You loved badly, I think. Love, even the love Maggie and I have, is not meant to be so isolated, so unique as you say your love for Lisay was. It had no room for anything or anyone else."

"Much as I love Maggie, it is just part of my love for the Church, for you and my other friends, and for Christ. Moderation, even in love, is a virtue, Peter. I love you differently than I love Maggie, but my appropriate care for you makes my love for Maggie more balanced and real."

Peter smiled at Max. "I love you too, Max. It is not something men like us say very often, but you say hard things you think and allow me to do the same. I suppose too that you have kept me from living a dull life!"

Max came very close to a grin. "Right. And now, go get to your duty; watching a lovely woman and answering her questions is not the worst task I have sent you to do."

"The dragon was the worst job, Max. Remind me to tell you about the dragon." Peter left the room letting the door slap back into the face of his friend.

Mary was tired of being in bed. It had come over her all at once that the time had come to make some decisions. She had listened for days now to what these people had to tell her. Of course, on the face of it all, they were clearly insane. She had grown up in a house where this apocalyptic and hyper-religious nonsense was all the rage so Mary Yurislav knew the drill.

How many impassioned sermons had she heard as a little girl naming the very Antichrist? Yet, somehow, here she was, staying in the very school where her mother had always prayed that she would attend.

"I made it, Mom, but I don't think I will graduate," she said to no one in particular. The only problem with her insanity theory was that it included Mary Yurislav. She knew that people under stress could see a great many things, but she could not deny what she had seen in Magog a few short days ago. If she wanted to do so, and she did not, she could have gotten out of bed to talk to Anastasia Romanov. If they were insane, then she was crazy as well.

Was she crazy? Jack Smith was a very good psychologist and he assured her she was not crazy, but then he believed the same things that she did. If she were nuts, then he was as well, but he did not seem crazy. The only weird thing that had happened to her so far was the total absence of identification in her briefcase. Her drivers license, her social security card, they were all gone. She would have to ask for them back.

In her deepest heart she knew these people were correct, but this still irritated her. Mary wanted some reason that justified her being wrong for so long about the most important things. Nothing had happened, after all, to weaken her argument against the very sort of religion all these folk practiced. There were huge, very big, even giant reasons that all fundamentalist Christianity could not be true.

Religion was possible in the modern world, but not this Middle Ages sort of religion, this faith in relics and saints. Worse still was the kind of faith-based religion that believed that some people spoke in other tongues or personally talked to God every day. Hadn't she outgrown all of it? Her pagan friends had been far nicer than the people she had known growing up in her home Church and, she noted with satisfaction, they had never stolen her Visa card.

Mary had a new thought. Perhaps it was her memory that

was at fault. Was she remembering her home church accurately? She began to wonder if she had been quite fair to all those folk of Faith Holiness. Had she stereotyped them, turned them into monsters, or dismissed their beliefs as the product of simple, bland piety only to suit prejudice?

Brother Simon, who was helping the group escape the law, did not fit the mold of the people she remembered as working at the Bible College during one of her many childhood visits. He was likable and, granted, his premises not stupid. She did some mental arithmetic and realized with a shock that Brother Simon had been at PHB when she was a child. Could she have been that wrong? Could it be that childhood conclusions might be wrong?

During his time with her, Father John had quietly discussed any of her questions about religion. He expressed his views strongly, but did not seem upset when she disagreed. He was as relaxed as any Socrates with his Glaucon. Father John did not fit the mold of priests or preachers she had met in college, but then, she realized with a shock, maybe those memories and judgments were also untrustworthy. Was Father Rob in college being patient with her questions rather than not knowing what to say? That was difficult to swallow.

Father John had nothing like all the answers and she had beaten him, she thought rather badly, in a couple of their Socratic dialogues. It was his faith, his theology practiced in his prayer that shook her. He knew God or he was mad. She had decided early on that he knew God.

Maximos was like that too. He was brilliant, of course, a fact everyone in the University was willing to concede. Brilliant people were not unusual in Mary's experience, but joyous ones were. In the end, it had been his love for his wife that won her grudging admiration, since his intellect and overly hasty opinions could be insufferable. His love for Maggie was pure and sincere without any posturing or irony at all. She could not share his archaic philosophy, but she could not help wishing that she could meet someone like him. Mary decided that she wanted to meet Max's Maggie to share a cup of tea and a long talk.

And then there was Peter Rupert Alexis. Again. Meeting Peter, suffering the ignominy of being rescued by Peter was galling. She hadn't thought of him enough in the last few decades to work up any real hatred, but he did annoy her. Even his name was stupid. What parent named their child after the last effective prime minister of Tsarist Russia and a cavalry commander in the English Civil War? Peter was sad and lonely (she could not help a trace of satisfaction at this), but also gentle and kind. It had been a long time since Mary had lived in a world with many gentlemen in it.

Being here was weird, too much like the freshman year in college she might have had and once thought she would have. She was here in Bible school and Peter was rooming down the hall. When was he coming to see her? Mary was irked at the thought. Why did she care when he was coming? She wasn't going to ask him to return the friendship ring she had given him and never gotten back. Mary stopped thinking about Peter, but was well trained enough to realize that thinking about stopping thinking about Peter was just another way to think about Peter. Being irked with Peter was another way of thinking about Peter … and she had not thought, very much, about Peter since she was seventeen and had stopped writing heart-broken poetry.

Mary knew that folks confined to hospitals begin to form attachments, but doing so after four days irritated her. Peter was not even her type. She was taller than he was by a good bit and she earned a lot more money. He was a bit gray and not very careful about his appearance. On top of that, he was petulant at times. And stubborn and opinionated people easily irritated Mary. He was often "down" and Mary liked cheerful people.

Of course, to be fair, in her old life, she reflected, she had used cheerful people as a sort of drug. She paused in their thinking: "Her 'old' life?" She was thinking like a convert in a cult! She would not become a mind-numbed robot listening to talk radio and voting for Bush. Peter had undoubtedly voted for W. They had argued about politics even back in the day. Peter …

What about Peter? No rational person fell in love in four days and he certainly was not hot enough for a quick fling, but she knew she wanted that man here now. He was her favorite "guard." Where was he anyway? She hated being alone, had told the group, and they had graciously agreed to sit with her in turns. She did not really need the attention now, but it kept Peter coming to her room so she did not change the arrangement. Count on Peter to be late. He had always been late when not kept on schedule.

"Let's face it," she thought, "however stupid it is, you have a re-run crush on Peter." Mary gritted her teeth at her lifetime habit of absolute honesty. She had always adopted the policy of getting what she wanted, but she was pretty sure Peter was not something she should want. She knew she was attractive, but she did not know if Peter agreed with this truth. If she was going to have a stupid crush, then she was not going to add the humiliation of being rejected again by a guy who had not realized his romantic ship was docking the first time. She knew men and was pretty sure that she should be able to win him back, but was less sure she should keep him or would want to do so if she did. Where was he anyway?

Mary made it a point of honor to always look good, but her recent troubles left her with no confidence in her present appearance. There was no mirror in the room, and she had only a dollar-store brush, borrowed on the sly from some poor student by Brother Simon. There was only one nightgown, Victorian with no secrets, and her robe. Still when he came, she tried. Fundamentally, the idea of flirting irritated Mary Yurislav, since the outcomes were so uncertain, but it did make Mary, the woman, very happy. She enjoyed being very happy and she would use Peter for that, if nothing else. What was wrong with a little romance in the middle of your troubles? In any case, she could get some of her own back from high school.

On one thing she was clear: No Christianity. She might have destroyed her career, wasted a few hundred millions, but no patriarchal religion. No head covering allowed. No meekly bowing to male priests or mimicking the Madonna and telling husbands "let it be done unto me according to thy will." She was not, and never would be, a "keeper at home." She had a perfectly good head of her own, and she would control her own body. If she wanted Peter's love, then he was free to give it. When she did not want it, he was free to move on.

# Chapter Five: The Great Waves

Mary knew her own religion had been pretty much of a disaster, but one need not go so far as to embrace the primitive faith of the people here. But what were those shadows in the pit? Were they real? What would her mainline pagan friends have to say about that?

Her door opened and her heart skipped a beat, which would have been irritatingly trite if it had not been so fun. Max had left just minutes ago.

"Time for Peter," she thought with a guilty cheerfulness. "It is all right. When this is over, I will go back to the real me." Mary put on her mask, brushed back her hair with a hand, but noted with disappointment, and then with alarm, that it was Anastasia.

That was a shock, since the woman had never come to her room after the first night. Mary had heard she spent most of the time in the chapel and she was sure this was true. Once, and no one knew this, Mary Yurislav had gone sneaking down the hall to see if Anastasia was real, or just a dream. The girl had been praying with her back turned to the door. The bayonet marks were visible on her neck. She was real, very Real.

Anastasia seemed very innocent, but she was no child. She had been a woman when she died. Mary had forgotten this fact, since most of the famous pictures of the family were from Anastasia's childhood, but growing up had not stopped in prison. Still, Mary was older than she was or had been by many years. It did not matter. Whatever had happened to Anastasia Romanov after death had changed and deepened her. Mary Yurislav felt her soul quiver under the kind eyes of the Tsar's daughter.

"You cannot do that, you know—you cannot go back." Anastasia was speaking to her and Mary began to panic. Max had told her that the Martyr-Princess rarely spoke. Her soul, it appeared, had been outside of time for the years since her death. Her body had been called back, and by the Grace of God, been reunited with her soul, but she was a living window to Heaven.

Anastasia, this Anastasia, had stood before the face of the Triune God. She knew things, that is, she knew anything God wanted her to know. It is frightening to stand before someone who knows and who cannot be controlled or silenced by any human means. She spoke excellent English, only lightly accented, Mary noted, and often stated she was here on a mission, though she had not yet said what it was. "Or so Max believes," Mary reminded herself fiercely. "Even in his theology saints are good, not omniscient."

"It is true, though Maximos puts it too simply."

"Stop that. Reading my mind and replying is unnerving!"

"I am sorry you find it so." Anastasia smiled. "You have no secrets from heaven or the company of Saints. You cannot go back to what you were, you know. You would become even worse than you were, though you were bad enough."

Mary bristled, "I did my best."

"You did not."

"What do you want me to do?"

"You have been under grace, up until now, due to your Mother's effective prayers, but soon you shall have to choose. If you do not become a Christian, then the demons that have left you will come back with seven times their number and you will become very vile. But if you come to Christ and the protection of His Church, then He has many good things for you."

This was going badly. Mary was not asking the questions and she felt out of control. This was forcing her into a corner when she wanted discussion, clarification, and equivocation. A saintly Russian Princess from the turn of the century was giving her marching orders. You can argue with a princess, but who can argue with a saint?

"I have been thinking about Christianity. I will take your message seriously." Mary tried to mix thoughtfulness with sincerity.

"No. This is no intellectual game or negotiation. The Holy Trinity demands your submission."

Mary could not breathe. She was dazed and knew that if she kept going she would soon be joining a nunnery and obeying some fat abbot.

"No. Your place is not in Holy Orders. You are not so privileged. Like most women, you are called to keep a home, to become mother to your children and to young women in your Church. If I am blunt, it is because you have been very wicked and are getting older that I must speak so. There is little time and opportunity left."

"Thank you. Some man will be so lucky." Mary said dryly.

"Not some man, but the man who is about to enter this room. God knows Peter Alexis has needed you and you need someone like him. Try not to be a Proverbial fool and marry him." Anastasia looked, almost, impatient, but then she stopped and thought for a moment.

Anastasia's countenance was peaceful again, "I am sorry I seem harsh, but your time is difficult for me. It is hard to understand these lies you struggle in, since they are so unique to your own little moment. It is like learning a new language to master them and a work of grace to be charitable to you. Confronting against such obvious errors is difficult, since it is like teaching you that it is right and proper to breathe."

"But, what do you know of love or marriage? You were just a child ..." Mary sputtered realizing what she was about to say.

Anastasia was just staring at her. The eyes were loving, unhurt, and unafraid. "The schools of heaven are even better than the tutors of Imperial Russia," she finally said.

Mary tried to be angry. Anastasia seemed to be majoring on the least important things and was spewing the very dogmas that Mary hated most. It was tyrannical of God: send in a "saint," have her announce God's will, then case closed. Damn. It was unfair. Mary was very angry now. She started to speak, found she was too mad to be effective, and stopped talking.

Anastasia began to move toward the door. "When you get to heaven, there will be no equality there... only liberty and love. I have seen Mary in the center of the Court of Heaven and you cannot know Her splendor. I have seen Nina, Equal to the Apostles, with a Kingdom at her feet. I have seen my own Aunt Elizabeth receive the crown of the Martyr. Saint Peter himself, splendid on this throne, has less glory than the Woman our Lord called Mother. But, Mary Yurislav, we are called mothers there, not one woman in all the Company of the Saints is called father.

Anastasia continued: "The Theotokos submits, and her Son,

a True Man, loves her with perfect love and gives Himself for her. We are consumed in Heaven with the passion of Order, Hierarchy that leads to Love. Make yourself fit to join us. Don't just believe, see it."

Mary had always had excellent vision, but now it was better, and for one brief moment, Mary Yurislav, not even a Christian, was given a glimpse of Heaven. She saw hierarchies of Angels, leading to Saint Michael, the Archangel. She perceived a Great Chain of saints of all Ages leading to the thrones of the Apostles. She glanced at the uncreated light that is the Throne of the Father, Son, and Holy Ghost, but could not stare as she wished due to its splendor.

Wherever she looked, Mary saw the humility and glory of lovers. She knew that love was in her longing to unite her soul with all those heavenly beings and transform her into her true self. Mary knew so much with one glance at Heaven that all her knowledge up to that moment seemed mere ignorance to her now.

She was offered a place, a low place, but still a place in the Great Company. It was all clear, just, and splendid. Her seat at the feast, the wedding feast, would find her just as permeated by love as the Apostles' thrones. She would be equal without being identical, and an individual without being alone. For the second time in four days, Mary wept.

When she began to cry, Anastasia, the holy martyr, came close to Mary. She leaned over the woman in the bed. The Martyr-Princess, the girl-woman, scars on her body from the bullets of hate, bent over and kissed the head of the engineer, provost, and vice-president of Douglass University.

Anastasia left the room, but did not leave Mary alone. She was with a great company of heaven and her heart had found rest in the beautiful vision of the energies of God.

Peter walked into the room five minutes later. He had gone down the hall to the bathroom to clean up a bit after talking to Max... realizing there was no use looking like a mess when he saw Mary. He might have to wear the same clothes every day, wash them out in a basin at night with hand soap, but he could be presentable. Peter admitted he was looking forward to seeing Mary, though he had met her again only three days ago.

When he went into the room, he could see that Mary had been crying. Peter had seen so little emotion from her since the destruction of Magog that this surprised him more than it should have. He had received endless questions from her agile mind as they sat for hours the last day or two. He knew some of his answers had not been nearly as good as her questions, because she had often dropped a line of discourse in minutes. Max could keep her going for hours on one line of reasoning.

Most of their time together, they talked about old friends from school. Peter told her about his life. She mostly wanted to hear about his adventures on Barterra, what that world was like, and the things he had seen and heard while he was there. Most of what he told her Peter had scarcely remembered himself so that telling her about them was almost as if he was experiencing them for the first time. They were memories, but very, very fresh memories.

"I know I was different when I came back," he had said to her at one point.

"Yes," she said, clearing her throat, "hurtful. You were," she smiled, "much improved in mathematics."

"Yes," Peter said thoughtfully, "I was."

"Mathematics, however," Mary said, "is not everything. I should know since I never saw the pattern of the cosmos and still got a higher Regent's trig score than you."

Peter and Mary both had laughed together.

He had told her about Lisay yesterday. Was it only yesterday? Had he only been talking like this to Mary for three days? What would happen when she left, and would she leave soon? Would he forget the feelings he was remembering?

"Are you all right?" Peter said to Mary as he sat in the chair by her bed. It was a pretty uncomfortable straight-back wooden chair, but he hadn't noticed that yet.

"She was here." Mary looked at him oddly as if she were sizing him up for an important job at Douglass.

"Anastasia was here?" That was potentially more revealing than Mary's tears. Peter was sure whatever Anastasia might say that it would be good and proper, but he dreaded finding out what it was. "What did she say?"

"I am not going to tell you," Mary spoke with an odd emphasis on that last word, "at least not now."

"What was it about?"

"Well, it was hard and it leaves me with a choice, if it was even true." Mary did not really question the truth of her own vision; she couldn't do that yet, but added the disclaimer from habit.

Peter had no doubt she believed Anastasia, but defended the Saint to have something to say. "It was true if she said it. Now if it had been Max talking, that would have been another story. You never know with Max. He might tell you something just to start an argument. Even when he is wrong or guessing, Max sounds Delphic."

"Max would have said more than the Martyr-Princess, but could not show me what she did." Mary looked searchingly at Peter again. "Tell me about Lisay, Peter."

"What do you want to know?" Mary was the easiest person in the group to talk with about Lisay, but the one person Peter wished would not ask about her.

Mary kept looking directly into his eyes, "What did she do to you?"

"Lisay did not mean to do anything bad to me. She loved me very much, but she wanted something else besides me and she could not have both. Someone very wicked whom she did not wish to believe was bad, promised both to her. She needed only to do a small thing, tell a little white lie really, in order to get it. Magic worked in that world, you know, and this man who promised her was a very powerful worker of magic."

"Did she get what she wanted?"

"No, he destroyed her and he used her little lie to do it. It also ended up destroying the city we both loved. I cannot imagine what the Tower looks like now."

"So from what I gather, this man is Bandor, a creature of human nightmares given shape by sixteen year old you. Dreadful thought that. Will this Bandor be the power behind the Anti-Christ and his prophet?"

"Yes."

"What was it that Lisay wanted, Peter?" The philosopher was silent. His jaw clenched. She could almost hear his teeth grinding together. He was not going to say.

Mary Yurislav had risen very high in a demanding profession and had run a good school well. She had done so with a first rate mind, good communication skills, and an ability to concentrate. She may have been frequently over-caffeinated, but she was in a Red-Bull fueled profession.

Mary did not know, however, that her greatest job skill never made her CV. She had quick insight and an ability to size up an employee or rival. Mary sometimes "just knew." Her mother had once told her that she had the "word of wisdom," one of many spiritual gifts in which Pentecostals romped. She brushed off the observation as a sexist compliment. She rightly refused any demeaning notion of "women's intuition" without realizing that might still be a woman who had intuition.

She looked at Peter and was wise. The truth was stamped in the fine lines that marred his face without adding character. "She wanted to have your baby and could not."

The anguish in Peter's eyes made her wish she had been silent. He finally blurted out, "Anastasia told you that?"

"No. She spoke of troubles and opportunities of my own. Your truth was easy to guess from other things you have told me, and from what you just said."

"Not so easy. Max hasn't guessed."

For the first time in her life she allowed herself a concession to a certain truth. "Max is not a woman, and he did not know you the way I did." She paused and then said with certainty, "His Maggie would have known in a flash."

"Well, however you know, you are right. Lisay could never have my baby. They had told her when we married that it has to do with the nature of their world, and it turned out to be true. I was in Barterra for four years, and when we fell in love she told me."

"Four years?" Mary said, "Narnia-like time!"

"Fictional time," Peter replied. "Time goes as quickly as the story you find yourself in. It was little to do with Earth time or a great deal. I never worked it out."

"I will have to think about that." Mary looked interested and then said, "How did you react when she told you?"

"What did I care? She thought it would scare off the Hero of Barterra but I loved her twice as much for it. I would have loved her twice as much for anything she told me. That was the way it was between us. Threat of damnation would not have slowed down my passion for her."

"Anastasia would not like that."

"Neither does Max, for that matter, but that was the truth." Peter was crying now. The tears were burning his contact lenses, but he ignored them. His greatest secret and pain was told. Had he failed Lisay? Had he looked, even for a moment, a bit disappointed when Lisay told him the news? Had he driven her to Bandor with unspoken desires?

No. It came to him that he had failed her in other ways, but not in that way. He did not realize it, but the hurt was beginning to heal. Mary caught the shadow of a change in his eye and dared to ask one more question:

"What was her lie?"

"She did not tell me she had been to see a warlock about her condition. She went there alone. Of course, it was Bandor, who turned out to be not just bad, but horrible. Lisay could not have known that." Peter was speaking very quickly. "I never knew about the warlock, and that turned out to matter a great deal as bad luck would have it." Peter looked very grim and seemed almost warlike, which was a bit comical in a middle-aged philosopher.

"I am so sorry, Peter. There is nothing more to say is there? I am sorry."

"Everybody was sorry, but Lisay still died."

"How do you feel?"

"I am sorry for it all, but it tore us apart on Barterra. We were not a couple by the time she died. I will always love and honor what she was, but only God could love what she became." Peter had nothing more to say, and Mary was wise enough to be quiet. They sat for a long time in stillness.

Peter finally spoke. "You ask me how I feel? I feel like it is finished." He looked younger then and rubbed his hand over his hair. Peter looked at her expectantly, as if she had his next move locked in her capacious brain.

It was at that moment that Mary Yurislav knew that she still loved Peter Rupert Alexis.

"Damn again," she thought, "this really is unfair." If he kept sitting there looking hurt, brave, and goofy, she would kiss him and she was not ready to kiss him. She might soon, but first there was more important business to finish.

Mary spoke as gently as she could. "I can't talk anymore. Could you call Father John? There is something I need to say to him."

Peter looked irritated and he rubbed his eyes. He groaned, almost a young man in his emotional overreaction. He said nothing, but he thought: "You cannot touch on that subject and then just tell me to leave! How can you rip me open and then tell me you can't talk anymore?" Peter's eyes hurt, his brain was frozen in place, and he felt like hell, but he could not pour out his anger on her when she was still sick in bed.

He looked at her calm brown eyes and one part of him whispered. "We should have left you in Magog." Most of Peter screamed, "No!" to that foolish idea.

Peter was glad she was here even if she was abrupt, nosey, and unkind. He looked at her and she just looked back at him. Why wouldn't she say anything? He felt like he should either storm out of the room or kiss her. What had made him think of kissing her? Mary just kept looking at him, waiting for him to leave, and his manners saved him when his emotions could not. He got up to leave and he had regained his composure. What kind of man would deny a sick woman her request to talk to a priest?

Somehow, Peter understood that Mary had made some kind of decision. He needed to get out of the way and let her do what she needed to do. His story about Lisay had triggered something in her, told her something she wanted to know. He could not storm out of the room, and he was out of practice when it came to kissing.

He wanted to help her, but she was somehow helping him. How? Peter was used to people who talked a lot, said everything they thought, and then explained it further, but Mary just sat waiting for him to comply with her request.

He got up, but never took his eyes off her. "I will get Father John. Thank you for talking to me as much as you did when you are so tired. I feel better. Having it all out is good. My memories returned last week and I have been trying to process them and make sense of them. You help, but then you always did help me."

He knew that sounded lamely like flirting, a reminder of sixteen thirty years late.

Mary smiled at him. She felt tears coming again and wanted him out of the room before she felt compelled to push the hair back from his forehead. "Get Father John, Peter." She closed her eyes.

Peter still stood staring for a moment at her closed eyes, but then regained the power to leave the room. In the corridor of PHB he realized he was shaking, but knew he also felt better than he had felt in decades. Where was Father John anyway? He felt slow on the uptake somehow. What was he missing?

He passed the room that they had turned into a chapel. He looked into it as he walked by and Anastasia turned her head. Her smile made him even more lightheaded. Without her saying a word, she showed him God as if she had preached a sermon. Peter knew that this woman saw his entire past and the trajectory of his life. She had the gift of knowledge and of prophesy.

He nodded at her, bowed slightly, and then heard her say, "Marry the girl as you should have in the first place, or you are a sorry excuse for a man." She went back to her prayers. For the first and only time in a life of adventure, Peter Alexis, Hero of Nimlandor and Master of the Narva Birds, fainted dead away.

# Chapter Six:

# The Philosopher King

22 January 2009, Thursday, The Day After the Destruction of Magog, 7:00 AM: Los Angeles California

He had missed the destruction of Magog the night he left Rochester, and he thought he would always be sorry. In later years, it would have made an excellent sermon anecdote, if he had been there, but he found out about it after landing at LAX. It was the smallest shock of his day.

Flying from Rochester to Southern California is like going from a black and white movie to Technicolor. Rochester is a handsome matron wearing earth tones. Los Angeles glitters under the hot sun, a woman sure of what she wants seen and not bothering to hide what she doesn't. The Reverend Doctor Robert DeLong fairly bounded down the skyway of the plane into LAX. He was glad to be home.

LAX seemed a bit run down, always under construction in the parts he used, nothing like Rochester's little jewel box of an airport. You had to ignore details like that in Southern California. If you could see the big picture and focus on the sweaty life of the town, you could not help but love L.A. It was the sun that always cheered DeLong up. One left the airport and got a good dose of it. Given the time difference, it was like getting three extra hours of life. "You have to believe in the goodness of God, in a place like this." DeLong reflected on this way to the cab.

It was a decent drive from the airport to Whittier Evangelical Seminary. The college had been moved to Richard Nixon's old hometown about the time the president-to-be headed to Washington. It had followed the typical Bible Institute to Seminary move under the pressure of the G.I. Loan and upwardly mobile fundamentalists.

Unlike several nearby schools such as Biola and Cal Baptist, Whittier Evangelical had managed to entirely shed its evangelical roots. It had grown up. W.E. had become more and more re-spectable, raised more and more money, and become less and less Christian in the process. The fourth President of the school had made most of the changes. He was the son-in-law of one of the founders and had earned a conventional degree. He was big, hearty, and had the energy of a used car salesman on Labor Day Weekend. "Everybody is part of WE. WE exclude nobody and love everybody. WE are the people Christ died to save." It soun-ded better when he said it, but not much.

Certainly, nobody listened to the handful of cranky alumni who were the only ones who even noticed the theological changes. The school was a success, and that is what counted. The carping of a few outsiders on right-wing blogs and aging alum al-ways sounded hollow next to the obvious success of the school. Even the most conservative alum were tempted to mute their cri-ticism as their Whittier diploma began to carry increased clout in the secular academic community.

At every step of the way, whoever was president would give a talk denying that Whittier was changing in its commitment to the "important" distinctive of the evangelical message. By now the school was glad to recall that evangelicals had been at the forefront of social action in the fight against slavery and industri-alism, but happy to forget that WE had been founded for more theological battles. Even DeLong was half-convinced that nothing essential had changed and the Founders would be thrilled with WE instead of anathematizing everyone in it. The Seminary was now in the forefront of other social justice issues. Nothing had changed.

"We have been faithful to our deepest calling," said the

current President in a Sojourner's article entitled "The Ascent of the Clergyman to Personhood." No one talked about the Founders of Whittier and it was rare for anyone to call it Whittier Evangelical. There were one or two convenient quotes about "the importance of learning" and "social responsibility" from the Founder and these received play in all the publications of the Seminary. Other than that, the Seminary felt it best to let the dead bury the dead.

It was the best job DeLong had ever had, and as the cab drove down Washington Avenue toward the campus he was thankful to have it. He knew that he was, in his way, a throw back, the token evangelical on the campus. He was amused by the frequent attacks he received from the right in his travels, when at WE amongst the faculty, DeLong was considered a bridge to the lunatic fringe of the religious world. A few professors still thought he did not belong at WE, but DeLong thought the situation was improving.

One professor from the Comparative Religions department had accused DeLong publicly of believing Hindus went to hell. DeLong had slipped the question with a bit of C.S. Lewis, but the damage had been done. He was still a bit suspect within the campus left, and many faculty members steered their more sensitive students around his lectures. It did not bother him mostly and he prayed often that he could be a better witness to the inclusive nature of Christianity.

His job was secure because the administration loved him. Their more conservative alum could be mollified by his star-quality and vocal presence in the evangelical world. One provost early in DeLong's career, when his presence was still a bit controversial, commented that Dr. DeLong saved the Seminary his whole salary just by keeping the widows of dead alum from removing the Seminary from their wills.

DeLong's recently published autobiography, Tell Me the Old Story, began: "I walk the middle way, the straight and narrow, between the intellectually easier paths of fundamentalism and total rationalism. The feelings I have when I hear the Old Story are things that my friends at the Seminary cannot explain or define with all their careful logic." DeLong was doing God's work at the Seminary.

The Seminary had been done in the faux-Spanish style that had been all the rage in the early seventies. The school had come into a large amount of money at the time, and the entire campus had been bulldozed and rebuilt. The faux-adobe was bright in the afternoon sun as DeLong pulled up to the campus in his cab. He paid the driver and tipped well. His large black dog, dear old Nero, bounded out of the car and began to run on the well-watered grass. It had been a good trip, but he was glad to be home.

DeLong waved at a student lounging on a bench, and began the short walk to his envy inducing office. DeLong had some phone calls to make before going home. He patted his jacket and found that his iPhone was still in place. He got out the phone and was startled to see a quick spark come from the phone when he touched the screen, but nothing seemed out of order. The professor moved his finger across the touch screen to unlock it and everything worked. "Static electricity," he thought.

He was glad the beautiful phone was OK. It had been an anniversary gift from his wife and the numbers in it were priceless. He had the private line of anybody who mattered in the religious world, left and right. He was on a first name basis with most of the religious leaders on the global A-list. DeLong was a man to whom most people would listen.

He was excited about one new project in particular. Peter Alexis, of all people, had given him the name of some people in Moscow, and these folk, the Evangelical Social Democratic Union, were working on the pivotal project of forming a new seminary in the former Soviet Union. In the two decades since the fall of communism, Russia had gotten her share of right-wing money and talent. She had her own on-the-ground leftist infrastructure, badly mauled by its association with the Old Regime, but the torn nation did not have the sort of healing sensible middle that kept America's religious extremes in check.

ESDU was an effort to present bleeding Russia with a middle way, and as a result, DeLong viewed the new seminary as having geopolitical significance. He would call soon. His dog came up to lick his hand and he patted it. The beast looked at him with big, gentle brown eyes.

He thought better of his schedule. He would call as soon as he could ... allowing for the time difference. After all, he had promised Peter to call soon. Nero licked his hand.

He opened the door to Meyer Hall. He did not see a shadow cross the sun from the east and pass into his office, but he did see the LA Times. He picked up the paper quickly and began to read. Nero settled down with his head on DeLong's knee.

27 January 2009, Tuesday, 11:52 AM: Pittsford New York

Maggie had been surprised at how quickly the story about Douglass had faded from the papers. It had started as if it was going to be an OJ-like cable-news-saturating story. Today she had found almost no mention of it in the D and C, which was dominated by coverage of the problems of President Obama's cabinet appointees. Rush wasn't talking about it and Morning Edition had only referred to it briefly. The national news basically had dropped the story. Maggie assumed nothing was going to be allowed to get in the way of the Obama first one hundred days.

She had moved to Susan's so that the children could come home from their grandparents' at Susan's request. Maggie was glad to have something to do to relieve her boredom, and happy to leave her house. The box still sat in her husband's office and the shadows continued to pour from it. The box could not be moved or destroyed. It had never been comfortable furniture, and had now become unbearable.

Tom Scott had come with her and insisted on driving back to help her after he finished his classes each day. He really was a good guy, and letting him try to help her distracted Maggie from her pain. She was not sure she wanted to live without Max, but she could serve others without him.

When the doorbell rang, the children had been doing their schoolwork in the kitchen. It was not going well. The boys seemed determined to fuss with each other. They had forgotten some score keys at their grandmother's house and were trying to decide whom to blame. Maggie had burned herself making break-fast, not used to cooking for four. She mourned Max and wanted a good cry, but could not for the sake of the boys and Susan.

Susan had called last night from the jail and that was bad enough news to ruin any good news. Solitary confinement had been ordered for her own safety and she had been interrogated every day. Last night was the first night she had been left alone and allowed to call Maggie. The grandfather clock in the front hall struck twelve loudly and the doorbell rang.

The doorbell rang and the clock stopped striking. Maggie opened the door in huff. UPS? Salesman? Avon calling? Did they do that anymore? Of course, she knew what it must be: reporters. Someone was going to get a piece of her mind.

The short, almost plain, woman in front of her looked famili-ar. She was too young to be going door to door really. What was there about this woman? Maggie was forgetting to speak. She kept looking at the eyes of the woman, such eyes ... pure color, could you have white eyes?

"That is it." Maggie thought. This girl is really pure, the way every mother wishes her daughter would be. With a start, Maggie realized that she had been staring and saying nothing and started to apologize, but stopped. Where had she seen this girl before?

Maggie realized that the longer she stared the more it was as if she was looking at a black-and-white photograph. The color was fading from the world around this stranger. The woman did not seem to mind the quiet or her impertinence in staring. She stood there waiting for Maggie to do something. The wind was kick-ing up again, but not a hair of the woman's carefully parted hair moved.

Maggie tried to smile, "Yes? I hope you are not a reporter. If you are, I have nothing further to say."

"I am Anastasia Nicolaevna."

Maggie did not even stagger. To her undying credit, she did not even stammer, "Yes?" The blood was gone from her honest face, but she looked right into the eyes of a Saint. And finally, "Won't you come in?"

"Yes, I must come in for a while. Thank you for inviting me

into this home. Don't be afraid, and don't worry about staring. I fear that I have that effect on everybody now."

She led the Martyr-Princess to the living room. "Will you sit down?" The woman sat down on the corner of the couch. Her back was straight, but she seemed utterly at peace. Maggie picked up some magazines littering the coffee table. She stacked them on a nearby ottoman. The woman watched her with a slight smile on her face.

Someone had given Anastasia a snow white, lace, ankle-length dress. She had walked, it seemed, all the way from the Bible College in the center of town. It had taken her hours, but she had wanted to see the twenty-first century first hand. It would be, she said with certainty, her last chance at a long walk.

When they offered to drive her, she had explained that her father had been quite a walker himself and had encouraged the children to exercise right up to the end. Maggie had known that already from reading Massie. It would be, Anastasia said, her only last chance at a long walk and she wanted to be able to tell her father.

"I make you uncomfortable. I am sorry." Anastasia looked at the older woman and smiled. "When you visit me in my Home, it will be more joyous."

"I am the one who should apologize. It is hard, however, to see someone you venerate standing on the front mat. I did not know what to do."

"I have an idea. Could you bring us a cup of tea?"

Maggie looked at the girl. She was going to like her, she decided with relief. You don't have to like the venerable, she realized with a shock, but Anastasia was likable. She hustled around the room, glad for something to do. She was sure she would like Anastasia, but in small doses.

She noticed the boys peering around the corner from the kitchen at their guest. How to explain this? It turned out to be easier than she thought. As she was leaving to get the tea, Anastasia spoke.

"I must tell you this first: Your husband is alive."

Maggie stopped on her way to the kitchen with her back to the Woman. The boys were staring past her into the room. Her heart had been broken and now it was whole. She leaned on the white frame of the door into the dining room, turned after a moment, and looked at Anastasia. For some reason she kept hearing Max singing to her, old show tunes mostly. Sometimes he would sing her the whole score to Camelot, her favorite. She could hear Max now: "If ever I should leave you ..."

Anastasia spoke. "He is alive. All of them are alive and hidden. They cannot stay where they are for long because Satan is closing in on them."

Just at that moment the front door slammed opened and Tom came into the room. He threw his backpack into a corner and said, "I am home! Anything I can ..." and saw Anastasia talking to Maggie. "What can we do for ..." Tom struggled to think of the right title for the Martyr-Princess. She smiled at him sweetly and Tom ended his sentence, "... you."

"Drive me back to Pentecostal Holiness Bible College."

"Of course!" Maggie replied and turning to Tom said, "Max is alive!"

Tom nodded and waited.

"Pack some clothes," Anastasia said, "for yourselves and the boys. You will never come back to this house again."

27 January 2009, Tuesday, 11:52 AM: Pentecostal Holiness Bible College

"Brother Berkeley."

Simon looked up. The ways of the Bible College are not subtle. If you were called by your first name it was good news. If by your last, trouble. This was very big trouble since it came connected to Elias Jones, D.Min. He was a man, Brother Simon reflected, who took all the fun out of fundamentalism.

Jones liked to suck the air through the gaps between his teeth and let it out with a whistling sound. It irritated Brother Simon, but irritation made him feel guilty about his lack of charity toward his co-worker so he had never said anything about it. The allegiance of alum could be told by whether their preaching style included staccato bursts or whistles.

Dr. Jones whistled more when he was upset, and he was very tuneful today. "I am very worried about those people upstairs, Brother Berkeley."

"What is wrong with them?"

"Who are they? I have never seen them before and I think, as your associate, I have the right to know who they are and what they are doing here." Jones was whistling like a teakettle at full boil now. "Accountability is important in any ministry and PHB has always had the highest standards, thanks be to God."

"One of them was a former student. You remember John "Jack" Smith."

"I remember no student of that name attending PHB."

"Come now, Dr. Jones, he married Susan Thomas ... she was, I believe, the Missionette of the Year in 1979."

"I have no idea what you are talking about, Brother." Dr. Elias Jones was annoying, but he usually had a good memory and this failure to connect began to bother Brother Simon.

"Well, trust me. He is a former student ... and ... he needs our help."

"I do trust you Brother Berkeley, but we are not a halfway house or a hotel. Either those of us connected to the Elder Board need to discuss this use of the facility or we need to clear them out soon. We are not a rich school and this, I am sure quite charitable, decision is costing us money." The final intake of air through the teeth was a B flat, Brother Simon decided.

"I will take care ... of ... it." Brother Simon shook hands with his colleague and showed him to the door. He was happy that Elias had not connected his guests with the terrorist events at Douglass University. Of course, nobody was talking about the events of that evening. Brother Simon wondered if the government was hushing up the attack given the drop in news coverage, though PHB students were not talking about it either and no government could control their speech!

As he walked up the back steps toward the third floor, Brother Simon realized that he really did not give too much thought to Jack and his visitors except when he was forced to do so. This bothered him, because usually Brother Simon was on top of everything. Old age was a reminder of why he had begun to prepare for a successor. He stopped in the middle of planning for the next president and said to nobody, "What am I doing? What, in heaven's name, could I want, on the third floor?"

Brother Simon turned and walked back down the steps.

On the third floor of PHB Peter was talking to Mary on a balcony that overlooked an alley with a scenic view of a brick wall. "This is not particularly romantic," she said, looking at him.

"No," he admitted, "but real romance, the possibility of actual romance, still seems unlikely to me."

"Right," the university executive replied, "as unlikely that I would find myself a Christian, or some kind of un-baptized almost-Christian, and in love with a guy whose picture I tore up in high school."

"Well," Peter said, "are you sorry?" Before she could answer Peter kissed Mary. "Are you sorry?" he asked again.

"Some unlikely things are good things," Mary said. "Are you sorry?" She kissed him back. "I am not an innocent princess needing rescue you know."

"You are in fact," Peter said, "rescuing me ... or at least my heart."

She laughed at him. "That is why I love you! Nobody has ever talked like that to me or anybody else in one hundred years. You mean stuff like that and actually say it." She looked at him as if he were a professor appealing a tenure denial. "Are sure you are not playing with my mind?"

"I am not," Peter said slowly, "playing with your mind."

"I still think I have gone crazy, but I am happy so it is a good kind of crazy."

"Everybody thinks we are dead, or criminals on the run, or both."

"To listen to the news I am not sure anybody much cares."

"Don't kid yourself. They care. Don't confuse media with police attention." and Peter smiled, "They may pull us apart, but we will always have Pentecostal Holiness Bible College."

"Don't," Mary replied, "My mother wanted me to come here to meet a man. I finally came here and met you."

"Your mother was right. I am sorry her last memories of me were bad ones."

"She never much liked you," Mary said bluntly, "thinking you too flighty in your faith commitment. She was wrong. But come on. My mother, and her prayers must be guiding us if Anastasia is right, forgives you, so we have much bigger things to be sorry about. How sorry are we? Let me count the ways ... I am sorry not to have a job, sorry to have built a monstrous machine that got hijacked by the devil, and sorry not to have a decent Internet connection. There is more, but that will do for a start."

"Would you be sorry to marry me?"

"Peter! Not yet," Mary said firmly, "I am not a girl to be swept off her feet and carried off to the altar."

"You can't blame a man for trying."

"Now that was an overused movie line," Mary said, "and I will not tolerate that kind of thing." She raised his chin slightly and kissed him again.

27 January 2009, Tuesday, 1:00 AM: Saint Petersburg, Russia

The "Church on the Blood" has not the site for a wedding or a funeral, but tonight it was haunted. A haunting is not rare in old places, but this was not an old place by Russian standards. The Church was in the fairy-tale onion dome style of the Kremlin, but it was much newer than that. It had scarcely been finished before the Revolution reduced it nearly to wreckage. It had been built for an Emperor, had been defaced by Bolsheviks, attacked by Nazis, and rebuilt by the love of the Russian people.

The famous mosaics glittered with any light that came into the windows, but nothing penetrated the man-shaped shadow that lay on the floor near a rail at the back of the nave. A tall man stood near the shade, but the man's own shadow was obliterated where it crossed the greater darkness.

The man was wearing an overcoat wrapped tightly around his body, though it was a mild 21 degrees outside. "I am uncomfortable meeting in a church," the man said at last. He did not act as if it was odd to speak to a shadow.

155

The shadow spoke: "The pain here is worse than any I have ever known."

"You came from Hades."

"My intentions make it worse for me, comrade, much worse."

"Then why meet here?" the man said to the shadow.

"Because this building was erected over a great triumph, the beginning of the awakening of real revolutionary consciousness in my life," the voice grew louder. "Most important for our present task, this ugly place contains one artifact that makes it valuable. My shadow now rests on a piece of nineteenth century road right behind the rail that has been preserved in this church. On that piece of street, a terrorist bomb murdered Tsar Alexander II. The street makes me feel alive. I need to be here if I am to gather my psychological resources to complete the work I once started."

"Russia needs you, Comrade."

"I need to escape Hades at any cost."

"You will help me restore my soul to my body, and then you will help me kill Anastasia ... again."

"Yes, Comrade Lenin."

The shadow lingered for a moment caressing the cobblestones. It began to grow, and moved toward the man in the jacket. He simply stared as it crept up his body toward his nose and mouth.

28 January, Wednesday, 4:00 PM: Pentecostal Holiness Bible College

Anastasia, Tom, Jack's three boys, and Maggie arrived like refugees from a war with suitcases in hand. They entered through a back door in the monstrous old Bible college building and saw no one. When the children were little, the Smith family had gathered all of the boys together and given them a "family hug." Jack had not participated in one since the first of his sons became a teenager, but when they saw each other both Jack and the children spontaneously revived the old practice.

"Your mother will be home soon," Jack said to them.

Doug replied, "We know, Dad. Anastasia told us she would be with us for Valentine's."

Chapter Six: The Philosopher King

"We aren't ever going home again Dad," Charles said quickly, "so I brought your Bills football cards, but I had to leave the rest of the good stuff at home."

"There was no room." John added.

"Of course we will go home again," Jack said to comfort his sons.

"None of you will see that house for many years," Anastasia said quietly, "at least in all probability. All of you will either be living at a new address or in Paradise with me before this month has ended."

Jack spoke slowly. "OK." He was surprised at how unconcerned his boys looked at this news. Evidently they knew more about it than he did.

"Dad," Doug said, "we are going on an adventure ..."

"Which means no homework," John added.

"And fewer chores." Charles finished.

Anastasia smiled and left the family to talk, something nobody in the Smith family ever had trouble doing.

When Maggie saw Max alive after a week of thinking him dead, she fixed his hair, straightened his tie, and kissed his lips–exactly in that order. The group scattered for a private teatime all over the third floor of the old building. Jack opened a new room for his boys and helped them settle in for what Anastasia had promised would be a very short stay. He scrounged up a copy of Fellowship of the Ring, Hitchhiker's Guide, and Left Behind to give them something to read in the afternoon. The boys played "rock-paper-scissors," best out of three, for first choice on the books and settled down to read. Jack promised to play some Horse with them in the school gym later that evening if there was time.

By early evening, the group sat in a decaying student lounge filled with ratty couches and overstuffed chairs with the stuffing showing. Peter sat with Mary, ignoring a raised eyebrow from Maggie, and a whispered follow up discussion between Maggie and Max. Mary was used to running meetings and so she took charge:

"Here we are and here we cannot stay. What is the plan? What are we going to do next?"

Max responded quickly. "Plan? We have no plan. We are not even sure what is happening."

"We know," Peter said, "that Bandor has come from Barterra. That is not good."

"To say the least," Barth agreed, "and we know Bandor can assume the shape of other human beings well enough to fool most people."

"Susan remains in jail," Jack added, "and I assume that means we are still wanted by the police for the destruction of Magog."

Mary frowned. "Magog was a multi-billion dollar project that has been annihilated. I cannot believe they could not have found us if they were really looking for us."

"I have noticed that we have faded from the papers," Father John said.

Maggie interrupted, "Perhaps they know we are not responsible for the destruction of Magog."

"Then why haven't they released Susan?" Jack wanted his wife out of prison.

"They will release your wife from prison very soon." Anastasia entered the room. The group stood to honor the Martyr Princess. She smiled at them and said, "Sit down, please. Let me tell you what I am permitted to tell you. The final conflict is nearly upon us, and knowledge is critical to our chances."

Max raised one grey eyebrow and asked, "Who or what is our foe?"

Anastasia was quiet for at least a minute and only spoke after bowing her head to pray. Her fingers worked a prayer rope given to her by Father John. "There exists a world that is a sub-creation of the human beings on this planet."

"Barterra!" Peter said.

Anastasia agreed. "Barterra. Perhaps Barth here could understand the physics of the relationship between the two realities, but I do not."

"Surely," Maggie said kindly, "you are being modest. You have been to the other side ..."

"Where I am still me," Anastasia continued, "and even at my best I was never very interested in math or sciences. Paradise intensifies who we are, it does not change our basic nature. Let me explain the situation the best I can."

"You have our full attention and we will be quiet until you are done," Mary said, giving a look to the gathering that had successfully silenced more difficult audiences.

"Barterra is a creation of the human imagination. As beings created in the image of God, we cannot create from nothing as He does, but we can give birth. This is not just true physically," Anastasia paused, "but spiritually. We can have imaginative children. If we were as we should be, this would be delightful and expand the possibilities of adventure and joy!"

"Unfortunately," Peter could not restrain himself, "we are not as we should be and the results of our imagination are not always good. Barterra is beautiful and twisted at the same time."

Mary looked stern. "Peter, dear, don't interrupt the saint," and Peter smiled and was quiet.

"Yes," Anastasia said, "Peter is right in saying that the human imagination is not always good. As a result of the Fall, God placed a gulf between Barterra and this world, which protects both places. Humanity is protected from the evil seeds they planted in the world of their creation and Barterra is allowed to work out its salvation without interference from dysfunctional parents. There is a great river of forgetfulness, Lethe that runs between the two. When everything is working as it should, it causes humanity to forget the worst human dreams and Barterra to forget the shame of their parents. In the rare cases, where humans or Barterrans have visited the "other," a drink from Lethe keeps them from remembering what they did in one world or another."

"Some of this is Plato's Timaeus," Max said, brightening up. "The text appears true in ways we did not suspect. Really, though, one wonders what Plato experienced ..." Mary shot Max her just-because-you-are-tenured-doesn't-mean-you-can-be-a-jerk look and he was quiet.

"I am describing this as best I can," Anastasia continued, "but this is only an image of the reality: a myth about a story. The Revolution of 1917 removed my father, the last Orthodox Emperor, and a great stone in the banks of Lethe was removed. The river began to leak into this world and some on Barterra began to re-member while many in this world began to forget. One of those who recalled what Is was the person in Barterra Peter named Bandor, Dragon Lord. He is obsessed with destroying the parents, the people of Earth, who did so much to harm their children. Eventually, Peter was sent to check his career as a kind of balance, but Peter failed."

Mary held her lover's hand, but Peter had come to peace with his memory.

Anastasia looked at Peter. "All has been forgiven, and Peter is still remembered by many with love and honor for what he tried to do. The failure, however, eventually gave Bandor the power to come here."

Father John interrupted. "Who sent Peter? Who governs this system?"

Anastasia took a sip of red wine that had been poured for her. "God governs, but others do His work. Some called them the Fates, but that is a dangerous term as it implies power independent of the Divine Will. They are not angels, Barterrans, or men, but a different race altogether. And though they do not rule humanity, they protect us through the tasks they perform. That is all I am allowed to say."

Father John bowed his head. "Bandor is here, and so he has overcome certain checks on his action. What should we do?"

Anastasia looked up. "Ultimately, he only overcame the barriers and the forgetting because humans built Magog. Magog opened the door and he came through it."

It was Peter's turn to squeeze Mary's hand. She was restless.

"I did not think of what might go wrong. I just wanted to touch the past," Mary said.

"You should have considered what you were doing more carefully," Anastasia replied, "but you have repented and forgiveness is absolute. The consequences remain. You intended harm mixed with much altruism, but your funders are another story. They desired to open the door to something else."

Mary was pale, but she was brave and she stated the facts. "We received a great deal of funding from Russian oil and gas concerns that had the money to give during the energy boom. I always wondered about it."

Anastasia looked on her with compassion. "Holy Mother Russia will produce great fools, sinners, and saints in the years to come and will birth a last Tsar and a last Antichrist, but that time is not yet. Men more fools than sinners wanted to bring back a strong man to save the land from weak men and they used your technology to try to reach his spirit."

"Whose spirit?" Max said.

"Lenin." Anastasia said briefly.

"Mother of God," Father John said in the silence.

"Did they succeed?" Mary spoke after what felt like minutes of contemplation of what she and her scientists might have done.

"Of course not," Anastasia replied, "the damned are spared any work that would increase their pain, but they believe they succeeded, because Bandor wishes them to believe it. He has taken their dreams and imaginations and shaped a shadow of Lenin. This shadow is wholly his creature and he hopes that it will be made incarnate through means he is devising."

"To what end?" Father John said.

"He will use his Lenin to seize control of Holy Mother Russia," Anastasia said.

Jack had been quiet. "And then he will rule that heavily armed nation through the Shadow of Lenin?"

"Bandor will try. His ability to confuse your perceptions is very great, but his greatest power comes from Lethe."

Peter was confused. "Lethe? How can the River of Forgetfulness help Bandor? Isn't it a good thing?"

"It is a good thing, but like all goods can be twisted. The destruction of Magog caused a vast backwash from Lethe. Bandor is using it to suppress every memory of the experiment so he can cover his own tracks."

"I remember Magog," Mary said.

Anastasia smiled, "You are with me, and nothing Bandor does can harm you. Sadly, Mary, you were not always under my protection and so I am afraid Bandor has ..."

Mary said, "I am no longer remembered am I? I get it. I get

it all. Nobody stole my identification. I have become a non-person."

"That is horrible," Jack said quickly. "You exist to us. You are still you."

"I know," Mary said, "and it is not striking me as bad. My old life was very messed up. I feel born again ..." and then Mary laughed at herself.

"If the memory of Magog is fading," Jack thought quickly, "why is Susan still in jail?"

"Inertia," Barth responded before Anastasia could speak. "People are slowly forgetting, but only slowly. Records are being cleansed, but only slowly. That is why the news of the destruction of Magog faded from page one to page three ..."

"And as of today has disappeared altogether," Maggie said, suddenly aware of the pattern.

"What about Susan?" Jack persisted.

"She will be freed." Anastasia promised. "Though it is more complicated than you might think. Soon there will be few records of Magog left and almost no recollection of what you did there," Anastasia said. "Bandor will remember and the Shade of Lenin, but he will not trust even his lieutenants with such knowledge. He is slowing wiping his tracks away ... slowly so that the forgetting is gentle and leaves little psychological trace. Only the holy places and a few holy men could remember. There might be a diary of some monk that will mention something of these events, but this is unlikely. Holy men do not often think of the news."

Father John nodded, "And even if they write of it future historians will assume the monk was mad and the worldly records accurate."

Anastasia agreed, "Most of history must be forgotten for humanity to continue or the burden of the evils we have done would destroy us. Only God can stand the memory of all that has been, is, and will be."

Jack suddenly felt relieved of a doubt. "That much I understand. There is good psychological sense in it."

"But I want to know the truth!" Max growled. "Will I never know the whole truth?"

"You will discover that the slow unfolding of the truth is one thing that occupies us in eternity. The whole truth is a bit much, but nothing is hidden that will not, eventually, be revealed. But you should know that though I cannot stop the leak of Lethe, I can harness it."

"Why can't you stop it?" Jack said. "You are very powerful."

"My power is limited to the Will of God," Anastasia was almost curt, "and His will is complex."

Mary laughed, "That sounds like making excuses for God."

"Exactly," Jack agreed.

Anastasia responded patiently, "What would you have me say?"

"Tell us why God allows the leak in the Lethe to continue." Maggie said.

"That part is simple: humans made it and so humans must fix it," Anastasia said.

"I think I understand," Barth broke in, "the equation must balance."

"The equation will balance and be beautiful," the Saint agreed, "and man will do good even if God must become man to do it."

"Yes," Father John responded, "even that has been done."

"It is being done," Anastasia spoke sternly, correcting the priest, "the Incarnation is now. It is Christ in you that will do anything good in this situation whatever else occurs. It was Christ in Peter that left hope in Barterra even when the Peter in Peter failed!"

"So we have two problems," Peter summarized, "Lethe and Lenin."

"You are forgetting Bandor," Barth pointed out, "though it would have spoiled the alliteration."

"I never forget Bandor," Peter said, "and Lethe and Bandor are connected. Beating Bandor back to Barterra bottles the bath, Barth."

"That was not very good," Mary said quickly. "Too forced to be truly witty."

"Finally a paramour," Max put in, "perceptive enough to punish Peter's puckish puns and putrid patter."

Maggie looked around the room, "Next failed attempt at an alliteration does not eat dinner."

Jack rolled his eyes. "You realize that I am now incapable of having a single thought that does not contain an alliteration."

"No exceptions," Maggie said firmly, "and that was self-referentially incoherent."

Father John attempted to get the group back on track. "Two things have occurred to me, Martyr Princess. First, are you really Anastasia or her Barterran image as "Lenin" is merely the imaginative shade of Lenin? Second, you said you could use the Lethe to your ends. How?"

Anastasia stood, "I have said almost all that can be said today. I am Anastasia. The heavenly host can be called to do good work. We do not need the mercy given to the damned.

"By the mystery of Heaven, I am in a new body like the one Adam possessed, but not as I will have in the great and general Resurrection. Mary Yurislav, you did that to me ... dooming me to a pain and sorrow that few persons have to experience twice."

"I am so sorry," Mary was stricken.

"What you meant for evil," Anastasia said, "... the Omnipotence turned to good. You could not have forced me here against the Will of Heaven, and Heaven gave me a choice. I chose to complete works that my family left unfinished."

"Charles Williams was right," Father John murmured, "... redemption works backwards and forwards in time."

"Of course," the Martyr-Princess said, "as for your second question about what good can be done with Lethe, that will perhaps come as a bit of a shock. I am harnessing Lethe to erase the memory of all of you from this time so that you can be sent to do another work. Bandor wants to erase memories of Magog ... and I am just stretching his intentions a bit! Only Tom, who has much to do in this world and had little to with Magog, will remain."

"Thank you," the young man said softly. He had been afraid that he would be called to leave Rochester, and suddenly he knew that he wanted nothing more than to keep going to church, going to Lyons, and helping his mother.

"You will be a seer," Anastasia said, "capable of dim visions of

Barterra. Your job will be the same as that of Max when Peter went to Barterra the first time. You will watch, learn, and mostly pray."

"Is that all? Can a seer do anything else?" Tom began, "Other than see I mean ..."

"Seeing is important, because you will be able to report to this world what the party is doing there. You will also have the capacity, a very limited capacity, to send objects, such as food, to the party."

"How?"

Max could not be silent for long. "Using the box."

Anastasia nodded and sipped her wine.

Peter sighed, "I remember. The box my father made. The box that after the bus crash..."

"Enough," Max said, "Tom just needs to know that some things can be sent to Barterra and some things can come to us from Barterra through the box in my office."

Tom looked puzzled, "What will I send?"

"People in that world need real food occasionally." Max said.

"Providing grub, not a very heroic job."

"I did it." the old professor replied.

Peter spoke: "If you can manage to send Diet Coke, something Max never managed, that will be heroic enough."

Anastasia raised an eyebrow at Peter, "The path between the worlds is not so easy to navigate, Peter. You will not be able to transport anything very technological or artificial. Diet Coke is out."

"On which grounds is my favorite drink excluded?" Peter asked. "Is Diet Coke too holy to move?"

Anastasia turned to Tom, "Everything owned by this group will be yours. You will soon be the owner of two houses ... and what I must confess are several apartments full of junk."

Maggie blinked, "We really aren't going home again?"

"Not for a great while and perhaps never." Anastasia said. "But for those of you who will return, if you return, Tom will hold your possessions. He need have no fear. I am weaving this world so that every document, every memory, including his own family's, will grant him what all of you have held as individuals."

"Aren't I a bit young for this much responsibility?" Tom was shocked.

"You will grow into it," Anastasia said, "and you are too young and unsure in the faith to go to Barterra. Stay here and prepare for a greater future work. Document what you see the party doing, though you lack the talent or name yet to publish it. Find someone to write it for you. Use the money you will find in Mary's accounts. You should not take out so many loans."

Mary said, "As for the money, you are welcome to it but I don't recall being asked for my possessions or if I wished to go on any quest! What happened to free will?"

"You don't have to go," Anastasia said, "... but Bandor has erased all trace of you from the memories of humankind by now. I saved what I could for you by transferring all you owned to Tom Scott as memories of you faded. Even your credit cards are his ... though eventually the banks will wonder why they gave so much credit to a college student and cut him down to size. Are you saying you wish to stay?"

"You know I want to redeem my life," Mary said seriously. "I just wanted to be asked."

"Heaven will always ask when it can, but you destroyed many of your choices before I could help you."

"I know. I am thankful."

"Will you go to Barterra?"

"I will," Mary said firmly, but her fingers were tapping nervously on the coffee table.

"Your mother," Anastasia said, "... is proud of you and Peter." She looked hard at him, "she says to be nice to her daughter."

"What of the rest of you?" Anastasia turned and looked at the rest of the group. "I erased memories of you to save you from your own impetuous actions, but you could stay. Tom could help you rebuild lives, though it might be complicated. Will you go to Barterra?" She looked first at Jack.

"My children?" Jack said.

Anastasia smiled. "They are eager to go and under the blessing

166

of heaven. Barterra will be a delight to their pure and baptized imaginations. Your wife did an excellent job in their schooling and they are very well prepared. No adventure will harm them ... though children," and she grew serious, "... are not always so blessed in this world." Jack was about to speak, but Anastasia raised her hand and continued. "Susan can go with you. She will be free by then, but you are the head of this house. You must decide."

Jack said, "We will go if Heaven desires it."

Anastasia turned to Peter, "What of the Sky-King?"

"Don't call me that."

"You are the King there, Peter. You should return and do your duty."

"Mary?" he looked at his new love. "Are you willing to go as the Sky-King's wife?"

"Really," she laughed, "Really? Sky-King?"

"I was sixteen, Mary," he said.

"I was sixteen then, too, and it would have made me laugh then. If I take you at all," she continued, "I will take you as Sky-King or as a poor man. But I don't know if I should or will take you. For now you will have to be content with my going with you."

Peter sighed and then turned back to the Martyr. "I will go," Peter said to Anastasia.

Max looked at Maggie. She smiled and took his hand. "We will go gladly," Max said. "Imagine an adventure at our age!"

"If you survive this adventure, which I fear you will not, you both will be very powerful on Barterra and could start a great academy if you wish," Anastasia said, "but try to be gentler to your students than you have been, Max."

Maggie and Max both laughed. They had stopped fearing death itself at least a decade ago and a promise of dying together took the last terror from it.

Anastasia turned to Barth. He spoke without being asked. "Where Peter goes I will go if he wants me. I am his friend."

"Thank you, Barth." Peter said.

"What of my flock?" Father John said as Anastasia turned in his direction.

"A messenger has been sent to the Bishop. He knows much and will guess a great deal more," Anastasia replied. "He is already sending your 'replacement.' The faithful that remain, and your congregation is so very small, will love him and never think of you. They will forget the past, and it was getting time for you to go in any case. You had taken them as far as you could, but perhaps you already knew that."

"Do they need me on Barterra?" Father John said.

"It is a world where vampires walk indeed." Anastasia said. "They always need a holy man."

"I will go then—and I will bring the garlic," the priest said.

"Then I leave you to your prayers," Anastasia said. "On the day of Saint Valentine you will see Barterra and try to heal the Lethe. I must prepare my own soul, and the days left to us to pray are almost too few. We have but two weeks to pray and pacify our wills to His! What we face will be terrible, but there is some hope." She got up and walked to the chapel.

"Living with a saint," Father John noted, "is a terrible blessing."

28 January, Wednesday, 2:00 PM: Douglass University

Bobby Kennedy was on a roll. There was no doubt about it and if he had been a happier person he would have been singing. Instead, he was tapping away at his computer keyboard and humming Glory Days. He had never seen a grant proposal come together so quickly. He had worked all through the weekend, even carrying his laptop into the bathroom with him. The proposal was brilliant, but even before seeing it, the University was offering him "every cooperation."

Evidently his reputation had reached a natural gas company or someone who worked for a natural gas company and they were eager to fund "any future research projects that might occur to Mr. Kennedy." Bobby knew his earlier ideas regarding time and information viruses were not ambitious enough for the money dangled before Douglass University. The provost would never forgive him if he asked for too little research funding. He had expanded his concepts into areas Bobby believed no scientist had ever considered: the relationship between memory, time, and history. What if one could bring objects or even people back from the past?

Even thinking about such a project would require huge amounts of money ... and conveniently for Bobby Kennedy, huge amounts of computer time. What could he call the project? Bobby considered carefully and then whimsically decided to name it "Gog." That would be apocalyptic enough to cause trouble with the fundies, which Kennedy viewed as a bonus. He hated working with religious fanatics. Gog the project would be.

Bobby's fingers paused over the keyboard. He felt vaguely uncomfortable any time he thought about the immediate past. "A scientist," he said to cheer himself up, "is a man who makes history, but is not controlled by history." His Gog experiment would prove that history was what people made of it. The Douglass President, the donors, and even his few government contacts were excited about his idea, which was like nothing (he recalled every word the President had spoken) "they had ever heard before."

29 January, Thursday, 5:00 PM: Saint Petersburg, Russia, EDSU

The room was darkened, and eleven of the Twelve sat around a table with their faces covered. The walls were covered in black velvet, the table was ebony, and black silk masks covered the entire heads of the members. Each man also spoke through a digital scrambler to disguise his voice and all wore gloves. One man, the leader, knew the names of the members, but no other individual knew even one other of his fellow initiates to Iskra. These were men who loved to mock the conventions of the Russian middle class, but delighted in the paraphernalia of the Revolutionary. There was not an ounce of self-irony in the room.

Iskra had been the name of an early revolutionary paper and was Russian for spark, a spark to light the flame of revolution in Russia again. The group killed any man or woman who dared to name it, but few knew enough to even whisper of its existence.

Iskra was rich with oil and gas money, but had never sought active political power. It bribed politicians to protect secrecy, but it would have been difficult to detect any other agenda to their corruption.

What did Iskra want? It wanted an end to Russian weakness, a restoration of the Soviet empire, and rebuilding the state apparatus that had birthed, fed, educated, and shaped them. They were loyal children of the Soviet bureaucracy, but as a result they were incapable of governing without a strong leader.

There was money in the room and a will to power, but an inability to exercise it over more than a small area. Each man dominated an industry, a region, or a party, but none of them could go beyond their petty fiefdoms to real rule. They knew it and they knew the dream of a new Soviet Union would die if they could not find a real leader.

Each of them had been close to despair since the fall of communism. Every potential member had been contacted by the mysterious founder of Iskra and found new hope. Joining Iskra was not easy, for their Leader, affectionately called Rookovodityel' or the Head, had made sure each passed through tests of loyalty matched for rigor and depravity only by those endured by in the legends from the early years of the Bolshevik Party. One man at the table had been asked to shoot a family member. He did it. Another man intentionally acquired a heroin addiction at the order of Iskra. Some failed their test, but these failures were murdered by the others as additional tests of loyalty for the Twelve. Each knew that every other member had committed everything to the Revolution and could be trusted absolutely.

Rookovodityel' was a hard man, and so he inspired little loyalty. He had the will to drive them forward and the power to compel obedience, but nobody could imagine him as the ultimate leader of the revolution. He would always remain their Head, but they needed a heart to inspire their cause. They had been shaped to do something, but were still unsure what that something would be.

At the urging of Rookovodityel' they had funded the Magog project in the United States. Only slowly had they realized the audacious plan behind the funding and it had thrilled them. Rookovodityel' wished to begin the Soviet Union again and wanted to bring Lenin back to finish the job. Lenin would be their Heart. Lenin would return from the dead and redeem the Revolution he had started from any taint of failure. The physics were spectacularly American and cutting edge, but it was the irreligion of the final step that appealed to many in the room and now that final step was close. Rookovodityel' had called this meeting after his return from America last week.

Rookovodityel' was fair haired and looked like a very young and innocent man, but to Iskra he was their local demigod through whom they hoped to reach the greater deities. As the only one in the room whose face was visible and whose true voice could be heard, Rookovodityel' seemed small and vulnerable as he stood to address the room, but this fooled none of them. Their head could kill any of them, or perhaps all twelve of them, in combat. No member of Iskra had ever discovered who Rookovodityel' was or from whence he came. One fool who poked about a bit too obviously had died most cruelly. Rookovodityel' seemed to have come from no place and to be nobody prior to 2006.

"Apostles of Iskra," Rookovodityel' said, "I have called you to this place in order to show you a success and a mystery." There was little sound in the room, but plenty of anticipation of what was next to come. There were few shadows in the black room, but near Rookovodityel' a dazzling light suddenly grew. It hurt the eyes, but when vision adjusted it was possible to see at the center of the fire that there was a man.

The man was a disappointment, at first glance as he looked like many middle-aged businessmen in Russia. He wore a well-tailored winter jacket and a fedora and was impeccably groomed, but once he turned to stare at them nothing else mattered. His eyes were gone, but they knew he could see all of them.

One of the Twelve spoke, "Is it he?"

Rookovodityel' answered, "It is and it is not."

Another voice worshipfully, "Comrade Lenin?"

Rookovodityel' was impatient, "Do not waste time. The body

is a disposable one, since it is one of you, one of the Twelve. I sent this man to be a host for Him. The body is not strong enough for both the souls it houses and soon will be consumed by the pain that our beloved Comrade Lenin feels."

A third voice, "Do you need volunteers? I will gladly die for the honor of hosting Him."

Rookovodityel' laughed, "You would not last long enough. Your sins are too great Vladimir."

The man in the overcoat continued to look towards them with his eyeless sockets. The leather covering the chairs of the eleven creaked as they shifted in their seats. Rookovodityel' had never used their first names in the meeting before this moment. How much else might be exposed?

A new voice, "What should we do?"

"You will continue to pay for what I do. We will find a body for Comrade Lenin."

"Which one of us?"

"None of you. We must find a soul reborn, but far from grace. We need a soul strong enough to stand the pain of the damned without dying, but one unclean enough to allow for a visitor."

"I am uncomfortable with taking religion so seriously."

Rookovodityel' laughed. "I am uncomfortable with taking you seriously." The Head reached down and pulled a throwing knife from within his jacket, threw it, and left it quivering in the chest of his critic.

"I prefer to deal with things as they are. Religion exists because it has evolutionary value. In rejecting it, we lose some of that value. The religious are weak in other ways, but they have certain strengths we need, but then none of you know the relevant physics or metaphysics. Any questions?" Rookovodityel' looked about the room. "We cannot actually possess such a soul, of course, but we can oppress it and use it to host Comrade Lenin."

"Use one of our priests?" one voice dared ask.

"No, the soul that hosts Comrade Lenin cannot be so far gone. The host must be very strong with few great flaws. He must be a man sincere in his commitments. He must nobly pursue bad ends. As you know, we lack the ability to access the technology here in Russia so it would help if he were a North American. There is the second project to consider in the long term. Yes, we need an American or a Canadian who loves God, but loves Him badly."

"I could help you steal the technology as I have done so many times in the past for Iskra. It is not so difficult."

"Yes, but there is risk. The change in administration makes our contacts nervous and, bluntly, we cannot easily build and staff it here in Russia without drawing the wrong attention."

The tenth spoke. "Surely the risk is a calculated one and worth it? White Russians are ready to sacrifice."

"Do you know what the second experiment must do to bring the other one back? The shadow is infinitely deeper, the pain greater, and the breach in the cosmos a gash. This present amnesia will be nothing compared to the full-blown senility that follows our second experiment. It will cover hundreds of square miles and it will stay in the United States of America."

The room burst into applause.

Rookovodityel' shook his head, "You are too easily placated ... if you only knew what would happen when your poor Head," he shrugged in mock self-deprecation, "is joined with this our Heart," he pointed at the host of Comrade Lenin, "and our Hand who will come."

The ten remaining cheered Rookovodityel'. "Wait, Comrades, wait. We must first place Comrade Lenin in the proper host."

"Is there such a man?"

Rookovodityel' said, "He is downstairs now."

29 January, 2009, Thursday, 5:00 PM: Saint Petersburg, Russia, EDSU

The Reverend Doctor Robert DeLong entered the EDSU building a bit jet lagged, but ready for God's business. He would be meeting with the head of the seminary today and he was already impressed by the scope of the ministry. The building was a remodeled late Tsarist era apartment building and everyone he met had treated him with professionalism and courtesy.

Usually DeLong could not have made such a rapid change

in his schedule, but the EDSU trip had been "a divine appointment" as his Pentecostal friends would have said. The President of his own seminary in Whittier had come to his office to say that he would take it as a personal favor if DeLong would go. His other appointments called to cancel. The Russian seminary was eager for him to come and offered to pay a good bit more than his normal consulting fee. They wanted him to help design a curriculum that would avoid fundamentalism and secularism and ultimately it was the lure of the ministry ... of starting a seminary with nearly unlimited funds and "doing it right" that got Robert DeLong to fly all the way to Russia with less than a weeks notice.

DeLong was used to thinking of Russia as a basket case and was taken off guard by the sheer efficiency and scale of the arrangements. His airline tickets had been first-class on British Air and had arrived by email minutes after he confirmed that he would come to Russia. The Los Angeles Russian consulate received his invitation from EDSU to visit Russia within a few more minutes and he had his visa within twenty-four hours of sending his passport ... all without using a travel agent or passport broker. Less than one week later he was in Saint Petersburg staying at a first-class hotel and admiring all that petro-dollars had been able to do since his last visit. The city was gleaming in the winter sun and DeLong wondered if it had ever looked so good.

An Estonian secretary, very blonde, brought him into the large waiting room outside the EDSU President's office. She also brought him Nescafe and a cookie and DeLong sipped the coffee and passed on the treat. He had not felt this excited in many years as he contemplated the scope of the project that had been described to him. A group of Russian business and political leaders were going to build the world's largest seminary. It would be ecumenical and inclusive, and they were asking DeLong to be part of the planning team.

DeLong was eager to see the President and impatient with the delay. The blonde secretary offered him something to read, but DeLong waved her away, pulled out his prayer rope, and distracted himself from noise with his prayer rope. As he prayed for mercy, DeLong remembered also to be thankful for the blessings God had sent him.

"The President will see you now." The Estonian said and DeLong entered the office and was not seen again for some time.

30 January, 2009, Friday, Feast of Charles, King and Martyr, 3:00 PM: Rochester, New York

Peter was tired of living on the third-floor of a Bible College, but he was not tired of walking down the hall every morning and seeing Mary. Actually, walking to see Mary was some of the last walking he did all day. She could not sit still for long and so, seeing her usually entailed some kind of exercise. Peter had struggled to stay on an exercise bike and so found doing "miles" walking and running around the third floor of PHB exhausting.

"We are having service tonight in the Chapel," he panted during today's run.

Mary grimaced, "I am at my limit of Church services for monarchs. Thank God for Jack ... at least he has more progressive political views."

Peter pushed back, "A memorial to a brave man who died defending the rights of his poorest subjects." Mary rolled her eyes and kept running.

Peter tried another approach, "If you come, we will get to sit together ..."

"Our present situation does not make it that hard to see each other," Mary noted. "And I have had more church in the last week than I have had in twenty years. Moderation in everything, Peter."

Peter kept chuffing after her and reflected on the bloodless martyrdom of marriage. He had always wondered about the bumper sticker in the Saint Michael Book Store, "Marriage a Pathway to Holiness," and hoped so. Attempts at engagement to Mary were proving only to be a pathway around the third floor of Pentecostal Holiness Bible College.

They stopped in front of Mary's room and agreed to meet in the lounge in a half-hour. Peter realized as he kissed Mary "good-bye" that he was perfectly happy. Despite facing exile back to Barterra and a world full of bitter memories, Peter was happy and he knew Mary was the reason. She was so dissimilar from anybody he had ever known since high school and he was delighted to have the difference restored to his life.

Mary had brought a cheap spiral notebook and a pen to the lounge. "I have a job for you," she said to Peter.

"What is it?"

"Tell me everything you know about Lethe, Barterra, and Bandor."

"That would take a long time."

"We have time and we need to get the group as much information as we can. I will get anything you give me into a good format and print it out for everybody. When we get to Barterra, we are going to need to know what is happening. You have told us stories every night about Barterra, but I want to get a more organized account."

Mary took notes as Peter told his story, "The Tower of Nimlandor sits at the edge of the world ... and I mean the edge. Barterra is flat and Nimlandor is on the Western edge of the disc that holds the great ocean of that watery world. There is an archipelago of inhabited and uninhabited islands scattered over the face of the World Shield."

"How can Barterra be flat?"

"I don't know. Remember Barterra is not in our "space." Wherever it is, you can get there from here, but the rules there are different."

"How so?"

"This is the world where our creations, our not-so-fictional creations, go to live out their lives. It is not a place you can reach on a rocket, but you can go there mentally. We sometimes do, Barterrans said to me, but passing the Lethe wipes most of our memories clean. We go there in our dreams, they told me. They see us then the way we see them when they appear here, as they sometimes do ... as ghosts."

Mary looked more than mildly excited. "So, Anne of Green Gables is there?"

# Chapter Six: The Philosopher King

"You have an earned doctorate in engineering and another in university administration and the first fictional character you think of is Anne of Green Gables?"

"My mother read it to me as a little girl and I don't care what you think." Mary began tapping her right hand fingers on her watch face.

"I am not mocking you, just marveling at you. In some ways you haven't changed at all since high school, but don't think I mind the similarities or the differences. I was just like you and would be so still if I had not been there. When I went there at sixteen, I was hoping to meet Sherlock Holmes or Frodo. No such luck. The archetypes of our fictional characters go there to live ... for example elves, but not particular elves from a story. The strangest race is the invisible warrior class, the Hongese."

"You are kidding." Mary's fingers froze in mid-tap.

"Didn't you ever have an invisible friend? They are real there. So Anne is not there, but there are plucky women like her. You will have lots of company when you get there."

"Thank you, Peter." Mary smiled at him.

"For what?"

"For not making fun of me and for being the first person I have ever met to use "plucky" in a sentence. At work they had a great many names for me, but nobody ever called me "plucky.""

"My plucky Mary Yurislav."

"I love you."

"I love you too."

"What about Lethe?"

Peter paused to collect his memories. "Lethe is born in a small spring beside the great Tower of Nimlandor. It flows from the castle over the edge of the world. All the oceans and rivers of the disc of Barterra empty over the edge and form the Great Sea. The spring of Lethe has mixed with the Great Sea that surrounds the world and imparted its properties to it. To touch the Lethe is to forget what you did that day, to bathe in it can easily wipe out a year, to be submerged in it for any length of time is to forget everything."

"What is beyond the Great Sea?"

"Their Heaven is beyond the Great Sea ... stretching in a series of domes above the World Shield. The cosmos in that place is geocentric, but more like that of Dante than the design of Plato. Some sages on Barterra claim that the Florentine was such a great poet that the very planets that circle Barterra were reordered after the Comedy was written to match it. I don't know about that, but great imaginations in this world can impact the history of Barterra. Shakespeare, for example, is much revered there, but so are people unknown to our history."

"They know our history?"

"Some of it ... at least our imaginative history. World War I is still discussed there. I have never understood how a Barterran knows what is happening here. They just do."

"You lacked that ability?"

"I was in Barterra, but not of it. They will not be able to kill us you know."

"I gathered that from earlier stories you told. I assume that is because we are their creators."

Peter nodded. "Something like that, but again I was only sixteen the last time I was there. It will be interesting what a better educated and older group makes of Barterra ... or sees there. We do have the power to shape them a bit, you know."

"Like wizards?"

"Nothing that grand, but we can, with great concentration, bend the will of some of them or even shift their shape. I was not very good at it, but I bet Max will be great at it."

"If there is a leak in the Great Sea, how in the world will we find it and know how to heal it?"

"There is one other thing you must know about Barterra. From the start, as each island or region is created from some volcanic imagination on this Earth, it receives a symbol in the form of a crystal bird."

"Why?"

"I don't know, but it was done by a very great Fire Wright. They are a kind of wizard who works with the elements, the greatest of which is fire ... as Heraclitus ..."

"Peter," Mary warned, "no distractions!"

"Right, the crystal birds were created by a Fire Wright named Shannon at the dawn of the world." Mary grimaced and Peter spoke more quickly, "I know. That is irritatingly vague and Genesis-y. Every Fire Wright was named Shannon, which, when you think of it, is an oddly informal name for something as severe as a Fire Wright. What exactly were the birds for originally?

I don't know, because these are just the kind of questions I did not ask at the time, but now wish I had. I was much more interested in not getting gored by a Goat-Stag or in riding my Pegasus Ariel. I have an amazing amount of knowledge about things that don't matter ... I was there two years, got married, fought battles, and lived a sadly unreflective life ... it is in this world I got all philosophical."

"I get it. You just accepted what you were told about things like history and geology."

"The way any kid accepts the physics he is taught in high school, yes. I was pretty excited and not very critical." Peter rubbed his eyes where his contact lenses had begun to irritate him. "They made me 'Sky-King' after all. It was a good deal."

"I am not attacking you! I just want to know everything I can. What about these birds?"

"Each region of the world has one of these birds; a Narva bird to use the correct term, and the fate of the bird and of the region are tied together."

"So if the bird were smashed?"

"I don't think that could be done," Peter said. "But if the bird were smashed an island controlled by the Narva bird would be destroyed. If the island were destroyed in natural volcanic eruptions, then the bird covering that region might suffer grave fire damage." Peter stopped and then said, "Throw a bird in the water and the island is Atlantis. There are rules for all of it known by the Wrights."

"O.K. I think I get it. How does this help us?"

"If we can get to the Tower, we will find the remaining Narva birds there. One is almost surely tied to the Great Sea. If the Sea is damaged, it will be damaged. We should be able to mend the Bird using our imaginations, and that will heal the Sea. If we grownups cannot heal the Narva, I am sure Jack's kids with their innocence would be able to do so."

"So, because we are creators, we can do things on this world that the people there cannot."

"Of course. It is a sub-creation of Earth."

"Why are only some of the Birds in the Tower?"

"Good question, but not one I am eager to answer. Originally the Narva were all kept in Temp-Andor, the greatest city on Barterra, but Temp-Andor is inaccessible."

"Yes?"

"The last time I was there, remember this was almost thirty years ago, I lost control of the City of Temp-Andor and the Narva stored there–to Bandor."

"That can't have been good."

"It wasn't, and the flight from the city was horrific. I took one case of Narva with me. It was all I could carry and stored them in the Tower. It was my last stronghold."

"You were a king there. It is hard to remember and believe. No offense, my love, but you do not seem very monarchial."

"I was a king there, but I failed. I wonder what is left of what we tried to do ... of the freedom we tried to win."

"Doesn't Bandor have the birds, the Narva, by now?"

"He may own the Tower, but Bandor cannot touch the Narva and like any Barterran his actions have no impact on them whatsoever. For him they simply report what is happening on the regions to which they are connected. In fact, no person on the planet has the strength to even pick them up. Unless some other visitor from Earth has moved them, they are still in the Tower."

"What if the Narva bird we need, the one that mirrors the Great Sea is still in Temp-Andor?"

Peter paused before he spoke, "I know it is not, because I know every Narva that is in the Tower. The great city and the entire island on which it sits is far below the Sea with every other island whose Narva were left in Temp-Andor."

"What? Why?"

Peter did not answer for several minutes. His vision was all turned inward and all he could see was the destruction of the place he loved.

He could see the great blue wave sweeping toward the city from the small Pegasus he rode. Below him the victorious fleet of the Lantern Alliance, his fleet, faced into the wave that would surely destroy them all. Horns sounded and bells rang, but it was useless. Nothing could save them. If they could fly, they might escape, but Lantern was finished.

Peter would live. He was the one man on Barterra who most wanted to die, but he could not die on this world. Nothing could kill him, but there was no protection for the thousands that lived in Temp-Andor and who had rallied to his cause. They had trusted him, and the leaders of the Alliance and Lantern's victory meant their doom.

Bandor had lost utterly, but in desperation had invoked the Myth of Atlantis. This story was almost, but sadly not quite, unspeakable and Bandor said the Words. He was going to drown the entire Isle of Originals and with it the Narva Birds that controlled the fate of the other islands of the world. If they sank beneath the waves, Peter knew that all the islands they controlled would soon sink with them and all the air breathers now alive would die.

Peter dug his heels into Ariel and the Pegasus plunged toward the palace. Over the entire Island of Originals, men and beasts were taking flight trying to escape. It was so unexpected, defeat on the day of victory, a massive heart attack on the day of the party. There was only one thing Peter must save, only one thing that only he could save, and he must act immediately.

Ariel hit the landing platform hard and Peter could tell she was tired. The wave was racing towards them and he did not have time to see if she was injured. He ran into his room and opened the great cabinet that filled one wall. In the cabinet, glowing and making a soft singing sound, were the hundreds of Narva birds, many species and innumerable colors. The Narva for the Isle of Originals could not be moved, it was the first bird made, tied to the island where it was crafted.

Peter could hear the wave now as it rumbled toward the Island, finally drowning out Ariel's impatient pounding on the roof.

"Where is Nimlandor's Narva bird?" he thought. Lisay was on Nimlandor, and so he had to save Nimlandor if nothing else. He grabbed the case that contained the master bird for the island of Nimlandor and the weight nearly made him drop it. Inside were over fifty of the tiny crystalline birds ... and the humming bird that represented Nimlandor was one of them. Fifty regions of the world around Nimlandor would be saved, but nothing else would be as it was this morning.

He ran up the stairs carrying the case ... knowing that Ariel could stand no more than this one case and his own weight, and also realizing that his choice had condemned most of the world to death by drowning. The wave was crashing on the beachfront as he rose high in the air above Temp-Andor ... the double eagle flag of the Sky Kings was ripped from the pole by the turmoil in the air caused by the sinking of the land and the tsunami. Peter tried not to watch the entire destruction of the city he loved and the victory he had won, but he could not always restrain himself. "How, by the love of the Lamb of God," he thought, "has Bandor learned the power of the Atlantis myth?"

"Sir," a young boy flew up to him on the family Pegasus, "you are the Sky King?"

"Yes. I am Peter Alexis."

"Sire," the boy was very serious, "what should we do? How do we fight back?"

Peter looked at the boy, realized he could not be more than ten, and said, "Where is your family, young man?"

"My father is in the fleet and my mother runs a shop in Temp-Andor. She sent me aloft on Robin here while she ran for help to the palace." He patted his Pegasus.

Peter looked down and saw that the city and the entire Island of Originals were slowly sinking into the sea. The wave had crashed through the cabinet and the magical cases that protected the Birds from the elements and made kindling of the magic cases. Most of Barterra was doomed.

"What is your name?" Peter looked at the boy and realized that he didn't seem to realize that all his family was gone.

"Robert, sir, Robert Combs."

"Well, Mr. Combs, let's gather up all the air borne we can and fly to Nimlandor or as far as our mounts can go."

"What about our folks, sire?"

"We must get to Nimlandor, Robert. We will discuss the situation there. Now gather all the flying folk you can and tell them to meet me in Nimlandor. I must go there quickly."

Peter watched Robert Combs fly away on Robin, and turned his own mount westward. He thanked God for the cases that kept the Birds from being effected by the change of altitude. How had Bandor known the Atlantis myth? How had he invoked it? Where had he gotten the manuscripts?

Peter just hoped Lisay was safe. The Sky King looked down and only saw a giant whirlpool stretching for miles where the Isle of the Originals had been. Dion, Rean, Trion, Danlar, The Free States ... Peter stopped listing what was gone. He had to get to Lisay.

Peter finally spoke to Mary. "Bandor destroyed the Isle of Originals and hoped to destroy the World Shield with it in the Sea. He knew the cases protecting the Narva could not last his great tsunami."

"The cases?" Mary said.

"Think about it. Why wouldn't every island in the world suffer an earthquake every time the birds in Temp-Andor were shaken? They would have, so great magical cases were constructing at the time the Narva were created to dampen any motion. There were extra spaces for when new islands were born.

If the cases had survived the shock of the wave, drowning the Narva would have done nothing. A few cases did survive, and those lucky islands remain eking out a perilous existence until the rot of the cases exposes their own birds to the peril of the Sea. When the birds are drowned, then the Island is drowned."

"Makes sense," Mary said, "assuming you decided to create such birds in the first place."

"There are several legends about that," Peter said smiling. He was remembering Shannon, his tutor and friend, expressing frustration with Peter's inability to understand Fire Wright teachings about a world where mythical thinking worked.

183

"But of course you could move the case and the birds in them," Mary said, "something the makers did not anticipate."

"Yes," Peter said, "and Bandor did not think of it either. I had discovered that I could move the birds by accident once, but that is a longer story."

"Nearly enough Barterra for one day," Mary agreed. "So Bandor decided to destroy the world with himself, but he did not." Mary looked at Peter. "Count on the skill, bravery, and cleverness of the Sky King."

"Bandor and his dragons would fly over an endless and landless sea, killing all they could find in the air ... until they became exhausted and died. He had lost, so he decided we would not win."

Mary took his hand as he paused. She was very quiet and very still.

Peter spoke again. "Imagine picking in a few seconds which peoples would live and which would die."

Mary held his hand and said nothing.

"You know who told him how to invoke the Atlantis myth," Peter said at last.

Mary knew.


14 February, 2009, Saturday, Saint Valentine's Day, 8:00 PM: Rochester, New York


Anastasia stood in front of Susan Smith's cell. The door opened and Susan walked out of jail. Nobody cared, because nobody remembered she had been there in the first place. She had noticed that her cell had been ignored more frequently. Sometimes she had to remind guards to bring her books or allow her phone privileges. They seemed very irritated to have to deal with her, but Susan had a strong will, a loud voice, and no trouble reminding others of her existence.

"Will someone let me speak to my lawyer?" she would demand. Nothing would follow, but she persisted in asking. In the last week, they would bring her food out of habit, but never let her out of the cell or do more than mumble at her. Her last day in prison, Saint Valentine's Day, had been the worst. Nobody came near her cell and she had not gotten even a card from Jack. Was Jack forgetting her too now? Susan was sad. There was no fancier word for it.

Starting the 28$^{th}$ of January she had received a letter every day from Maggie and so she knew how the group interpreted their situation. Maggie did not mention Jack directly at first or PHB where they were "hiding," but Susan caught on quickly. As the two weeks passed, Maggie became bolder until her last letter, received yesterday, was really an essay that amounted to a booklet on the present situation as Max, Peter, and Jack saw it. She could never get anyone in the county lockup to take her seriously enough to mail a letter, so she could not ask all the questions she had.

She had been started in solitary in the county jail since she might be a dangerous terrorist, but this had only increased her isolation when she was forgotten. It was a lonely Valentine's Day and she reread Jack's insert to her in Maggie's last ... and she reread it.

Susan tried to make sense of her situation by sorting through everything she had been told. She understood from the letters that her identity was essentially being erased from people's memories. She irritated her jailers with her presence, because she forced them to remember something every inclination in their being wanted to forget: Susan Smith. She did not cry often, but she had a good weep when Maggie told her that Jack had given their house to that college student Tom. Evidently the bad guys did not know about him so his identity was fairly safe, Maggie's was too, but she had chosen to "vanish" with her husband.

Susan was now officially homeless. Essentially nothing of her old life was left to her. She had always thought that if Jack and the children were fine that nothing else would matter, but it did matter. Jack and the children's safety were paramount, but the other things were the outer sign of her love for them. Now all the signs were destroyed. She had heard that victims of fires and robberies sometimes felt this anger and displacement, and it helped to know she was not just being materialistic or selfish.

Susan had loved her home and had worked hard to make it

lovely. She had sacrificed her time the way a mother bird sacrifices her own feathers to make her nest warm and inviting to her family. She cared. And if she ever caught up to the people responsible, she was going to make them pay.

She wasn't even sure she could keep track of the bad guys anymore. The letters unfolded what the Forgotten understood about the situation as they learned more. Some of it was obvious, but other parts were mysterious. Susan thought she understood the Russian side of things pretty well.

Some Russians had funded an experiment at Douglass University to bring back Lenin to "save the Revolution." This was the experiment the group had tried and failed to stop. That made a Twilight-Zone-kind-of-sense, but evidently they were not going into the past at D.U., just poking a hole between the world of men and the world of the imaginative children of men without knowing it. They saw what they wanted to see, Barterra and Bandor made sure of it, but they had not gotten what they wanted to get.

It was our bad luck that our imaginative world, Barterra, was ruled by a no-good named Bandor, and he had come to Earth earlier as a result of their poking at the cosmos in ways only dimly understood. Bandor plus Lenin plus Russian mafia money equaled trouble for civilization, but the main problem was Bandor. He was the one who was using the power of the Lethe, forgetfulness, and he was the real leader behind the Russians. All his power was coming through this hole between the worlds, and soon, she and the rest of the group, now calling themselves the Forgotten, were being sent to Barterra to fix the hole.

"It is humanity's great blessing," Father John had written in one note, "that Anastasia, real Anastasia, came through the hole with Bandor." Jack had added, "When everyone has forgotten us totally, then she will come for you and we will be together."

Susan turned on her side and tried to sleep but could not do so. She tried to read her pocket New Testament, but could not concentrate. She turned to face the cell wall in her room and began to cry. She wanted to be with Jack on Valentines. She wanted her house back and to watch Enchanted on her new television cuddling with her husband. If God was all-powerful,... but she checked that thought. Why had she been stuck here for two weeks? What was her husband doing? Jack was probably studying some abstruse problem and had forgotten today was Valentine's.

Susan was a strong woman, but had finally come to the end of her strength. She thought of praising God, but could not think of any songs appropriate to jail. She wanted to be thankful her family was safe, but she did not want to go on adventures. Everything seemed stupid.

"The Lord rebuke you," Anastasia said as the jail door opened, and Susan immediately felt better. "How are you, dear Susan? I have come to get you." Anastasia was standing in the doorway. As she looked tenderly at Susan, tears came to her eyes.

Susan dried her own eyes on the sleeves of her orange jumpsuit. "I am fine. I assume you are ..."

"I am Anastasia."

"Why are you crying?"

"I know prison, and I often wished that some angel or saint would open the doors in Yekaterinburg and set us free. Grace is allowing me to do for another what could not be done for me. It is painful, but good."

"Can we go to Jack and the children now?"

"We are going to Jack and the children. Tonight you will go to your new home far away from here."

"Anastasia?"

"Yes?"

"Thank you."

"Praise the Holy God, Holy Mighty, Holy Immortal. You have allowed me to see the high mercy of heaven. I knew it, but now I see it."

14 February 2009, Saturday, Saint Valentine's Day, 11:30 PM: Rochester, New York, PHB

"We have spent two weeks talking, and we have read everything Mary has prepared from Peter's discussions," Max said, "and we still have no real clue what we will find when we get to Barterra."

"We will know soon enough," Barth said, "and I can't wait. This, Peter, is better than our old Dungeons and Dragons games in college."

The Forgotten were all standing together with their suitcases on the third floor of Pentecostal Holiness Bible College. Anastasia was going to send them up and out of the Earth and into Barterra. There was no promise that they would ever come home again. They had spent the last two weeks doing what they could to prepare for that move as the Earth forgot their existence.

They had transferred all their possessions to Tom Scott while enough memory of them remained for legal documents to be executed. Anastasia had helped by carrying their written instructions to banks, lawyers, and title companies. Whether it was her Imperial manner, her puckish sense of humor, or her sanctity, she was hard even for a lawyer to resist and so, at the end of two weeks, they were indeed the Forgotten, and Tom Scott owned a house in the City and in Pittsford.

They had paid their bills, Barth had protested the necessity of this, but Anastasia insisted, and settled the residue on their new friend: Tom Scott was now a wealthy young man. Anastasia had a long talk with the young man's mother and when she left, Tom's mom seemed to accept the new financial situation as if it had always been the case. For the rest of his life, nobody would ask Tom how he came into his possessions and even his mother felt a strong distaste for going near the topic.

"Tom had his wild days, but since he got saved, the Lord has blessed him," she would say to neighbors. That was what Anastasia told her, and it was precisely true. It was all she ever needed to know. Tom was the proud owner of several houses, but it was Max's that contained the most important surprises. The young man had feared the old scholar would find it hard to part from the place where he and Maggie had spent so much time, but if this was true it did not show on the older man's face earlier in the week when they had snuck to Max's house for one last visit. Maggie had refused to go, saying that it was no longer her home and she had no desire to risk becoming "a pillar of salt."

# Chapter Six: The Philosopher King

Max had handed the keys to his house to Tom without any hesitation, "You will find that I have lived an interesting life."

"Sir?"

"There are a great many books in here that you will find no place else. And then there is this." Max pointed to the dark wood hope chest in the corner of his study. The ornate carving was not ancient, but more Victorian, and at first it was hard to notice it. Later Tom realized how noticeably hard to notice this box was. There was a mirror on the top of the box, but when he first looked at it, the glass was frosted.

"Is that the Orichalcum?"

"It is," Max said, "a portal between Barterra and this world. On the great feast days, Easter, Pentecost, Christmas, you can send some small objects to the Forgotten. In the glass, a true seer can tell what is happening in Barterra. For a short time, I managed to see into it, but I lost the power when Peter returned." Max was very quiet for a moment and then spoke again.

"Can you seen into it now?"

"Yes, Professor. I can see a field, a pool of water, and a great tower."

"You see the Tower of Nimlandor. I suspect that this is where Anastasia will send us. It will follow us, I think, but you will have to use your interpretative gift to make sense of our movements."

"Anastasia says I will have a rough idea what is happening to you."

"And you must send us things through the box."

"What will you need, sir?"

"We will need food mostly. We cannot live on Barterran food indefinitely, and what we take with us will run out eventually. Even a tiny amount can sustain us for a long time if added to Barterran "shadow food," since as the Timaeus points out ..."

"Anastasia has given me instructions about that Professor."

"Yes, I am sure."

Max and Tom discussed Tom's duties the rest of that day and most the night. Not all of what Max said agreed, or at least agreed easily, with what Anastasia told Tom at other times, but he felt he knew enough to get started. Today was the day his job as Seer would begin. As Tom looked around the room at the group ready to leave for Barterra he still felt badly about taking their money.

"I will keep what I can, invest what I can, and hope to return you more than you gave me, if you come back for it," Tom had told them.

"Have you been reading the paper?" Max said. "My portfolio is down twenty-percent since the start of the year. We are leaving, Maggie," he said, looking at his wife with the Eye of Maximos, "just in time."

"So we are," she replied, "though I wish I had just gone ahead and visited Israel. We will not have the chance now and there was no reason to save the money!"

Barth spoke to Max. "I understand why we cannot bring guns to a world that does not have the technology ... I grew up on the 'prime directive,' but why no swords?"

Max laughed. "Other than Peter's restored memories would any of us know what to do with a sword?"

"No, but it seems better to have one than not to have one." Barth replied.

"You also know that Anastasia said that we were to bring no metal work, no watches, nothing beyond our most personal possessions. We will be given what we need there or we will know we do not need it."

Father John had been praying. He looked up and said, "I think we should be quiet now. The time has nearly come."

Peter and Mary were sitting together and Peter looked up at the clock. It was almost midnight and they would be in Barterra before Valentine's Day was over. "Saint Valentine, pray for us," he said, looking at Mary, but she had her eyes closed. In reality, the tension was making her restless leg syndrome act up and she was trying to control her movements. She would have no access to her medicine on Barterra ... not that the treatment helped much anyway.

Jack and Susan told the children to stop their Uno game. Doug, who had won three hands in a row, protested the enforced quiet. The children had been happy to see their mother, but that had been an hour ago after all ... and they were not going to Barterra yet. Jack told Doug to be quiet and the family stood waiting for Anastasia.

Barth stood behind Peter and Maggie perfectly happy. He was leaving nothing he cared about behind and was going on an adventure with all the people he care about on this Earth. He was content and ready to start.

The third floor of Pentecostal Holiness Bible College was quiet. Nobody had come upstairs from the school in days and most of the students were out for Valentine's Day. They were shocked when the door opened and Brother Simon entered and not Anastasia.

"I remember now," he said smiling. "I remember, because God wills it and I have prayed through to knowledge."

Jack walked over to him and shook his hand. "Thank you, Brother Simon."

"I came up, Mr. Smith," the old pastor said as he looked at his former student, "to tell Susan that I was wrong about you."

"I know, Brother Simon," Susan said with a laugh.

"No! Wait," Brother Simon spoke quickly, "Let me finish. I love the both of you and I have brought you something." He handed them a worn King James Bible. "This is the Founder's Bible and it contains the Greatest Story Ever Told. Take it with you to the land of stories and read it. It will be as true and powerful there as it is here. I know."

"You are right," Anastasia walked through the door behind him. The old dean lowered his head to acknowledge her. "You are right and I bless you." He bowed his head and the Martyr-Princess signed him and prayed for him. "Help Tom Scott here. When he graduates from Lyons, he will come to this place as a student, but the real purpose will be to be mentored by you. He is your replacement and the best days of Pentecostal Holiness are ahead. The third floor will not be empty for long!"

Brother Simon smiled and said, "I have always known our best days are ahead."

The Martyr-Princess turned to the group. "God go with you. My work is on this side of the Lethe and I cannot come to that place, but my family and I will remember you always in our prayers. Pray for Russia and Peter ..."

Peter looked up at Anastasia and saw she looked hurt, "... pray especially for your friend Robert DeLong. It is his soul I must warn and try to save before it is too late."

It was simple when it happened, nothing like the journey Peter had taken as a result of his father's experiments. One minute they were looking at Anastasia and the next moment they stood next to a river at the bottom of a grassy hill on top of which was a great green tower.

"The Tower of Nimlandor on the banks of the Lethe at the end of this world," Peter said, and the group began to walk up the hill.

# Chapter Seven:
# Dazzled by the Sun

(At the advice of early readers this chapter has been removed. The world, as another author once said about a similar incident, is not yet ready for what it would reveal and it would distract from the central message of the text.)

# Chapter Eight:
# On the Decay of a City

In the Twenty-Fifth Year of the Interregnum: The Tower Hill,
Nimlandor

Jack watched his children run through the fields under the
Tower. They had been in Barterra for a few hours and the shock
was wearing off. Susan was trying to control the kids, but neither
parent could keep three boys still for long. Everything was green
on the island and fresh and the field in which they had arrived
looked like it had been designed for soccer. Jack wondered if Tom
was already watching them in the box in Max's study.

The pool where the Lethe began was dark blue shading to
green in the center. A stream ran out of the pool toward the edge
of the world where it tumbled over a cliff and into the Great Sea.
When Jack leaned over the cliff and looked down, he could see
the bottom, but it meant little to him as he could scarcely see the
white caps of the waves in the sea beneath him from where he
was.

When he had picked a small blue flower in the field, a tiny
fairy flew out of it and spun quickly away from him. When he
had started to caution the group to watch where they stepped,
Peter had told him that flower fairies were very nimble and almost never trodden down with their flowers. Jack knew that the
Tower contained the object of their quest, the Narva bird that
controlled the River Lethe, but it was hard to concentrate on the

mission. Barterra was too interesting ... Nimlandor reminded Jack of Letchworth Park if "the Grand Canyon of the East" had been on an island.

Jack had discovered that by concentrating as hard as he could, it was possible to change the color of the flowers from blue to a darker blue. It was not possible to change a flower from blue to pink. Jack knew this because he tried the experiment. He called to Peter. "Hey, Sky-King! Look what I can do!"

"Jack, don't call me that too loudly and, yes, you can change the color of flowers ... though you might not want to do so with any flower you want to keep alive. You make them unfit for the ecosystem. Flower fairies will not go to a modified blossom."

"Don't be a kill joy. Aren't you excited to be back?"

Peter looked up at the Tower, the place where Lisay Macbor died. "No, I am not glad to be back, but I am ready. The memories I lost have returned, and the job I started is still not finished."

Jack nodded. "We do have a job to do, but I don't think it is going to win us many local friends. We have to save our own planet by trapping the evil monster that rules this world permanently on Barterra. They may take a dim view of us here on Barterra."

Peter pushed up his glasses and laughed. "I wonder what they think of me after almost thirty years. You know it is tough to return to Barterra with bifocals, but the contacts were not going to last here."

Max walked up behind Peter and said, "There is no sign of any guards or traps on the road to the Tower. Perhaps we should head up to it unless we want to sleep in the open. What is inside?"

"The Tower is a country home for the ruler of Nimlandor and is part fortress and part hunting lodge. If Bandor kept a Macbor in charge of the country, he wouldn't be here at this time of year, but the house would be maintained. We would have many friends amongst the staff, as the people of Nimlandor are very independent. Bandor might also have destroyed the Macbors and simply installed a drake on the grounds to guard the birds. There is nothing else on the island worth a garrison."

"There surely will be a guard around the Birds in any case. Though the Barterrans cannot touch them, Bandor would be worried about a creator, that's us, coming back and stealing them. Having them in his power would give him instant intelligence about the health of any region of the world ... it is almost certainly how he first learned the barrier between our world and the Lethe had been breached."

"Should we walk up and see?" Mary asked as she walked over to the group with Barth.

"Perhaps we should leave Maggie and Susan with the children?" Max said.

"Or Barth and Jack," Mary said quickly.

"Let's discuss it," Max said, and the smaller group joined Maggie and Susan in the field.

In the end, Maggie stayed with the boys while Susan went with Jack, swearing that she was not going to sit on the sidelines for another two weeks doing nothing. Max and Peter led the small group up the broad road that led to the top of the hill. It was obvious that traffic was much lighter than in the days when Peter had lived with the Macbors in the Tower. The road was still used, but it had grown over in places and was much narrower than it had been.

"The condition of this road strongly suggests that the Tower is not in daily use," Peter remarked.

"I agree," said Father John looking closely at the road. "There is no indication of much foot traffic, let alone the wagons needed to maintain a large household."

Mary pushed Peter forward with a laugh. "Come on, Sherlock, let's see what's up there."

The Tower soared over a large brick house. A brick wall covered with ivy and pierced every twenty feet with an iron gate surrounded the house itself. Peter saw the familiar wrought-iron gates with the crest of the Macbors, a shield with a fallen lamb, and felt sick. He remembered the last time he walked through those gates leading an exhausted Ariel, but not the last time he had left the Tower. He had been out cold, carried by his few remaining friends. The next time he remembered what had happened in the Tower almost thirty years had passed and he was in Penfield, New York.

Mary took his hand. "I am not Lisay," she said.

"I know, but I am Peter Alexis ... the fifth of that name to be proclaimed Sky-King and it was here that I failed my people and had to be sent home."

Father John cleared his throat. "The only unpardonable sin is one for which we will not receive Christ's forgiveness."

Peter walked to the gates and touched the lamb on the shield. "Have you ever noticed that in most adventure stories, even the religious ones, everything depends on the hero doing the right thing? It isn't true, you know."

Father John put his hand on Peter's shoulder. "No, they mostly are not right, but the fairy tales were, Peter. In those better stories, humility and acceptance of God's destiny helped ..."

Barth interrupted. "Peter, do good dragons exist in this world?"

"Yes, but mostly not. Why do you ask? Or should I ask?"

"If you look through the gate to the right," Barth said, "you will see the end of a tail. This tail is remarkably like spiked and deadly tails pictured in the better books on dragons."

Peter spoke softly. "Well, that is a drake."

Max whistled. "A wingless dragon. Very fierce."

Mary raised an eyebrow and said, "How in the world do you know that? Ph.D. in dragon biology?"

"It is dragontology and I am no expert ... and would not have to be one to recognize a drake tail. The spikes, however, are remarkable. They are surprisingly long and appear more dangerous looking in person than in my dragon books at home."

"A drake is almost surely on Bandor's side ... and given their hearing, he knows we are here. In fact, he probably knew we were here minutes after we arrived in the meadow. I am not sure why he has not turned to confront us."

"He?" Max asked.

Peter replied, "The female does not have spikes on her tail."

"Peter," Barth said quietly, "the tail is moving. The drake is going away or turning around. Just thought you should notice."

The Forgotten watched with fascination as the drake moved into a nearby outbuilding.

"What about turning around and running? Does anyone realize that we are standing here talking about a dragon that could be preparing to crisp us?" Mary said.

"Of course, you must not forget that this drake cannot kill us in this world, though if what Peter said is true, he could knock us out of action by causing us intense pain. As creators we would heal eventually ... but it would be most unpleasant. Many drakes spit acid, and over short distances I assume a beast that size can run as quickly as a horse." Max stopped when he saw the expression on Mary's face.

"What should we do Peter? I assume you have the most actual experience with dragons," Barth said quickly.

"Wait. If he has not attacked us yet, then we might try talking to him. Dragons are quite hierarchical; he might be interested in knowing that I have returned. Most dragons do not like the Sky-Kings, but they are not like the vampires, either. They respect the position, and you can talk to them before they try to kill you. A dragon will have a chat with us, then attack, and if he can injure us would mourn disfiguring a king."

"I always suspected dragons had a sense of honor." Max said with satisfaction.

Peter nodded, "All of you might try to concentrate on the mind of this drake. We can trouble his mind. Father John and Max in particular might be able to soften his feelings towards us."

"These are not the droids you are looking for?" Barth suggested hopefully.

"More like, 'you gain honor from speaking to us.'" Peter said.

"No more Star Wars references, gentlemen," Susan said, "and that includes you Jack."

"I was just going to say that our Jedi mind tricks are unlikely to work on that more-than-Jabba-size beast anyway." Jack said to Susan.

"No, Jack. Don't start. Restrain your inner nerd." Susan replied.

"Peter, is it wise to reveal who you are?" Father John said, getting the conversation back on track.

"We need to get Bandor back here and find out if I have any

friends left. My army chief of staff was in Nimlandor thirty years ago. Did he survive? Did ..."

"You know," Mary said sharply, "I am realizing that a weakness of sending a party of academics to a Medieval world is that we talk and don't do."

"What would you suggest, Mary? There is no sense running. This drake can catch us where ever we would go."

Peter stopped talking because the drake had come out of the great barn and was now coming towards them. Not many people still living on Earth, sane and sober, can claim to have seen a living dragon, and the Forgotten wished they were not sober now that they were seeing one. Protected by modern weapons, it is easy to forget the fear generated through the raw power of a beast that is as tall as a giraffe, but more massive than three elephants. The glistening multicolor armor plates on the drake made it obvious that even if they had been armed, which they were not, few things short of an elephant gun would have penetrated his hide. Over his chest he had put on a massive golden medallion bearing Bandor's symbol of the blazing Sun. He opened his massive jaws in an ostentatious yawn and spoke, "Who approaches the keep of Bandor, Lord of Samov and Earl of Nimlandor?"

Peter held up his hand. "Greetings, Lord Drake. May I ask your name?"

The drake showed sharp, yellowed teeth, "You have asked, but you must tell me your name. What boon do you ask of the Most High?"

Peter laughed at the drake. "I ask no boon of Bandor, though you might ask mercy of me. I am Peter Alexis the Fifth, King of Dragons, and I have come to greet the Macbor as a friend of his house. You owe me obedience as master of all your kind."

The drake nodded seriously. "I thought that some powerful science had brought you to the meadow by the Lethe. We have long thought you might return when the Most High entered your world. The Most High reads my thoughts and knows you are here. I am His servant and none of your own."

"I honor you in your position, Lord Drake, and so must ask if you have any words to your Lady before you die at my hands."

The drake smiled again. "I know I cannot kill you, but you know I can make you wish that you could die over the next few months. We also know you have no Lady Wife, Sky-King to send a message before I incapacitate you, which I suspect is more likely than my own death."

Mary started forward and started to speak, but Peter waved her back: "You will know by now also that all my party are creators and that we have power over your will."

"Some power. I feel it, but it is not enough. One of you is quite annoying. I will burn him last to dishonor him for his invasion of my privacy."

"Do you think we would come to Barterra unarmed? I know Bandor is the great power in Nimlandor and you know I am not stupid."

"There is something to be said for that line of reasoning ... but those are the chances I must take."

"At least have the courage to tell me your name before battle is joined, Peter said."

"I am Ferus, hatchling of White Ferus and Lady Foxfire, and husband of the Lady Feria."

The drake reared on his hind legs and opened his mouth. Peter's right arm remembered old habits and swung for his sword, his mind realized he had no sword, and he wondered again why Anastasia had not provided him with one, all in the two seconds it took the Ferus to spew his fire. Peter got ready to hurt.

15 February, 2009, Septuagesima Sunday: Rochester, New York

Tom sat in Max's chair and pondered what he had seen in the surface of the Orichalchum. He felt he knew exactly what the old scholar was doing on Barterra. He jotted down some notes, the party had not really done much yet and sipped a cold lemonade.

He had gone to his own church in Pittsford that morning and it still shocked him how everyone accepted his "new" car and residence. His Pentecostal pastor was no spiritual fool and looked absentmindedly at Tom for a long time as if he was occasionally remembering something and then forgetting it. It embarrassed the college student to realize how superior he had once felt to the pastor.

He looked at the gun over the mantle and wished Max could have taken it with him. The group had gone unarmed. This seemed illogical to Tom until Peter had explained that no technology beyond that of a certain period could be brought to Barterra. Mechanical watches might make it, but not watches powered by batteries. On the other eight planets there were worlds where the science fiction imagination was allowed free reign, but not Barterra. Barterra was only for the deepest and oldest human myths. Tolkien had influenced it, though not as much as Charles Williams, but Isaac Asimov had no power there.

Tom had asked about the eight planets and Peter had patiently explained that the Sun and Moon counted as planets with the other classic spheres in the geocentric cosmos of Barterra. Pluto had recently appeared, but Neptune and Uranus had never captured any imagination powerful enough to make the worlds come into being in Barterran space.

Why not some swords? Tom knew some Renaissance Faire people from Lyons who could help, but Anastasia had refused them permission. "You will go to live there with no weapons from this world. Take only those possessions iconic to you ... even too much clothing is imposition on that world. Metaphorically, the matter is too dense. You will find what you need there. By Saint John the Baptist, Tom can send a few things more, but not very much." That was that. Tom had wanted to ask "why," and Anastasia would have been happy to dialogue, but he feared the discussion would include a Bible verse, and his faith did not feel up to that much religiosity yet.

Tom turned up the gas in the fireplace, afraid yet to burn "Max's wood." He figured he would live in Jack's house eventually since it was more up to date and in his hometown, but Max's library was a great place to study and he knew the Orichalcum must stay there. He thought he might be able to convince his mother to sell her house and move into his "city house" and take care of it for him. Both couples had told him to use their things, sell what he did not need, though all of them had begged him to spare their books if they could. Tom was a Kindle guy, but he understood the feeling.

Tom felt uneasy in his spirit, got up, and walked over to the Orichalcum. It cleared and suddenly he **knew** the Forgotten were fighting a dragon. He began to pray, then stopped himself with self-irony: "I am turning into a religious extremist." He thought about it and then smiled. He was sitting in a house while his friends and Anastasia fought a Dragon Lord who was using Lenin to take control of the world. Why even pretend to be anything other than a religious extremist?

"Lord have mercy on my friends who are forgotten by the world, but not forgotten by you ... Give them wisdom to know how to respond to the dangers they will face." He had soaked up more religious language in Sunday School than he thought.

15 February, 2009 (Septuagesima Sunday) Moscow, Russia

Saint Petersburg has a man made magic, while Moscow has deeper and more natural mystery to it. The form of DeLong walked toward the Mary and Martha Convent. He wanted to see how the construction there was progressing. It irritated him to see the statue of Saint Elizabeth, the New Martyr. It hurt him to see the garden growing up in her name. Workers scurried all over the site like beetles building a mound of dung. It annoyed him to see people still enthralled with reaction and private charity years after all of it should have been swept away by something better.

"Lenin" knew he was a shadow of the shadow of the great man. He knew that Bandor had created him by dark arts to satisfy the needs of Iskra. Bandor, the Rookovodityel', had created him to be the heart of the Iskra movement as Bandor was its head. He knew that he contained every expectation of the Eleven for Lenin, every fact that could be gleaned from history books, and every trivial detail contained in the collected letters and works of the tyrant. He was a perfect copy of Lenin, but he was not Lenin.

This galled him and made him irritable. He hated being a shadow of Bandor, because he knew Bandor himself was the creation of thousands of human imaginations. He wanted to be **real** and knew he was not autonomous. He wanted the freedom to rebel against his creator that the stupid worker smoking a cigarette across the plaza took for granted.

DeLong's soul was also causing Lenin trouble. DeLong had been a naïf and no Christian, but he was not a bad man. His soul kept trying to reach out to God and it was all Lenin could do to squelch prayers that rose up in his brain. Lenin was in full possession of the brain, but DeLong still owned his soul and could confuse issues occasionally. This could be very frustrating. It was hard enough being Lenin, without having objections from DeLong rising and confusing issues. DeLong persisted and endured as an epiphenomenon rising over his own brain, but Lenin was still in control.

Lenin watched people enter and leave the main church of the monastery. He would not enter, since leaving the Church on the Blood and taking the body of DeLong he could no longer tolerate even the smell of churches. The smell of incense stank and made DeLong's body sick. Churches weakened his hold on the body and he could not risk losing all control. He should not be here at all, but he was eager to recruit a new member for Iskra, a new member for the Eleven to replace one of the recently dead.

He saw the monk, his target, leave the main church, and his heart beat more slowly. There was a bad man, a very bad monk, who was a leader of the Ultra-orthodox faction of the church. He was wearing the most conservative of monkish attire and was fingering a prayer rope, but to Lenin it was obvious that this was no Christian. He could see the marks of luxury of the soul and easy living on the face behind the gaunt signs of fasting and the self-importance as he prayed the Jesus prayer. This man tormented the body, but allowed his soul free reign. The Lord had no mercy on the monk, because he did not really believe he was a sinner. His extreme piety was a cover for his decadence.

Lenin-DeLong walked up to the monk as he stood praying silently before the white statue of the New Martyr. Workers for Iskra had long ago approached the monk to sell unimportant information on his friends and superiors, and Brother Nicholas had gone along. He needed money to indulge his acts of charity. Lenin spoke softly. "May I help you?" He saw Brother Nicholas turn to him with bright eyes and knew that he would gain a new convert that day.

"You pray for Russia?" Lenin said to the monk, knowing the answer.

"I pray for Russia every day in this holy place," the monk said.

"Follow me," Lenin replied, looking at Brother Nicholas with DeLong's eyes.

Brother Nicholas left everything and followed Lenin.

1 New Month, in the Twenty-Fifth Year of the Interregnum: The Tower Hill, Nimlandor

It turned out that it was good that they had brought a psychologist. Peter looked for a sword that was not there while Max futilely tried to control the drake's mind. Barth grabbed the gate to swing it open, hoping to at least land a blow. Susan and Mary ran up behind Barth to follow him. Jack did not move, staying absolutely, clinically calm. Back at PHB, Peter had explained that Barterra was built around the four basic elements: earth, water, air, and fire.

"Air," Jack thought with his two seconds, "is the second lightest element on Barterra, but the easiest to manipulate. It is hard to keep anything in an airy state. Fire is the lightest, but very fine. What can be done with fire?"

As fire began to pour from the great drake's mouth, Jack forgot about manipulating his mind and thought more about condensing fire. The fire shot toward them. They could feel the heat, and then they were all unceremoniously soaked with water. Ferus moved backward on his giant haunches in surprise.

"Anaximenes!" Max shouted.

"I always get him confused with Anaxagoras," Peter responded.

"Will someone tell an Earth trained scientist what you two are burbling about?" Mary panted.

"I condensed the fire coming from the drake's mouth," Jack said.

"It is as Anaximenes said it would be, given Barterran physics. Fire condenses through air to water and water would rarefy to fire ..."

"Sky-King, you have a great Fire-Wright with you!" Ferus said with a bow.

"Of course," Peter said, swinging open the gate, "what would you expect?"

"We have not seen a Fire-Wright since Shannon disappeared with you."

"This is Jack Smith, a great doctor in our world. He is displeased that you would not even ask his name before attempting his hurt." Peter said politely.

The drake, Ferus, fell to all four legs and backed up further. "I meant no disrespect to the Smith."

"You will let the Fire-Wright pass through to the Narva Birds to perform his tasks."

"This I cannot do, even if it costs me my life, but I will not fight with a Master of Fire." The drake spoke with great humility.

Peter raised a hand and said, "We honor your obedience. We shall retire to the meadow and consider how to give you an honorable death if you cannot obey the Sky-King and his Fire-Wright."

Peter turned around and motioned the Forgotten to follow him back through the gates, down the road, and toward the meadow. The drake sat watching them the entire time. When they had reached a safe distance, Peter let out a long breath.

"That was a near thing," he said.

"I know what I did ... what I meant to do in changing the fire to water, but I don't know how I did it."

"No," Peter replied, "you would not. You have the skill to be a Fire-Wright, but not the training. There is no guarantee your untutored mind could do it again."

"I am frustrated I did not think of it," Max said.

Barth said, "So Jack was lucky?"

"Partly, and partly under extreme stress he picked a task in his mental power," Peter said.

"I know I was lucky," Jack replied, "but I was also funny. Here we are exploring a new world, but sopping wet by being squirted by a water-breathing dragon!"

"Could I turn the road to water?" Mary asked, ignoring continued banter between Barth and Jack.

"Maybe a little bit of it," Max said, "but rarifying a thing is harder than condensing it."

"Shannon could never teach me to do it," Peter admitted.

"How can the Barterrans do it?" Susan asked.

"I don't know," Peter admitted. "Another question I wished I had asked when I lived here, but I think some of them are 'sub-sub-creators.' That is one way of describing a Fire-Wright's job."

"We can safely assume none of the Barterrans would be as good as Jack if he had training in how to use his 'creator' power here," Max said.

"What kind of things can we do, Peter?" Mary asked.

"I don't know for sure," Peter answered, "because I am not very good at any of this actually. Jack just did something greater than I ever achieved when I was here."

"We can change this world, even radically, by developing a powerful new story or, as the Barterrans would call it, "myth," but that requires the talents of a Shakespeare. Any of us might be able to shift the properties of an object that are not essential to it. These accidental features are more pliable ... something like the shade of blue in a flower can be changed. We can also increase or decrease the desire of a person to do a particular thing. You just saw that we can rarify or condense the basic elements of Barterra: earth, water, air, and fire. We are lucky the dragon attacked with a simple element."

Jack's children ran up to greet him as they approached the meadow. They told their father that Maggie had worked them hard to dig a fire pit, bring some dry wood from a near by forest, and prepare for a fire for the evening. They had found few edibles and wanted to know what Dad was going to do about dinner. Doug was blunt: "I am hungry and I want something to eat."

"That is where I can help," Barth said. "Father John and I did not have many personal items that we wanted to bring with us to a new world, so we brought food instead."

Father John warned them not to "over expect" as the dried meat, fruit, and protein bars were not much to feed all eleven of them, but the children were overjoyed. They caught Maggie up on their adventure with the dragon and, of course, the children wanted to see the dragon. Susan said, "No," and got a fierce argument. Jack pointed out to the children that they would see the drake soon enough unless they were very lucky, and that quieted everybody.

"This is fun," Barth said as they sat around the fire. It was growing dark and they had been experimenting with their "creator" powers. All of them could do a bit of "magic," as the children called it.

Jack was the best of the group at the process he called "condensation." He could also move elements in the other direction, but not consistently. He could change tiny amounts of air to fire, but he was best at moving fire to water, and water to earth. He got the most consistent results of any of the party. His kids loved his ability to occasionally send out sparks of light like fireflies shooting from the air over their hands merely by concentrating.

Max could not condense substances at all, but he could occasionally move them in the other direction, a process he called rarefaction. Mary was best at small shifts in shape in substances. She could make the edges of a flower waver, or make a spherical shape slightly less spherical. She suspected, and Peter confirmed, that none of them could change the stuff of which they themselves were made. "Creators" were immune to certain kinds of change in Barterra, which was one reason they could not die.

Barth was the best at making tiny bits of matter invisible. He managed to make one tip of a leaf disappear. Barth wasted a good bit of time trying to make parts of the fire invisible, but eventually realized that he only had the power to make "earthy" solids fade from view.

All of this provided great amusement to the Forgotten, but the excitement of the day began to wear on them, and they began to nod as the fire died down. Peter had gone for a long walk with Mary as the evening's festivities wound down hoping, he said, to find some allies. "Our only communication should not be with a dragon," Peter noted and nobody was tempted to disagree, but he and Mary walked for a long time in the forest by the Lethe pool without meeting any living soul.

"Barterra is pretty empty," Mary said to Peter.

"This part of it always was, but don't be fooled. Temp-Andor was a pretty big city. It had well over a quarter of a million residents."

"Still, even that is not New York City." Mary tapped her fingers nervously, "and there doesn't seem to be anyone here at all."

"This area was the country home for the Macbors, rulers of this island of Nimlandor. I don't know what happened to them. Judge Macbor could still be alive, though I doubt it."

"Why?" Mary started to say more, but stopped when she saw a light hovering near a tree. It was multi-colored at first, but became a piercing blue as they drew closer to it.

"Peter? What is that?"

Peter's eyes never left the light as he said with excitement, "That is a fairy! A full grown fairy!" He bowed in the direction of the light and waited. The light moved toward them and Mary could see a fairy straight out of Kate Greenway fluttering in the center of light. She was beautiful and appeared very delicate. Her movements were like those of a paper doll moving in a breeze. Mary laughed. "Bad special effect, Peter! That doesn't look real!"

The fairy sounded a long high note. Peter bowed again.

Mary whispered, "What is happening?"

"She is speaking to us, but I cannot speak the language of Fairy. Just wait ...and don't insult her again."

The two stood with heads bowed and then heard a voice sing, "Majesty!"

Peter had tears running down his face and Mary took his hand. The word had been welcoming, loving, and joyful at once. Peter felt at home for the first time that day. He finally spoke out. "Here I am. What is your name, fair lady?"

The fairy sang again, "Shah!"

Peter bowed his head again to acknowledge the trust of being told part of the name of a Fairy. Mary was not watching the Fairy Shah because she could not get her eyes off the transformation taking place in Peter's face. He did not get younger, but love was casting out fear. Mary could believe that the face in front of her was that of a King. She listened to her Lord as he began to tell Shah about the Forgotten and the situation they faced.

Peter and Mary walked back to the camp an hour later, hopeful for the first time since morning that they might win in their struggle with Bandor. Meeting a Fairy usually has a positive effect on people unless they want something silly, like money or marriage, from the Fair Folk. Peter and Mary held hands and were even tempted to sing, but thought better of it as the wood grew darker.

Shah hadn't given Peter and Mary much good news, but she had promised help. Judge Macbor **was** dead. Peter had cringed to hear it, but his son was in the mountains to the South. The new Judge was hiding more than he was resisting since Bandor had occupied Nimlandor. Fortunately, the island was unimportant enough to be ignored. It merited only a drake and a few guards scattered over its surface, since except for the Narva there was nothing much on it to guard except sheep.

Most of the other islands were underwater or had been conquered by Bandor. The dwarves in the Krak were unconquered and the fleets of Second Danlar kept that island and a few other tiny states and colonies free, but most of the world was making do as best they could under the Dragon Lord. The Lantern Alliance was shattered, though people still hoped for Peter's return. Things were bad, but fortunately the Dragon Lord did not have much interest in ruling, so the poor islands were left pretty much to pay taxes and suffer quietly. Bandor was often gone and when he was not on Barterra, his Empire would crumble at the edges.

The Fairies and much of the forest folk were still untouched by Bandor, though their numbers were slowly declining. Bandor had not yet bothered to eradicate those foes not living in cities. The price of the conquest was high and the spoils not worth the effort. Most of his magic and his energy had been turned elsewhere for the last twenty-five years. General Gala, Peter's old chief of staff was still alive, and reckoned Bandor was trying to follow the

Sky-King to Earth. The distraction was keeping a bit of freedom alive.

Help was on its way to the Forgotten. Shah had promised to go to the Earl, the new Judge and Heir of Macbor, young Simon, and tell him that the Sky-King had returned. She could not promise useful military help, but was sure he would send some men and supplies. As for the dragon, Shah was less helpful. Only dragon fire is hot enough to kill a Fairy, and so, having a drake in the neighborhood had kept Shah and the few friends she had left in the forest quiet.

Before she left, Shah had asked one hard question. "Why did you leave, my Lord?"

"When I lost control of the Narva, my body fell into the control of Bandor, and Shannon was only able to save me by sending me out of Barterra and back to the creators."

"Why so long to return?"

"The Lethe wiped all memory of Barterra from my mind."

"It is as we thought. Some humans have lost faith, but the Fair Folk knew you would not leave us forever."

"Does Gala still hope for my return?"

"Gala hopes and acts in the name of Lantern. The Dwarves and the Empire of Danlar acknowledge the Alliance in words, but without the Sky-King will do nothing in deeds."

"Is this area safe other than the drake?"

"No. It is the home of a band of vampires. They have slain all the humans to increase their numbers near the Tower and they are slowly snuffing out our light. Can you help us?"

"Is our party safe for now?"

"I believe so, but you should be on guard after nightfall. One bat looks so much like another to us, we cannot be sure which is undead."

Remembering this part of the conversation disturbed Peter's equanimity. Talking to Fairies could be too comforting and it was time they returned. In fact, the closer they came to camp and the further from their experience with Shah, the more uncomfortable Peter grew. They really had been gone a long time. The group was inexperienced with travel in Barterra and he needed to get back.

"Mary, I think we better run."

She agreed, a tight facial expression replacing her look of peace. They took off toward the camp, but stopped as they came to the edge of the forest and looked at the fire. It was hard to see in the dark, but the scene around the fire was lit like a stage set. The Forgotten were sleeping before the fire and a large man stood near it with a woman, probably Susan, in his arms. Father John, crouched in front of the tall man, appeared to be the only other person awake. "Vampire?" Mary said.

"Yes."

"Movies help here more than science," she replied.

"Movies help form the science here," he said briefly.

"Should we get a stake?" she said looking at the trees for an oak.

"No, we are not strong enough to Buffy the vampire."

"What can we do?"

"Pray and bluff."

Peter walked toward the fire shouting at Father John. "Father, we are back. Who is this undead dog?"

Father John did not take his eye off the Vampire, but his voice was as steady as if he was saying mass on Sunday. "He is wholly unclean, but paralyzed before the Holy Cross and a relic of the blessed Anastasia."

Mary could not take her eyes off the woman in the Vampire's arms. It was surely Susan. This was nothing like a movie since there was nothing romantic about the blood lust in the eyes of the undead creature. She admired Susan and could only think of saving her. She heard Peter running hard just behind her.

"Drop her." He could hardly get the words out as the running winded him.

The Vampire turned his head and looked at Peter and Mary running toward his position. When he smiled, a bit of Susan's blood showed on his teeth. They were very close now. The Vampire was lean and tall, but a bit stoop-shouldered. He was cradling Susan like a lover, but his eyes were on Mary. She could not take her eyes off his. She knew she should pray, but she could not find the words. The Vampire continued to stare at her and finally, as if she had fallen asleep in mid-charge, Mary fell to the ground.

Peter reached the Vampire, but stopped as the Vampire turned his gaze to Peter. Peter staggered under the blow of the look. The dragon was a noble being in the service of evil, but this beast-man was a foul thing wishing only to be fouler. He wanted to kill Peter because it hated the living and their God.

Father John spoke. "Have courage, Peter."

Peter looked down because he could no longer stand the revelations of his own evil read in the eyes of the Vampire. The red eyes of the beast humiliated him, but when he looked down he saw Mary on the ground. Mary was sleeping like most of the Forgotten and it jolted Peter. His gaze was steady as he looked up. The Vampire spoke. "Sleep."

"No," Peter said, jumping forward and wrapping the Vampire in his arms. Knocked free, Susan rolled to the edge of the fire. The intense heat woke her up, but she acted as if drugged and could only grab her neck and roll away from the fire.

The Vampire and Peter tumbled to the ground. Peter realized as he felt the weight of the Vampire on top of him that he had no plan for what to do next. He grabbed the monster by the throat to keep the fangs from his neck, but the Vampire's hands grabbed at his arms and they were much stronger than he could have imagined. He felt his jacket tear and felt the sharp nails of his foe tear at his skin. He could not hold on much longer, but there was nothing to do but hold on.

The scream that burst from the throat of the Vampire stunned Peter. He instantly felt the grip on his arms vanish and the weight pressing down on him lift. He saw Father John standing over him and swatting at a large bat flying away. In the priest's hands was an Image of the Royal Family that he had pressed into the skin of the undead. When Peter grabbed the Vampire, the old priest had managed to come closer with his sacred relics. The slightest touch of the icon had driven the Vampire away from the fire and the Forgotten.

They were safe for the moment at least.

Father John adjusted his cassock. "That was new."

Peter was grim. "But it will not be the last time. We met a friend, a fairy really, in the woods, and she reported a party of vampires."

"We will have to be on guard then," Father John said.

Peter told the priest there was little reason to wake the rest of the Forgotten. They would wake up with the rise of the sun.

"It is Susan who is the problem," he said.

"She cannot die or become like him?" Father John responded.

"No, as a creator she is fairly safe, but she can be deeply oppressed by the bite of this Vampire. Nothing good will come of it, Father John."

Father John had walked to Susan and examined her injury. He was pleased to see it was shallow. She did not resist his touch or shrink back from the cross around his neck. Susan's thick hair was disheveled and her skin mottled. Father John realized he had never seen her with even a speck of dirt under her manicured nails and now she was covered with debris from around their campsite. "What should we do, Peter?" he said.

"Do?" Peter said absentmindedly. "Do?"

"What should we do about Susan?"

Peter knelt down next to Mary and cradled her head in his arms. She was sleeping peacefully now. He found it hard to think about his friend, Susan, when Mary was dreaming the bad dreams that her Vampiric sleep would produce. He knew Mary would be fine, but fine was not enough for Peter.

"Peter," Father John repeated, "What about Susan?"

"Susan," Peter said looking up at last, "needs the Eucharist."

"They have the Body and Blood in this World?" the priest said.

"They have an image of it, but of course you as a creator of fiction have access to the form from which their Image is derived. No evil on this planet can long torment us before the reality of the power of the Eucharist. Any evil here is a shadow of a shadow against the absolute light of the Body and Blood."

The priest turned and reached into his cassock. He opened a small box in which was the intictured Host. He pressed it against the wound on Susan's neck and saw a marvelous thing. The wound vanished as if it had never been ... a nightmare of a dream that was gone in the morning. Opening her eyes, Susan saw her priest leaning over her. She said, "Father, forgive me for I have sinned."

He signed her then with the sign of the Holy Cross and said, "Remember, woman, that thou art dust and to dust thou shalt return." He placed the Host on her tongue, she swallowed, and fell into a deep and restful sleep.

"All is well," Peter said, "but we should not let that happen again. There is no real bread here or real wine ... only the shadows of both. We can eat and be sustained here, after a fashion, but the bread and the wine of this world cannot support the power of the Eucharistic mystery. Be sparing with what you have because there will be no more while we are here. It is far too great, complex, and real. Even we are nothing before the Body and Blood."

Nodding, the priest nodded and closed his little box. The fire burned and the two friends sat guard over the Forgotten.

The morning light came over the Tower of Nimlandor. Peter and Father John saw the drake stretched on a length of wall turned in their direction. Peter waved. The Forgotten began to stir and stretch. They were in a bad mood, as the sleep of the Vampire gives no rest. Only Susan woke refreshed.

"I want to go home," Doug said to his father.

Looking at the boys, Peter got up and spoke to the group. "Just at dawn on Barterra, if I remember just what to do, we will hear something very special." Turning toward the drake, heclifted both hands and spoke softly: "I am the Sky-King, heir to the Pirates, but also of the Lamb. John Blackbeard was my father's father, but the Lantern Bearer is my Name. Sing! Sing, Barterra!" The Forgotten turned to look to the East and saw the giant lizard raise his head. From the distance they could not see him open his mouth, but they all heard the drake begin to sing.

The rays of the sun lit the dew on the grass, but the sweet sound of the drake-song filled their ears and then reached deep into their minds. It was not an evil song, but the song of a beast that for a moment knew his place.

Every note was like a French-horn calling to hunt or to battle. Just as the intensity of the dragon trumpeting reached a climax, it was joined by the woodwind sound of the oboe. From the forest came a band of Fairies who responded with trills and wild abandon to the singing of the Drake. Deep in the forest, the Forgotten heard a thrumming bass sound as the Vampires sang and retired to their graves. Voices none but Peter could recognize sounded from the forest until a whole orchestra hymned the morning light. Finally, Peter sang the Old One Hundred, and the Forgotten joined him as they forgot their sorrows in the morning light of Barterra.

> Praise God from whom all blessings flow
> Praise Him all Creatures here below
> Praise Him Above Ye Heavenly Hosts
> Praise Father, Son, and Holy Ghost.

On Earth, Bandor the Rookovodityel' shuddered and for the first time thought about going home.

# Chapter Nine:

# The Tyrant

March 4, 2009, Ash Wednesday and the Start of Great Lent for the Western Orthodox: Saint Petersburg Moscow, Cathedral of Saint Peter and Saint Paul

Anastasia stood before a grotto at the right of the entrance to the Cathedral. It was strange to see her name engraved on the wall. Heaven had taught her own unworthiness, and the grace of Christ that had been borne in her through martyrdom. She did not know fully why she had been allowed to return, but in the mystery of grace she was here to help redeem the past.

She gazed at the Icon of her family that sat at the center of the room and saw her family not as they were portrayed, but as they are. She saw them in Paradise cleansed of every stain, aware of every mistake, and active for the good of mankind. One corner was dark to her where her own image was placed. She was not in heaven and so that window was closed.

The tourists behind her pushed, demanding that she move out of the way. Digital cameras flashed, but Anastasia was not annoyed. There was little harm in the crowd and much potential for true piety. Heaven had taught the young Princess to forgive everything that could be forgiven.

She saw one American tourist hesitantly drift to the front of the crowd and briefly kneel. He was tired looking and she knew, as Heaven always knows, the troubles that oppressed him.

This middle-aged man was burdened by his own sin, sick of himself, and in poor health. He had come to this shrine to pray, but instead of quiet and religious contemplation, he found only tourism. After kneeling, he got up looking vaguely disappointed. There was more Disney than Massie in this room and he had not found what he was looking for.

Anastasia turned her back to the place to which her bones would return and caught the man's eyes. It was just a second, but he knew, or guessed, and tried to doubt, but went back to knowing it was she. The young woman in front of him in the long jacket and with the pulled back hair was not just another Russian tourist. She raised her hand to bless him and as the crowd pushed them apart, he stumbled backward, healed in body and heart. He looked around wildly, but she had slipped away and his tour group was heading for the bus. The American stopped. He could not remember the Woman's face or what she had done just now, but he could not worry for long. He was overflowing with love from God. He was nearly drunk with the knowledge that Jesus had shown mercy to a sinner through His servant, Anastasia.

Anastasia stood near the tomb of her grandfather and grandmother, newly moved here from Denmark. She knew their souls were safe with God, but longed for the reunion of their blessed souls with the dust housed in these crypts. She alone of all the Romanov family she had known, was again in the body ... for a little while longer. She felt sorrow for the separation, but greater pity for the man she had come to save, and for Russia, still bleeding from the wounds of 1918. Only those fully justified by grace can stand to know the full truth, and she knew her own family was responsible, even if unintentionally, for many of those wounds without for an instant minimizing the monstrous crimes of the revolutionaries. Standing in the Cathedral of dead Tsars, Anastasia accepted that all had sinned from Tsar Peter to President Yeltsin, and the wages of that sin had been death.

Anastasia knew she faced the test of Trajan and she gave her will to God. Anastasia Nikolaevna Romanova, passion bearer, heard the prayers, the impatience, the hunger, the anger in all the tourists and pilgrims that filled the room. She was uninterested in the gilt and the grandeur because the Icons kept drawing her eyes to the action of Heaven. Beneath her feet, the wails of the unrighteous dead, some interred in this room, added the bass note to the Cathedral chorus.

She began to sing under her breath in harmony to what she heard:

> We praise you, God:
> we acknowledge you as Lord.
> All the earth venerates you
> as the eternal father.
>
> To you all the angels,
> to you the heavens and all the powers:
> to you the cherubim and seraphim
> sing with unending voice:
>
> "Sanctus, Sanctus, Sanctus
> Dominus Deus Sabaoth.
> Heaven and earth are full
> of the majesty of your glory."
>
> The glorious chorus of Apostles praises you,
> the praiseworthy number of prophets praises you,
> the white-robed army of martyrs praises you.
>
> The holy Church gives witness to you
> throughout the whole world
> as the Father of immense majesty;
> your true and only Son who is to be worshipped,
> and also the Holy Spirit, the Paraclete.
>
> O Christ, you are the king of glory.
> You are the eternal son of the Father.
> Undertaking to liberate humanity,
> you did not dread the womb of the Virgin.

By overcoming the sting of death,
you opened the kingdom of heaven to believers.
You sit at the right hand of God,
in the glory of the Father.

We believe you will come as judge.

Therefore we ask you, assist your servants,
whom you have redeemed by your precious blood.
Make them to be numbered among the holy ones
in eternal glory.

Save your people, Lord,
and bless your inheritance.
And rule them,
and lift them up into eternity.

We bless you every day;
and we praise your name for ever,
and throughout all ages.

Keep us, O Lord,
without sin this day.
Have mercy on us, O Lord,
have mercy on us.

May your mercy be upon us, O Lord,
since we have hoped in you.
I have hoped in you, O Lord:
may I not be confounded for ever.

March 4, 2009, Ash Wednesday and the Start of Great Lent for
the Western Orthodox: Saint Petersburg, Moscow

"There exists," said Bandor the Rookovodityel', "some chance of
failure."

The Twelve sat together in the Petersburg headquarters of

Iskra and listened. Their newest two members were the only ones without the traditional hoods and masks. Lenin in the body of DeLong sat atvthe right hand of Bandor the Rookovodityel' while the monk Nicholas sat on his left hand.

"The body for our Strong Hand is here," said their Head, pointing to the monk, "and he is willing to receive the soul we must call up, but the machine will not be ready for some time to bring it from my world."

"We do not have much time. She is here." Lenin spoke. He used every ounce of the rhetorical skill and practiced eloquence that DeLong's brain had for him to command. The other members of Iskra stirred. They had been briefed, and they knew the name of the woman who had somehow slipped into Russia from the United States.

"Why do we fear this woman?" A very brave, or drunk, member spoke.

"She is a power, and she is in touch with the powers. It is enough that we fear her. If that is true of our Head and your Heart, then what does that say of you who fear both of us." Lenin spoke as if he were a gun spitting out bullets.

"There are other problems that cut right to the source of our power." Bandor spoke hesitantly. His young face was drawn as if the Dragon Lord could use a better night's sleep. "My base and the place from which comes the Heart and the Hand are under attack."

"Who would dare?" asked another of the Twelve.

"An old foe," Bandor replied, "who thinks he can seal me in this world cut off from my power or draw me back to that world and close the gate forever between us."

DeLong's mouth moved. "We could never permit that, Comrade Rookovodityel'! Could we, Iskra?" The Twelve pounded their hands on the table and Lenin smiled with DeLong's best grin. "How can he be stopped?"

The Head of Iskra spoke. "I must return to my own world and stop their schemes. My servants there are inadequate for the group that has come. You, Comrade Lenin, our true Heart, must finish what you started so long ago. You must execute Citizen Romanov."

The monk, Nicholas, actually spoke. "Is it wise my, Lord, to leave us when we have so much at stake?"

"It is not wise, but it is necessary," Bandor said.

"What do you mean?" the monk replied.

Bandor was very passionate: "I mean that there is no other way to stop their plan. Much must be risked to gain much."

Again the table vibrated under the fists of the men who wished to show their support. "She is powerful, but I will meet her in a place where she will have only unpleasant surprises." Lenin leaned forward and continued. "She died by my command once, but this time I will personally shoot her on the spot designed for her bones by traitors to the Revolution."

The room burst into cheers as the Twelve celebrated the second death of Anastasia.

1 New Month, in the Twenty-Fifth Year of the Interregnum: The Tower Hill, Nimlandor

Maggie Maximos looked from the forest past the hill of the Tower to the great field next to Lethe where they had camped. She watched as the drake entered the field and headed for the small group of scholars that waited for the giant beast. Maggie gathered John, Doug, and Charles to her and asked them to pray. John and Doug were quiet, but Charles kept trying to change the color of a bluebell and probably was not going to be much use as a prayer warrior.

Maggie knew that this day would determine their fate on Barterra. Today Peter and the other Forgotten would try to find the Narva birds that he had placed in the Tower twenty-odd years ago. Today Peter would try to heal the Narva that controlled the Lethe, cut off its flow to the Earth, and pull Bandor back into Barterra. Tomorrow Peter would begin the fight to free the people of Barterra, or tomorrow Peter Alexis V would be dead.

It was Maggie who had the idea about getting past the drake. Maggie hated killing anything, and after the song of the dragon the previous day she had refused to imagine that there was no alternative. It was this that got her thinking and the group had approved her plan, if not her passivity regarding dragons.

"Look," she argued, "none of us have swords or are in the physical condition to fight a dragon, and the corpse would make a stinking mess anyway."

Max laughed, "You just don't want to lose such a beautiful singer."

"I hesitate to kill anything," Maggie sniffed.

"You would not hesitate to kill a dragon if you had seen them at the sack of Second Cor." Peter said.

"You know, friend," Barth replied, "It is that kind of cryptic pronouncement that gets old. We don't know what Second Cor is, you know."

"Second Cor was a colony of ..."

"Wait!" Barth yelled, "Could it be First Cor?"

"Actually," Peter said, "the Empire refers to it as simply Cor or Mother Cor."

Max interrupted. "That is not much better, Peter, and we need to get going."

Max had kissed her good-bye and that was the last she had heard from them. All she knew was that she was hidden safely in the woods and that they had challenged the dragon to a dual in the meadow as she had suggested. Maggie crossed herself and then her fingers.

In the meadow, after returning from hiding, Maggie and the boys in the forest nearby, things had gotten interesting quickly for the rest of the Forgotten. The fairy Shah had arrived to inform Peter that the men of Nimlandor were marching toward the Tower. The fastest riders in their tiny cavalry might reach the meadow by late afternoon, but a full force could not arrive that day. As far as the drake was concerned, the army did not matter because the partisans would be too lightly armed for a battle with a drake. "Still it would be good to have a sword again," Peter thought, though unlike riding a bike, fighting with a sword was a skill you lost with time.

"He is coming," Father John said as he saw the drake move gracefully down the hill.

"Of course he is coming," Peter whispered, "he could not resist an honorable challenge and he knows that I will not allow anyone to slip past his position if I have promised not to do so."

Shah had delivered their message to Ferus and now flew ahead of the drake to the meadow. She was humming sadly to herself as she flew, but Ferus, mostly, was silent with only the sound of his massive feet creating a disturbance in the harmony of the scene.

Peter looked up at the sky which was a very pale blue. He had forgotten how deeply Nimlandor had been impacted by the imaginations about Scotland. The breeze was fresh off the Edge of the Shield and made him feel younger than his forty years. There was always a bit of the Lethe mist in the air of this meadow that made a man forget his troubles and feel more at peace. He was sixteen again remembering the eleven-battle campaign that had won a kingdom on Barterra and all the glories of the great cities, treasures of conquest, and freedom for all folk. It was the first time since he had regained his memories that any of his victories had seemed meaningful, but nothing he found on Barterra had ever made him happier than being on Nimlandor. The little rocky island was home.

"Are you ready, Jack?" he said.

"Ready," Jack answered and he spat on the grass and condensed it to ice. It sprinkled in the sun before it melted.

"Good trick," Peter said and looked at the Forgotten stationed at different points at the edge of the pool of Lethe. "Are all of you ready? Father John?"

Father John raised his Cross and blessed them: "May God save the right! Saint George and Saint Michael fight for us today."

"There is something I never thought I would hear," Barth laughed.

Shah spoke, "Ferus has come and is honored to conquer or die in the face of the Sky King." The fairy flew to the side and hovered, waiting.

Bowing to Ferus, Peter strode forward. The massive drake towered over the Forgotten. This time he would use no fire, a useless weapon against any Fire Wright, but would hammer them into the ground with his massive tail and grind on them with his teeth. The dragon knew he could not kill his creators, but he could incapacitate their bodies. He would damage them so badly that it would be months before their mighty creator souls could reform their bodies.

Peter Alexis did a very strange thing. He walked up to the dragon as it loomed over him and struck at his iron hard belly with his fist. Peter rubbed his hand and Ferus laughed at the Sky-King.

"What are you doing, little King?" the dragon chuckled.

The River Lethe slammed into the open mouth of the drake. The combined mental powers of the Forgotten succeeded in lifting a huge amount of the Pool of Forgetfulness and hurtling it into the dragon's mouth. The drake involuntarily swallowed and immediately his eyes grew peaceful. He lowered himself to the ground and stared at Peter.

"You are a dragon master. I can sense it. Who are you?"

"You are Ferus, hatchling of White Ferus and Lady Foxfire, and husband of the Lady Feria and I am your rightful Lord: Peter Alexis Fifth, King of Dragons and Sky-King of Barterra. I am a creator here, but a creature of the Almighty," Peter answered.

Ferus put his belly down on the field. "I submit to your rule."

Peter put his hand on the head of Ferus and said, "I bind you to obedience."

"With a dragon's heart," Ferus said.

"You have had a drink from Lethe. Do you remember the powers of Lethe?"

"I do, though all my life before this moment is a peaceful dream, some of it I recall."

"More will come to you in a few days. You have swallowed much water and it will take time for your memories to return. Some may never come back to you. Do you remember Binding Oaths?"

"No," Ferus closed his great eyes, "I remember nothing of the Oaths."

"We cannot trust you then," Peter said calmly, "to come with us to the Tower. You must stay here in the meadow and guard the path behind us. Vampires may come at night. You must greet them with fire."

"I will, King Peter." Ferus got up. Peter nodded at Ferus and spoke softly to Shah. "Go to the forest past the Tower and find Maggie and the boys. Tell them what has happened and guard them from any harm if you can. Also, urge them to avoid the drake even if he seems safe now and to stay where they are." The fairy bowed and flew toward the Tower and the forest beyond.

Peter turned to the Forgotten who were standing quietly behind him and said loudly, "Follow me to the Tower. Our plans are proceeding apace, but the Lord Ferus has swallowed too much of the Lethe and must remain behind."

Mary smiled. "You are not going to start saying things like 'our plans are proceeding apace' or I am going to get very sarcastic."

Peter grinned. "Something about the air here makes me talk like a junior high Dungeon Master."

The group walked silently up the path toward the Tower. Not a word passed between them until they were well out of earshot of the drake, and then a general sigh signaled that the entire group had been holding its collective breath.

"Well done, Peter," Jack said.

"It was Maggie's plan," Mary pointed out.

"I suggest we walk quickly." Max said. "If Peter's memory is right, the drake should be on our side for days, but I don't trust Peter's memory."

"Good idea," Susan said. "We should get to the Tower and get this job done."

"Are you sure you can heal the Narva bird?" Barth asked his oldest friend.

"I am sure." Peter wasn't confident of much, but he knew his power over the birds. It had come with the anointing balm of the Kingship.

"Why do you have such powers over dragons?" Mary asked her lover.

"I don't know," Peter replied. "Just as you may discover special 'creator' powers here, I discovered a special affinity for dragons. They trust me. Dragons need an overlord to function here. I have that capacity and it is one reason, amongst many, that I was made Sky-King. Bandor and the Sky-Kings have dueled for their rule for a long time."

"Bandor isn't going to turn out to be your father or something?" Jack said laughing.

"No," Peter said, giving his best young Luke Skywalker impression, "Bandor is partly a sub-creation, partly not, and his chaos is a very old one. He cannot master us, but he can," Peter looked pained, "outwit us."

They approached the great gates of the Tower and opened them. The stone pavement under their feet was free of all weeds. They walked toward the grass of the green where a flock of sheep was munching away. Ferus had kept a ready food supply and his lair reflected his high social status. The flock was fat and numerous since dragons are excellent shepherds.

Peter spoke. "Dragons keep their homes very neat. Of course, Ferus was too large to go into the inner rooms, but we will find them orderly. There will not even be dust on the tables."

"Magic?" Max asked.

"No, well, sort of," Peter began but then stopped as he approached the wooden stairs that led up to the great door of the Tower. The door opened and the Forgotten saw a strange sight.

"A robot!" Barth exclaimed as he saw an obviously mechanical man holding open the door. The short mechanical man was more Victorian than futuristic. It was golden in color and had an obvious wind-up key coming from the back.

Peter bowed his head. "I am home, John."

"Of course, Master Peter." The voice that came from the mechanical man was very precise, but otherwise perfectly natural.

"How," Mary asked, "is that possible in a medieval world?"

"The myth of mechanical men is as old as Homer's Iliad or Plato's Symposium." Max was warming to a lecture, but John smoothly diverted the conversation.

"Exactly, Sir, and I look forward to hearing from a knowledge creator the details of my creation. Hephaestus made me, dear Lady, a very long time ago. Who are your guests, King Peter?"

Peter introduced the Forgotten and said, "We are in a bit of a hurry, John. The Lord Ferus has forgotten his allegiance, but may recall it at any time."

"I understand, Sir. Will you be wanting dinner?"

"We will be wanting an excellent dinner," Peter said, "but first I would ask you to have the staff lock all the doors and gates and for you to take us to the Narva birds."

"We cannot hold the Tower against Ferus, Sire." John said by way of reminder.

"It will not be necessary, John. Just have the staff lock up and prepare a meal in Homogene's Hall."

"Yes, Sire."

John pulled a bell rope next to the door and a slender silver robot appeared out of a small door in the hall. "Miss Prudence, our King has returned." Prudence bowed to Peter, and John gave her instructions. When he was finished, he turned back to the Sky-King. "I must say that is good to have humans back in the Tower, Sire. You will find everything in order, but it has been quite tedious preparing for nothing."

"How much food is available?" Peter asked the butler mechanical.

"We have kept the outer fields and husbandry active," John said, "but I fear trade has come to a stand still so we only have the most basic food in storage."

"Could we stand a siege if the castle were manned by one hundred men?" Peter asked.

"We could," John spoke apologetically, "but I fear that you would not enjoy the food. The wine cellars are untouched as the Lord Bandor wished it so for his own pleasure. There would, however, be something a trifle incongruous in eating plain bread with very fine port."

"It will be fine, John. Now show us to the Narva room."

John walked down the hall and Mary nudged Peter. "Did you know about this?"

Peter nodded. "The staff has always come with the castle and helped give the Macbor family status that ruling this little island would not have normally given them. The mechanicals are excellent servants, but they will not fight anyone. They cannot disobey a command from a living soul. When Ferus was here, they would have obeyed him."

"I will like living here," Mary said, looking at the perfectly orderly halls with their tapestries and simple wooden furniture all in perfect order. She touched a dark oak chest and found it dust free. She could smell the polish on her finger.

"You will have to marry me first."

Max groaned, "We have a dragon in the field who may remember to come back and crush us at any time. We are on a planet where most of civilization is controlled by a very evil being. Can you just hurry us to the Narva and stop the flirting?"

Peter laughed at Max. "Relax. I'm starting to enjoy myself."

They followed John up several flights of stairs and down numerous hallways. The Forgotten were sure that they would never be able to find their way back, but as they walked each was joined by a mechanical that introduced itself and said it had come to serve.

"Well," Barth said to his silver aide named Tim, "is it possible to get a bath in this place?"

"I will draw one before dinner, of course, and draw appropriate clothing for your rank from the stores." Tim paused, "What is your rank, sir?"

"What is my rank, Peter?"

"You are the Sky-King's Friend as are all the rest of you." Peter noted as they reached the top of a final flight of stairs.

"Very good, my Lord." Tim said with a bow. The Forgotten observed that all the mechanicals except for John were silver. Susan asked Peter about this and Peter replied that John was the original mechanical and had built all the rest himself.

"How was it done?" Susan asked.

"By a process known only to myself," John sounded more mechanical than usual, "and we find a discussion of it a bit," a pregnant pause, "a bit inappropriate. No offense meant, my Lady Susan."

"I am sorry, John," Susan said sincerely, "we do not know your ways yet."

"We take no offense." John answered. "We only point out our

customs. You may do as you will. Lord Bandor ignored the proprieties," John imitated a cough, "all the time."

Eventually the group reached two double doors made of what appeared to be mahogany. A double-headed eagle was centered on the doors with a head and wing on each of the two doors. There was a great iron lock on the door. John selected a key from the large ring he carried around his waist and opened the door.

The Forgotten gasped at the sight of the room, for in this entire remarkable day and in the long astounding week, they had seen nothing like it. The room itself was a great vault stretching to fan arches over their heads. Eleven banners hung from the arches. The floor was black marble and every other paving stone was a hendecagon. In the center of the room there was a golden table, also eleven-sided, and on it was a case containing the Narva Birds.

The room was filled with the music of the Birds. Each sang out the health of their region of Barterra, whether island, sea, or pole. The sound was overpowering and the Forgotten stood in the room amazed. Peter walked toward the hendecagon in the room and the case he had placed on it twenty-five years ago. A few steps from the case he stopped and looked down. The stains were still on the floor despite John's attempts to clean it.

Peter looked up and resumed walking to the table. His mission was almost complete. He would pick up the Narva bird for the World Sea and heal it. Bandor would be trapped on Earth without the power of the Lethe to aid him. Finally, he stood at the table and moved to open the great case.

"Peter," Max was speaking behind him. "Peter, turn around very slowly."

Peter turned around and saw that between himself and the Forgotten was the rapidly solidifying form of a man. There was no doubt whom. Peter still had no weapon, and Bandor was sure to be armed. He thought quickly. "John, leave us. Shut the door and lock it behind you. The rest of you follow John out of here." He looked at Mary. "All of you leave now."

"We will not leave you," Barth said, looking at his friend.

"You will leave me. You don't know Bandor's powers here.

Only I as the anointed King can hope to survive him in his rage. Leave quickly and wait for the scouting party that is coming."

They still hesitated as the body of Bandor grew more complete. "Peter is right," Max said. "We should go. Remember what he told us about Bandor before we came."

"You really must go if the Sky-King asks it," John said sweeping them toward the door.

Mary looked at Peter firmly. "I will stay."

Peter answered, "You will not."

"Please, Miss." John sounded like he was begging.

"Fine, I will go. But remember, I am going against my will." Mary turned around and walked out of the chamber.

"Guard the gate," Peter called after them. "General Gala, the Macbor, and our allies will be here soon. We must hold this Tower against the time when the drake realizes his mistake." Peter turned back to the table and opened the cabinet. Bandor was nearly formed, and Peter heard the great doors swing shut behind the Forgotten. As he reached for the World Sea Bird, a great gull, he saw that it was wounded in the heart. Water poured from its side where it had been pierced. He heard the lock click in the hallway.

"Peter Alexis." It was Bandor's voice.

Peter was trapped in the room where Lisay had died. Just as before, he was holding a Narva and looking at the man who killed her.

"Eleven victories over me and eleven banners in the room," Bandor laughed. "A bit much isn't it?"

"The people of Barterra were happy to be free. Many nobles raised the money amongst themselves and presented me this room as a present right before ..."

"Right before I made an Atlantis of the Isle of Originals."

"Yes."

Peter realized with a shock that there was one difference from the last time. Then Bandor had looked older and his injury had made him appear sinister to the young king. Now, Peter was middle-aged, but Bandor still appeared twenty-seven or so, in his prime. Peter was older now, grayer, and more tired than the Dragon Lord. It was a debilitating switch in perspective.

"It will take you time to heal that Bird, and I will not give you that time." Bandor stepped toward Peter. Peter looked at the Narva, which had water dripping from it unto the floor. He focused on it, but Bandor easily blocked his thoughts, as he had always been able to do.

Peter looked up at the Dragon Lord now standing uncomfortably close. "You cannot kill me, Bandor."

Bandor laughed. "You will wish I could." The Dragon Lord pulled a large flask from his very expensive London tailored suit. "Drink this water, my old friend. I have concentrated it just as I did before, though I don't have so beautiful a servant to administer the medicine."

Peter did not flinch. "Let me put down the Narva so there is something left of this world when our fight is done."

Peter carefully put the crystalline bird down on the table. As quickly as he could, Peter flung the water that had dripped over his hands from the Narva into the eyes of his opponent. Bandor staggered back. The Narva bled Lethe water, and contact with it dazed Bandor. For a moment he could not remember where he was. A moment was all Peter needed to fling himself on his enemy. He pounded Bandor with all the rage he had.

Bandor dropped the flask of Lethe concentrate which landed unbroken on the floor. His nose was broken and his lip cut by Peter's fists, but he still did not fight back. His one good eye was misty and he looked ready to cry. Peter feared his opponent's tricks and kept pounding, hoping to knock him out, but the scholar had too little muscle and long forgotten training.

Bandor's blue eye became clear and he flipped Peter over and got to his feet. Peter was on the floor looking up at his foe. "It is time to take your medicine, Peter. You have made an effort. Now drink." Peter lunged at Bandor's knees, but the Dragon Lord kicked him in the face.

Peter could not move from the stunning pain.

Bandor spoke. "What will you gain even if you defeat me? Your grand Alliance is twenty-five years gone, and one of my lieutenants would take my place as Emperor and Dragon Lord." Bandor picked up the flask and moved it closer to where Peter lay gasping on the floor. "I will keep you because I cannot kill you, Peter, but I will keep you as my jester. You will be a perpetual blank slate for me to write upon until your soul longs to escape." Peter tried to lash out at him, but Bandor simply kicked him again.

"You will heal so quickly here from these wounds, Peter. It is almost not worth inflicting them." Bandor knelt down and wrapped one strong hand around the Sky-King's throat and began to choke him. The other hand pinched Peter's nose shut. "You will open your mouth." The bottle of Lethe water was on the floor next to them. Peter knew that eventually he would have to open his mouth and Bandor would fill his mouth with it. There was nothing he could do.

The choking was not the worst of the pain Peter experienced. The same spiritual oppression that had clouded his mind in Penfield was renewed. He was full of doubt, self-pity, loathing, and hatred. He could not think through the cloud of emotions that Bandor was releasing on him. The Dragon Lord was slowly gaining control of his mind just as he had twenty-five years ago when Peter had lost everything. This time Bandor had needed no trick to betray Peter into his hands.

Bandor waited for Peter to begin to gasp for breath and took even greater control of the Sky-King's mind. He was surprised at how frail his opponent had become, how much less optimistic. This was easy. Bandor moved through the lower parts of the soul and reached for the nous, the inner core of Peter's being. Suddenly, a blinding flash of light nearly made him loose his grip on the King.

Peter was aware he was losing control of his body and his soul. He knew there was nothing he could do, but the man had one advantage over the boy. Peter had practice in failure. He began to pray as he failed, just as he had learned to do first from Max, and then later from Father John. It was a prayer of the inner man. His breathing slowed as he rested in God's grace. There was nothing he could do, but God was good. Years of grace received on his knees at Saint Michael Church were there to buttress his prayer, as they had not been twenty-five years ago. His deepest mind was filled with light that had never been created.

Peter had nothing left but that Light. It shone on him and set him free. He knew that he could not be killed, but that he could give up his life for the good of Barterra. Nobody could take his life, but he could give it and so defeat the schemes of his enemy. Bandor would reach to control his mind, but find only the grace God gives a martyr. Peter hoped he enjoyed it.

It was an easy call, and Peter received the grace to die.

Bandor was ready to take one hand off Peter's throat and reach for the bottle of Lethe water. Peter had stopped struggling. Mentally, the Dragon Lord prepared to complete the possession of his old foe. Bandor sacked the mind of Peter Rupert Alexis. He saw memories of Lisay and dreams of Mary shrivel before his touch. He pushed aside friendship with Max and Barth. Slowly, Bandor came to the core of Peter's being, and then his mind was stunned. There was a gate to Paradise there; the real Peter was leaving, and drawing Bandor after him.

The Dragon Lord shrieked in horror. He could not face that light and yet he could not look away from it. It was beautiful and terrible and he was not ready for it. His soul was too small for the visions he was seeing. A bearded man and a tall wife stood watching from a distance as Peter's soul drew closer to Heaven. Stop! He must let go of Peter and get out of this room, but he discovered that he had no will to do so. The vision was too beautiful to turn away. Even if it killed him, Bandor had to see what Peter was seeing.

He had won only to discover that his final victory over Peter Alexis Fifth would be his last. This King would be dead, but some other Sovereign would replace him. Bandor's mind was blue screening as he tried to cope with the crash of all he had believed. He could not think and now he could not let go of Peter, though the King was now breathing deeply through his mouth. Bandor was being drawn into the presence of the Almighty and the beauty burned him like Hell.

When they had been expelled from the room, the Forgotten stood outside the doors of the chamber unsure what to do. They had obeyed Max out of instinct and left Peter to face Bandor, but now felt useless. "We must pray," Father John said. "We can help Peter best by praying for him."

"But shouldn't we do something?" Jack said.

"What can we do?" Barth was eager to act.

Father John was severe. "The only doing he needs from us is praying." Max started to talk, but Father John looked at him severely. The Forgotten dropped to their knees before the door as the mechanical man stood watch and waited for his next command or duty. They began to pray for Peter, for Barterra, for Earth, and for their own families.

Mary was extremely annoyed with Father John and Max. She did not drop to her knees with the rest. She wanted to save Peter and was angry at the typical reaction of academics to a stressful situation: They wanted to talk about it. In this case, it was talking to the Almighty, but it was still talking. "The Lord helps those who help themselves," Mary thought. Secular academics started committees when they faced problems; Mary saw that Christian ones had prayer meetings.

She was going to act. "Open the door, John." She was Queenly, tall and powerful, as she pushed through the kneeling Forgotten toward the door and Peter. She was furious with herself for ever leaving her dear Peter alone with Bandor. She was not a fairy tale Princess. Max caught her arm as she went toward the opening doors. "No!" he said.

"I am going to help the man I love even if I die doing it," she replied, gently but firmly detaching his hand. Max looked at her with sorrow, but did nothing more to stop her.

"That deed which you are about to do, do quickly," Father John whispered as Mary slipped away. John closed the door behind her.

Bandor knew he was doomed and that he had been trapped by his own confidence. He was going to die in the uncreated light that would burst forth from the martyr-Sky-King as he went into the face of God. The pain grew intense and Bandor longed to let go of Peter's neck, but he could not. Neither Peter nor Bandor would have heard the end of the world, let alone one woman pounding across the room to save her beloved.

Mary landed on Bandor's back and her long fingernails scratched his face, drawing blood. She was screaming at Bandor, beating him with her other hand. With relief, the Dragon Lord rolled off Peter. He felt the Sky-King's concentration vanish and the tensions in his mind lessened.

"Mary," Peter sighed as the Vision retreated before her violence, "No."

"I will not," Mary cried, striking at Bandor, "let you down like she did." She was pounding at Bandor's face, but he hardly felt it compared to the relief from the mental pain he had been experiencing.

"You don't understand!" Peter was hardly audible as he struggled to his knees.

She saw the vial of concentrated Lethe water Bandor had dropped in the struggle. Mary was no fool and she knew it was nothing of Peter's. Whatever it was, Bandor had brought it with him. She grabbled it, rolling off Bandor in the process. Bandor pushed himself up and stood. Still dazed from the Light, he was looking for a weapon, but could find nothing in the room with which to battle two people. Mary looked at the vial and opened it. It looked like water and suddenly she made one of those lucky guesses that had made her such a good administrator.

Peter looked at Mary and suddenly understood what she was going to do. Too late he shouted, "No!" Mary had already thrown the concentrate in Bandor's face as he stood gasping for breath.

Bandor stopped staggering and swallowed reflexively. The water of Lethe helped him, though it also confused him. He was lost in his own thoughts, still hurting with a mind badly scarred, but unable to remember the source of his pain. He forgot Mary and Peter and tried to remember his own identity and what it was that he wanted in this room only to fail. He only could recall that he should go home. It would be safe at home.

Bandor concentrated all his thoughts on Samov and his room there. He looked up at the light streaming through the massive clear gothic windows of the chamber. Samov was out there. He kept looking up as his body slowly lifted from the ground and soared faster and faster into the air. The Lord of Dragons rose, smashed his way through one of the windows and was gone. His confusion and pain might take months to heal, but he was headed for home and safety. The glass fell down like crystal rain while Peter and Mary watched it fall on the other side of the room as if they were honeymooners looking at Niagara Falls. They saw the sights, but hardly noticed.

Peter looked down and saw that Mary was standing on the stained tile on the floor. It was the same, he thought. Love had betrayed him again, but then he realized the differences when Mary turned her gaze from the shattered window high above them. There was not a shadow of selfishness in her glance. She had meant to do right.

"Peter?" she said, "Are you alright?"

"I am fine," he said. "Are you?"

"If you are," she said sternly, "I will be fine."

The sounds of the outside world could enter the chamber now that the window was broken. Peter heard a bird singing and then he heard something else, soft at first but slowly growing louder with a raucous defiance that cheered his heart. Mary heard it as well.

"What is it? Is it our friends?" She looked so happy that Peter could not help loving her for it. It was obvious now that they were hearing the sound of bagpipes playing a tune Peter knew well. The men and fair folk of Nimlandor were coming to the skirl of **To the Rescue of Desque**. He did not have to be there to see the outriders racing across the meadow and the companies of the Macbor marching out the woods behind them.

"If I am not mistaken, it is Gala and the Macbor. They have come to save the King. Thanks to you, there will be a king to save."

Mary glowed with happiness. He would have to tell her later, Peter supposed. There could be no love based on a lie, but for now he had a more pressing job. He heard the door swing open behind him as he walked to the Narva birds, and picked up the Gull again. Pressing the Bird to his heart, he prayed as only an anointed King can pray for his land and for his people.

Stepping up, Max put his hand on his protégé's shoulder and added his prayers. Father John crossed himself and joined them. The others just watched as the water dripping from Peter's hand began to lessen and the sound of the Gull grew sweeter and less shrill. Finally, Peter held the Narva over his head where it flashed in the light.

The Forgotten cheered and Susan rushed over and gave Mary an encouraging hug. Suddenly the castle shuddered as if the world had shifted ever so slightly, but the motion passed as quickly as it had come. Peter placed the Narva carefully down in the case before him.

They had won a partial victory and he must be thankful for it, but it was hard to have seen Paradise only to return. Still the same vision made him incapable, at the moment, of the slightest regret or bitterness. Things were as they were and God would bring good of it. The wound on the Narva bird had closed, the gap in the foundation of the River Lethe had closed, and Bandor was trapped on Barterra away from Earth.

Mary took his hand. "You are alive, lover. Alive to fight another day." Peter looked at her with admiration for her courage, and with gratitude for her love. She was a good woman and would make a great Queen if he could finally gain her consent.

"You are right, Mary. We will fight another day." He took her hand and said to Max, "We'd better go to the gates to meet Gala and see what can be done about that dragon."

4 March 2009, Ash Wednesday and the Start of Great Lent for the Western Orthodox: Saint Petersburg, Moscow

Anastasia sat quietly in the empty Cathedral, feeling a momentary weakness. She knew something had gone wrong on Barterra because Peter was not in Paradise. Anastasia sighed. She understood since she once would have thought the rescue of her family would have been better than her death. God knows she remembered praying with her mother for hours for some officer, any officer, to remember them in Siberia. None ever did.

That someone had loved Peter enough to save him did not irritate Anastasia. It made her a bit sad. Someone had swerved from the best to a lesser course, but all was not yet lost for the Forgotten because love had motivated the error. God would take the events He was given, events in some mysterious way He foreknew without controlling, and make a different, but better story of them.

She knew the cost of the delay in Peter's death. As she sat in the corner of the Cathedral, she was lonely. The shrine was so artificial; even most of the stone around her was not real, but wood painted to look like granite. Russia was no longer as wicked as it had been in 1918, but it was much less Russian and much more fake. As one who remembered the last of Holy Mother Russia, Anastasia would not be sorry to leave this place.

Tonight was going to be hard and she needed to prepare. She flexed her fingers and looked at them. It was not a glorified body, or even a fully human one, but it was part of her now. She had grown used to the feel of a beating heart and to the weight of her body on feet. Magog had created this shadow of a human body, as the great machine reached into the human imagination to grab something from what they wrongly believed was the past. Heaven had allowed the actual soul of Anastasia to fill it and she was thankful for that grace.

Her family was being allowed by the backward redemption of Heaven to heal some of their own errors. She was being allowed to undo some of what they had done badly. This work was always being done in prayer before God, but Anastasia was being given a rare, though not unprecedented, chance to do so in the flesh. There was much she had been allowed to do. She had been allowed to tap the deeper physics and metaphysics of the world and witness what present science would call a "miracle." She had nearly completed her task when she had placed the security of this building in a state of forgetfulness. If the recordings on the security cameras were ever viewed, no human being would see anything. She knew the angels could see them, but she was not worried about angels or devils.

When she was alive the first time, Anastasia thought, she had often forgotten that even the Lord Jesus had asked the bitter cup to pass. Her memories of Heaven were clear and she was not afraid of what was coming, but she did not look forward to it. One might know that a nasty job was necessary without wanting to rush into the task. "If it be your will, Father," the Martyr Princess began, but never finished.

Two men walked out from the shadows, pushing down the velvet rope that separated the crypt of the last Romanovs from the rest of the Cathedral. Walking up to Anastasia, they looked down at the young woman sitting on the bench. She was sitting in a plain coat and looked up at them with serious eyes.

"You cut us off from the Rookovodityel'." The taller of the two men was speaking. He was good looking in a flashy American way.

"I did not, but my friends have done so."

The little monk next to him said, "You cannot keep him from us for long. Already we are preparing to open another door."

"I know," Anastasia said, "but my family will be there to help close it when you do."

"But you will not be," said the American man.

"No. I will not."

The American spoke, "Do you know who I am?"

"I know who you pretend to be."

"Then you know what I did to you and to your family. What I gladly did ..."

"And I forgave Lenin for it at the gates of Paradise. You took a family of sinners and made us martyrs."

Lenin made Delong's body jerk to attention. "Your bones must return to where they belong."

"My bones are still there. This body is wholly a product of Magog."

"We will restore the Revolution in Russia and then bring it to the world."

Anastasia laughed. "There will be one more Tsar and then an End will come, though whether it is the last of all days or not, no man knows."

"Why are you here? What do you hope to do? You cannot stop the power of Iskra."

Anastasia looked at Lenin in DeLong's body. "I came to save you, Robert DeLong."

Lenin's mouth sagged, and DeLong's soul fought to regain some control of his own body. Anastasia simply sat looking at him as the soul of the weak-minded man fought to regain possession of his own body. He failed as he always did, but this time not without some hope, because Anastasia still looked at him with love.

"You cannot do this thing," Lenin said, and pulled out a gun. The time had come to end this crisis and keep the plan moving. They needed to free the Head from Barterra and bring the Hand from the past. He pointed the gun at the Grand Duchess.

Anastasia had never seen this particular model or make. It made the guns of Yekaterinburg look like museum pieces. She looked at Lenin calmly and said, "Reverend DeLong, in the name of Jesus Christ, do you wish to be free?"

The face before her jerked into motion and spoke. "Oh, God, yes."

Anastasia raised her hand in the sign of the cross, the gun fired, and Reverend DeLong fell to the floor. The Grand Duchess felt the bullet enter her body and knew she did not have long to live. The shadow bodies of human imaginations died much more easily than the real things. It did not, she observed, make her feel any better. "God help me," she thought, "this hurts."

Anastasia could feel herself slipping from her seat toward the floor. It would be funny to lie with Lenin on the floor of her crypt.

The monk spoke to her as she slumped on the bench. "Would you like last rites?" He was mocking her pain, but that was unimportant compared to what she knew must follow.

"You are a false priest, and I would not receive any sacrament from you, but I will pray for you if you wish it."

He looked at her as she fell to the floor of the tomb and mocked her. "I do not need your prayers. You are dying."

"Look at your leader, Father Nicholas."

The priest-monk was startled to hear his name from someone he had never met. He was more than a little afraid of even a wounded Anastasia Romanova, but, he thought quickly, she was simply Citizen Romanov to him. He did glance at Lenin-DeLong and was startled to see a black shadow creeping from the nose of DeLong. He dropped his gun.

"My God," He said.

"He was once." Anastasia could scarcely be heard, but she was still looking at him with those big eyes. He saw the shadow creeping from Lenin toward his feet. Surely he was slated for the Hand and not for possession now. But if not him, who? Father Nicholas became frightened and crossed himself in superstitious terror.

Two times was not enough to get good at dying of gun shot wounds, and Anastasia discovered it. She was hurting horribly. She could not breathe, and her eyesight was failing, but still she prayed for the soul of DeLong, for the soul of the false-Lenin, and for the stupid monk before her. She saw her mother again with the look of horror on her face as she saw the bullets dance off the diamonds in her corset. She saw her father's bloody head. This did not grieve her, because she had seen the transformation. One moment there was horror and the next moment there was Jesus.

She looked at the dark shadow slithering toward the priest-monk, and spoke one last time to Father Nicholas who stood in stunned silence. "May your silver perish with you, because you thought you could obtain the gift of God with money! You have neither part nor lot in this matter, for your heart is not right before God. Repent, therefore, of this wickedness of yours, and pray to the Lord that, if possible, the intent of your heart may be forgiven you. For I see that you are in the gall of bitterness and in the bond of iniquity."

Anastasia died again.

The shadow jerked the monk's body around as it entered, and the soul of Lenin found a new home which only imminent death or a very powerful exorcist could force him to leave. He rooted through memories and realized they had chosen well. Father Nicholas was an excellent subject for possession. His baptized, though apostate, soul was strong enough to handle the strain. It was true that he was not as powerful as DeLong, but a soul one step from the nether gloom could not be choosy.

Lenin regained his composure and saw his enemy dead at his feet. He called a number on the monk's mobile that only he knew. "Come. Execute Tobolsk Initiative." He was satisfied that the Gog project in the United States would get them on track.

The Head was missing, but that could be fixed. The Hand would need a new body, but Stalin would not be picky. How Lenin longed to see Bandor and Stalin join him in forming a new trinity! He rubbed his head to silence the protests.

The body of DeLong had been spiritually stronger, of course. The integration of the body and soul was more complete. Perhaps they had made a mistake in picking this particular monk, but it could not be helped at the moment. Lenin closed the mobile and started to leave. He felt decidedly odd. It was only then that Lenin remembered the feelings associated with his first stroke.

# Chapter Ten:

# The Story Will Save Us

16 March 2009, Great Lent: Rochester, New York

The newspaper was very ragged. It had been trapped in the brush next to the road since the twenty-fourth of January. It read, President's Fame Gives Him Grace Period. Kennedy picked it up and tossed it in a nearby University trash bin as he walked into the building. By now most students and faculty were sick of politics and talking about politics. He adjusted his tie and walked into the science building. He would soon have a spacious new office to reflect his increased status. The search for a new vice-provost was likely to open up all kinds of desirable University real estate.

Bobby Kennedy opened the email that had arrived in the ten minutes since he had last checked his Blackberry. Lately, the good news never stopped. Not only had his initial grant request been approved, but also the Russian foundation Social Democratic Union was asking if increased money would help speed up program implementation.

They also wanted to send a liaison to make sure the project went according to plan. "We have had bad experiences with projects going off task in the past." This was less good, but Kennedy assumed that it was the cost of doing business with this foundation. He was lucky that he had not deleted their initial contact email because their description was in none of the standard grant agencies books. He suspected Russian mob ties, though why the mob would want to invest in impractical physics experiments was beyond him. They seemed well connected enough to get through the normal Homeland Security hassles and in this one area, Kennedy approved of "don't ask, don't tell."

Gog would be built, and with proper funding the experiment could begin in record time. Kennedy already had his eye on a large empty set of offices in the basement. He could find no record of its ever being used since it had been a sunken volleyball court in an earlier iteration of the building plan. With a few modifications, the pit for the court would just about hold the main tank for Gog. He could use the office space that surrounded it for the computers and other paraphernalia. It was surprising that the space had never been repurposed, but Universities were like that. Lately he found it easier to simply not think about certain things. Whenever he did this, he felt happier and this unexpected happiness was better than drugs. He would go on not wondering.

He hit "reply", and told SDU that he could use more funding and that he would happy to work with any aide they suggested. "My goal is total cooperation with the laudable social goals of your fine foundation." He smiled at how nicely he had manipulated the entire situation.

16 March, 2009, Great Lent: Saint Petersburg, Russia

Lenin was strapped to a hospital bed, unable to move or talk. He was in a private sanatorium owned by one of the Eleven of Iskra. When the Tobolsk Team had arrived to clean up the mess, they had found the monk sitting on the ground. He had tried to tell them he was Comrade Lenin, but they could not understand anything he said. His communication skills deteriorated from there.

The body holding Lenin had been signed in under his monastic name and was receiving the best of care. None of the Eleven were eager to risk the death of the monk and the transference of Lenin's strong soul to a new body. They needed someone less wicked next time, stronger, but like DeLong, apostate enough for transference to work. Without the Rookovodityel', they did not dare even look for a new candidate.

The council member assigned to watch Lenin had taken the code name Nagorny. He would have to watch the monk, but he was still not going to give out his real name. Nagorny checked his email and noticed that their American contact was being cooperative with their plans. It was difficult to work with Americans, but the Rookovodityel' had thought it important and, given the dangers associated with their next task, wanted it off Russian soil. This seemed sensible: the effects of the last experiment had wiped thousands of memories clean all over the world. Only the protection of Rookovodityel' had saved the remnant of the Eleven. Nagorny supposed that only a few people in the entire world remembered the project at all.

The body of Father Nicholas stirred and he began to move his fingers under the straps. Nagorny knew that if his hands were released, he would begin to claw at this own face. Though his nails had been trimmed nearly to the quick, the hospital felt it was better to leave him in this state for now. Nagorny was sure that many of the physical problems of their patient were not due to the stroke.

They would decide what to do with the body after they reestablished contact with the Rookovodityel'. There was good hope for the future, but much that concerned him. When the Tobolsk team arrived at the Cathedral of Peter and Paul there had been only the body of Father Nicholas. Anastasia had disappeared entirely. The body of DeLong had also been missing, but the Tobolsk group had found it in a regular Petersburg hospital.

Nagorny had decided against the immediate termination of DeLong. First, he apparently was being treated as a stroke victim. He showed no signs of remembering any of the events related to his time at the Seminary, and in fact seemed eager to chat with officials from that Iskra front. Second, DeLong had been a useful carrier of Iskra's Heart and, until Nagorny knew why Lenin had transferred himself to Father Nicholas, he was not eager to kill such a potentially valuable ally. In any case, given their extensive Los Angeles organization, it would be no problem to deal with

DeLong here or at his home. Iskra was going to have to get used to working in the United States.

A doctor entered the room and Nagorny looked up. "Mr. Nagorny?" the doctor said.

"Yes, doctor." Nagorny smiled at the medico.

"We have hope," said the doctor, "that your friend will make some kind of recovery. Really the damage to the brain is much less than you would think from his present symptoms. He could recover very quickly at any moment, or the process could take many months. Strokes are very unpredictable."

"That is good news, doctor." Nagorny was pleased. "He is a good friend and also one of the leaders in my gas and oil company. Spare no expense in helping him."

"You can be sure that we will do whatever we can."

16 March 2009, Great Lent: Rochester, New York

Tom was trying to get used to a new routine. Every day he would drive from Max's house to Lyons and take classes. His philosophy class was much less interesting without Professor Alexis, but nobody except Tom seemed to notice the difference. He would be glad to graduate and start taking classes at PHB. He saw Brother Simon as often as he could and it was good to talk to the only other person he knew who retained some memories of his missing friends.

It was a bad time to sell real estate in Rochester so he was going to rent his mother's old house for now. She was moving into the Smith house as soon as Tom had Jack and Susan's possessions moved into storage. He had changed his mind and was planning on living in the city. It made his commute worse this semester, but it would be perfect for studying at PHB in the fall. Besides, what was happening in the window of the Orichalcum and the stories it stirred in his mind were too interesting to miss for long. He spent every night documenting the lives of the Forgotten on Barterra.

Fortunately, the combined wealth of the Forgotten gave him plenty of money to deal with problems. He had moved Peter and

Barth's things out of their respective apartments quickly and the managers had already filled the spaces. Their limited possessions filled Max's capacious attic. Nobody was asking any questions. It was not just Bandor's toying with time and the forgetfulness of the Lethe, but also Anastasia's careful knitting together of a new history to explain as many loose ends as possible. Anastasia had done her job well. His friends were truly forgotten.

He had heard nothing from the Saint since she left for Russia. After he had seen her final victory in the mirror, she had disappeared. There was much Tom still did not understand about the Saint and her adventures. When he asked her how she planned to get on a plane without any identification, she had only smiled. He asked for her prayers nightly and felt his prayers were heard.

Tom knew he needed to settle down. Adventure and excitement were over for him for a good long while, at least if his friends continued to be successful. His ability to discern the pattern of events in the window of the Orichalcum was growing, but it was also a tiring process. He had written pages about the work of Anastasia and the Forgotten.

He was getting used to checking the stock market every day and hoped it had found a bottom. Tom smiled at himself, he was still not used to having investments. Some of his new possessions were more difficult than others. He was unsure what to do with the gold bullion that Max had shown him in a safe in his office. The old scholar had been a bit of a survivalist.

Before he could totally move past the adventures of the last month, there was one more job to do. He looked at the thick manila envelope that Professor Alexis had given him, now a good bit thicker with his additions. It was prepaid Federal Express and the agent would arrive before 10:30 today. He could remember his conversation with Peter.

Professor Alexis had smoothed his hair back, as he usually did in class before making an important point, and looked at Tom. "You will take care of my papers? You will send them to the man I mentioned? Everything has been arranged with the carrier."

Tom said, "Of course, Professor Alexis," and he smiled and shook his friend's hand.

"We appreciate what you are doing for us." Professor Alexis looked as if he wanted to say something. "It is possible that we will neither fully succeed nor fail. The Martyr has suggested that in this case it would be good for someone not connected to the group to know our story."

"I understand, sir."

"You should call me Peter, Tom."

"Yes, Peter." Tom thought that he would always think of "Peter" as Professor Alexis. Why did professors always do this?

"It is very important that this be published as a fictional story."

"I understand."

"Well, I am not sure any of us understand, but if it is published and taken as fiction by the right person, it might help us on Barterra. Human imagination does funny things there. I don't know anyone who writes well enough to do the job, but a better writer might read the tale if it is widely disseminated and have it spark his or her imagination. I have discovered that most of my own friends have a deplorable lack of literary talent, but John Mark's imagination will at least be excited enough about this story to get a manuscript out.

"Of course, I cannot even be positive of that. You must watch for publication. If he does not write a book within the year, you must risk calling him and push. If he fails, there is a second copy of these notes in the safe. You can monitor him easily as I have made you his friend on several social networks using dummy accounts. Here is that information. If he fails altogether, I am not sure whom else you can try, but you will have to find someone. Do you understand?"

Tom laughed. "I understood the first of the several times we have gone over this. Is there anything else, Professor Alexis?"

"Nothing. I am sorry you are left here holding everything together."

"I want to stay. There are things I need to learn, and Brother Simon has agreed to teach me. Besides, I am not married."

"There are women on Barterra."

"Not real women, sir."

"No." Peter had smiled a bit sadly. "I suppose you are right.

You should stay. Perhaps you will see Barterra someday. It is worth seeing."

"I hope so."

Peter had smoothed back his brown and gray hair again and offered Tom his hand. They shook and Peter added, "We could have been good friends, I think."

"Yes, sir." That had been the last extended conversation between the two. Since then the package had been in the safe with the other copy, along with Max's pile of Eagles and Loons. He had not opened the Fed Ex package or the copy except to insert his own pages and was surprised by his own lack of curiosity.

Tom heard the doorbell ring downstairs and picked up the package. It would go to a Biola University professor who had known Peter in high school, though Tom assumed he no longer remembered it. He wondered what this fellow would make of it. He would be sure to check his Twitter feed carefully over the next few months.

16 March 2009, Great Lent: Saint Petersburg, Russia

DeLong was tired. He looked at the monitors beeping near his bed and was thankful for his first-rate Seminary medical plan. He remembered going in for his meeting at the Russian seminary, but evidently he had some sort of stroke. He couldn't remember a thing after that. Fortunately, he had received rapid medical attention and was feeling much better. From looking on-line he knew how important the right medicine was after a stroke and he had been given the proper stuff right away. He really was doing remarkably well. The doctors told him that he could go home to LA soon; in fact, the Russian government was insisting he go. He assumed he was not going to be able to help with the Russian seminary project. He was just as glad.

DeLong supposed that this stroke was a sure sign from God to slow down. He knew he had been pushing himself lately and that stress might be one factor in bringing on a stroke. DeLong ruefully realized he had also smoked his last cigar.

The handsome professor looked at his Bible, which had served to pass the time in the hospital. DeLong suddenly realized that the last few weeks were the most time he had spend just soaking in the book for years. He wondered if he been too spiritually busy as well as physically overactive. Something would have to be done about that!

DeLong determined that he would take the yearlong sabbatical offer his University had wired him. He would go home and focus on his therapy. As soon as he was fit, he would go on retreat for a month or two. He felt the need to get back in touch with his childhood faith and simpler things.

He felt lighthearted and approved of his own doubts. No fear of fundamentalism, of course, but perhaps he had overreacted in the other direction and become a bit politically correct? Likely he had. A man should never stop challenging his own assumptions, DeLong thought. He should keep dialoguing with the Master until he saw Jesus clearly in the breaking of the bread. He turned to the passage in Matthew and started to read.

15<sup>th</sup> day of Sky-King's Return: The Tower Hill, Nimlandor

Two weeks after his encounter with Bandor in the chamber of the Narva, Peter stood by the source of the Lethe and looked up at the keep of Nimlandor. He was feeling pretty good and was no longer sorry to be alive. The memory of Paradise had faded, if Dante's imagination had failed to describe Heaven, Peter's certainly had done even worse. There was no sense talking about it and no need to dwell on what could have been. There were, he thought, things to see and do in this life.

The gold flag with the black double-headed eagle flew over the Tower for the first time in a quarter of a century. The Macbor was back in his chamber and the tiny area around the castle was once again under the control of a renewed Lantern Alliance. "We have freed roughly a square mile. Only the rest of the planet to go." Peter had said as they raised the flag and renewed old oaths. They hadn't done much, but still it was good to see the Eagle back in its place.

All over Nimlandor, people felt hopeful. Fairies, Peter told the Forgotten, were the mobile phones of Barterra. They had been on Barterra for two weeks and Shah told him that the fairies were spreading the word as fast as possible. By now, most of the beings on the planet were aware that he was back and were trying to decide what they thought of it.

Peter Rupert Alexis felt like taking stock himself.

There had been little celebration when General Gala rode up to the castle with twenty-five light cavalry two weeks ago. The young Macbor had followed Gala with seventy-eight well trained men and a dozen local farmers who knew how to use arms. The rejoicing was muted, because even if Bandor himself was incapacitated for a time, his lieutenants were not. Messages were going out through Fairy couriers to the Krak and to the Empire to see what aid they might expect.

The Forgotten were mostly getting along well. The boys had settled in quickly; Gala had adopted all of them as honorary grandsons. The Macbor had started a training program in riding and fighting and when Susan had started to protest that Charles "at least" was too young "by far" to fight at ten, the Earl of the Tower had silenced her by saying that he had started as a page by age seven. She knew that her boys would have to learn to live in this new world, but had no intention of abandoning her role as home-school mother precipitously.

"You can teach them," she said to the Earl, "if I can learn along with them."

"But, my Lady Susan," the Macbor began, "some of these arts are not appropriate to a lady."

"Then I will participate where propriety allows and watch when it does not. I want to **understand** this world from the ground up."

Jack intervened. "If I were you, Earl Macbor, I would concede the point. In the world of the creators there is no greater or more fearful wrath than that of a home-school mother."

"It is not, I think, so different on Barterra. The Lady Susan is wise and a mother and I defer to her decision."

All the Forgotten had continued to stretch their limits in dealing with the elements of Barterra. Jack was now able to condense small objects in about a quarter of his attempts. His best trick was to extinguish a candle at night, though Susan quickly grew tired of it. Jack generally refused to make ice to cool their drinks, as he said that such repetitive use of his powers gave him a headache. Susan had yet to discover any particular "creator" skills, and none of the children were old enough to manifest them.

Max's power to rarify was much less consistent than Jack's ability to condense. He could turn earth to water and had totally dispensed thereby with washing his hands, but that was about the limit of what he could consistently do.

"It is age," he said to Peter and to Maggie one night in their rooms after dinner. "If only I had come here with you twenty-five years ago, you would have seen something. Right, Maggie?" She refused to even try to do any "magic."

"With great power would come," she began before Max swatted her with a scroll he had been studying.

"We shall have to be content," Max said to his wife, "with being oldest and wisest."

"You are the oldest, anyway," she said and Peter had laughed at them both.

Barth was delighted with his continued experiments in invisibility. "By bending light," he began one evening when he and Peter were trying archery, "I can create the illusion that I am not here."

"You can create the illusion that a part of you is not there. Wait until you meet the Hongese. They can fight invisible. Besides, I don't see much call for the illusion that you have no thumb."

Barth rolled his eyes, shot, and actually hit the edge of the target. This put pressure on Peter since neither of them had done this yet. The Sky-King concentrated and aimed his bow. Releasing the string, the arrow flew true and hit just inside the outer ring ... palpably better than Barth's shot. Peter was about to turn to gloat when his arrow vanished.

"Well," Peter said, "that was an obvious trick."

"Trick?" Barth said. "You missed and lost your arrow."

"You saw me hit the target!"

"I see nothing ..." his old friend began in his best Sergeant Shultz manner. Fortunately for their friendship, Barth's concentration slipped and the arrow reappeared.

Mary had surprised them all by being able to shape shift, a very rare gift amongst Barterrans and the only one that Peter could not do at all. Strictly speaking, it was not shape shifting, as she pointed out her actual appearance had not changed, but she **was** able to create an airy illusion around her body. She could **appear** to be something other than what she was, though at the moment her ability was limited to a form roughly the same size as her actual appearance. The smaller the change in her appearance the easier it was to maintain it.

She and Susan had discussed the ethics of using this skill for some time. One night she **appeared** to be wearing her customary red nail polish with a splendid manicure at dinner. Maggie and Susan had noticed, but nobody else had. This was irritating, but she supposed she had not expected much else from their hapless lot of male academics.

In the middle of dinner, the illusion failed and she noticed she had not washed her hands very thoroughly. She could even fool herself! This was very interesting and she spent several hours experimenting with changing her dress appearance in numerous ways before the ridiculousness of it all made her laugh.

Could she, should she, remove certain lines that had crept around her eyes in the last few years? Mary had decided against it because she was not sure where it would stop. Makeup was at least obvious and had to come off sometime, but living in even a small illusion seemed too much. It was a good skill and was obviously useful, so she kept practicing. She discovered that so far her longest illusion, a very small change to the shape of her nose, lasted only twenty minutes. Greater illusions lasted shorter times.

She decided only to change her appearance for the good of others. She had told Peter all about it and he agreed with her decision. Shape-shifters on Barterra, and there were a few amongst the residents, were often very unhappy beings.

Peter was the anointed King and so could bond with Dragons. He could do a little bit of everything, but not much of anything. In short, Peter thought, so far the Forgotten, including himself, were not an intimidating lot. The Lords of Samov and Second Metcalf had no particular reason to fear them. Any second year apprentice Fire Wright might do better.

In short, they were comfortably settled in a well-maintained castle. As long as their needs were simple, the mechanical staff could provide it. Braver young men were moving back into crofts in the area and would appear on any given day to swear fealty to the Macbor and ask for protection against the Vampires. The undead had appeared to be their biggest short-term problem, until Peter had talked to Ferus.

Ferus the dragon faithfully guarded the castle for almost a week, but the power of the Lethe began to fade and the group knew they needed to do something with him. Peter could not simply command him to drink more water. The dragon was forgetful, not stupid.

"You can lead a dragon to the Lethe, but you cannot make him drink," Peter had said during a council regarding Ferus, which had earned him a withering eye roll from Mary. Peter was comfortable using Lethe water in battle, but not for mind control.

This had started a long discussion on the use and misuse of Lethe. The Macbor had several ideas on how they might overcome certain tendencies of the water to lose its potency over time. Peter had dozed through parts of it. Strategists had been trying to bottle Lethe as a weapon for the entire history of Barterra with little success. Bandor could keep a concentrate for a short period of time, but only at a terrible cost to his own psychical energy. Generally, it was easier to simply kill your foe than to make him forget unless, as in the case of Ferus, he happened to be conveniently standing next to the Lethe.

"Given his age and experience," Peter said, "Ferus was unlikely to stand by the same river twice." Barth groaned, and suddenly the physicist remembered high schools classes with Peter, prankster extraordinaire. Barth realized that Peter's restored memory had brought back a character trait that had disappeared since high school. Peter was the once and future bad joke king. He had told Peter that he was glad to see him happier, but worried that the Sky-King was going to start shorting sheets.

Peter grinned. "I am shocked you could accuse your liege lord of such a thing." He shook his head sorrowfully. "You might have noticed that Barterrans do not customarily use sheets, Dr. Science. Now, if Barth is done sharing his personal terrors, we can get back to discussing the drake." They hadn't come up with much, but the general agreement was that, as a dragon master, Ferus was fundamentally Peter's problem.

The dragon would be a problem in any siege. They did not need to kill him yet, and so patience seemed the better part of virtue. Ferus was not powerful enough to enter a guarded castle with working catapults and they could not fight him in the field with light troops.

Eventually, they hoped, a well-trained Fire Wright would come and help them deal with Ferus. Peter remembered that even talking to the drake had been difficult when he had regained his memory.

As duty demanded, Peter had been there when Ferus had come to his senses a week ago. When the dragon had looked at him, Peter had seen that Ferus knew what had been done to him.

"Trickery is unexpected in a Sky-King." Ferus over enunciated every word.

"I am sorry for it, but there was no other option."

"Do the ends justify the means?" The drake was irritable as people often are when they come out from under the power of Lethe water.

"No," Peter said honestly, "but rules of combat are not moral laws."

"That is the kind of sophistry that old men use."

"I am an older man and no warrior now."

"So I see. You are standing here so I assume you know that I cannot reach the Most High. He is cut off from us and his mind is confused."

"Yes, I thought that would be true."

"You have been bound to me by my own choice," Ferus shook his great hand sadly, "but my binding to Bandor is deeper. You are very fortunate that he cannot speak to me. Our bonds will hold until he breaks them, for my binding to him is deeper than that to my Lady Wife. I will not attack you until the Most High orders me to bring you pain sophistical creator-man."

"I understand, and am sorry to have lost your respect."

"You will lose more than that if I can help it. May I assume you are still the enemy of the Most High?"

"I am the sworn enemy of any being that does true harm to dragons," Peter said with a smile.

"A cryptic answer that confirms your duplicitous nature. You are my commander until he speaks, but at least show the integrity to allow me to depart into the deep woods."

"You may, but you must hunt Vampires there."

"This I do not mind. They are servants of the Most High that I find most distasteful. He uses them because he must."

"Do the ends justify the means, Ferus?"

The dragon smiled, which is a frightening sight for any man, and nodded.

"You **are** a sophist. You know better than most why the Most High finds certain wicked creatures on His side and His true feelings about them, so I will not bandy useless words with you. I will no longer regret causing you pain."

Peter bowed, and Ferus ambled into the deeper woods. Many Vampires would die over the next few months, and the woods would be more peaceful than they had been in some time. Still, soon, Ferus would return to his devotion to his Most High. Peter would never understand the relationship of certain families of dragons to Bandor.

A week later Peter stood by the Lethe and continued to muse about Ferus and his relations with the Tower.

Having a drake in the woods was **really** going to be a problem if they stayed, but at least they would know **exactly** when Bandor regained control of himself. Peter still marveled at the drake's annoyance at being cheated out of a "fair fight." How could such noble beasts serve Bandor? Perhaps it was their pharisaical tendencies. They remained a major source of his power and the dragon clans that served him did so with all their soul. Their Lord's inability to respond to their mental cries must be causing confusion all over the planet.

He knew that dragon mythology placed the start of their relationship deep in time and that dragons refused to discuss clan secrets with an outsider, which the Sky-King definitely was. They viewed the Sky-Kings as interlopers and morally equivalent to Bandor's empire. There were some ancient reasons for this odd fact. Each dragon carried the memories of all their ancestors and some clans had very unhappy memories of John Blackbeard, the first of the Sky-Kings.

It was a good reminder that the early Sky-Kings had been pirates and not noblemen, while Bandor had grown worse with time, the Kings had grown better. Bandor, as Shannon had once told him, was a complicated topic, and there had been little to choose between the Alliance and the Empire in terms of virtue in the early days. The Free States, independent of either side, were an outgrowth of that time, but so was an alliance with Bandor by most of the leading dragon families. Shannon said that they were lucky, given what he knew about the history but would not repeat to Peter, that any dragons were in the Alliance at all. If Shannon was still alive, and Gala had been unsure, he looked forward to watching Max and the Fire Wright Talk.

Should he stay at the Tower? One strategy was to run and slowly gather strength over the planet. Gala and the Macbor thought that this was best and they knew the state of the planet much better than he did. Leading a resistance and slowly building up a new army was safer and so appealing in one way, but would lead to a great loss of life as Bandor began the process of hunting him and using reprisals to get information.

Peter had an idea, a wild idea, to strike a bigger blow. When he suggested it in council, Gala had opposed it outright. The old General was unwilling to risk the Alliance on one great throw of the dice. He had gotten used to losing and was unwilling to lose the hope he had just gained in the last two weeks. Peter was cautious to overrule the general before he knew more, but he also knew Gala's limits. The old soldier was the master at organizing and mobilizing an army, but he was slow to use it. Gala knew the power of the Sky-King as a rallying piece and wished to use Peter as a king in chess. Peter thought of himself as more active than that metaphor would allow.

Max was walking down the hill with Mary and Peter walked away from the brink of the pool to meet them. Max and Peter had told Mary the entire story of what had happened in the Narva chamber. She had taken it differently than either Max or Peter thought she would.

"I would do it again, if it meant Peter were alive."

"Many, many people will die now that Bandor has escaped."

Mary spoke quickly. "First, I did not know the situation. I did not know that Bandor was about to die. For that matter, you did not know what was happening either, Max. Father John would sit and pray if lifting a finger would save the planet. That is not my personality.

"Second, Bandor's actions are his moral responsibility and not mine. He may kill more people, but he was going to kill Peter. My responsibility was to prevent a certain evil and not to sit passively by in case action would be worse than inaction.

"Finally, I would not do what I did, maybe," Mary was honest enough to pause, "I might not do what I did if I had known everything that was happening, but since Peter did not know himself before Bandor arrived, I acted on what I knew. I would do it again knowing what I knew then!"

Max nodded. "There is something to all of that, but you might learn with time an inner quietness that would change the moral calculus."

"Yes, but I haven't learned it yet. When I learn inner quietness," her finger nails were tapping rhythmically on the table, "I will let you know." Suddenly her hands stopped moving and her face twisted up. "Besides," and like a Narva wounded there was water flowing from her eyes, "I don't think I could stand to see Peter die."

Peter sighed at the end of that memory and realized that standing near the Lethe always made him too reflective. Lethe cheered him up, but the mist in the air also freed his mind to wander. He waved at Mary and Max and moved further up the path toward them. His mentor and his beloved were arguing as they got near him.

"Peter is right," Mary was saying, "the Sky-King needs to do something. He must act."

"He must act," Max replied, "but prudence ..."

"Will only get us killed more slowly. We should play to win."

Peter interrupted their conversation: "I don't know what I am going to do yet, but I suspect Mary is right, Max."

"Maybe," Max turned his famous eye on his protégé, "but exactly how do you plan to rescue the remaining Narva when you saw them head to the bottom of the sea?"

"That is a problem, though we could appeal to the Sea Peoples."

"The Sea Peoples are not under your rule. They are not to be trusted. Why would they reduce their dominions? We are lucky they do not smash the rest of the cases and sink more islands."

"Enough for now!" Peter begged. "Could you leave us alone for a bit Maximos?"

Max smiled agreeably and turned back up toward the Tower. He had brought Mary down for the sole purpose of leaving her with Peter. He had recognized the expansive mood of his former pupil at breakfast so was counting on good things. As he said to Maggie, "Faint heart never won fair lady and Peter has a strong heart today!"

When they were alone, Peter picked a blue fairy flower and watched as the fairy circled Mary's head. "Not even a hint of grey," he said to her, taking her hand.

"Wait until we have been here a month or two," she said, "and hints will come."

He laughed. "We will be equals, then."

She kissed him. Both of them had gotten used to the height difference and were, Peter thought, getting good at this. They started to walk by the Lethe.

"I want to marry you," Peter said.

"Not yet," Mary looked at him and loved him.

"Why? Just marry me! Is it my job prospects?"

"No, it is my impact on you and your job prospects."

"What do you mean?"

"It is something Anastasia said to me before we left. She said to me, 'Mary, never forget you are certainly a danger to that man. He loves you absolutely and you return it fiercely. Such love can blind your wisdom."

"What?" Peter was confused.

"As gently as she could, without exposing anything that is not already public knowledge, she said that her mother loved her father too much to make a good Tsarina. Alexandra allowed passion for her family to harm her nation, though she was also a great patriot. This was a great pity ... and Anastasia warned me of it."

"I don't see the parallel at all," Peter said hotly.

"You don't see it, because you don't know how much I love you. I am not so good at expressing my passion in words as you are. I am afraid," Mary paused, "I am afraid I would kill anyone who tried to harm you without a single thought."

Peter looked at her and said, "I feel the same way about you."

"No, I don't think you do. You were willing to die for Barterra and leave me. I would not have been willing to lose you for the sake of anything ... or I fear I would not have been willing. The Alliance can go to hell if it costs me you." Mary was speaking in a matter of fact tone, but she could not hold still she was so upset. She was walking so quickly that Peter could scarcely keep up.

"Alexandra loved Nicholas more than Russia. I love you more than Earth and Barterra. That is not right in an Empress, and it would not be right for your wife."

"I am willing to risk it."

"I am not."

"Do you think it is hopeless?" Peter looked hard at Mary. She stopped walking and offered him her hand.

"It is not hopeless if Father John can teach me some of the quietness of spirit he is always chattering about."

"He has a lot to teach both of us."

"I love you, Peter. I just don't want to hurt you by hurting Barterra and causing you to fail. Maybe," she looked uncertain for the first time since Peter had known her, "Maybe I have caused you to fail already."

"Nonsense," Peter said. "God is bigger than you, Mary Yurislav."

"Peter, I want to marry you, I want to help you, I want to be your strongest supporter and partner. I want ... God knows I want too much. What's next?"

Peter saw the green hills of Nimlandor and took Mary's hand. "I have a lot to show you," he said to her.

"I cannot wait to see it," she replied, and though they remembered all their pain, they were still happy.

# Epilogue:
# A Note From the Author


Evidently I grew up with Peter Rupert Alexis, but I have no memory of it. A diary, a prayer journal, and some papers arrived at my office in the Torrey Honors Institute in February of 2009 outlining an adventure much like the one you have read here. Like everyone else, I have no memory of any of the unique events it describes.

I did attend a Christian high school that is now closed in Penfield, New York, and Peter said he attended as well. He is not in any yearbook, and none of my friends have any memory of him.

According to Peter, we lost touch after high school, but he had followed my career with some interest. At some point, he claims, we were Facebook friends, but he doesn't have an account now. We are much alike, both being Orthodox Christians who venerate the memory of the Martyred Tsar. While Peter had little faith in my literary skills, he did trust me to get the "message right" and "accurately preserve the essentials of our adventures while shielding the innocent." Since I have now proven I am no novelist, I can only hope his positive expectations have been satisfied.

If the story is to be believed, the Forgotten Eleven—Peter, Mary, Barth, Max, Maggie, Father John, Jack, Susan and their children (Charles, John, and Doug)—are now on Barterra. Tom waits in Rochester for their return, but I have no idea what his actual name is. At Peter's request I have changed the names and locations of certain events in the book enough so that there is no easy correspondence with actual places in Los Angeles, Saint Petersburg, or Rochester. To cite one easy example, Pentecostal Holiness Bible Institute does not exist and does not directly correspond with any of the fine Bible programs in Rochester, certainly not to Elim Bible Institute. I knew where the events unfolded, but at Peter's request, the story had been changed to protect the Forgotten, and the original documents were burned in my fireplace here at Saint Anne's on Orthodox Ash Wednesday 2009.

I decided to write a fictionalized version of these documents when I found an old notebook buried in a stack of papers from high school. It had been in storage in my parents' house in West Virginia, and when they moved out here ended up at Saint Anne's. My wife Hope and I spent several enjoyable evenings laughing at late seventies and early eighties clothes and hair in the yearbooks and other items found in the box. We even found a note that I had written to Hope expressing interest in her in tenth grade!

That turned out to be only the **second** most improbable find in the boxes. A blue three-ring binder contained the beginnings of a novel, **The Lantern Iliad: The Sky King's Heir**, that centered on the adventures of a sixteen year old, **Peter Rupert Alexis**. It is in my ninth grade handwriting and in my usual florid style, but I don't recollect writing it. I find it difficult to attend to the book, and have not been able to read all of it as a result. My mind resists dealing with any manuscript other than the one that Peter sent me.

It is evidence of something, but I am not sure of what. My brother, Daniel, and one other person saw the original papers from Peter, and I still have the notebook so I do not think this is all a product of a deranged mind! I will leave it to my readers to decide what it is.

Is Lenin still alive in Russia? Is Gog an operational project? What is the exact relationship between our world and Barterra? I don't know, but I hope some day to meet Peter Rupert Alexis and ask him. If he left this world, he can return as he did once before, though I trust with a happier outcome for himself, and with his memories intact.

Most of all, I trust that I will meet the Blessed Anastasia face-to-face and thank her for her prayers and her suffering. Whatever the merits of this story, history records her martyrdom in 1918 and the recognition of her glorification as a passion bearer by the one Holy Catholic and Apostolic Church.

I covet her prayers and yours,

John Mark Nicholas Reynolds
Saint Anne's
Feast of the Martyred Tsar 2009
La Mirada, California

CPSIA information can be obtained at www.ICGtesting.com
Printed in the USA
LVOW131742061012

301786LV00001B/5/P